## The Pretender

"Funny and touching . . . totally entertaining."
—Julia Quinn, *New York Times* bestselling
author of *Romancing Mister Bridgerton*

"Bradley beautifully manipulates the sinfully sensual yet delicately romantic relationship . . . into an irresistible and supremely satisfying love story."
—*Booklist* (starred review)

"Bursting with adventure and sizzling passion to satisfy the most daring reader."
—*Romantic Times Bookclub* (Top Pick)

"A charming heroine and a dashing spy hero make *The Pretender* a riveting read . . . entertained me thoroughly from beginning to end."
—Sabrina Jeffries, *USA Today* bestselling
author of *After the Abduction*

"An engaging, lusty tale, full of adventure and loaded with charm."
—Gaelen Foley, *USA Today* bestselling author

# The
# *Rogue*

*(Book Five in the Liar's Club series)*

## CELESTE BRADLEY

St. Martin's Paperbacks

THE ROGUE

Copyright © 2005 by Celeste Bradley.
Excerpt from *Surrender to a Wicked Spy* copyright © 2005 by Celeste Bradley.

ISBN: 0-312-93115-8
EAN: 9780312-93115-5

Printed in the United States of America

St. Martin's Paperbacks edition / June 2005

St. Martin's Paperbacks are published by St. Martin's Press, 175 Fifth Avenue, New York, NY 10010.

10  9  8  7  6  5  4  3  2  1

This book is dedicated to the first person who read the first words I wrote . . . and then asked for more. Thank you, Joanne.

# Acknowledgments

I would like to acknowledge all those who keep reading and reading and reading. . . . Keep reading!

As always, my thanks to my friends and family, my editor and agent, and my darling Bill. You make it work.

# The
# Rogue

# Prologue

It was time to come to a decision about the gambler.

The man in the darkened room slouched in a chair placed before the glowing coals in his hearth. His feet were up on a stool, his eyes were closed, and he gave every appearance of relaxation. However, if one were privileged to see the workings of his mind the view would be a busy one indeed.

The gambler . . .

The gambler could be useful—and, indeed, had already been so. The gambler could also be a handicap if the fellow's weaknesses overcame him. He knew a great deal. It could be dangerous to leave such a piece on the board. And while the gambler's loyalties had never actually faltered, they had never truly been tested either.

A pawn, so far, limited to moving in only one direction. Yet he was a pawn who could be promoted to a knight—or who could cost the match.

The coals glowed and the house settled and creaked with the advancement of the crisping autumn night. The clock on the mantel chimed the third hour. The man remained sprawled comfortably in his chair, thinking.

Yes, the gambler could yet be useful.

One last time.

# Chapter One

Lady Jane Pennington was feeling rather hunted. The ballroom was beginning to seem like a forest with impoverished bachelors waiting in the blinds, and she was the doe.

Jane propped herself up against the wall, half-hidden by a potted palm. She didn't think her toes could bear any more dancing.

Instead, she spent several minutes seeking out her five female cousins, the girls commonly known in Society as the Maywell Mob. Lord Maywell was the host of this evening's perspiration works—er, ball—and he was also Jane's uncle.

The gentleman was nowhere in sight, of course, being far more interested in cards than he was in trying to further the acquaintance and marriage possibilities of his five daughters. Jane allowed herself to fume without betraying it in her expression.

Supplying escort and introductions for his daughters was the least the man could do, especially after saddling the poor things with the Maywell nose, not to mention the Maywell propensity to overindulge.

With only her overworked aunt, Lady Maywell, chaperoning all five daughters, the girls had been known to get themselves into some very silly situations.

She spotted her youngest cousin, Serena, shyly watching

the dancers. At fifteen, Serena was far too young to be out, but that decision was not up to Jane. Lord and Lady Maywell had thrown their daughters wholesale at the Marriage Mart, evidently hoping that one would stick.

Abandoning the safety of her palm for a moment, Jane made her way to Serena and surreptitiously adjusted the girl's sash and tucked a wayward strand of strawberry-blonde hair, much like her own, back into its arrangement.

"You've a stain on your bodice, dear," she whispered to Serena. "Re-pin your silk flower over it."

Serena gulped and nodded, then turned to run for the ladies' retiring room. Looking across the room, Jane noticed that Augusta, the eldest of the five, who was still not quite twenty, had found a glass of champagne somewhere. Lady Maywell was nowhere in sight so Jane moved swiftly.

A young man stepped into her path. "Lady Jane! May I beg this dance?"

Jane blinked at him. What the blazes was the little rotter's name again? She'd been introduced to every male under fifty since coming to London three months ago and could scarcely recall a single individual.

They all remembered her, more's the pity. Lady Jane Pennington, richly gowned and unwed and therefore a catch for any enterprising fellow who thought himself poorer than he should be. The attention had at first been bewildering, had briefly been flattering, but then had dissolved into annoying when she realized that there was only one reason for the adoration.

Her irritation must have leaked into her expression, for the young man actually took a step back. "My lady?"

*Billingsly.* The name popped into Jane's head from nowhere in particular. "Mr. Billingsly—please forgive me." She forced herself to be polite. After all, it wasn't Mr. Billingsly's fault that he was one of the most boring fellows it had ever been her pleasure to have her slippers trod by. "I'm sorry, but I've just found that my aunt requires my presence."

That was true enough, if one considered that if Aunt
Lottie knew of Augusta's actions, she would certainly
wish Jane to act on her behalf. "But I see that my cousin
Julia is available for this dance."

Disappointment chased the fellow's smile away. Rally-
ing, he bowed. "Of course. The pleasure will be all—"

Oh, horse apples. Augusta had drained the flute dry.
Jane brushed past Mr. Billingsly with an absent nod. "You
will excuse me, I'm sure."

By the time Jane had maneuvered her way around the
dancers, Augusta, who as far as Jane knew had never im-
bibed a drop of wine in her life, was already blinking
dazedly at the shimmering chandelier above her head.

"Look, Jane," she said when Jane approached her. "It
makes little rainbows on the ceiling!" She hiccupped,
then giggled. "Isn't champagne divine?"

Oh, glory. Jane pulled her cousin away from her amaze-
ment and down the length of the ballroom. "It is time for
you to get some air, dear. It's far too warm in here."

Augusta blinked and came willingly enough. "I am a
bit dizzy."

"Have you eaten anything today?"

Augusta shook her head virtuously. "Oh, no. I wanted
to get into this gown. Don't I look fine?"

Jane sighed. This was going to get worse before it got
better. "You look lovely, dear heart. Now here we go. Out
through these doors . . ."

A few moments later, the champagne was in the
bushes and Augusta was on her way to her bedchamber
with a maid, suddenly more than willing to bring her evening to an end. Disaster averted.

Jane remained outside on the terrace, breathing in the
cool evening air. She herself wasn't willing to reenter the
stuffy ballroom either. She was only willing to go so far
to satisfy Mother.

*"Follow your uncle and aunt carefully. You've little ex-
perience at these things."*

Of course, that was then. Now she had three months of experience behind her and all she could say for it was, this was the most bored she'd ever been in her life. Her days were filled with girlish giggles and her evenings were filled with sore toes and false fawning.

She recorded every bit of it dutifully in her daily letters to Mother, although she couldn't imagine why Mother would be interested.

Taking advantage of being completely unobserved for a moment, Jane indulged in a languorous stretch. Rubbing the back of her neck while rolling her head from side to side, she wondered if she'd fulfilled her obligation to attract young men for her cousins' benefit for the evening. She was tired, and someone ought to look in on Augusta . . .

A wayward glimmer caught her eye. She looked up at the house before her, shading her eyes from the glare through the ballroom windows. There it was again.

High in a third-floor window—the second from the left—she saw another gleam of candlelight. There was something furtive about that candle. Wasn't that the room her uncle had closed off, declaring the chimney structurally dangerous?

It certainly looked solid from here, but then, Lord and Lady Maywell were still able to maintain the appearance of prosperity. The house seemed elegant and richly appointed, although Jane knew for a fact that it was a decaying pile.

So if that room was dangerous—what was someone doing in there with that furtive candle?

Jane backed up a few steps, trying to see into the window. The terrace ended in a balustrade that ran to curving stone stairs to the left and right. Jane lifted her skirts with one hand and ran lightly down the stairs and out onto the lawn, never taking her eyes off that window.

The angle was still too severe. What a pity. For a moment, she'd thought she actually had something interesting to tell Mother.

She cast a look behind her. At the edge of the lawn, just outside the circle of light cast by the ballroom windows and terrace lanterns, stood a grand old elm.

Jane liked that tree, for it was the only thing in her relations' tightly maintained garden that reminded her of the old wild groves in Northumbria.

Once upon a time, she had been an accomplished climber of trees. She cast one last thoughtful glance at the window. Was the candle gone?

A flicker of light from the upper window encouraged her. The sturdy-looking branches of the elm virtually dared her.

Jane smiled to herself and crossed the lawn to the tree.


The ballroom was crowded with predators intent on sensual fulfillment, virgins intent on a triumphant match, and chaperones determined to keep them apart—usually an interesting mix, certain to provide an evening's worth of cynical amusement.

At the moment, however, Ethan Damont—gambler, rampant bachelor, and gainfully unemployed counterfeit gentleman—only wanted to find the back door.

Over the years, Ethan had learned that it was always best to leave by the less obvious exit after a lucrative night, in case someone belatedly decided that a certain professional gambler had been . . . well . . . "cheating" was really the only word for it.

It wouldn't do to have his sleeves and pockets searched at the moment. Ethan was very proud of his unbroken record of evident honesty and he wasn't about to tempt fate now by sailing out the front door in full sight.

A crimson glove caught his arm, forcing him to pause. A dark-eyed lady with a memorable bosom smiled up at him.

"Why, what a pleasure it is to see you again, Mr. Damont." The last was said in a bedroom purr. For a moment, Ethan fondly recalled other names she'd called him in that very tone.

Of course, the lady's husband hadn't been very happy to hear cries of "Faster, my stallion!" coming from his wife's bedroom during that best-not-remembered house party.

But it was time for him to leave. With a last wistful look at the aforesaid bosom, Ethan bowed and smiled regretfully. "I must beg your leave, madam. Urgent business, you know."

He hadn't taken more than ten strides when another gloved hand caught him short. This one was clad in emerald silk that perfectly matched the stones around the neck of a statuesque blonde.

"Darling, I didn't know you were here!" She inhaled deeply. Miraculous things happened within the structured bodice of her jet-black gown.

Ah, the Widow Bloomsbury . . .

The nights—and mornings, and afternoons—he had spent in the widow's bed shone with a fiery glow in Ethan's memory. So very limber!

Ethan kissed the back of that gloved hand. "Another time, another place, pet," he murmured. "I must be off."

He turned away to see a vaguely familiar lady in sapphire blue moving toward him with an intent gleam in her eye. Bloody hell, perhaps this ball didn't contain any virgins after all! He dashed around the dancers to avoid her.

This time he kept his head up and his eyes peeled. He managed to detour around the next several ladies heading in his direction and make the door to the terrace without having to stop again.

Breathless and feeling rather like the fox before the hounds, Ethan cast one last desperate look behind him, then slipped outside into the dark garden.

Evidently what Lady Jane Pennington's mother had often

told her was true. One never knew when one would be
glad one wore a fresh pair of knickers. Thank goodness
she'd donned a brand-new pair this evening. When one
was hanging upside down from a tree, the condition of
one's knickers and garters became of vital importance.

Jane stopped trying to fight back the skirts that hung
over her face and arms and hung quietly by her knees
from the tree branch, swinging only slightly in a pensive
manner.

The ground—too far down to simply let go and fall.
The branch—impossible to grasp when her upper body
was sheathed in her own inverted skirts. " 'The new sil-
houette is very narrow, miss'," Jane quoted the absent
dressmaker viciously to herself. " 'Small steps are all the
rage, miss. Elegance first, miss'."

Right then, time for another try. Carefully bunching
the fabric in her hands as she went, she worked the hems
of her petticoat and gown up to her elbows, then higher,
this time successfully freeing her face and shoulders.
Taking a deep breath of cool night air, she shot a leery
glance at the ground just a bit too far below her.

The worst of it was that it was all for nothing. The
glimmer in the window was long gone now and she
hadn't seen anything worthwhile.

Taking a deep breath, she swung her body back and
forth, reaching upward at the top of each arc to grasp for
her limb with both hands. Her fingers slipped on the
crumbling bark the first and second times. She swung upward once more.

The branch let out a threatening cracking sound at her
burst of activity. Jane froze. Her moment of inattention
allowed the layers of muslin to cover her once more.

The thick limb had seemed sturdy enough when she'd
clambered up onto it. If her formal dancing slippers had
not been so slick and useless that she'd been unable to
keep her footing, she would have been fine.

She was still fine at the moment, since her legs were

strong from country living and her head wasn't pounding too severely yet, but if she didn't find a solution to her problem soon, she was going to have to face a fate that currently ranked somewhat worse than death.

She was going to have to call for help.

Ethan Damont left Lord Maywell's lovely ballroom with his pockets full of Lord Maywell's lovely money. Since he'd been assured by reliable sources that Lord Maywell was a very bad sort of man, Ethan had even enjoyed the evening's card game.

The refreshing thrill from a pastime that had mostly left him cold for the last year put an additional spring to his step as he crossed Maywell's expansive grounds.

Sauntering down the gravel walk leading to a rear wall that hopefully wouldn't be too high to manage, Ethan heard a sound that made him freeze in place.

Somewhere, not a dozen yards away, a woman was cursing softly and creatively.

A woman? Out in the dark alone? Ethan's lips twitched. Who said she was alone?

He began moving again. Far be it from him to interfere in someone else's mischief. He certainly wouldn't want to be disturbed at such a moment. At least, not as he re-called such moments, dimly though that was.

Female companionship was something else that had lost its previous glow this past year—at least as far as the sort of women Ethan had once fancied.

There had been a time he'd liked his entertainment en-thusiastically shameless, the more so the better. Wine, women, and song. When money ran thick like honey through his fingers, he'd had no trouble finding playmates aplenty. And when times were lean, his charm had been enough for at least an occasional tumble.

Then one day the wine turned to vinegar, the women became loud and blowsy, and the song began a discordant resonance deep within him. It suddenly felt as though he could see far, far into his future—and all it held was more of the same.

He'd kept up the pretense for a while, but then lost interest even in that. It wasn't until he'd been dragged from his house a few weeks ago by a dark-haired beauty on a mission that he had felt his own heart beating in excitement once again.

Of course, who could blame him? She was a fine and revitalizing creature, was Rose Lacey—that is, Rose Tremayne, for she was now married to quite possibly the last friend Ethan had left in the world.

Which was probably for the best. Ethan had little to recommend himself to a woman so principled. Ethan could honestly claim that his own life was devoted to the redistribution of wealth—into his own pockets.

He wondered without much interest if it was going to be a very long life.

Then he heard it. *Sniffle.*

"Oh, no," he groaned to himself. "Not that." His spine weakened. He tried to stiffen it by sheer will.

*Sniffle.*

"Bloody hell," he whispered, slumping in resignation. Turning around, he retraced his silent steps until he was opposite where he believed the woman to be. The hedge was old growth and sparse between the thick gnarled trunks. Ethan wriggled through with commendable lack of noise.

The grounds here were dark, but Ethan could see the black trunks of trees silhouetted against the better lit area nearer the house. The earth was soft under his feet, so he was able to approach the ladylike sniffling unheard.

Finally, Ethan was treated to such a sight that he simply had to pause. With a deep breath, he took a moment to appreciate it fully. Long, bestockinged, truly superior legs were wrapped firmly around a jutting tree branch. It was damned erotic, that's what it was. Ethan felt like letting go a bestial growl of his own.

He stepped closer. In the light from the house he could see the milky gleam of thigh skin peeking over the tops of the pair of rather battered stockings. The calves that were crooked over the limb looked plump and fully strong enough to hang on to him—er, the tree branch—all night long.

There was nothing else to see but yards of muslin swathing the rest of her. No difficulty there.

Ethan had ever been a leg man.

Just then, the branch Ethan had been envying gave out a loud, groaning crack!

Ethan lunged forward, grasped the muslin bundle by what he judged to be a waist and tugged the whole lot, legs and all, into his arms. His damsel in distress let out a yelp of surprise and sent an elbow deep into his stomach.

"Oof!" That had hurt! Just for that, Ethan put her down far more slowly than he otherwise would have. After all, one didn't happen onto this sort of view every day. With his arms wrapped around her, the act of turning her over caused a few "unavoidable" liberties to be taken.

"So sorry. Do forgive me," Ethan said without much urgency. He let the luscious legs down first and watched wistfully as the muslin shifted allegiance and tumbled down to hide them. He was left with a struggling, protesting bundle of fallen hair and slapping hands.

"Get—off! Oh! *Oh!*" The woman gave him a last hearty shove and Ethan released her.

"You're welcome," he drawled, and dipped a low ironic bow, then turned to walk away. Heroism never paid. "I do hope the branch doesn't fall on your head," he called to her, his tone not terribly concerned.

Red-faced and gasping, Lady Jane Pennington, well-known Society heiress and recent rescuee, straightened and brushed her hair partially out of her eyes. The light of the house was behind her, shining on a broad back that was swiftly disappearing into the darkness.

Oh, thank heaven he was leaving! If one could catch

fire from embarrassment and humiliation, she would certainly be a living torch right now. The fact that someone had seen—oh, she could die!

Still, a lifetime of taking pride in her good manners forced the words from her throat. "Thank you, sir," she said. The words choked a bit, but fair was fair.

He turned to look at her, then slowly stalked back toward her. Jane abruptly doubled her embarrassment as the light fell onto his face. He was not only tall and strong, but manly and handsome as well. All in all the worst possible candidate for rescuer she could imagine.

He came close, then closer still. Jane backed up a step in alarm. Her hair still hung over her eyes and her face was in shadow, but it wouldn't do to be recognized.

The fellow came so near that she had to tilt her head back to look into his face. Her breath caught at the impact of his fine face and form. So near . . .

Only then did a shiver of alarm pass through her. She was alone, in the deserted garden at night with a man who had seen her drawers.

Even the most gallant of rescuers might gain the wrong impression.

His gaze was narrowed as he cast it down on her. "I'd rather an honest 'get-thee-gone' than that grudging thanks, gazelle," he said, his voice low.

Jane twitched. She'd had a long night and was in no mood for this man's opinion. "And I would rather you be on your way than coming back to mock me."

"Ouch." He smiled slowly. "You have teeth. Perhaps you aren't a gazelle after all." He dipped his head near hers, until if she turned her neck she could brush his cheek with her lips.

"Are you a predator?" His voice feathered warm and soft in her ear. "Is that why you were in the tree, waiting to pounce on some unsuspecting male?" His tone made it clear that he was more than willing to be that male.

Oh, bother. He was one of *those* men. Jane snorted.

"Does that load of horse apples actually work on women? Or am I the first one you've practiced it on?" She folded her arms. "Because I must inform you that it will never succeed."

He pulled his head back to look at her. His eyes were in shadow. Jane could not tell his reaction. Was he offended? Did she care?

"Of course not." His tone was flat, almost bored. "What was I thinking? I'm awaited at home, in any case."

Then he plucked a leaf from her hair and tucked it into his weskit pocket. "My token, fair maiden," he said mockingly.

He turned his back on her and strode away. Just as he stepped into the deeper darkness of the rear garden, the stranger sent her a flashing, wicked grin over his shoulder and pointed up to "her" tree.

"Nice limbs," he called. "A fellow could lie among them all night." With an insouciant salute, he turned away again and was gone.

Jane clapped one hand to her mouth at his shocking jest—then snorted with laughter despite herself. He was a wicked, wicked fellow.

She picked up her skirts and ran for the house. She hoped she could make it to her room before anyone saw the condition she was in. As she scurried through the dimness, she wondered about her handsome, wicked rescuer . . .

Perhaps she wouldn't tell Mother about this one.

# Chapter Two

Ethan was not awaited at home. That had been a lie. There was no one to greet him but his silver-haired butler and his looming sour-faced male cook. Ethan Damont descended from the hired carriage to the front steps of his prized Mayfair house. Despite the lateness of the hour, his ground-floor windows blazed with light, as did the rectangle of open door that waited him.

If he wasn't mistaken, his new butler had somehow known to open the door before Ethan had even been driven into his own square. Such punctilious attention to duty was a bit alarming. Ethan certainly hoped he wasn't expected to reward it with timely pay and Christmas bonuses. Gambling was a chancy career, at best.

Things were fine now, of course. It would take even a devoted hedonist like Ethan a long while to run through the generous reward he'd received for helping to rescue Collis Tremayne's stout old uncle . . .

It occurred to Ethan for the first time that he'd never caught that uncle's name. Then he shrugged the thought out of his fogged mind. He wasn't drunk, of course. One couldn't cheat well if one was drunk.

Well, that wasn't necessarily true. Ethan could and had, more than once, but it was very bad form. The marks didn't like it when they couldn't blame their losses on their own relative inebriation. It caused suspicion, which was very bad for business.

But he wasn't drunk tonight. Merely tired, tired of the whole bloody game.

He let out a breath and climbed his own steps with much less enthusiasm than the lovely house deserved. He'd won it in his salad days, from a man so rich he'd simply shrugged and bought another, finer one the next day.

Ethan loved his house, loved every scrap of gilded molding, every square of marble on the floor, every mouse in the cellar, and every damned bat in the attic.

He might not be a gentleman, and he might not be a worthy—or even a vaguely good—man, but he had a bloody fine house.

In the front hall of said house, Ethan's butler stood at the ready in dignified if nauseating splendor, all tricked out in the hideous new official pink and violet livery of Diamond House. Ethan had picked it out rather face-tiously when pressed past his patience by the man's insistence on proper uniform—well, he hadn't dreamed the bloke would take him seriously!—and now it seemed he would be staring at it forever.

Oh, well, what was one more mistake in a life that held so many? The butler wore it with imperturbable dignity all the same.

He gave the butler his gloves and hat. "How did you know it was me? It was a hired carriage."

The butler didn't shrug like another man might have. He merely nodded respectfully. "I simply knew, sir."

"Yes, but how?"

The butler blinked slowly, his gaze never faltering in its level, mystic calm. "I knew because it *was* you, sir."

"That's frightening, do you know that?"

"Yes, sir."

Ethan shrugged out of the greatcoat he'd worn against the September fog outside. "Well, stop it. You'll give me nightmares."

"Indeed, sir."

Ethan shot the man a sharp glance, but the cool reserve remained in place. That had not been humor. With a barely concealed shudder, Ethan took himself off to his study.

Although it was nearly morning, he didn't even attempt to go to bed. Sleep never came until he was so bloody tired his eyes wouldn't stay open. He might as well stare at the fire and sip brandy until that happened.

The brandy decanter was nowhere in sight.

"Jeeves!"

The butler appeared miraculously at his study door, making Ethan jump. "Sir, my name is P—"

"Jeeves, do I pay you well?"

"Obscenely so, sir."

"Too right." For the moment, anyway. "So, if I want to call you Jeeves, and you have no objection to Jeeves other than it isn't really your name—you didn't have a dog named Jeeves, or an enemy, or any such thing, did you?"

"No, sir, indeed I did not."

"Well, then. I like calling you Jeeves. It's easy to remember when I'm tired or drunk, or tired and drunk, and I like it. I feel most lordly when I say it. Say it with me, Jeeves."

The butler—damned if Ethan hadn't forgotten his real name already—serenely repeated it with him. *"Jeeves."*

"So, Jeeves, the reason I called you in here is that my brandy is missing."

"Yes, sir, it is."

Ethan took a sigh. It seemed he was going to pay for the Jeeves thing. "Did you put my brandy somewhere else?"

"Yes, sir, I did."

"And this somewhere else is . . . ?"

"In your sitting room, sir, just off your bedchamber."

Ethan waited, but Jeeves won. With his knees weak with surrender, Ethan folded. "Why did you put it in my sitting room as opposed to my study, Jeeves?"

"Why, so when you drink yourself into a useless stupor, I may only have to carry you the distance of one room, as opposed to two flights of stairs, sir." Jeeves gazed at him with no sign of unease or distress at such flagrant insubordination. "If you refuse to allow me to hire the staff that this house requires, I must find other ways to do my duties to your expectation."

Ethan gazed back at him in shock. Then a short laugh burst from him without his consent. "Jeeves, you're a man of good sense. I'll take my brandy in my sitting room from now on. Point for point, wouldn't you agree?"

"Indeed, sir. It will interest me who wins the day, sir."

Ethan laughed again and turned toward the stairs and the sitting room where his brandy awaited. Then he stopped. "If you could hire one person, who would it be?"

"A cook, sir," Jeeves said promptly.

"I have a cook."

"You have a tattooed sailor who spits in your soup, sir. You rarely eat at home, sir, but I do."

The man had a point. "Very well, then. You may choose a new cook."

Ethan continued up the stairs, then stopped again. "Jeeves, what sort of tattoo?"

"Twins, sir. Voluptuous ones, in the altogether. Apparently, it was a memory worth preserving forever."

Ethan whistled. "I'll say. I'd like to see that."

"He's very proud of it. He would be more than willing to show it to you on request, sir, but I'd advise against it."

"Why is that?"

Jeeves looked up at him with ancient eyes. "The young ladies in question reside on each of Cook's buttocks, sir. Your food will never taste the same, I promise you."

Ethan was still laughing as he poured himself a drink. Sitting by the fire with his brandy, he had to admit that Jeeves was the first sign of life his house had seen in a very long while.

The glints of firelight in the brandy reminded Ethan of

the faint light glinting from the tangled hair of the girl in the garden. He absently rubbed the ribs where she had sent her elbow into them. She had an admirable swing, he had to give her that.

As he tipped back his glass, he wondered how she had explained her state of dishevelment to her companions. He took out the leaf that still lay tucked into his weskit pocket and slid the cool red and orange slickness between his fingers.

He hadn't asked her for her name, which was probably for the best. He hadn't behaved very well. Of course, neither had she.

Who was she and what in the world had she been doing up a tree? The questions so possessed him that he quite forgot to pour himself another brandy.

He wondered if she had a beau.

"Eeny meeny miney mo, which of these will be my beau?"

The many and varied daughters of Lord Maywell shrieked with laughter at the saucy rhyme and crowded forward to see which sketch of the current crop of bachelors that Augusta, the eldest, had landed her finger upon.

Lady Jane Pennington flopped back on the counterpane of the bed she shared with her youngest cousin, Serena, and tried mightily to suppress her boredom. She'd not returned to the festivities after her mishap, for there was no chance that she could remove all the damage from her dress and person in order to prevent comment. She'd been quite prepared to plead headache or some such when the rest of the girls came upstairs.

It turned out that no one had missed her.

Well, the girls had been entirely overstimulated by the evening, and her aunt had had all she could bear keeping an eye on them. It was a statement of faith and high esteem that her relations hadn't had to monitor her every move this evening.

As it turned out, it had been a blessing as well, considering the events in the garden. Jane put that from her mind. It was too embarrassing and . . . well, somewhat stirring.

The giggles swelled to scandalized shrieks. Jane winced.

The Maywell Mob, as they were known in less reverent circles, were generally rather dear girls but exhaustively focused on one single group goal. Marriage, for all five of them, as soon as possible.

Of course, if Jane had grown up sharing beds and hairbrushes and a single harried ladies' maid with five sisters, she might be in a bit more hurry to leave home. As it was, however, Jane had no home to speak of. Her father's estate had gone to his brother Christoph, who had become the new Marquis of Wyndham. Fourteen-year-old Jane and her mother had been whisked off to Northumbria to the "Dowager House" on the lesser estate.

Jane shook off those thoughts as well. A sheltered young heiress ought not to bother herself with such things, much less brood over them. Instead, she ought to be playing silly girlish games. She took a deep breath and shut off darker memories, turning a tolerant smile upon her cousins' antics.

They were all intent upon their game. The pity of it was, this game of marriage was a deadly serious one for them.

The girls were not likely to marry at all in this war-depleted Marriage Mart. The shortage of eligible young men had made the infighting fierce and the Maywell Mob were not highly ranked by the bachelors available.

Lady Maywell, in her infinite wisdom, had decided to launch all five girls at once. "Best to bait all the traps straightaway," she'd reasoned. "All the more likely that at least one of them will marry."

The fact that they all five sported the Maywell nose was only part of the problem. Jane herself was more likely to be called "handsome" or "elegant" than "beautiful," although that was perhaps due more to her wardrobe than anything.

The Maywell Mob, on the other hand, was near to breaking his lordship by requiring gowns, such as they were, and entertainment to entice eligible men. There wasn't much left with which to bestow dowries.

In contrast, Jane's wardrobe alone could provide for several daughters. She wore only the finest gowns, fitted to perfection, with everything a woman needed to ride in high style into this do-or-die-unwed battlefield.

All a sham, of course, but for Jane a reminder of a life long ago. All the years of stringent survival seemed to have leached all excitement from grosgrain ribbon and batiste pantalets.

The giggles rose in volume and velocity. Jane winced. From Augusta right down to Serena, the cousins didn't share an ounce of sense between them.

Still, they were dear girls, who had welcomed their estranged cousin cheerfully. By all rights, they ought to have envied her trunks full of lovely things. The sisters were forced to trim and retrim the same gowns, passing them from sister to sister in hopes they'd not be so easily recognized.

A veritable shell game of fashion misdirection.

Yet despite their own lack, they had gasped and admired without reservation when Jane had unpacked, with not the slightest hint of resentment.

Now, the game went on around her, reaching such levels of giggles and squeals that Jane decided to sleep elsewhere. Rolling over, she tried to crawl off the bed between Serena and Bedelia, who ranked fourth—or was it third?

Bedelia gasped. "Oh, Jane, look what you've done, you silly creature!"

Jane blinked. That was a bit of kettle-blacking, if one were to ask her. Then she looked down to see one of the sketches crumpled under her elbow. Rising, she put the paper over her knee and tried to smooth it out.

The sketches were Serena's and were really rather good. One didn't disrespect a talent like that, especially when poor Serena had so little to recommend her otherwise. Not terribly clever, not notably pretty, and as Jane could attest, she kicked horribly in her sleep.

The drawing smoothed out to portray a face that made Jane's movements slow and her breath quicken. High of brow and wide of cheekbone, with his overlong hair worn loose and defiant, the man in the sketch made Jane think of a weary medieval hero who had just removed his helm after slaying the dragon and freeing the princess.

It was the man from the garden. "Who is he?"

Augusta sniffed. "Oh, him. He's naught but a place card."

"A what?" That could not mean what it sounded like.

"A place card is what Mama calls gentlemen that merely round out the seating at a party," Bedelia explained. "Ethan Damont isn't a gentleman or anything. He's just a handsome face with which to fill the table."

"And Papa likes to play cards with him," Serena added. "He says he's going to keep playing him until he figures out how the Diamond is cheating."

Invited but unwelcome? It was actually worse than Jane had thought. She felt rather sorry for him. Then Serena's words caught her attention. "The Diamond?" Jane turned to her cousins. "The gambler that the Voice of Society is always talking about?"

Augusta rolled her eyes. "The gossip makes more of him than he is. No name and no fortune at all. Serena only put him in the pot to make an even dozen."

"A place card," Serena said, giggling. "And he has pretty eyes."

The man on the paper gazed up at Jane. Serena was sometimes more talented than she knew, for in her blithe hurry to provide the game pieces, she had set down more of the man than she likely would have had she thought more about it.

Ethan Damont did not have "pretty" eyes. He had lost and tragic eyes—eyes that spoke of loneliness and wry resignation. Jane felt something twist ever so sideways in her chest. *Ethan Damont, the Diamond.*

He'd been shockingly forward and free with his touch. Oh, not in any truly obscene way, but she'd been quite aware how he'd taken his time setting her to the ground. A man of physicality, that one. Tall, glib, and outrageously behaved—just as one would expect from an opportunistic card player of common blood.

She looked back down at the drawing. His eyes . . .

Why did she have the feeling that there was much more to Mr. Ethan Damont than met the eyes?

# Chapter Three

The next day, Ethan was back to his usual self. He strutted down the Strand in full rake regalia, walking stick and all. He hadn't a worry in the world at the moment. He'd banked a pile of notes from Lord Maywell last night, which he'd added to the reward he'd recently received from that portly uncle of Collis Tremayne's.

Ethan had never been told why Collis and his uncle were beaten and chained in a dungeon-like chamber of an arms factory—but then, he'd never asked. He'd never even asked the uncle's name, but had blithely dubbed the fellow "the Codger" and left it at that.

There were times when a bloke needed to know the score and there were times when he was better off in the dark.

So with his pockets full and his questions firmly squelched, Ethan resolved to enjoy the new day and his fresh state of solvency. What sort of delicious trouble could he find on this fair afternoon in the greatest city in the world? He took a deep, satisfied breath. The possibilities were endless.

Ethan loved London, every sooty, grimy, shady bit of it. He despised having to leave it. He'd been dragged off to house parties on country estates a few times, where he had established a reputation as a hunter and rider, and had spent the rest of his time fighting off complete boredom by charming many a lady of the house directly out of her knickers.

Then of course there had been those memorable occasions when his boredom had been alleviated by fleeing a jealous husband or six . . . ah, well, those were fine times.

Nevertheless, breathtaking run-for-one's-life excitement aside, he'd always been glad to come home to the city. When he was here, the invisible lines between people blurred a bit, doors opened a crack, and he was able to pass back and forth between who he was and who they all thought him to be without much effort.

He caught a glimpse of himself in a shop window. Never averse to admiring a job well done, he paused to congratulate himself on presenting every evidence of being a gentleman. The hat, expensive sleek beaver with the latest narrower brim—tipped at precisely the right careless angle, of course—the frock coat and weskit, cut in the latest highly fitted manner, all in the finest fabrics. Gray kidskin gloves made just for him, grasping a walking stick he neither liked nor needed.

He fancied boots over stockings and slippers, himself, although he could claim a decent pair of calves all on his own.

Yes, from head to toe, he was quite the picture of the gentleman about town. Everything in place, not a single clue of his real origins apparent to remind those around him that he didn't—not quite—belong.

Of course, everyone knew. He'd decided long ago it was better to reveal the matter early on, and then work like the devil to make them forget it.

*Why?*

To be truthful, he didn't even know anymore. He'd been trained from birth to pass in Society, immersed in lessons from the early years on, governesses chosen from the penniless gentry, tutors as well, no expense spared to teach him riding and shooting and all the varied amusements of the class that did little but amuse themselves.

Looking at his own reflection now, Ethan had to admit that his father had done one hell of a job of it. Ethan Damont, born of a clothmaker father and a seamstress mother, looked every inch the aristocrat his father had wanted him to be.

Of course, his father's goal had been to raise the entire family to a higher level of society. Pity the old man hadn't realized that by making sure his son was a true aristocrat, i.e., to-the-bone lazy and useless, he'd virtually guaranteed that Ethan would have little or no interest in the design and production of mattress ticking.

Or in becoming the stepping-stone in his father's social-climbing ambitions.

The old fellow hadn't taken that one well at all. Nine years ago the elder Mr. Damont had cast his only son from the house, proclaiming him worthless and unbearable. Remembering what a devilish sot he'd been at twenty, Ethan had to admit his father had likely been correct.

Well, one would never know it now. A fine house in Mayfair, servants who looked as though they might actually stick around for a while, and every appearance of gentle indolence—at the moment, the worthless and unbearable part was entirely invisible to the naked eye.

A pair of ladies passed behind his reflections, accompanied by a heavily laden footman. Two bonnets turned his way, then back toward each other. Scandalized giggles emerged from both. Ethan became aware that he was gazing thoughtfully into the window of an establishment that sold ladies' unmentionables.

Chuckling at his own gaffe, Ethan was about to continue on his way when another motion behind him caught his eye in the reflection. A small, tattered man was scuttling down the street, his back to Ethan.

Ethan blinked, then shook his head. The city was full of shabby people of the streets, many of them small, many of them tattered. There was no reason to think . . .

He turned and went on his way, leaving with only a glance at the pretty items discreetly displayed. Only swatches of fabrics and lengths of lace were visible, as if the materials only became unmentionable—and unviewable—after they were cut and sewn.

Lace spread over creamy satin jogged Ethan's memory, bringing last night's adventure to mind. As he walked on, he allowed himself a moment to warm himself on the memory of long lovely legs . . .

He hadn't seen her face. Ah, it was just as well. Not just any face could have lived up to the promise of those silken thighs. A woman would have to be entirely stunning to merit those limbs. Her hair would have to be golden—or raven black, like Rose Tremayne's hair. Exceptional hair.

Last night's lady had a mass of hair all right, but Ethan couldn't recall the color precisely. Not golden, not dark. Something in between, no doubt. In between and entirely ordinary.

Except that it had reminded him of firelight on creamy silken sheets . . .

Her figure in general had been adequate, if he recalled the dimensions correctly from his elusive moment of handling her down from the tree. Trim waist with acceptable amount of bosom, if not generous. She'd reacted to his fresh behavior with distaste and sarcasm, but with an added patina of innocence she was likely not even aware of. Unmarried? A virgin?

Well, there was no point in wondering. He hadn't seen her face and she'd made sure of it. Obviously, she wanted no one to know of her predicament.

Curiosity nagged at him. In his urgent desire to flee the scene of his cheat, he'd not lingered to learn how she'd managed to get herself into such an unlikely position. Or her name, or her family.

No point, old man. She was at Lord Maywell's ball. She was aristocracy and therefore out of his reach. He'd

always been most circumspect about that particular in-
fringement. Dallying with a bored wife would merely get
him beaten and evicted from the estate. Toying with a virtuous daughter of Society would get him shot at dawn—at
least, it would if he were a gentleman. A man such as himself wouldn't be afforded such a dignified end. More
likely he'd simply be found dead in a ditch. Of course, if
he were a gentleman, such actions would more likely get
him married.

Frankly, he'd rather be shot.

Whistling away that particular disturbing image, and
cautioning himself against any more memories of the
previous night, Ethan continued on his way.

The day was very fine, indeed, and he suffered no
more interruptions of his peaceful frame of mind until he
neared his own street. Pausing before crossing to allow a
carriage to go by, Ethan happened to glance back the way
he had come—just in time to see a small, tattered man
duck into a doorway.

Scowling, Ethan strode back down the walk and
plucked Mr. Feebles from his hiding place with one hand.

"Oy, guv'nor!" The pickpocket Ethan had met on his
previous adventure with Collis Tremayne and that group
of rabid do-gooders, the Liar's Club, flapped both hands
sheepishly. "Whot you doin' here?" the little man said in
hastily manufactured surprise.

"Being followed, apparently," Ethan said grimly.
"Why?"

Feebles shrugged as well as he was able, considering
Ethan's grip on his collar. "Don't know what you mean,
sor."

Ethan made a disgusted sound and released the little
man, setting him back into his doorway with a slight
shove. "Stay away from me," he said. "All you lot, just
stay away."

He strode off, his grip on his walking stick tight with
fury. Those damned Liars . . . getting mixed up with them

had nearly got him killed once before. Ethan wasn't fond of getting killed.

Bloody bastards, bloody sneaking, invisible bastards—

Ethan halted, then turned back. He strode to Feebles's doorway to find the man leaning comfortably against the wall, idly picking his teeth. "You weren't following me, were you?"

Feebles flicked his toothpick past Ethan into the street. "No, sor. If I'd been followin' you, you'd never have seen me."

"You wanted me to see you. Why?"

"Don't know, sor. I was told to be seen around every corner, I was." Feebles grinned. The elfin smile didn't do much to ease the impression that he was eerily odd. "If I was you, I'd be thinkin' someone wanted to keep an eye on me and wanted me to know it."

"Lord Etheridge?" The leader of the Liars wasn't someone Ethan would have ever met under other circumstances, being far too high above him and far too upright a fellow to invite a gamester to his home for amusement. If Lord Etheridge wanted to see him socially—well, he wouldn't. Which meant it had something to do with those bloody pikers, the Liars.

Ethan turned back to Feebles. "What—"

Feebles was gone. Ethan was quite sure he wouldn't spot the little man again. He was also quite sure Feebles would still be there.

Over breakfast in Lord Maywell's chilly breakfast room, Jane toyed with her fork as her cousins chattered endlessly about the previous night's ball.

Even now, Uncle Harold ignored the chatter and chaos about his breakfast plate, instead absorbing himself with the day's news sheets. Poor Aunt Lottie, always left to handle things on her own. Jane shot her uncle a disapproving glance.

He didn't see it.

She cleared her throat.

He turned a page.

"Uncle Harold!" Her voice echoed through the break-fast room. She wouldn't have believed there could be a break in the madness, but of course, there was, right at the moment she'd chosen to speak. All eyes turned to her, even her uncle's.

"I say, Jane," he muttered. "You do have a set of lungs on you."

"Tsk-tsk, Jane." Aunt Lottie shook her head. "I know you've been brought up in the country, dear, but there's no need to yodel *here*."

Jane narrowed her eyes at them all. "I only meant to speak above the noise, Aunt Lottie."

Six pairs of female eyes regarded her with complete innocence. "What noise, dear?" Aunt Lottie seemed seri-ously concerned with her sanity.

Uncle Harold was already diving headfirst back into his news sheets.

"I intended to ask Uncle Harold what he thought of the young gentlemen who attended last evening," Jane said. "I did not meet them all to speak to, and I value his opinion."

Uncle Harold blinked. "What? Oh, that useless lot. Bunch of simpering second sons without a hope in hell of inheriting anything useful. Boring too. You girls ought to be glad to see the last of those fellows."

"The last?" Augusta seemed horrified by the very thought. "What do you mean, Papa?"

"No more balls, hosting or attending," Uncle Harold said bluntly. "Can't afford more dresses and you and your sisters won't wear anything twice."

Such an unjust accusation silenced all the women at the table for a long indignant moment. Still, Jane had to admit that her uncle had a point. Even though the girls had been the unofficial hostesses of the evening, and therefore entitled to first pick of the gentlemen, they'd scarcely been able to fill their dance cards.

The man from the garden had not danced, she was sure of it. She would have noticed someone so fine.

"That is too bad, Uncle," she said, answering his declaration above the wails and protests of her cousins. "You did seem to enjoy your cards so much last night."

"Hmph!" Her uncle grimaced over his eggs. "Only two players were any good—and one was married and the other is ineligible."

Aunt Lottie blinked. "Who was married? I only invited single men."

"Tremayne," Uncle Harold said. "Went and got himself married on the quiet."

Aunt Lottie gasped. "Not nice Mr. Tremayne!" The wails erupted once more. Jane thought that was a bit much, since everyone knew Mr. Collis Tremayne had been moon-high out of her cousins' reach even when unmarried.

"Who did he marry, Papa?" Augusta asked tearfully.

Uncle Harold shrugged. "Black-haired girl, the one he quit the game to dance with."

"I saw her!" Serena declared, as outraged as if the girl had stolen Tremayne from under their very noses. "She wasn't even pretty!"

Jane had seen her as well. The new Mrs. Tremayne was not a classic beauty, it was true, but Jane had thought her quite arresting and especially graceful. However, Jane had slightly more pressing questions on her mind at the moment. "You said the other interesting gentleman was ineligible?"

"Oh, Papa must be talking about Mr. Damont," Serena said knowledgeably. "You remember, the place card?"

"Serena, that's enough," Aunt Lottie admonished sharply. "We do not discuss our guests in that manner."

Uncle Harold grunted. "Don't know why not. It's only the truth. He won't be a guest of ours again. Bloody piker took the pot!"

"Harold!" Aunt Lottie gasped.

Jane didn't know why Aunt Lottie still bothered to object to her husband's vulgarisms. One would think after twenty-odd years of marriage that nothing would surprise her aunt.

Unfortunately, Uncle Harold ran the house, and if he said that Mr. Damont was never coming back, then it was so.

Unless . . .

"Quite right," Jane said stoutly. "You certainly don't need a fellow like that coming around to beat you so soundly at cards. It would be much wiser to stay away from anyone so much more proficient."

Uncle Harold slid a cold glance in Jane's direction. She blinked in dismay. Suddenly, she had a deep desire not to be seated at his right any longer. It would not do to underestimate this man.

"I never said he was 'so much more proficient,' Jane girl," he said, his voice low. "And I'll thank you not to tell me whom to invite to my own house and whom to exclude."

Jane nodded quickly and looked away. "Of course, Uncle. Forgive me."

Uncle Harold grunted and turned back to his eggs. "And he didn't beat me soundly either. I almost had him. I'll bring him back to play again tonight and this time I'll thrash him, see if I don't."

"Of course, Uncle," Jane agreed carefully. At least it seemed she'd had the ban against Mr. Damont lifted—

Abruptly, Jane caught herself. Why had she done that? Wouldn't it be best if Mr. Damont never darkened her doorway again? He'd seen—well, nearly *everything*.

She'd been particularly counseled by Mother not to call that sort of attention to herself. *"You must seem as decorative and demure as possible. Outspoken women are too often the object of curiosity."*

What if he spread the tale about? What if even now he was entertaining his friends with the story of how he'd plucked Lady Jane Pennington—if he had indeed recognized her—from a tree like a piece of indecently clad fruit? Mortification heated Jane's cheeks at the thought of his hands on her, lifting her down, and the way her body had slid against his, and the way he'd leaned close enough to—

Mortification, definitely. Nothing else. Pure, unadulterated embarrassment.

He wouldn't tell, *he couldn't*—yet Serena had said he was not a gentleman. He was just an ordinary man, who could not be expected to live up to the finer code of ethics demanded by a gentleman's status. He might very well tell the story, having no idea that he should not. How would he know better, after all, a man of his background?

And yet, he'd not pressed his advantage, not exactly. He'd been a bit fresh, of course, but then again, she'd been very rude not to thank him more sincerely. He seemed—

There was no help for it. She truly had no idea what sort of man he was. She needed to meet him again, speak to him, gain some assurance that he would never, ever, speak of what had happened.

Of course, the fact that she burned to look into Mr. Damont's eyes and see if Serena had been correct about that lonely, soulful gaze had absolutely nothing to do with it.

Nothing at all.

# Chapter Four

Ethan was bloody tired of being followed.

Although he himself had never officially joined the private gaming hell called the Liar's Club, he knew he'd find Collis Tremayne there. Collis and that bloody intimidating uncle of his—the other one, not the friendly, stout old sod Ethan had helped rescue—had something going on in that club. Ethan didn't know what, he didn't want to know what, he didn't bloody care—but he wouldn't stand for being watched like this.

He stormed past the doorman, who merely bowed and opened the door swiftly—which only fueled the fire more. The doorman knew him, and didn't the bloke look familiar from that riverside jaunt they'd all taken to stop that ship? Ethan shook it off. He didn't want to know. He just wanted to be left alone.

He let the doorman take his hat. "I want Tremayne," he demanded brusquely.

"Yes, sir." The bland-faced doorman nodded, then turned away.

Ethan stomped into the main gaming room and threw himself into a chair at an empty card table. The club was just beginning to fill. This sort of place was dead in the early evening, though if he recalled correctly it was lively enough in the early morning hours. A drink was set down before him. He took a sip, just to tell. Yes, his preferred label of brandy.

Bloody spooky lot, these Liar's Club blokes.

He toyed with a pair of dice from the craps table, rolling them simultaneously through the fingers of one hand, as though they were traveling from fingertip to fingertip of their own volition. Then he amused himself by making them disappear and reappear.

They felt odd to him, so he idly took a throw. They rolled to a stop an inch before they ought to have. He picked them up again and examined them closely. He kept track of every make of dice used in the more popular hells and made sure to bring his own whenever possible.

He had never seen this particular make before.

Collis Tremayne slid into the seat beside him, although Ethan's old schoolmate had not been in evidence before. "Good evening, Damont," Collis said easily. "I've been expecting you."

Ethan tossed the dice down and leaned back in his chair, his arms folded. "You bugger, Tremayne."

Collis grinned. "Sorry, not to my taste. But in this part of town, I'm sure we could arrange for it."

"Stop grinning at me, Collis. I didn't come here because you wanted me to. I came here because I want your bloke to stop following me."

"Feebles? He's just keeping an eye on you. We don't want anything to happen to you, Ethan."

Ethan narrowed his eyes. "What happens to me is not your business, Tremayne. Other than past friendship—getting farther in the past by the moment—I have no ties to you and your lot of—of— What do you blokes *do,* anyway?" Then he threw up his hands. "No, don't tell me. I truly, deeply *don't* want to know."

Collis looked around them. "Ethan, we cannot talk here. Come with me."

Ethan raised a brow. "No traps? No dark cellars with chains on the walls?"

Collis grunted. "No chains. Besides, if I recall correctly, I was the one chained, not you."

Since that was true enough, Ethan let his resentment subside long enough to follow his old friend. Collis showed him to a small empty private dining room off the game room, the type where business might be discussed without interruption. Nothing out of the ordinary. It was paneled in warm woods and pleasingly lit by a crystal chandelier.

Ethan turned to Collis. "So, what is it you want from me, Tremayne?"

A deep voice erupted from behind him. "Not him. Me."

Ethan's heart nearly stalled. "Bloody hell!" He whirled to see the other uncle, the imposing one, standing where there had only been an empty room seconds before.

Lord Etheridge's lips twitched. "Sorry to startle you."

Ethan scoffed. "No you aren't!" He whirled and headed for the door. "I hate this bloody club. The spookiest damned place—"

Collis held out one hand, stopping him. "Ethan, I think you should stay."

"Yes," said Lord Etheridge. "Stay."

Ethan would have preferred that the invitation not sound quite so much like a command. He'd been careful to never put himself in a position to take orders. A sensible plan in all. He wasn't any good at obedience. Orders made him twitchy with the desire to do just the opposite.

Lord Etheridge looked as if he were in the habit of expecting obedience. Ethan felt jumpy already. Not a promising sign of things to come in this encounter.

"Your dice are loaded," he accused bluntly.

Etheridge nodded. "An inventor friend of mine makes them for us. The fight against Napoleon is expensive. The Liars pay their own way." He eyed Ethan narrowly. "You have some objection to cheating the few for the good of the many?"

Ethan shrugged. "No. Personally, I cheat for my own

good. I only thought better of a gentleman such as yourself."

"The needs of the nation overshadow niceties such as personal honor," Etheridge responded easily.

Ethan eyed his lordship narrowly. Etheridge didn't sound like any lord he'd ever met before.

Unpredictability could be a bad thing in a situation such as this. Even knowing that could not have prepared him for what Etheridge said next.

"I've received approval from rather high up to impress you into our service, Mr. Damont." Lord Etheridge's lips twisted. "You belong to us now, such as you are."

Ethan's jaw dropped. Then he recovered, protesting even as he stood. "That is impossible. I am a free man!" That was true. He owned his home, had no debts, currently had enough blunt socked away to indulge in fine brandy for at least a year—

"I am afraid you are not," Lord Etheridge said slowly.

Collis jumped in. "Ethan, listen to us. You've not time to waste."

Ethan gazed from one to the other, his inner alarms clanging. "I'm not interested." He turned to go once more. The sooner he left this madhouse, the better.

"It seems that you are not a taxpaying sort of man, Damont. Your house could be seized."

Lord Etheridge's mild words stopped Ethan in his tracks. He whirled. "You cannot touch my house. I won it, I own it, free and clear! I can pay your bloody taxes today, if you like!"

"Then we shall appeal to your better nature." Etheridge sat at the gleaming table. "Please sit, Mr. Damont."

Collis joined his uncle. "Ethan, give us a quarter of an hour," he urged.

Ethan wanted nothing less, but he pulled one of the chairs apart from the others and sat. He watched both men narrowly. "You have thirteen minutes left."

Collis looked toward his uncle. "Dalton, convince him."

Dalton—Ethan decided upon the insolent familiarity with grim glee—steepled his fingers. "Mr. Damont, we find ourselves, and you, in a very . . ."

"Awkward," Collis supplied helpfully.

Dalton slid the younger man a quelling glance. "A very awkward position. By no fault of your own, you were pulled into a recent event that you had no right or responsibility to interfere with."

"Oh, that's nice," Ethan said sourly to Collis. "Saved your arse, I did."

Collis nodded in full agreement, but Dalton held up a hand. "It was an emergency, you were deemed trustworthy by long acquaintance with Collis, and I'm still trying to decide if Mrs. Tremayne acted wisely."

Ethan planted an elbow on the table, and his chin on his fist. "You weren't there when she needed you," he said bluntly. "*I* was minding my own ducks in my own house when Rose dragged me out by the hair." Ethan shrugged. "Not that I minded." He turned to Collis. "How is your lovely wife these days? Fierce as ever?"

Collis began to answer eagerly, but Dalton cleared his throat. Almost as one, Ethan and Collis rolled their eyes and turned their attention back to Dalton.

"Do not digress, if you please, Mr. Damont," he said shortly. "Then, you again assisted us in the distraction of Lord Maywell last evening while we—ah, investigated him."

Ethan snorted. "Cleaned out his safe box, you mean." He leaned back in his chair. "You've only nine minutes left, my lord."

"In short—"

"I beg of you," muttered Ethan.

Dalton darkened. "*In short,* Mr. Damont, since you know both dangerously much and yet even more dangerously little, we find ourselves in the position of having to decide what to do with you."

Ethan leaned toward Collis. "Is that the royal 'we'?"

Collis coughed back a laugh, but kicked Ethan under the table. "This is bad, Ethan."

"*We* are the Liar's Club, Mr. Damont," Dalton said with his teeth clenched in obvious irritation. "We work for the Crown. Intelligence, counterintelligence, espionage. Spies, Mr. Damont."

Too late, Ethan clapped his hands over his ears. "I told you I didn't want to know!"

Dalton watched him carefully. "You must have suspected."

Ethan cursed and put his hands down. "Suspecting is one thing. I *suspect* my cook is spitting in my soup. *Knowing* means never eating soup again."

Collis looked green. "Ugh." He raised his hand. "I move we eat no soup today."

Dalton ignored him. "Mr. Damont, enough dancing around the issue. We have decided to make you a Liar. You have intelligence, skills, and you have already proved your discretion. Despite my reservations, even I must admit this solution is vastly safer than letting you run free knowing a handful of half-truths."

"Tell him the best part," Collis urged.

Dalton gave a put-upon sigh. "Upon deliberation, it has been decided that you may forgo the majority of Liar training and apprenticeship. You have already secured an excellent education and you are financially independent— in a manner of speaking. Your talents are ideal for infiltration. As a professional gambler, you are accustomed to taking risks, you know how to read people, and as we observed a few moments ago, you are adept at sleight of hand."

He'd been watched, even then. "From now on I'm only using the privy in the dark," Ethan muttered.

His lordship did not pause. "Your profession provides the perfect cover to wander the Continent as a secure courier. Other than a few courses to round out your skills, you could be vested as a full Liar immediately."

Collis beamed. "Isn't that superb? Normally, the only way to join the club is through months of training or apprenticeship." He glanced puckishly at Dalton. "Although we have acquired some astounding talent through marriage."

Dalton shushed Collis with a sharp gesture and focused on Ethan. "I see you as primarily information acquisition," Dalton said, "and counter-espionage infiltration." Dalton's lips twisted with wry reluctance. "For your first mission, you are to go back to play a few more hands with Lord Maywell. We believe Maywell could be the opposition's mastermind here in London. The lads have dubbed this leader the Chimera . . ."

Ethan listened in horror as Dalton mapped out the rest of his life for him.

"We want you to string him along by his apparent compulsion to gamble. Whether his love of cards is real or merely a useful cover, he should welcome your presence at his game. Never let him win enough to salve his pride, or lose enough to cause him to exclude you." Lord Etheridge leaned back in his chair. "We cannot get into Maywell House again. He redoubled his number of guards today and canceled most of his family's social engagements for the last few weeks of the Season. Obviously our first intrusion last night has already been detected. He is incredibly particular about who he lets in, and now he will be more so." Etheridge gazed sourly at Ethan. "You, on the other hand, have already received an invitation to dinner and gaming tonight."

Ethan rubbed both hands over his face in an effort to clear his mind. "So, you connive to get me here this morning to ask me—nay, *tell* me—that like it or not, I am now a *spy*? And how do you know what invitations I've received?"

The situation was too eerie for words. He shoved back from the table and stood. "Your time is up. Good day, good sirs. I appreciate the kindness of your offer—no, actually I

don't and I think you're both barking mad—but I respectfully decline. Translate that as *'I'm getting the bloody hell
out of this madhouse!'* "

He turned to go, finally and at last. This time he made
it all the way through the card room and was stepping into
the front hall when Collis caught his arm.

Ethan pulled away angrily. "You won't convince me to
stay and listen for one more bloody minute, Tremayne."

Collis shook his head. "I'm not trying to. Come to me
if you have any questions, won't you, Ethan? It wouldn't
do to be seen around the club again. You might not get another chance to walk out."

"Is that a threat?"

Collis sighed. "Ethan, my former valet knew about the
club. He sold some newsy tidbits to the Voice of Society."

Ethan swallowed. Already he could see where that
would be a very bad idea. "Did the Liars kill him?"

Collis shook his head.

That was a relief. Ethan breathed a bit easier until Collis shrugged and said, "We haven't found him yet."

Bloody hell. Ethan stared at the man he'd thought was
his friend. "Whose side are you on?"

Collis sighed. "I'm a Liar, Ethan. My loyalties lie here.
I'm asking you to think seriously about this. I'm hoping
for an outcome that won't force me to choose."

"You recall that 'better nature' he mentioned?" Ethan
shook his head. "I just remembered—I don't have one."

With that, he took his hat and coat from the doorman
and left the club.

Jane dipped her quill tip into the inkwell and daubed it
absently on the side. She put pen to paper.

"Dear Mother . . ."

There she stopped. Normally, she blithely reported
every tiny detail of life here with her relations, right down
to naming every caller and delivery. Mother wanted to
know everything, so Jane did her best to serve.

So why could she not bring herself to tell Mother about the fellow Ethan Damont?

She was afraid that Mother might misunderstand, for one thing. How could she describe the way Mr. Damont had been skulking about the dark garden during the ball without making him sound much worse than he was?

Of course, she didn't know that he wasn't . . .

Frustrated with her own indecision, Jane gave up on her letter and cleaned her quill. As she stoppered the ink bottle, she resolved to find out for herself what sort of man Mr. Damont was.

She would see him again this evening when he came for supper and cards with her uncle, provided he responded to the invitation.

Jane absently brushed the feather tip of the quill down one cheek. She didn't know what to do about the locked room either. It bothered her no end that someone had been in there. Of course, it could have been a servant dusting—but during the peak of the ball? Unlikely.

It really wouldn't be appropriate for her to let herself into a room her uncle had expressly forbidden them all to enter—but Jane was full up to her eyebrows with "appropriate." She'd never realized how much freedom she'd had living in seclusion at the Dowager House until she'd come here to London and taken on the life of the pampered Society lady.

Despite the rigors of country living on a tiny stipend, she now recalled fondly those days when she'd had all the fields and moors to roam freely.

Here, she could not even set foot out into the street—or into a locked room of the house—without permission.

She never would have let that stop her before. But Mother had done so much for her, and she owed Mother complete obedience.

Then again . . .

Mother would want to know what was in the locked room, wouldn't she? Wasn't Jane supposed to be including every detail of her life here? And finding out that curious little tidbit for Mother would make Jane feel better about keeping her encounter with Mr. Damont a secret.

Even knowing that she was rationalizing without restraint, Jane smiled eagerly to herself. Finally, a bit of action!

# Chapter Five

Back in his house—his freely owned house, by God!—Ethan went over that morning's stunning disclosure in his mind again and again.

Collis Tremayne was a spy for the Crown. In the midst of pouring himself a drink to wash down that bit of news, another development struck Ethan, stopping him cold with the decanter still tilted in his hand. "Well, I'm damned," he whispered.

Rose Tremayne must be a spy as well.

After a moment, he finished pouring his drink, then absently left it on the decanter tray and walked away from it.

He'd known that, of course. He'd *suspected*.

Yet somehow, knowing for certain was something else altogether. Lively, lithe Rose . . . a *spy*!

Well, it was a good thing they'd never come together then, wasn't it? Ethan wanted nothing to do with spies of either side, thank you very much. They were mad, all of them.

What the hell would make someone want to risk their life for the abstract concept of "patriotism"? Oh, England was all right. He certainly didn't want to harm England, but he didn't see any reason why he should help her either. After all, what had England ever done for him?

No, that sort of bizarre black-and-white thinking

might work for honor-bound blokes like Etheridge and Collis, but Ethan liked his shades of gray just fine. Why fight when he could walk away?

Ethan went through the front entrance hall toward the stairs. He was going out tonight. He went out every night. He much preferred it to sitting about this deathly quiet house.

As usual, there was a pile of invitations on the hall table. Out of curiosity, Ethan stopped and sorted through them, looking for one in particular and frankly dreading finding it.

And there it was. "Lord and Lady Maywell, requesting the presence of Mr. Ethan Damont for an evening of cards. Supper will be served at nine . . ."

Feeling an uneasy prickle on the back of his neck, Ethan dropped the thick card back on the table. He wasn't going and that was that. He had no one to please but himself, no matter what Etheridge had to say about it.

As he went upstairs to dress for his evening out, one thought kept going through his mind.

Rose Tremayne . . . a spy.

Who would ever think that a woman could be a spy?

Ethan had first met Rose when she'd banged on his door at the ungodly hour of noon one day. She'd demanded his help on the basis of his schoolyard friendship with Collis, pumped him full of coffee, and dragged him, red-eyed and hung-over, into the most frightening and exhilarating adventure of his life, rescuing Collis and his fat relation from the bowels of a traitor's munitions factory.

Of course, he'd hated every minute of it, except for the reward he'd received from Collis's dear old Uncle Codger. And except for every minute he'd spent in Rose's company, of course. He'd taken a fancy to the extraordinary Rose but, as usual, it had been Collis who got the girl in the end.

Later, Ethan examined himself in the cheval mirror in

his dressing room. Jeeves tied a mean neckcloth, that was certain. Ethan could find no fault in his butler's arrangements. "I could seduce a widow at a funeral," Ethan marveled.

"A worthy pursuit, I am sure, sir." Standing behind him with a clothing brush at the ready, Jeeves betrayed no sign of irony.

Ethan pointed one finger at him. "Don't disparage my methods, O Butler Mine. You'd be surprised at the gratitude one can inspire at such moments."

"I am in no doubt, sir. It sounds like the true path to happiness indeed." Jeeves put away the unchosen garments with blinding efficiency. "May I inquire as to your destination tonight, sir?"

Ethan tugged at his cuffs. "Not to Maywell's, that is certain," he muttered resentfully.

Jeeves blinked mildly. "Indeed, sir? Did his lordship not invite you for cards this evening?"

"He did." Ethan blew out a breath, then turned to his butler. "Jeeves, have you ever been forced to do something you don't want to do?"

"Daily, sir," was the prompt reply.

Ethan blinked. "Really? What is that?"

"I very much dislike dusting, sir. It makes my eyes water."

Ethan narrowed his eyes. "You're fishing for more servants, aren't you?"

"No, sir. I am simply answering your question."

Ethan closed his eyes. "Very well, Jeeves. You may bring in a housemaid."

"Thank you, sir," Jeeves said mildly. "However, I'd prefer to bring in a footman. A young fellow about the place would be most useful."

Ethan's lips twisted without humor. "Reluctant to bring a young girl into the house? Which is no reflection of your opinion of me, I'm sure."

Jeeves did not respond, but only kept his gaze level.

Ethan gave up. "Very well. I assume you have one in mind?"

"Yes, sir. It happens I do. A very sturdy young man by the name of Uri."

"Does this mean I may drink in my study again, now that you have Uri to roll me up the stairs?"

Jeeves went very still. "If the master insists, sir."

Ethan sighed. "Oh, never mind. I'll keep the brandy in my sitting room."

Nothing actually resembling relief crossed Jeeves's face, yet Ethan had the distinct impression the old fellow had dodged a near bullet. Why were Ethan's drinking habits of such importance to him?

"I'm off, then." He took his hat and gloves from Jeeves's ready hands and donned them in front of the mirror. At the very last, he flicked his hat with one finger to add just the right jaunty slant to the brim.

"Have a very enjoyable evening, sir," Jeeves said. "Oh, sir . . ."

Ethan paused. "Yes, Jeeves?"

"I always find the best path to take when someone is trying to force my hand is to do precisely what I would have done had they not attempted it."

Ethan was startled. "Good God, Jeeves, did you just offer me an actual personal opinion?"

Jeeves only gazed at him serenely. "Why would I do that, sir?"

Ethan shook his head. "Right. Sorry. My mad imagination at work, I suppose. Besides, I cannot go to Lord Maywell's. I did not accept the invitation."

"Have no fear, sir. I took the liberty of accepting it for you."

Ethan closed his eyes briefly. "That doesn't mean I'm going, Jeeves."

"Of course not, sir. Have an enjoyable evening, sir," Jeeves said calmly.

The hired carriage stood outside, as ready as if it were

his own. Truly, Ethan had never commanded such service before he'd hired Jeeves. The man was, indeed, a treasure, just as advertised by his previous employer, Miss Lillian Something-or-other.

Ethan wasn't one to look a treasure in the mouth.

Settling into the seat, he gave his gloves a final tug and pondered his evening. He'd half-decided to try his luck at the Liar's Club tables tonight, just to show that lot that he couldn't be railroaded into anything—but Jeeves's words kept floating through his mind. *"Do precisely what I would have done had they not attempted it."*

And the fact was, if Etheridge had kept his annoying gob shut, Ethan would have at this moment been on his way to answer Maywell's challenge and take some more of his lordship's lovely money.

With swift decision, Ethan rapped on the ceiling of the carriage. The small trap flipped open. "Maywell's, in Barkley Square!"

The carriage paused, then the driver began to turn. Ethan slouched back onto the emerald velvet seat. He would go to Maywell's and do his best to get thrown out. That would show those manipulative bastards what!

Jane took a bit more care than usual with her hair tonight. When she was done, despite the fact that she'd been dodging Serena's elbows for brief glances in the looking glass over the vanity, even she had to admit that she looked especially fine.

Every hair was in place, bound by strings of tiny pearls and ribbons so sheer one could see right through them. The length was twisted elegantly into a knot high on her head, which showed off her neck to great advantage.

"Ooh, Jane! You do look nice!" Serena blinked innocently at her. "Have you set your cap for someone who is coming tonight? Tell me, please do!"

Jane paused in the act of applying finely ground rice

powder to her face. Set her cap? Is that what she was doing, setting her cap for Mr. Ethan Damont?

That was ridiculous, of course. Why would she be dressing up for some gambling, womanizing rake?

*If not for him, then who?*

When she couldn't answer that question, even to herself, Jane pulled every pin from her elaborate hairstyle. While Serena looked on in horror, Jane brushed out the silken reddish-blond mass and twisted it up into a simple knot on the back of her neck.

Passing by the pale lavender confection of silk and lace that lay ready for her across the foot of the bed, Jane went to the wardrobe and removed the plainest gown available. Of course, the leaf-green silk was still very fine and fatally elegant, but it was the least flirtatious thing she had.

Now dressed more befitting a casual dinner with family, Jane left Serena to her primping. The male guests were already gathering in the smoking room downstairs, so Jane went into the garden for a bit of clear air and hopefully a bit of clear thinking.

If Mr. Damont appeared this evening, she would not have much time to discover whether or not he could be trusted. At any moment he could say a few words that would destroy her chances to fulfill her responsibility to Mother. Being revealed to the world as a hoydenish wanton would most definitely get her sent away from here.

The thought crossed her mind that she would then never be forced to dance with any more clumsy young men—but that was not the point. Mother had expectations of her. Jane wouldn't let Mother down for the world.

*"You must never appear too obvious. Subtlety will get the job done where candor will not."*

Unfortunately, she had not been very subtle last night—neither before the rescue nor after. If Mr. Damont thought her wild and abandoned, he'd have good reason to.

Jane smoothed her plain skirts and took the path through the garden that did *not* pass beneath the elm tree.

For the second time in twenty-four hours, Ethan found himself making his escape from Lord Maywell's. The smoking room was full of tender youthful louts here to pay homage to one of the young marriageable ladies of the house. Ethan had obviously been invited to keep his lordship occupied with cards while the other fellows pursued their marital goals.

*They might invite you to supper, but they wouldn't want you to marry their daughter.*

Not that he was surprised, of course. Society had been this way since time immemorial. Why would it change?

Ethan closed his eyes and inhaled deeply of the chilling evening air. He toyed with a cheroot but did not light it. He did not so much smoke them for his own enjoyment as use them as one of his many distractions for his prey.

There was no one here to perform for. No one but the sculptures and the shrubbery to see him pass one hand over his face in weariness. So tired of keeping up his game . . . so tired of being charming and dashing and useless.

*Then join the Liars,* said that voice from within. *Be of use.*

Ethan snorted at his own conscience—if indeed it was his conscience and not the first sign of incipient madness—and replied out loud.

"What use would I be, a man who cannot be trusted?"

A sound came from the garden at his words. No more than a rustle, swiftly silenced, but enough to bring something into focus in the darkness.

What Ethan had believed to be another bit of shrubbery was in actuality a woman in a green dress, standing against the deeper emerald of the foliage. Her pale face shone dimly, as if it were nothing more than a bit of marble statuary among the other figures that stood so incongruously in this urban sylvary.

Ethan rose slowly from his slouch against the wall, all the while keeping his gaze hard upon the woman. It would not do to lose sight of her—although he was not quite sure why it mattered so.

She made no effort to escape him as he approached. Indeed, as he neared her he was forced to reevaluate his assumption that she was trying to remain hidden, for she was simply standing there in full sight. It was a mere accident of coloration and light that had made her seem to emerge from nowhere.

He bowed courteously. "Good evening, ma'am. Ethan Damont, at your service."

She curtsied with all due politeness, but did not speak. Ethan peered more closely at her, but for all of him he could not place her.

# Chapter Six

The world seemed suddenly so quiet around them. Even the night insects were quieted, with nary a flutter of moth wings to be heard. The sounds of the male laughter faded and Jane became very aware of the beat of her heart.

Her pulse pounded, in fact. How silly. She was neither frightened nor nervous. She willed her breathing to slow and her heart to follow. Mr. Damont stood quite calmly before her, offering no threat. His head was tilted slightly to one side as he waited for her to speak. Surprisingly, he gazed at her with complete lack of recognition.

Could that be? True, her hair had been hanging everywhere . . . and her back had been to the dim light coming from the house.

Realizing that made her suddenly loath to speak. He had heard her speak, and Jane had been told more than once that her voice was quite distinctive. It would be best to remain quiet for the moment, and it might prove most interesting to see how such a man would behave in the present situation. To be truthful, she was reluctant to condemn him for his behavior last night, for she had been rude first.

Tonight provided a fresh start. What would he say? How would he behave toward her? So far, he had introduced himself—a social imposition, but not one that she found important. After all, what was he to do upon finding a strange woman standing alone in a garden at night—ignore her?

To her surprise, he suddenly smiled and offered his arm. "The dew is falling. Your slippers will be wetted. Shall we adjourn to the terrace?"

Bemused by his easy tone, Jane placed her hand lightly on his arm. They turned and crossed the lawn as sedately as if they were strolling in Hyde Park in the middle of the afternoon. Jane lifted her hem slightly to mount the three steps to the terrace and found that the dew had indeed dampened her gown and slippers. He seated her upon the stone bench, then braced one foot upon it and leaned an elbow on his knee.

"Forgive my impertinence, ma'am, but have we ever been introduced?"

Jane shook her head. It was not a lie. No one had ever formally introduced them.

"Then I am shockingly forward, I fear," he said with a rueful smile. Heavens, he was a handsome one, wasn't he? Jane fought down the increasing rate of her pulse once again. She was only here to discover whether he was the sort to divulge her embarrassment to the world.

"Are you a guest at this party?"

Jane shook her head. She was one of the hostesses, but she could hardly explain that with hand signals, now could she?

Mr. Damont seemed to take her answer in a somewhat different light. He visibly relaxed. "Ah, one of the unwashed multitudes, then, like myself. I'll wager you're chaperone or companion to that mob of daughters in there."

Jane blinked, suddenly wondering if that, indeed, was her role in that house. Goodness, the thought had never occurred to her—but otherwise why would her uncle bring in another girl to marry off, when he already had five to worry about?

Ah, but she was the only one who stood a chance, wasn't she? She was an heiress, unlike her cousins. She was quite suddenly wryly sure of what her role in that family was . . . she was bait. Bring in the men, attract the eligible bachelors, so that the sisters might have a shot at bagging one of the extras.

Mr. Damont took her silence for assent and relaxed further. "They're nice girls, for their sort. I'm only glad I'm not on their list." He smiled down at her. "Common as a cart horse, that's me."

Jane went very still, mesmerized by the sudden warmth in his eyes. He was looking at her as if she were simply an ordinary girl—not "my lady," or "the heiress," or even "wealthy customer."

If she was not mistaken, no man had ever looked at her like that in her life.

She smiled shyly back up at him, a real smile, without a smidgen of social reticence in it.

His eyes warmed further. "You as well, eh?"

Her gaze went to his fine cravat, tied in the latest style, ruby stock pin glittering in the folds. He followed her gaze, glancing down at himself with a wry grimace.

"Protective coloration," he explained. He nodded at her severe silk gown. "Like you. If you went about in rags, you'd only draw attention. You must put half your pay into keeping up appearances," he said sympathetically.

Jane looked down and smoothed her skirts. Did she really look like a governess in this gown? True, it was cut very simply.

She was suddenly overcome by a wild desire to own something daring and bright, something that would make Mr. Damont's eyes pop from his head—

Not that she cared what he liked. Not at all. But there was that sapphire-colored silk she'd seen displayed at the modiste's . . .

Ethan gazed down at his companion. Aside from that one unfettered, surprisingly contagious grin, she'd scarcely been able to respond to him at all. She was a funny, shy creature, wasn't she?

Of course, that explained why she was lurking in the garden tonight. Still, shirking her duties that way made her a bit of a rebel as well, and Ethan was very fond of rebellion. He encouraged it, in fact.

He leaned close to her ear. "Stay right here," he whispered. "I shall return in a moment."

With a wink, he quickly let himself back into the house. It was the work of only a moment to abscond with two glasses and a bottle of wine left to breathe in the butler's pantry.

When he returned to the terrace, his new friend was standing at the edge of the lawn as if she were contemplating making a run for the shrubbery. Tucking the wine under his arm, Ethan went to her and held out his hand.

"You cannot leave me now," he said with a smile. "If you go, I'll have to go back in as well." He put on a mournful face. "A fate worse than death, you know."

That got a tiny laugh from her, hardly more than an amused breath, but Ethan took encouragement nonetheless. Taking her unresisting hand, he led her back to the bench. "You and I," he said, "are the only two people in the world, as of this moment."

She was gazing at him in wry disbelief, her opinion of his madness plain. "Oh, I know," he said. "You think me mad, but look at it from this perspective. If we are the only two people in the world, then there is no one to condemn or decry us. No one else to whom we owe a farthing, or a favor." Or a house.

Ethan shook off any thought of the Liars and their deal with the devil. "I want an hour of freedom," he begged his companion with a smile. "Doesn't that sound grand?"

She glanced away, biting her lip slightly. The motion called Ethan's attention to the fact that she had a very pretty mouth—a nice bow to her upper lip and her bottom one was full enough to impart a hint of secret sensuality. Now that was interesting.

Being that he was no kind of gentleman, Ethan wasn't above stealing a kiss from a pretty lass. A pink tip of tongue flicked out to soothe that bitten lip.

No, indeed. Not above that at all . . .

His rebel governess turned back to gaze at him with a challenge in her eyes and a glass in her hand.

Ethan grinned. "That's my girl." He poured them both a few inches of wine. "Now, sip that slowly—"

When she quickly brought the glass to her lips, Ethan stopped her with a hand on hers. "There is no race," he said softly. "This is about savoring a moment of time out of time. Sip slowly and pretend that there is no tomorrow, no yesterday, no expectations—"

He halted at the soft sheen that came into her eyes. She blinked quickly, but the startled expression on her face gave him pause. He hadn't meant to upset her—but perhaps it was not his words that made tears threaten.

If what he was saying struck such a chord with her . . . well, perhaps they had even more in common than he'd first assumed.

He set his own glass on the bench and took her hand in both of his, glass and all. "Don't take on so," he whispered. "I know it can be hard to make your way where you do not truly belong—to walk in their halls and live in their rooms—and it must be doubly hard for you, lost between, who is neither servant nor equal—"

Jane could not withstand the sweet sympathy in his voice, the warm comfort of his hands on hers. To her complete disbelief, a single hot tear broke free from her control to roll down her face. Why? She had no such burden! She was Lady Jane Pennington, without a care in the world.

And yet, until that moment, she had never before realized how truly alone she was. Lost between—yes, that was precisely how she felt. Few women in her world were her equal, either in status or in competence. Her own mother used to look at her as if she were not quite sure where her daughter had emerged from. Everyone looked to her when difficulties arose, but no one ever paused to wonder if she had any difficulties of her own.

Men knew not what to make of her, for her very competence seemed to turn them away. She was unfeminine, unwanted except for her wealth, which was more of an ironic joke than she'd ever dare admit.

Mr. Damont liked her . . . but Mr. Damont didn't know her. She let her hand relax within his warm ones. He took her glass away, setting it beside his. His eyes shone with sympathy for the plight of the shy governess. If she spoke now, revealed herself, he would—

What would he do? She found him entirely unpredictable. He was by turns charming and caustic, kind and cynical. He obviously had no love of the aristocracy.

Therefore it was very unlikely that he would continue to like her, to talk to her, and certainly not to hold her hand so comfortingly in his large warm ones.

She had no right to that comfort. It was undeserved and unwanted. She tried to pull her hand from his.

His fingers tightened gently about hers. "Shh," he soothed. "Don't be vexed. One tear does not an ocean make." He reached to brush his knuckles down her cheek, drying the path of that tear with a single caress. Jane nearly started. When had anyone ever touched her like that?

He flicked his fingers open in the air. "See? It never happened. No one will ever know. Besides, no one else exists tonight, remember?"

Jane nodded slowly, unwillingly charmed by the notion. That way she would not have to wonder, What was Lady Jane Pennington doing sitting in the dark with a common gambler, drinking his wine and holding his hand?

The door to the house opened, shattering the moment. "Ah, Lady Jane, here you are," the footman standing there said. "Her ladyship is seeking you."

Jane went quite cold. Her gaze shot to meet that of Mr. Damont. He dropped her hand and stared up at her as if she had suddenly turned blue.

Jane stood, never taking her gaze from Mr. Damont's shocked one. "Thank you, Robert. Tell her ladyship I will join her shortly."

When the obviously curious footman shut the door and left them in the dark once more, Jane clasped her hands before her. "Do please forgive my deception, but it was necessary to ascertain whether you were the sort of man to expose the embarrassing incident the other night—"

"You? That was you?" He seemed most distressed. "In the tree?" His eyes narrowed. "Who are you?"

Jane lifted her chin. "I am Lady Jane Pennington, daughter of the late Marquis of Wyndham."

Mr. Damont shot up from the bench. "You're a bloody actress, that's what you are! What sort of game is this?" He was indignant and angry, which she'd expected, but also visibly hurt, which she had not.

Jane took a breath. "I had no intention of misleading you, sir—"

"The bloody hell you didn't!" He ran a hand over his face, obviously reaching for control. "See here, Lady Jane, do you have any idea what sort of trouble a bloke could get into for trifling with a woman like you?"

Oh, dear. That possibility had never crossed her mind. "I've—I've no intention of making trouble for you, Mr. Damont."

He turned away, shaking his head. "I thought you were someone I—" He turned back angrily. "I suppose now we're going to play 'Call the magistrate, I've been assaulted,' am I correct?"

Jane drew back. "Of course not—"

"Why not? You've quite a case against me. I've held your hand, held you in my arms, touched you in all sorts of improper ways. I've even seen you in your knickers, lovely legs and all, haven't I?"

Jane swallowed. She hadn't meant to inspire such a rage—

*Lovely legs and all?*

Shocking. Bawdy. And very gratifying, in a secret feminine way that she would never admit. Did she have attractive limbs? Perhaps she did. How would she know, after all?

Ethan drew a deep breath. Calm down, old man. If the wench were going to call down the law upon him, she could have done so already. One scream and the house would have descended upon them and hauled him off her.

Instead, she had tricked him, lied to him—

Well, that wasn't strictly true. She hadn't spoken at all, but Ethan was in no mood to be charitable. Lies by omission were lies all the same. He ought to know, he'd practically invented the method.

Damnation, all he had wanted was a moment where he wasn't who he was . . .

*Perhaps that was all Lady Jane Pennington had wanted as well.*

Ethan wasn't willing to allow complete forgiveness, but his anger settled slightly. He turned to her. "I think it is time you went home. I'll have a footman fetch your carriage—"

"I live here," she interjected. "I am Lord Maywell's niece."

Ethan closed his eyes in complete surrender. "Of course you are." This was going to make his bloody blasted "mission" even more difficult. Ethan found himself very near laughter. "You are a lady, an heiress, the daughter of a marquis, the niece of Lord Maywell—and I've seen your knickers."

Lady Jane Pennington folded her arms. "I fail to see what you find so amusing, Mr. Damont."

Ethan laughed out loud. "Of course you don't!" He swept her a deep, mocking bow. "Back into the house with you, Lady Jane, or I'll tell every man in there what color your garters are!"

"Oh!"

She had the pure gall to be affronted. The lying schemer. She drew up to her full height—which was rather nicely tall, in fact, for she nearly reached his chin. Ethan had ever preferred tall women—and stalked away from him, shutting the terrace doors behind her with a decided slam.

Ethan let his head hang and rubbed one hand over his face. His fingers left a damp trail on his cheek.

Her single tear. Lady Jane Pennington, who had nothing to weep over as far as he could see, had left a single, hot teardrop in his hand.

Ethan touched his dampened cheek with curious fingers and wondered what he had said that would bring a woman like that to tears.

Ethan expected supper to be excruciating. These things usually were. Now, with the addition of the "matter of Lady Jane Pennington" to make him feel the breath of aristocratic retribution on the back of his neck, it looked to be a nightmare from hell.

Ethan's usual manner of passing the time at boring events was flirtation, but that would be impossible at the Maywell table. With the Maywell Mob making up nearly the entire list of attending ladies, there would be no safe targets for his charm.

Flirting with a young Society girl would mark him as unsafe—ending his parasitic career with one fell blow of the hammer. So far he was tolerated, even encouraged, because he'd never crossed that line. Oh, he'd had some playful encounters with married women, and a few memorable widows, but he knew what he was—and he knew what he wasn't.

So the Society daughters he treated with cool politeness, careful not to allow the slightest hint of attraction even to the most stunning of them. They weren't for the likes of him. They weren't even supposed to be breathing the same air.

When he was ushered into the main salon of Maywell
House, Ethan saw that his fears were realized. The only
ladies present were the five daughters of Lord Maywell
and their cousin, Lady Jane Pennington.

After leaving the terrace, he'd returned to the smoking
room and listened more carefully to the discussions floating about him. His impression was that Lady Jane Pennington was an heiress trolling for a duke at the least, for
she'd given short shrift to any lesser fellows.

The young blokes about town had dubbed her Lady
Pain for her manner of delivering her refusals. When
anyone met with her guardian, Lord Maywell, to plead
for her hand, Lady Jane had immediately shot back a
scathing refusal letter to each. Ethan didn't blame her for
seeking a higher match, but such cruelty could not be ex-
cused.

The most he could hope for this evening was to be
seated next to Lady Maywell, who was far too sensible to
flirt and might even offer some interesting conversation.

Instead, he found himself between the youngest—and
possibly the silliest—daughter, Serena, and Lady Pain
herself.

Of course. He sighed deeply, hiding it beneath the act
of sitting down. It was going to be a very long evening.

Lady Jane looked very much the proper heiress now.
Ethan was quite sensitive to the secret code enacted in the
nuances of dress and manner. Here in the full light, it was
obvious that Lady Jane's gown was finer even than Lady
Maywell's in cut and fabric.

He must be slipping, to ever perceive her as a lowly
governess.

The first course of soup was served. To his left, Miss
Serena Maywell promptly tipped her spoon onto her
bodice. Ethan suspected it was because she'd been staring
at him and not her soup, but he'd been careful to not quite
meet her eye.

He continued to act as if the spreading stain on her gown

were invisible, along with her tiny humiliated sniffles. He would have liked to charm her out of her upset, but she was so young that she'd surely take his attentions wrong.

Damn, the girl couldn't be but sixteen! She ought to be dreaming in her schoolroom, sneaking peeks through the banister at what the adults were up to! What were her parents thinking to throw her out onto the Marriage Mart at her age?

On the other side of him, Lady Jane cast fretful glances past him—or rather, *through* him—at Serena, but there was little she could do from where she sat. Finally Ethan, unable to bear the small hiccups now accompanying the sniffles to his left, turned helplessly to Lady Jane.

"Is there nothing you can do?" he asked in a low voice.

Lady Jane shook her head without looking at him. "I fear not," she murmured. "She cannot leave the table and I dare not call further attention to her now. We can only pray that no one else notices."

She was kind to her cousin, at least. Perhaps her spleen was saved for encroaching gamblers and overly ambitious suitors only. Still rather ill done of her, but not entirely nasty. Ethan tilted his head slightly toward her once more. "Then I fear I must make sure no one else notices."

Ethan leaned forward to speak to the table at large. "Have you all heard the latest about the Prince Regent? There's a driver who knows a footman who knows a chambermaid who swears she heard a donkey bray from the royal bedchamber—"

Jane sat back and watched Mr. Ethan Damont capture the attention of the entire party with one skillfully ribald tale after another. He was shocking, outrageous, and entirely entertaining without ever going over the line of innuendo and rumor. If she hadn't known his purpose, she would have thought him presumptuous and flashy— just the sort of fellow she could not bear.

But as she watched him engage everyone there, distracting them enough so that Serena was able to dab secretly at her gown with a damp dinner napkin—*rescuing* Serena like a knight charging in on a white horse of gossip, for pity's sake!—Jane found that she could bear him very well indeed.

He was angry with her, however, that much she was sure of. His manner was nothing like his teasing behavior before.

She could leave it at that, if she liked. He'd proved to-night that he would not willingly allow a lady to be embarrassed. It was possible that she could simply trust his nobler instincts . . .

No. It was no good. She'd never been one to bear suspense well. She had to know if he could be trusted with the truth. She would pin him down directly after supper.

# Chapter Seven

Once the ladies had left the dining room, Ethan made his escape into the hall, past a footman who stood guard against interruption, and around the corner. If he could just make it out of this madhouse, he would go back to the Liar's Club and tell Lord Overbearing that he could take his little spy ring and—

"Mr. Damont, I wish to speak to you."

Ethan nearly jumped out of his skin when the girl popped up from nowhere. "Good God, my lady!" He clapped a hand over his heart, not actually pretending. "Have pity, if you please!" He blinked at her, then dropped his charm like a hot rock. "Oh, it's you," he said dismissively.

Lady Jane drew herself up. "I do not see why you are so testy yet. I had a perfectly reasonable explanation for my actions. I needed to ascertain whether or not you could be trusted."

Ethan regarded her hotly. "And the verdict?"

Jane clasped both hands before her. "I found you charming and kind. Pity that I turned out to be so very wrong."

"Hmph." Ethan could not help feeling gratified that she had liked him. He had liked her as well, until—

"What do you mean, you were so very wrong?"

Jane fought back a smile. She'd certainly managed to get his attention. "Oh, very well. I suppose I wasn't so much wrong as I was . . . misled."

"Misled!"

She spread both hands against his outrage. "Truce! I shall admit it, I was not wrong." She dropped her hands and gave him a slight smile. "Why is that you take no affront when someone accuses you of cheating at cards, yet you took great offense when I said you were not charming?"

Ethan folded his arms defensively. "Well, I . . . I put a great deal of effort into being charming . . ."

Jane tilted her head. "And less into resisting the impulse to cheat?"

"What? No, I mean— Damn it, you are twisting my words about!"

Jane nodded. "I am. I don't know why. You seem to bring out the devil in me."

Ethan laughed out loud, a swift bark of surprise. "You and the devil have not the slightest acquaintance, I'm sure."

"Why not? Did you not earlier accuse me of lying?"

"That wasn't lying. That was a mere sin of omission." He grinned at her and she couldn't help but smile back.

Then Lady Jane folded her arms and narrowed her eyes. "Why didn't you talk to me during dinner? It was very rude of you to ignore me."

Ethan couldn't answer that one, since he hadn't ignored her at all. He'd been exquisitely aware of her every movement, her every breath—especially the way said breaths caused her bodice to tighten over her succulent breasts.

He abruptly wished he could smack himself on the head. How could he be so entranced by the mere act of inhaling and exhaling? It was only breathing, for pity's sake! Yet somehow when she did it, he was captivated.

Jane took a deep breath, then halted when Mr. Damont let out a heartfelt moan. "What is it? Are you ill?"

"Yes," he said faintly. "I am evidently a very sick man."

She leaned closer and peered into his face. His eyes widened in something that might almost be called fear, then shut tightly.

"Only breathing, only breathing . . ." he seemed to be muttering over and over. He backed away, still blind. Jane grabbed his arm before he could collide with a marble-topped hall table that contained a fine Chinese vase she was fairly sure was older than England itself. She gave Mr. Damont a sturdy yank to pull him back from danger.

He stumbled, coming up against her, chest to breast. Jane froze in surprise at first, then forced herself to stand still. For some reason, she found herself quite desperate to get Mr. Damont to truly *look* at her, the way he had outside. Perhaps being entirely without propriety would get his attention.

He was holding himself quite immobile as well. Then slowly, with an air of quiet purpose, he inhaled deeply. The act brought his hard chest more firmly against her. With a mixture of shame and exhilaration, Jane felt her nipples harden within her bodice. Could he feel it?

His gaze, which had shot off to one side when they impacted, slid slowly back down to where their bodies met. Dizzy with her own lack of breath, Jane inhaled as well.

Ethan's mind went entirely blank when he saw her creamy breasts swell against his chest. Then the blood rushed from his brain completely, apparently needed by other portions of his anatomy as he felt the jewel points of her nipples boring through his waistcoat. One would have thought the layers of fine silk and linen would have fended her arousal off, but no. The fact was undeniable.

Lady Jane Pennington possessed a burning desire for him, Ethan Damont.

Bloody hell. With a graceless nod and an unintelligible mumble, Ethan ran for the card room where the other gentlemen waited.

There was safety in numbers, after all. Ethan was feeling

the need for a bit of safety from the audacious Lady Jane
Pennington.

He'd wriggle his way out of this "mission" later.

Jane knew her uncle would be occupied with his card game
after supper. All the men had left and the women—mostly
Lady Maywell and the Mob, since inviting women to supper would only defeat the purpose—had retired to the
drawing room and were listening to each other play and
sing, or perhaps playing a few hands of cards themselves.

Jane begged off, claiming the headache—which wasn't
far from the truth. Something was pounding indeed.

Mr. Damont had run from her as if she'd suddenly
sprouted horns, leaving her standing oddly bereft and
slightly chilled in the hall.

What a strange, tense moment that had been. She'd
never been so close to a man, standing chest to breast that
way . . .

She pressed a hand to her flushed face. She should be
very much shamed by her own behavior. She wasn't.
Stimulated, perhaps, and a good bit disturbed, but there
didn't seem be a bit of shame in the mix. It seemed she
had little of that organ left.

Her obvious flush helped her case, fortunately. Her
harried aunt only nodded assent, looking slightly envious
as she did so. Jane tried to cover her story as well as possible when she went to her room, even by sending the
maid for a cool cloth and then telling her she didn't want
to be disturbed.

She mussed the bed artistically and even donned her
own night rail and wrapper, so that if she was caught she
could say she was looking for something to read herself
to sleep.

Then, when she was sure that the entire household was
occupied elsewhere, Jane made her way to the seldom-
used wing of the house. The room where she'd seen the
glimmer of candlelight was here.

One by one, she entered each south-facing room and counted the windows. This wing was not kept well heated and Jane was glad for her thick brocade wrapper. The first room was an unused chamber that looked as though it had been meant for a music room. The second was smaller and more charming, reminding Jane of her mother's morning room where her mother had done the menus and her correspondence. Each of these had two tall windows to the south, so the next room must be the one, just as she'd thought.

The door to the next room was locked. Jane pondered the lock for a long moment. She'd heard of picking a lock with a hairpin, but that was a skill she'd never acquired.

Lady Maywell kept a key ring, as did the housekeeper and the butler. Jane dared not venture belowstairs for fear of being caught far out of her place, but Lady Maywell's bedchamber was not far from her own. Padding as swiftly and silently through the halls as she could, Jane paused outside her aunt's door. If her aunt's maid was present, Jane would have to come up with some pretense for entering, a pretense that might come unraveled later.

Still, faint heart never won piddle-squat. Taking a deep breath, Jane pressed open her aunt's door.

There was no one within. If she hurried, she ought to be able to use the key and get the key ring back to her aunt before anyone saw it was missing.

Jane turned and left the room, forcing herself to walk sedately, and perhaps even a bit weakly, until she reached a hall where she knew no one would be about. Then she ran, her slippers making a sound like bird wings on the runner.

Jane hurriedly tried the first five keys at random, until her nervous fingers dropped the ring to the carpet and caused her to lose all track of what she had tried.

"Oh, horse apples!" she hissed to herself. Then she forced herself to slow her frenzy. Methodically using one key, then the next, then the next, she worked her way around the key ring until only two remained.

The second-to-last key slid easily into the keyhole and she heard the tumblers within give a well-oiled turn. The door was open.

Quickly she picked up her candle and slipped within.

Lord Maywell's house was very fine, although Ethan had detected a bit of crumbling about the edges, but one could tell that it was in his lordship's card room where truly no expense was spared. The fine plush chairs, the deep emerald felt on the card table—even the chandelier was one especially commissioned to shine downward onto the cards without creating a glare for the players. Ethan knew this because he'd fancied installing one just like it someday.

It was clear that his lordship took his card playing most seriously.

Ethan seated himself at the remaining empty chair with a nod of apology to Lord Maywell. "I beg your pardon, my lord."

Maywell stared at him for a moment, obviously waiting for an explanation, but Ethan had none to give. He could hardly tell the man he'd been rubbing body parts with Lady Jane, could he?

The cards were dealt and Ethan began to get down to the business of playing. He'd no backup cards on him tonight, for he'd sworn he wasn't coming here. He was reduced to using the basics—observation, distraction, bluff—to create just the right environment for Lord Maywell to begin to win.

Surely if his lordship beat Ethan Damont at cards, he'd lose interest in extending any more such invitations. Without such invitations, the Liar's Club couldn't very well expect Ethan to continue with this madness?

Except Maywell wasn't winning.

Ethan watched the cards and the other players carefully. The fellows at the table were all cut from the same cloth. They played with careless panache, the way gentlemen were supposed to play. One didn't quibble over the loss of a few or twenty pounds at the tables. To even consider such a trivial loss would imply that one wasn't entirely flush—a deadly fate in Society.

No, it couldn't be that one of them was interfering with his control of the game. That only left himself—and while his heart wasn't truly into it, he was still capable of manipulating such an easy table—and Lord Maywell. Finally, Ethan gave in and allowed his lordship to lose. As the pot was gathered, the vowels totaled, and the cards shuffled, Ethan sat back and contemplated Lord Maywell through the wafting tobacco smoke.

Maywell was contemplating him right back.

Well, this wasn't going quite as planned. Ethan would have to come up with another way to never be invited back. "Your niece seems a fine young lady," he said conversationally.

Maywell nodded. "We've grown very fond of Jane," he said tonelessly.

Ethan raised a brow. "Grown? Were you not fond of her before?"

The other blokes froze at that impertinence, sliding their wary gaze between Ethan and Maywell, who both sat cool and relaxed, leaning back in their chairs in an open manner.

Maywell only grunted. "Never knew her before this Season. She's my wife's sister's daughter. They'd not talked for years. Then one day here comes Jane with a carriage full of trunks, to stay with us for the summer."

Ethan could tell the others were fascinated with any tidbit about Jane. That bothered him a bit. He ignored it. "That must be very nice for you all," he said, in a voice implying he could not care less. "She's not much to look at though, is she?"

The others began to protest avidly. Lady Jane was the loveliest, brightest, most delightful—blah, blah, blah. None of them had actually spoken to the acerbic, opinionated Jane, that was obvious. For a moment, Ethan almost felt sorry for the girl. He knew what it was like to walk around with a sticky label on one's forehead, telling the world in precisely which slot they were to fit one. Of course, Lady Jane's slot was velvet-lined and diamond-studded, so Ethan didn't bother feeling sorry for long.

Maywell didn't change expression. "We've had no complaints," he said calmly.

Ethan shrugged carelessly. "It matters not a jot to me, of course."

One of the others laughed disbelievingly at that. "Well, of course it wouldn't, Damont! I mean, really!"

Ethan slid an even glance the speaker's way. "Right. Thank you so much for reminding me."

"No thanks needed, old man," the speaker said earnestly.

Ethan was barely able to refrain from rolling his eyes. Maywell only looked amused. "What good company we have tonight," he said in a lazily jolly tone.

The other blokes—Ethan was just going to think of them as the Suitors from now on—the Suitors all looked very pleased with themselves. Ethan hoped Jane did pick one of these idiots. He'd like to watch her trample such a husband all the rest of their days.

Except that she really was too good for this lot. Even with her odd ways and cruel reputation, Lady Jane Pennington was of a higher order altogether. These half-wits hadn't a chance in hell of winning such a prize.

Maywell didn't think so either, Ethan could tell. Why did his lordship surround himself with such trivial young men? Didn't the fellow have anyone his own size to pick on?

Ah, yes. Enter himself.

The discussion turned political. Only Lord Maywell himself kept silent on the subject, surprisingly.

All Ethan had to do was to endure the rest of this evening, then he could go back to the Liars and tell them they were wrong about Lord Harold Maywell.

*But what if they aren't?*

Well, that wasn't his headache, was it? If the Liars wanted to believe the word of a halfhearted gambler they'd indentured into their little ring, then that was their complaint, wasn't it? After all, they were idiots to be trusting someone like him—he was a *cheat,* for God's sake!

*Can you really let Maywell go free without knowing for sure?*

"Just watch me," Ethan muttered under his breath.

"What was that, Damont?" Maywell blew out a smoke ring.

Ethan patted his pockets idly and took out one of his own special cheroots. One of the Suitors had evidently heard of this particular habit of Ethan's, for he protested immediately. "Not that, Damont, I beg of you!"

Ethan blinked innocently. "I say, do you blokes object if I smoke this in here?"

The Suitors objected. Strenuously. Ethan didn't blame them, for his cheroots were the foulest creations under the sun. It was a tobacco blend of his own invention, one he kept for just such occasions.

He had yet to meet another player who could bear the smell of it, and pulling one from his jacket pocket never failed to elicit a unanimous call for a break and a polite request that Ethan take himself and his cheroot elsewhere. Ethan usually only used it when he thought he might be losing. It gave him a chance to replace any necessary toys of the trade, not to mention the chance to sneak a peek at his fellow players' cards when leaving and reentering the room.

Ethan bowed to the other players. "My lord, sirs—if you gentlemen will excuse me for a moment?"

Maywell narrowed his eyes, but nodded shortly. The man obviously disliked any interruption of his gaming.

"Don't get lost this time, Damont," Lord Maywell growled around his cheroot. "I'll be wanting to win a bit of that back."

Ethan was only winning because Maywell was arranging it, but still Ethan delivered a fairly respectful nod. He couldn't toady very well, but that only seemed to make Maywell regard him all the more highly.

Once outside on the terrace, Ethan drew out his cheroot again and lit it, drawing only lightly on the bitter smoke. He needed to make this last, by God. He needed time to think.

As he pondered his lordship's behavior, Ethan narrowed his eyes against his own smoke. God, these things were foul.

Perhaps it was not so surprising . . . if his lordship was conducting some sort of test.

*"Charm him,"* the Liars had said. *"Get him to let you in."*

It was a gamble, trying to make a guess as to what Lord Maywell wanted to hear. Choose rightly, and he'd find himself drawn into his worst nightmare—responsibility. Chose wrongly, and he wouldn't be invited back.

Ethan grinned. Perhaps it was not such a gamble after all.

As he turned to put his cheroot out with a sense of olfactory relief, Ethan happened to glance idly up at the opposite wing of the house, the one that Maywell had mentioned was rarely used.

A candle flickered in one window.

# Chapter Eight

Jane was frustrated. There was nothing of interest in the tiny room. It was obviously meant for linen storage, but the shelves were nearly bare and the built-in drawers were empty.

There was a tiny hearth with a kettle hook jutting out from one side, so that one could swing a kettle over the coals to heat. Perhaps it was a sort of staging area for tea trays and such?

All was empty now. So what had someone been doing in here, skulking during the ball?

From the unswept floor, something tiny gleamed in the candlelight. Jane knelt to pick it up, rolling it in her fingers close to the light of her candle.

It was nothing but a shimmering clear glass bead, the tiny sort that was sewn onto ladies' gowns. Well, this house was full of ladies, so that wasn't much of a clue. This could have landed in here months ago.

Abruptly Jane realized she'd been in here long enough. She covered the candle with her hand as she moved past the bare uncovered window on her way to the door. Her eye was caught by a figure standing out in the lawn, dimly visible by the light of the house behind him.

It was him, Ethan Damont, renowned gambler and

rogue, midnight rescuer, and generally delectable individual—and he was gazing directly up at her with his arms folded disapprovingly.

Jane stepped into the library and carefully closed the door behind her. Mr. Damont stood staring at the cold hearth with his back to her, a looming shadow against the candelabra he'd lit. With her back to the door and her hand still on the knob, she waited.

"Lady Jane Pennington—one can find her in the oddest places," Mr. Damont said without turning.

Jane took a breath. "Yes, well, I do live in this house."

He turned and grinned at her with his hands stuffed in his pockets. "So what is it you were doing in the empty wing—" He took in her attire and raised an eyebrow. "In your wrapper, yet?"

"You look worried, Mr. Damont," Jane said. "Is that a problem?"

"Damn it, it is if anyone finds us together and you know it!"

Jane nearly laughed at his discomfort. "Are you a prude, Mr. Damont?"

With a flash of annoyance in his eyes, he folded his arms. "More so than you, apparently. Although I ought not to be surprised, I suppose."

She stiffened. "Oh, really? Why is that?"

"Why? Your penchant for high places, I suppose. Not to mention states of undress."

She blushed and looked away. "You may remember the occasion, Mr. Damont, but it is indelicate of you to remind me of it."

"Indelicate?" Ethan thought a moment. "Yes, I do think that is one of my attributes."

"Well, what do you want from me? Your pantomime 'Meet me in the library' was quite good by the way. I especially liked the motion you made for 'book.' Why did you wish to meet me here?"

"To warn you, of course."

"Warn me? About what?"

Ethan rubbed the back of his neck. "Well—"

"Yes?"

"Well, for one thing, it isn't advisable for a young lady to be skulking about in the dark!"

She blinked and drew her brows together. "Whyever not?"

Ethan found himself distracted by that surprisingly attractive expression. She wasn't a beauty exactly, but she did possess rather striking eyebrows. Fine, arched, and light brown, they perfectly expressed her every irritation—

Ethan blinked, pulling himself back to the moment. Idiot, mooning about some irritating chit's eyebrows. He'd ordered her here for a reason—he only needed to recall what that was.

She did look utterly charming in her wrapper with her thick reddish-blonde braid trailing strands of hair along her cheek. And freckles? Adorable.

But that was beside the point. The point was that she kept being where she ought not to be, and that could be dangerous in this house.

He could not tell her about the Liars' suspicions of Lord Maywell, not without explaining all about the Liars—which, if he was any judge of the ruthlessness in a man's eye, would cause Lord Etheridge to give a very unpleasant order regarding poor old Ethan Damont. So, no telling the girl.

No explaining himself to her at all, now that he thought about it. He'd meant to chastise her, to warn her, to scold her and demand that she keep herself safe—

But there wasn't one thing he could say.

Actions spoke louder than words, did they not? Ethan picked up the candelabra and, never taking his gaze from that of Lady Jane, blew out one candle.

Ethan Damont had ever been a creature of impulse. Looking back later, he would definitely come up with a better reason for his next action than the fact that she looked utterly charming in her wrapper. And after he'd thought it over some more, he would come up with the idea that getting himself driven out of Maywell House at the end of a horsewhip for meddling with one of the young ladies would most definitely make him useless to the Liars.

He moved toward her, with a slight smile on his face. Her eyes widened and she drew back, but there was nowhere for her to go. Her back was pressed to the closed door. He blew out another candle, then another. There were only two left.

Now he could see the frank panic skittering across her face. One more step. One less candle. Now he was a mere arm's length from her with only a single candle standing between them and the intimate darkness.

Ethan smiled at her, a purposely sensual, dangerous smile. "Lady Jane, you ought to be in bed," he whispered softly, heavy on the innuendo.

"If—if you s-say so," she stuttered. Then, quick as lightning, she pulled the door open—

Only to hear Lord Maywell's voice in the distance. "We'll be in the library. If you can find Mr. Damont, please have him join us there."

Within seconds, the room was dark, the unlit candelabra was back on the mantel, and the library was empty of anything other than books.

Jane was quite breathless. Mr. Damont was a very efficient man.

Of course, if she were inclined to be critical, she might find fault with his choice of hiding place. There was a true lack of space for one here under the cloth-covered library table. Two made for close quarters indeed.

Behind her, Mr. Damont shifted uncomfortably. "Are you sure it is quite proper for us to be alone together here?" he whispered.

She slid him a sideways glance. "Worried for your virtue, Mr. Damont?"

"You ought to be worried for yours, my lady."

"From you? Hardly." She turned her attention back to the slit in the fabric that showed the library most clearly. Uncle Harold was lingering in the hall with someone. She could hear their voices but not their words.

Ethan was oddly affronted. "What are you implying?"

"Hmm?" That other voice didn't really sound like any of the younger men who had been at dinner. Who was Uncle Harold talking to?

He tapped her on the shoulder. She turned her head again. "What do you mean, 'hardly'?" he insisted.

Jane sighed with resignation, then twisted her body slightly in order to look at him fully. "I imply nothing but that my virtue is utterly safe in your hands," she reassured him in a low voice.

"It is not!" he burst out in a loud whisper. "Take that back!"

She was surprised into a soft laugh. She felt him stiffen with affront. Oh, dear, Mr. Ethan Damont was getting testy. Jane made a tiny scoffing sound.

"I heard that," he hissed. "Now take that back!"

"Very well," she drawled. "I take it back. I live in fear that your manliness will overcome me," she chanted dutifully. "Pray, control your magnificent steed."

He growled. "Snot."

"Lecher," she retorted. "Better now?"

"Just you wait, Lady Pain-in-the-arse," he growled. "One day you and I will be alone together in a dark room—"

"Like now?"

He made a noise like a frustrated bear. Jane stifled another chuckle. "Honestly, men can be such—"

He dipped his head and kissed her. It was a swift kiss, with only the slightest lingering on the parting. Still, it sent a bolt of mingled fire and fear through her.

"What?" he whispered against her lips. "Men can be such—what?"

Jane turned away, back to her vigil at the slit, and drew her shoulder high between them. Mr. Damont said no more, though Jane could feel his warm breath stirring the small curls on the back of her neck. She bit her lips together, trying to erase the lingering memory of his warm mouth on them. It did no good. There was something growing within her, a newly awakened heat that she had no idea what to do with.

Now the darkness was no longer comfortable. Now his presence behind her was no longer that of a companion in distress.

Now, he was a man, and Jane had never felt more like a woman in her life.

The library door opened at last. The butler entered bearing candles, then Uncle Harold and another, smaller man entered. "I have the information, my lord," the other man said, standing with his back to Jane.

"Fine, fine," Lord Maywell said carelessly. "I'll look at it later." He sat before the fire, leaving the other man standing without an invitation.

Jane slumped. Obviously the new man was just a servant of some kind. The door opened and the butler reentered with a pot of coffee.

"Mr. Damont is nowhere to be found, my lord, but his hat and walking stick are still here," the butler informed him.

Jane turned to give Mr. Damont a disbelieving look. *Walking stick?* she mouthed. He grimaced, obviously not open to criticism of his personal style. She grinned. *Flash,* she accused silently.

"He's a slippery fellow," Uncle Harold said to no one in particular. The visitor merely nodded politely.

Uncle Harold waved the coffee away. "If Damont isn't joining me, then I'm off." He rose heavily. The smaller man did nothing to help him, which rather surprised Jane.

A servant would have. The fellow might be something more. A man of business, perhaps?

She would ask Serena tomorrow. The lovely thing about Serena was that she always answered truthfully, yet never asked why you wanted to know something. Jane knew without a doubt that she herself had never been that trusting, likely not even as an infant.

Uncle Harold strode from the library, followed by the smaller man, then by the butler carrying the untouched coffee tray.

Jane started to move immediately, but Mr. Damont put a restraining hand on her arm. She went very still, her heart thudding. The heat of his touch through her clothes plunged her directly back into that kiss.

They waited a moment longer, then they crept out into the empty room. Jane straightened her skirts with shaking hands. She clasped them behind her to hide the trembling.

"Well, Mr. Damont, I fear it is time for me to say good evening and allow you to take your leave."

His lips quirked. "So formal. Very well, then, my lady. I will take my leave, as you so subtly request."

She nodded shortly and turned to go.

His voice stopped her before she'd taken five steps. When had his very voice become like a leash to her will?

"Lady Jane, I believe there is something you should know about me."

She took a deep breath and turned, but a small polite smile was the best she could do. "And what is that, Mr. Damont?"

"I haven't a sou. Not really." He waved a hand over his own rumpled but fine attire. "All flash, no substance—just as you said."

That confession was the last thing she'd expected. If one could say nothing else about Mr. Ethan Damont, one could say he was very honest—for a card cheat.

The stories she'd heard about him—well, yes, she'd asked about him, just out of curiosity—had that his father was a wealthy clothmaker who had disowned Ethan when he'd proved ungrateful.

"What happened with your father?" Goodness, had she just blurted that question out like that? Curiosity was one thing, but now she was embarrassing them both!

He didn't seem embarrassed, however. He tilted his head, gazing at her calmly. "I was disowned, tossed out, etcetera."

"But why? What did you—" She stopped and bit her lip. "This is none of my affair. My apologies."

He shrugged. "I think it's best if you know. What did I do?" He shook his head. "What didn't I do? I was not only a disappointment, I was a grand failure. I should know. I worked very hard at it."

He didn't sound particularly sorry, but Jane had the feeling he wasn't really telling her everything. He went on.

"I had my share of fine feeling and disappointment, as does any young man. After one particularly wrenching drama, I spent several weeks staying as drunk as possible. That bit of wallowing was the final straw for my father. He tossed me out on my sodden arse and told me never to return."

How terrible for him. Jane missed her own gentle father dreadfully. She could not have borne such disapproval from him, she was sure. "Did you ever return?"

"No." Ethan looked away. "He took ill soon after. I didn't hear about it in time—probably because I was still very drunk—so I never saw him again. My mother retired to the country and some distant cousin took over the factories."

"But aren't they yours?"

"Oh, no. My father did live long enough to write me out of everything. It isn't like it is in your world, my lady. The common man chooses precisely who inherits his wealth. Leaving it all to the eldest son is still the usual, of course, but it is by no means the law. If a man takes a particular dislike to his own offspring, he may leave his accumulated blunt to anyone he likes." He took a long breath. "I assure you, a rat in the attic stood a better chance of inheriting than I. And likely deserved it more."

Jane frowned. "But did you actually want to inherit the factories?"

He grinned wryly at her tone. "What, can you not imagine me as a merchant? Can't you see me keeping my books with my ink guards about my sleeves while working my poor employees into their early graves?" He shook his head, laughing slightly. "No, I can't picture it either."

Jane took a breath. "Thank you for telling me all this, Mr. Damont. I ought not to have asked."

He shook his head, chuckling. "My dear Lady Jane, give me this much—you did not bring it up. I did."

She pursed her lips. "That is true. Why did you think this should concern me?"

"You are on the hunt for a rich husband, are you not?"

*Hunt?* Jane blinked, then recovered. That was her express purpose in this house, after all. "Yes, I suppose I am on the hunt for a rich, *titled* husband, since you insist on putting it so bluntly." She raised her chin. "Do you mean to take yourself out of the running with this confession of alleged poverty?"

"I only wish to warn you against becoming attached." His eyes were shadowed. She could not see if he was in his teasing mode. By the sobriety of his tone, she feared he was quite serious.

The arrogance of his assumption was more than enough to return her equilibrium. She tilted her head, clasping her now dead-steady hands before her. "Mr. Damont, I assure you, becoming attached to you would require lengths of strong rope and quantities of glue."

She whirled and went on her way, pausing only to look back over her shoulder at him. "And even then, sir, I would not wager on it."

The quiet rumble of his laughter followed her down

the hall like a friendly dog, at once comforting and annoying. Still, she was glad they were back on familiar, maddening ground.

That meant she could put thoughts of that disturbing kiss behind her. And she would. Soon.

It was a pity that she must, however. It had been a very nice kiss.

Moreover, it had been her first.

Ethan arrived home early, unannounced and in a shabby hack.

It did him no good. Jeeves was waiting on the front steps to take his hat and stick.

"You exhaust me, Jeeves," Ethan said to the butler as he alighted from the cab.

"Yes, sir," Jeeves replied evenly. "Will you be going back out, sir?"

"No, Jeeves. You can relax now." Ethan entered his house and headed for a brandy. He was halfway across his study before he remembered that his brandy had taken up residence in his chambers.

"Never mind," he muttered to himself. The fire was mesmerizing enough and his chair had been pulled invitingly close to the hearth. Rubbing his brow against the tension that tightened there, he flung himself into his chair without looking.

Only to jump up with a shout when something small and squirmy shot out from behind him with a strangled squeak.

Ethan swept up the poker and brandished it in the direction the nasty thing had gone. His study door opened.

"Is there a problem, sir?"

"Jeeves, there's a rat in here!"

"Yes, sir. What color is it, sir?"

"Color?" He blinked. He'd only had the merest glimpse. "Why . . . sort of orangish, I think." Which was ridiculous.

He watched as Jeeves calmly crossed the room and

reached beneath the settee. Impressed, Ethan lowered his weapon. "Hellfire, you're certainly a man of parts, Jeeves!"

"Indeed, sir," Jeeves replied calmly. He serenely patted around in the dark space for a moment, then drew out his hand. "Is this your rat, sir?"

From the butler's grip dangled a thin, stringy-tailed, struggling . . . kitten. Ethan recoiled. "No, by God! That's worse!"

Jeeves turned his wrist in order to gaze into the kitten's face. The little monster batted him gently on the nose. Ethan shuddered. "Take it away, Jeeves."

"Yes, sir." Jeeves stuffed the thing into his pocket. The tiny tail flipped this way and that from the top rim of the pink pocket. "Shall I send it back to Mrs. Tremayne, sir, or merely toss it into the alley?"

Ethan went still. "Mrs. Tremayne? Rose brought that thing here?"

"Yes, sir. This evening while you were gone. I assumed you wished to have a pet cat, sir, or I would have refused it on your behalf."

The kitten was a gift from Rose.

Now what was he supposed to do about that? Ethan closed his eyes in resignation and hung the poker back on its hook. He reached out his hand. "I'll take the kitten, Jeeves."

"It is no trouble to dispose of it, sir. I'm sure there's a rain barrel about somewhere . . ."

Ethan laughed, a soft, helpless gust. "Oh, shut it, Jeeves. You wouldn't do such a thing and we both know it. Now give me it."

"Yes, sir."

The kitten was dropped into his hand. It weighed nothing at all. Ethan closed his fingers entirely around the little creature's belly. It didn't struggle, but simply hung there tensely in his grip, little paws spread as if it could only prepare itself for a fall.

Taking pity on it, for he'd felt that way a few times in

his life himself, Ethan brought it closer and put his other hand beneath it to support its feet. The kitten went limp then, melting into his hands like warm taffy.

Ethan took Rose's gift back to the chair with him and sat, holding it carefully before him as if he weren't sure it wouldn't go off. In fact, he wasn't. Other than horses, he'd never spent much time around animals.

There had been no pets in the Damont household. His father had always treated creatures as commodities, to be bought and sold, and only valued for what work they could do.

"Don't feel bad, little moggie," Ethan whispered to the kitten. It blinked large sleepy green eyes at him. "He quite felt the same way about me."

So, he was no longer alone. A butler, a new cook, and a tiny morsel of fur. He brought the kitten to his chest and tucked it into his waistcoat—but only because his arms were growing tired. A loud rattling purr erupted from the scant little thing.

"I hope you don't expect me to give you the best pillow, or buy you liver, or . . ." What else did one do to spoil a cat?

He'd have to ask around.

# Chapter Nine

Ethan woke up to the smell of something heavenly beneath his nose. Breakfast was usually not a happy event for him, so he waited for the customary morning-after queasiness to surge.

Instead, his stomach growled voraciously. He cracked one eye open the tiniest possible slit. Oddly, the morning light did not slice into his brain like a knife. Ethan raised one hand to his head, but there was no pounding there at all.

His stomach made another, less polite request. Damn, something smelled good. Opening both eyes was rewarded by the sight of a tray at his bedside, silver covers fogging slightly at the edges from the steaming delights within.

The kitten sat on the table beside it, stringy tail daintily curled about its feet, wide green eyes fixed on its own image reflected in the gleaming silver.

Ethan sat up quickly and reached for the tray. Before he could pick it up, Jeeves appeared in the edges of his hunger-focused vision and placed the tray upon Ethan's lap for him. The kitten reared onto hind legs, pawing at Jeeves's cuff links as they passed over its head.

The lifting of the silver domes was enough to do in a lesser man. Eggs, coddled to perfection and steaming from beneath their sheen of fine sweet butter. Sausages posing seductively at the edge, like plump thighs slightly parted. Caramelized pears gleamed at him from another, smaller plate, winking shyly in their sweet glaze, and wickedly black coffee appeared in a fine china cup to round out the trio of tantalization.

Delighted, Ethan grinned up at Jeeves. "Who knew breakfast could be so provocative?"

Jeeves raised a brow. "Everyone who stops at one brandy the night before, sir."

Ethan gestured with his fork at the ready. "You may have a point." Then he hesitated. "Jeeves, who made this?"

Jeeves folded his hands before him. "You need not worry, sir. There is a new cook in residence." Reassured, Ethan ate.

The food was magnificent. Ethan stopped stuffing his face long enough to inquire, "You found someone so quickly?"

Jeeves maintained an innocent expression. "I hired one first thing yesterday morning."

"Appalling efficiency, Jeeves," Ethan muttered. "I thought we talked about that."

"Yes, sir. I shall endeavor to improve."

"Have you found me another tattooed sailor then, Jeeves?"

"No, sir. The lady has no visible tattoos, nor has she shown any propensity to swear."

Ethan blinked. "A woman? In this house?"

"Yes, sir. You seem upset, sir. Do you by chance possess an allergy?"

Ethan swallowed. "She isn't by any chance . . . young, is she?"

"Oh no, sir. She is quite satisfactorily middle-aged. Although I pray you do not repeat that, sir. I do so enjoy my coddled eggs in the morning."

A bit of sausage evaded Ethan and rolled from the plate. The kitten flew across the counterpane in a flash of ginger to snap it up.

Ethan laughed. "Look at that! Like a bolt of lightning from the hand of Zeus himself!"

Jeeves scooped the kitten up in one hand. The little creature sent a pink tongue across his whiskers while keeping his gaze fixed on Ethan's plate, alert for more escaping sausage.

"I think the young master might prefer a saucer of milk in the kitchen, sir," Jeeves said, as if he did not have a handful of squirming fur.

Ethan shook his head. "The young master can eat with the old master. I'll give him some cream from my tray." He went back to his pears. "Be sure to tell Cook—"

Jeeves cleared his throat. "Might I suggest, sir—as she is a respectable woman of great talent—that you address her as 'Mrs. Cook,' at the least?"

"Mrs. Cook, it is," Ethan announced. "You may tell Mrs. Cook that these are the best bloody eggs I've eaten in my entire sodding existence."

"Yes, sir."

"Jeeves? That's word for word, mind you."

Faint agony crossed Jeeves's aquiline features. "Yes, sir. Of course, sir. I'll leave you to your meal, sir."

Ethan snorted into his coffee as Jeeves left the room. He ought not to tease Jeeves like that. He really, truly ought not to.

Then again, life was short.

After he had woken at an hour decided upon by Jeeves, eaten a breakfast selected by Jeeves, and donned a suit chosen by Jeeves, Ethan was beginning to wonder who served whom in his house.

He trotted down the stairs to stand undecided in his own front hall. "Jeeves!"

The butler appeared like the bursting of a soap bubble, inevitable yet still startling. "Yes, sir?"

Ethan fidgeted. "I'm never awake this early. What am I supposed to do with myself?"

Jeeves didn't so much as blink. "I believe most healthy

young gentlemen enjoy a turn about Hyde Park in such
nice weather."

The park? Ethan couldn't remember the last time
he'd been in the park, at least not in daylight. There was
that time he and Collis had ended up naked and singing
in a tree—

"Naked" and "tree" reminded Ethan of Lady Jane Pennington. Now he was sorry about that kiss—well no, actually, he wasn't. What a missed opportunity that would
have been! Missing opportunities wasn't Ethan's usual
style at all.

As if Jeeves were reading his mind, the butler said, "I
believe there are many ladies partaking of fresh air in the
park at this hour."

Yes, a bit of pretty companionship would do him good,
for he was beginning to obsess about a certain pair of
milky white thighs. Ethan nodded decisively. "The park it
is. Would you mind fetching my—"

Jeeves brought his hands from behind his back. One
held Ethan's hat, the other held the gloves that matched
his suit. "Have a nice walk, sir."

Ethan sighed. There were no words. One didn't berate
a servant for doing an excellent job, after all. Still,
Jeeves's attention to detail made the little hairs on the
back of Ethan's neck stand up.

Outside, the day was something altogether new and interesting. People were much friendlier at this hour, for
one thing. Ethan was greeted with polite, assessing nods
from the gentlemen who passed him, and polite, admiring
glances from the ladies who passed.

Furthermore, there were children around. Hyde Park
abounded with them. Wee infants in prams, chubby tod-
dlers taking unsteady steps, laughing boys and girls chas-
ing dogs and balls and apparently anything not tied down.
Pausing to think, Ethan realized he had not seen an actual
child in years. Folks usually didn't pack their offspring
along to gaming hells and brothels, or even ballrooms.

A small, lace-covered whirlwind slammed into his legs as he stood there. Without thinking, Ethan swept her up into his arms before she ricocheted to the ground.

"Hello, darling," he said with a smile, automatically turning on the charm. Female was female, after all.

Wide blue eyes stared at him from the depths of a lacy bonnet. "You ran into me," the child accused.

Ethan blinked, then set her on her tiny booted feet with a deep bow. "Indeed, my lady. My deepest apologies." He plucked a clover flower from the lawn while he was down there and presented it to her. "Please take this token of my profound regret. May I hope you will ever forgive me?"

She took the flower and sniffed it, considering him carefully. Then she answered his bow with a very pretty deep curtsy. "You are, of course, forgiven, kind sir."

Then she grinned at him, showing a charming lack of two front teeth. "But you're much too familiar," she scolded, and ran back the way she'd come, little feet kicking up a froth of lacy skirts.

Ethan sighed. "I hear that a great deal," he murmured.

"She's a bit young for you, I think," said a teasing voice behind him. Ethan turned to see the face that still haunted some of his more domestic dreams.

"Rose!"

Rose Tremayne stood there, looking the picture of inborn grace in a sprigged frock with a parasol crooked over her shoulder. A trim young maid stood behind her, but Ethan wasn't fooled by the uniform and cap. The girl was one of *them*. Still, Rose was a far cry from the woman he'd been very nearly kidnapped by, desperate, dirty, and clad in boy's trousers. Yet the irreverence for all things Society still twinkled in her hazel eyes.

Ethan was very glad to see her. "What are you doing here?" he asked. "Not that I'm complaining, mind you. Are you on a mission?" He pointed warily at the parasol. "Is that thing loaded?"

She laughed. "It isn't a weapon, Ethan, it's a sunshade."

Then she poised it before her, considering. "However, now that you mention it, I do see potential."

Ethan took her hand briefly in greeting, but refrained from holding it. It had never been serious, his infatuation for Rose, but damn if she wasn't as magnificent as ever.

The fact that she was mad for Collis Tremayne and always had been had set a limit on his feelings, for even Ethan didn't make a pass behind a friend's back—although if Rose had shown him the slightest encouragement he might have broken that unwritten rule.

No, it was more that she almost allowed him to believe that there was someone out there as perfect for him as she was for Collis.

She was looking at him now with utmost concentration. He could almost see the wheels turning in her head. "I hear you turned down Lord Etheridge's offer," she said bluntly.

Ethan smiled. Rose never wasted time. "I did indeed."

"Then why did you go back to Maywell's last night?"

He started. How had she known—oh, right. Feebles. He snorted. "To prove to you lot that you couldn't force me to—Wait, that doesn't sound right." He frowned to himself. "Damn, it made sense when Jeeves said it."

Rose tilted her head. "Who is Jeeves?"

"My new butler."

She looked at him oddly for a moment. "Jeeves," she said to herself. Then, "Take a turn about the path with me?"

Ethan offered his arm in response. They walked in silence for a while. Ethan knew she was trying to think of some way to convince him. It wouldn't work of course, but her company was enjoyable and it was a very fine day. He could think of worse ways to waste the morning.

The morning was half gone and Jane still had not finished her daily letter to Mother.

So far, she'd included seeing the mysterious glimmer of candlelight and even a cheerful bit about her adventure into the locked room.

After that—

She hesitated. She could hardly tell Mother about the kiss! And really, what was there to tell about Mr. Damont? All he had actually done was play cards with her uncle.

Bending back over the page, she dutifully listed all the gentlemen who had joined her uncle in the card room last night, slipping Mr. Damont's name casually into the middle of the list so as not to call extra attention to him.

After all, who knew what Mother would make of Mr. Damont's attentions? Besides, if she explained about Mr. Damont, she would also be forced to go into detail about the incident in the tree—something she'd really rather not do!

Oh, yes! Jane remembered something else she could put in the letter.

"Uncle Harold's man of business arrived late last night with some information for him. Uncle Harold received him in the library. He was a smallish fellow, with a round face, dressed in a brown wool suit." Mother liked to know that sort of thing. "Simms served coffee, but Uncle Harold and the man of business did not stay in there long."

There. Everything she'd said was the truth. It simply wasn't all of it.

The fact remained, however, that Jane felt guilty as she sealed the letter. She owed Mother so very much. The only thing that had ever been asked of Jane in return was that she tell Mother every little detail of her time in London.

Mr. Damont was the problem.

Jane ruthlessly examined her feelings about the tall, sardonic gambler. He was very handsome and charming, in an exasperating sort of way.

He was outrageous, shockingly forward, and generally irreverent. He was also kind. Simply look at the way he'd rescued Serena. A little thing, true, but so innately gallant that Jane counted it quite highly in her assessment of him.

She liked him.

He was entirely unsuitable. She ought not even speak to such a rogue.

He was the most interesting person she had met in all her months in London.

He was arrogant. And deeply, permanently objection-able.

Yet, she still liked him.

Jane let her head drop to her hands in frustration. How did one solve a problem like Mr. Damont?

*"You must learn everything about someone before be-coming too drawn in with them. You cannot always trust what you see on the surface."*

Jane sat up with a smile. Absolutely true! More excel-lent advice from Mother. She knew exactly what she needed to do next.

It was time to find out more about Mr. Ethan Damont.

The graveled walk trailed through the center of the park, taking them on a tour of English leisure as they passed people from all walks of life enjoying the day. Rough men in workingman's clothes lounged on blankets with women in fulsome calico, while sturdy children climbed over them. Long-limbed fine-blooded horses pulled phaetons occupied by dashing young men and giggling young ladies, often with a patient lady's maid tucked into the drop seat behind them.

If Ethan was a marrying sort, he'd be taking notes on an excellent way to steal a kiss or three. Unfortunately, the ladies he was accustomed to kissing didn't go out in public much, unless you counted Mrs. Blythe's Pleasure Balls. No, courtship was for other men—men with expec-tations of a good living and, of course, the support of the girl's family.

Not a possibility either way for him. Not that he was truly interested. It was merely a passing thought.

After a prolonged hesitation, Rose gave a sigh full of

irritation and turned to him. They were pausing at the footbridge crossing the Serpentine. Ethan thought she looked very appealing framed by the narrow lake stretching out behind her.

"Ethan, you aren't going to listen to a thing I have to say, are you?" she said in an exasperated tone.

Ethan turned away from her and leaned both elbows on the railing. Pretending blithe unconcern, he gazed happily around him at one of the last fine days of the year.

"Not a bit of it," he replied absently. "Would you care for an ice? I think the parlor may still be open." He grinned at her over his shoulder. "If not, I shall raise my sword and force them to open for your pleasure."

Rose stood her parasol on the planks of the footbridge and rested both hands on the pommel. "I cannot today, I fear. There is a great deal to be done, you know."

Ethan knew she was speaking of much more vital things than overseeing her new household. "Tell me something, Rose—why would a nice sort like you want to be a spy?"

She grinned at him, a sudden flashing smile that transformed her from merely attractive to stunning. "Because being a spy is the most excitement you'll ever have in your life."

Excitement? He'd never quite thought of it that way before. Despite his piqued interest, Ethan laughed. "I doubt that, dear lady, but I'll not dispute with you." He shook his head. "Remember, I have some outrageous experiences to compare it to."

"Quite so," she said, laughing. Then she focused that intimidating intensity upon him once more. "Do me one favor, Ethan?"

He straightened, then bowed playfully, refusing to let her pull him into her fervor. "Anything for you, lovely one."

She narrowed her eyes. "Just once, I'd like you to seriously ask yourself . . ."

He waited for her to demand some grim and responsible thinking from him. He wouldn't listen. They could keep their little club and their danger and their intrigue. He would remain free until he died of it.

Rose leaned close and a wicked twinkle suddenly gleamed from her eyes. "I simply want you to ask yourself; *Why the hell not?*"

Ethan blinked at the unexpected playful challenge. Rose pressed a kiss to her own gloved fingertip and transferred it to his lips. "Sleep on that, won't you, Damont?"

With that, she turned and sauntered back the way they'd come, her long legs swinging her fashionable skirts just a bit too wide, her movements as lethally graceful as a cat's.

"When I grow up, I want to wed a woman like her," Ethan whispered to himself.

Not that that would ever happen.

Excitement, hmm?

# Chapter Ten

Jane dabbed at her forehead with a handkerchief. She'd not realized that Mr. Damont's house was quite this far from Barkley Square. She was becoming quite warm from the walk, but she was much better off than Robert, her uncle's footman, puffing along behind her.

Although Robert was quite used to carrying parcels for Aunt Lottie and the girls, Jane would wager that he'd never been put to quite the pace she had set today.

Jane simply didn't see the point in dallying. Her swinging country-bred stride might not be top form among the *haut ton,* but it got Jane where she wished to go.

At this moment, Jane wished to see where Mr. Ethan Damont lived. You could tell a great deal about someone by their residence.

As she walked, she looked about her curiously. She ought to be nearing Mr. Damont's address now—and she was a bit surprised by the elegance and refinement reflected by the neighborhood.

Mr. Damont had claimed to be all flash. All Jane saw around her was substance. Tasteful, stately homes looked down on her, their generous windows reflecting the unusually fine September day.

Now, according to her directions, Mr. Damont's street was two next after an oncoming row of intriguing little shops. Jane peered down both ways, interested despite her mission. There was a tailor and a seamstress, a milliner and a teashop—how lovely! What a clever idea, to set up so handy to these wealthy residences. Jane quite envied the convenience of it all.

She turned to look down the other direction—

And saw Mr. Damont strolling down the street toward her.

Oh, horse apples! Jane grabbed Robert by the arm and yanked him into the first doorway, the milliner's. A little bell tinkled above the door as they entered. Jane dove to one side of the door to keep watch through the window.

Mr. Damont had continued his easy pace, looking about him casually—a gentleman out walking on a fine day. Nothing unusual there. What was unusual was Mr. Damont's faintly surprised expression. It made Jane wonder what he usually did with his afternoons.

He did paint an attractive picture though, didn't he? His caramel-brown coat contrasted nicely with his butter-yellow waistcoat. The cut of it didn't do the breadth of his shoulders any harm either. No padding there.

His long stride closed the distance between them swiftly despite his easy pace. He did have long legs, didn't he? His dark brown trousers ended in highly shined boots, showing his muscled thighs off nicely.

And the fit of those trousers . . .

There was no way to be sure, of course, but Jane strongly suspected that Mr. Ethan Damont didn't find it necessary to pad a single thing.

She let her gaze travel back up his form to his face—only to find him looking directly at her.

Oh, no! She jumped back from the window, but it was too late. He was crossing the street toward the shop, a curious smile on his face.

Jane quickly grabbed the first bonnet she saw and plunked it on her head. There was a mirror on the wall opposite the door. Jane pretended to be examining herself in the bonnet, but actually she was eyeing the door behind her in the reflection.

She saw a slice of yellow waistcoat through the glass door panel. Blast, he was coming in! She busied herself with the ribbons of the bonnet, tilting her face down to hide behind the brim.

She saw booted feet come to stand behind her in the mirror.

"Hello, Robert," Mr. Damont said in his lazy way.

Jane cringed. She'd forgotten about Robert. Of course Mr. Damont would recognize the footman from the Maywell household. Robert always served the card room.

There was no help for it. Jane raised her head to see Mr. Damont smiling at her. She feigned surprise. "My goodness! Fancy meeting you here, sir!" She cringed inwardly at her own clumsy dissembling. Goodness, could she be more obvious?

Mr. Damont didn't seem to think so. His gaze was full of repressed laughter, heightened by a decidedly wicked twinkle. Eek—he hadn't caught her examining the cut of his trousers, had he?

"Good afternoon, Lady Jane," he drawled. "Did you see something you like?"

Oh, no. He *had* noticed where she was looking! How dare he say such a thing—and with that naughty gleam in his eye!

She sputtered in panic. Then she realized he was gesturing about them at the contents of the millinery. He grinned down at her. "Are you quite well, my lady?"

Jane gaped at him. He'd known precisely what she'd been thinking. She could see it on his face. Oh, he was wicked!

Ethan couldn't take it anymore. He leaned closer to whisper to her. "You are too easy, Lady Jane."

Abruptly, she laughed. Rather, she snorted helplessly.

Ethan smiled in satisfaction. Lady Jane Pennington was not quite the Society paragon that she liked to portray. Beneath that elegant exterior was a rather mischievous sense of humor.

He shook his finger at her. "You shouldn't laugh. Don't you know that proper ladies aren't supposed to laugh at my sort of jokes?"

Jane turned away to hide her smile. He was quite correct. She spent a moment pretending to adjust the bonnet, until she'd composed herself once more.

Mr. Damont cleared his throat. "Well . . . that's very . . . fetching."

The extreme doubt in his voice made Jane look closely at the bonnet in the mirror for the first time.

It was awful, dripping stuffed silk grapes and layered leaves. She looked as if she were carrying a basket from the vineyard on her head. Then she saw the knowing look in Mr. Damont's eyes in the mirror and stiffened. "No one ever did say you had any taste, sir."

He nodded easily. "Too true. No one ever did."

Jane removed the bonnet—really, she could not get the awful thing off fast enough to suit her—and placed it reverently on its stand. "I do love it so, but I'm afraid it's too dear." She smiled apologetically at Mr. Damont. "It was very nice to see you again, sir, but I really must be going." She tried to step past him, but she found him directly in front of her once more.

"Ah . . . Lady Jane? If it would not be too far out of your way . . ." He hesitated, then looked away, his insouciant manner disappearing.

Jane stared at him. Was he actually nervous? "Yes?"

He took a breath and smiled diffidently. "Well, I . . . I only live a short way from here . . . and if you have nothing to do this afternoon—"

Jane drew back, horror creeping through her. "Mr. Damont, I realize that by seeking you out this way I have left you with a bad impression of my standards, but—"

"Oh! No!" He went wide-eyed and held both hands up before him. "No, that isn't—I don't—I only thought you might like to see my—"

"*Oh!*" Jane backed away toward the door. "I think I've heard enough!" She felt sick. Mr. Damont thought she was— Oh, she couldn't bear it. She turned, nearly running from the shop. She heard Robert huffing behind her. That was too bad for him, for Jane was so embarrassed that she felt fully capable of running all the way back to Barkley Square.

Ethan stood in the milliner's shop, rendered quite breathless from the swiftness of Lady Jane's getaway. "To see my new pet kitten," he finished lamely. Good God, the woman had sped away like a racehorse! "You're really slipping, old man," he muttered to himself. "It usually takes at least a quarter of an hour before you drive them away."

But what was that she had said? *"By seeking you out this way."* Lady Jane Pennington had been seeking *him* out? Whatever for?

Unless her uncle had set her onto his trail.

Lord Maywell would never involve an innocent girl in his machinations, would he? Then again, perhaps he would. Maywell had quite a ruthless air about him sometimes.

For the first time, it occurred to Ethan that Jane and her cousins might be in danger living in a traitor's house, especially if Maywell was the ringleader the Liars thought him to be. The thought of Jane in peril was unacceptable. A fierce wave of protectiveness swept over Ethan.

It was an unaccustomed sensation, what with the hardening of his jaw and all. Rather dizzying, actually. Perhaps that's why he found himself suddenly leaving the shop, his long, determined stride taking him directly to the one place he'd sworn never to set foot in again.

The stout doorman of the Liar's Club greeted him dubiously. "May I help you, sir?"

Ethan glared at the younger fellow. "Tell Tremayne—
*I'm in.*"

Collis was jubilant. "I knew you'd come round," he crowed as he led Ethan up the stairs to the second floor of the club a few moments later. "You won't regret it, mate. This is the grandest adventure of all—"

"I'm not here for adventure," Ethan groused. "I'm here because Maywell is a lout for putting his family in danger."

Collis raised a brow. "Oh? Doesn't Maywell have a passel of daughters?" He grinned. "You gallant old sod! Ethan Damont, knight errant!"

Ethan scowled. "Shut it, Collis."

Collis let out a great, false sigh. "That's all I hear about this place, day and night. You'd think all these great minds could come up with something a bit more original."

Lord Etheridge appeared at the top of the stairs. "Shut it, Collis."

Collis shrugged. "See what I mean?"

Ethan disregarded his friend's glee to glare at Lord Etheridge as he came level to him. "I'm here. I'll do it, but not because you tried to force me. And I want my house out of hock."

Dalton nodded, unsmiling. "Done."

Ethan drew himself up. "What do I do first?"

Dalton gestured for Ethan to follow him down the hall. "First, we assess your skills. There might be a few lessons you'll need to take."

Ethan balked. "School? I don't think so."

Collis grinned. "That's exactly how I felt." He became more serious. "If truth be told, I'm glad I studied. It all came in handy at one point or another." He clapped Ethan on the back. "Luckily, you'll be taking lessons here and not at the school we have nearby. I'm not sure your fragile personality could stand up against being surpassed by fifteen-year-olds."

Etheridge slid Collis a quelling glance. Ethan was surprised to see his friend settle immediately. Good God, Collis really was the good little Liar, wasn't he?

"Mr. Damont is a special case," Dalton reminded them both. "Our situation requires us to get someone into Maywell's immediately. There will be very little training."

They'd arrived at the end of the hall. Ethan expected them to step into one of the rooms to the right or left, but instead, Collis and his lordship faced the back wall. Etheridge pressed something, Ethan heard a click, and the wall slid aside.

"So that's how you sneaked up on me in the dining room," Ethan muttered.

Dalton smiled, almost. "I enjoyed that."

*I'll wager you did, you mad bastard.* Ethan was beginning to regret his decision. Lord Etheridge didn't want him here, that was plain enough.

The next stretch of hallway was much like the first, only a bit more worn. Ethan saw rooms to either side, one of which contained large rolled papers stacked in cupboards to the ceiling. "Maps?"

Etheridge stopped. "We use them and make them, especially our scouts out on the front lines. You won't be operating there, but it wouldn't hurt to be able to read and follow the simpler ones."

Ethan pursed his lips. "I think I can get by," he said drily. "I did have the same formal education as Collis." He folded his arms. "And it happens that *I* actually studied."

Etheridge looked to Collis for confirmation. When Collis nodded, Dalton gestured for them to continue. "Moving along then." They stopped at another doorway, where a pale young man in spectacles looked up from the work piled on his desk, blinking myopically at them. "This is Fisher. He's our code master."

Fisher blushed. "Only until Mr. Atwater returns from Portugal," he said apologetically.

A red-haired young woman stood up from behind the file cupboard she'd been delving into. "Hello, my lord, Collis. Is this Mr. Damont?" She smiled at Ethan, who automatically grinned back. She was a pretty thing, with her short, brilliant curls and friendly grin.

Etheridge nodded. "Mrs. Cunnington, Mr. Damont," he said. He turned to Ethan. "Phillipa's husband, James, is my second, and the sabotage master, but you won't be working with him."

Phillipa smiled, but Ethan thought he saw a flicker of worry in her eyes. "He's out on the front lines, blowing things up," she explained, her voice cheerful despite her concern. "He and Papa won't be back for weeks."

"Damont won't be using code, since his post is right here in town," Etheridge continued. "But he'll be bringing you anything he might find on location. You're to give it top priority, Fisher."

Fisher cast a despairing glance over his already piled desk, then raised his gaze to Etheridge's. "Right, my lord. Top priority."

They went on, but not before Ethan sent Mrs. Cunnington another grin. She was quite the stunner.

"Back off, Damont," Etheridge said without turning around. "James is the jealous sort."

Ethan was not discouraged. He'd had no idea that there were any lady Liars besides Rose. This could end up being rather delightful. They turned a corner and Ethan saw a slim, dark-haired lovely pinning a sheet of paper up on a large notice board in the hall. She turned and smiled as they approached. Now, there was a fine-looking woman! She reminded him of Rose, without the athleticism. Ethan straightened and prepared to turn on the charm.

"Hello, darling," Etheridge practically cooed. "How are you feeling?"

The woman gazed up at Lord Etheridge in absolute adoration. "Better. Kurt made me soup and soda crisps." She smiled ruefully. "I think I'm going to give up on breakfast altogether."

Ethan deflated. Wife. Treasured and expectant wife at that. He disliked Etheridge more than ever, the lucky rotter.

"Clara, I'd like to introduce Mr. Ethan Damont, who will be joining us. Damont, Lady Etheridge. *My* Lady Etheridge," he said pointedly.

Ethan slid Collis a look. "What have you been telling him about me?"

Collis shrugged. "The truth."

Oh, hell. No wonder Etheridge was bristling like a hedgehog. Ethan smiled diffidently at Lady Etheridge. "My lady," he greeted her quietly, infusing it with no charm whatsoever. "May I wish you improved health?"

Clara smiled back. "Why, thank you, Mr. Damont. What a polite young man." She sent her husband one of those wifely aren't-you-ashamed-of-yourself looks.

Etheridge's lips twisted as he gazed at Ethan sourly. Ethan blinked innocently back.

Collis was peering at the notice board. "I say, Clara, you've captured him exactly."

Ethan leaned forward. "Who?"

"Later," Etheridge practically barked. "Clara, you should go rest in the attic. I'll check in on you later."

Lady Etheridge only looked indulgently at her husband and shook her head. "Mr. Damont is not going to importune me, Dalton. You've made yourself very clear." She looked at Ethan. "Hasn't he, Mr. Damont?"

Ethan nodded emphatically. "Yes, my lady. You are Lady Etheridge and I am not suicidal."

She turned back to say, "There, you see?"

Etheridge only grunted. "Move on, Damont."

"Yes, my lord," Ethan retorted briskly. "Anything you say, my lord."

Etheridge drew a breath and considered Ethan for a long moment. "I think we'll start with Kurt."

When Ethan followed Collis and his lordship down the back stair to the cellar, his first thought was that this place went on forever.

When he saw the scarred, shirtless giant crouching in a fighting stance in the center of a vast mat, Ethan's second thought was that he ought to have been more polite to Lord Etheridge.

An hour later, Ethan was flat on his back on the mat, out of breath, out of ideas, and out of any will to go on living. Kurt stood over him. The giant grunted and held out one hand to pull Ethan up.

Lord Etheridge entered the room as Ethan made it to his feet.

"How did he do?"

Kurt folded massive arms over his enormous chest. "Not much of a boxer. 'E never laid a finger on me. Went down after one blow."

"I see." Etheridge looked disappointed but not surprised. If Ethan hadn't been so breathless he might have been insulted.

Kurt grunted again. "Fast though. Took me an hour to land a hit."

Etheridge looked stunned. "An hour?"

Kurt nodded. " 'E could teach me a few things about dodgin' blows."

Ethan braced his hands on his knees, his chest heaving. "I'm a runner . . . not a fighter. All those irate . . . husbands."

Etheridge turned to Collis, who was perched on a pile of equipment. Collis shrugged. "I wouldn't have believed it either, but it's true. He survived an hour against Kurt." He shook his head. "I've never seen anyone move that fast in my life. He was a blur."

Ethan could tell Etheridge was impressed, but his lordship only nodded. "On to Feebles, then."

Collis jumped down and threw Ethan his shirt. "Don't worry," he said with a grin. "This won't hurt."

# Chapter Eleven

Feebles looked odd indoors, like a wild creature unsure of its surroundings. The little man's eyes kept flickering to the door as if to make sure it was still open.

He and Ethan stood in a room that at first glance looked like a storeroom and at second glance like some medieval dungeon.

It was all locks, chains, safe boxes. There were even several grimy doors leaning against the walls, their keyholes shiny with use. And in the middle of the floor, being regarded with misty eyes of love and admiration by Mr. Feebles, stood a brand-new modern vault.

Ethan had managed the door locks after a bit of coaching and the padlocks were no match for the set of picks he was given. To tell the truth, he was enjoying himself immensely. There was something very satisfying about opening something that was meant to stay locked—about breaching something that was made to keep him out.

Now, however, it was time to tackle the vault. It was just the sort of thing rich men installed in their homes to hold valuables. Ethan regarded it uneasily. It was nearly as tall as Feebles himself and looked as impenetrable as solid stone. The entire thing seemed cast of iron. Even the hinges on the door were as thick as a fist.

"This be the new Valiant numerical-lock vault," Feebles said reverently. "The same one Lord Maywell had delivered to Barkley Square yesterday mornin' after he twigged that we'd been in his hidey-hole durin' the ball. Ye can't drill it, ye can't smash it, ye can't even move it without six men and a draft cart."

"Right." Ethan stuffed his hands in his pockets. "Can't be opened—got it."

Feebles tilted his head and smiled gently at the vault. "Oh, ye can be opened, can't ye, my darlin'?" he cooed.

Ethan eyed the strange little man carefully. He'd always rather liked Feebles. Nevertheless, he took a surreptitious step away. "How?"

Feebles put a finger to his lips. "Shh. All you have to do is listen to her."

"Right." Ethan took another step. Kurt had been one thing—a giant with fists like hammers, but certainly fathomable. Feebles was just plain eerie. He looked as though he were going to kiss that big iron box.

Feebles was leaning closer and closer, stroking his hand down the door to the complicated-looking latch.

"Uh . . . Feebles?"

Ethan drew back as Feebles pressed one cheek adoringly to the iron door and caressed the lock as delicately as if he were toying with the tips of a woman's breasts. This was getting a bit too strange for Ethan. He wondered whether Feebles was going to come after him next—

The door to the vault popped open.

Ethan blinked. "I say, Feebles, that was amazing! Do it again."

After a few more demonstrations, Ethan had his own cheek pressed to the iron door and was twiddling the lock as enthusiastically as he'd ever tickled a bosom.

Feebles hovered. "Listen . . . listen . . ."

Ethan glanced up at him. "Do you mind?"

Feebles raised his hands apologetically, but kept

bouncing on his toes around Ethan. Ethan ignored the little man, devoting as much attention to listening to the tiny clicks inside the lock as he ever had to interpreting the music of a woman's ecstatic cries.

It took several tries, but finally Ethan heard the last tumbler click into place. "Come on, lover," he whispered. He lifted the lever and the latch came loose. The door swung open in a heavy congratulatory wave.

The clapping of many hands came from the doorway. Ethan turned to see Collis, Clara, Phillipa, and Fisher applauding him with smiles. Kurt glared approvingly as well, but Etheridge only gazed impassively at him over the heads of the others.

Feebles, however, was transported. "You've a natural touch, sir, a real natural touch!"

Ethan bowed slightly. "I had a good teacher, Mr. Feebles."

Etheridge stepped forward. "Very well, then, Mr. Damont. You've passed the most important tests. I think it's time you and I had a talk."

"Jane, my dear," Uncle Harold called from his study as Jane passed the open doorway. "Do come in for a moment."

Jane had walked past Uncle Harold's study a thousand times since she'd come to London. He'd never so much as looked to notice her before.

This couldn't be good. As she swallowed nervously and entered the study, she wondered what Robert had told Uncle Harold.

Well, what was there to tell? She'd told Robert she wanted to walk on such a lovely day. He'd certainly witnessed some vigorous walking. He'd seen her enter a shop, try on a bonnet, speak to a man she'd encountered in her uncle's own house, and then walk home.

Blast, she ought to have tried to hide her disturbance

more cleverly. Mother had warned her to watch out for gossipy servants.

*"Never underestimate what a household retainer sees and hears. It usually does not take much to persuade them to carry tales."*

She moved to stand before her uncle's desk, willing her hands to stop shaking. That didn't work, so she clasped them daintily behind her back.

"Yes, Uncle Harold?"

Her uncle peered up at her, his usually dour face creased into something he probably thought more pleasant. Jane's stomach flipped over. Her uncle never smiled. What was afoot here?

"I've been meaning to ask you, Jane—have you had a pleasant Season here with us?"

Jane relaxed slightly. Uncle Harold only wanted to know if she was going to stay or go home to Northumbria now that the Season was nearly done.

"I've had a very nice time, indeed, Uncle. Aunt Lottie and the girls have been lovely to me."

Uncle Harold nodded. "And Society at large? Have you met any young fellows who piqued your interest?"

Oh, dear. That whole husband-hunt pretense was coming back to haunt her now. She painted regret onto her expression. "No, I'm sorry to say that I have not formed an attachment to any of the gentlemen I've met." True enough, for Mr. Damont was no gentleman.

Not that she was attached to him—of course not! He was an enigma—a puzzle she was interested in solving, that was all.

Uncle Harold blew out the sides of his fluffy white moustache. "Oh, dear. That is too bad. I so hoped you'd find the love match your mother was expecting for you."

The last thing Mother was interested in was a love match, but Jane only nodded sorrowfully.

"If you'd like to accompany us to Scotland for the

hunting season, you certainly may. Then there will be
Christmas and all that rot. Perhaps you'll meet someone
interesting at one of the house parties we usually attend?"

Jane smiled, relieved that the topic of particular gentlemen was closed. "I'd like to stay, Uncle Harold.
Mother has said I might if you invited me."

"Well, then, the matter is settled." He nodded and
waved her genially away. "I'll tell your aunt you'll be
staying."

Jane turned to leave, happy to go. Gruff, indifferent
Uncle Harold she was accustomed to. Genial, warm Uncle Harold was a bit much for her nerves.

"Oh, Jane?"

She turned back. Blast, she'd almost made it out of the
study. "Yes, Uncle Harold?"

"My dear, you'll need to do some shopping for the
winter Season, yes?"

Jane blinked. That was true. She could hardly wear her
light muslin and silk frocks this winter—and she certainly couldn't be seen wearing her gowns from last winter. "Yes, Uncle, I will."

He nodded. "Then you had best give me your bank account numbers so that I can pay your expenses for you."
He smiled. Jane nearly drew back from the show of teeth.
"You can hardly traipse along the Strand with cash in
your reticule!"

That was also true. Jane hesitated, but could come up
with no legitimate reason not to give her uncle the bank
information. Likely he could get it from the bank anyway,
being her eldest male relative as he was.

She nodded. Mother wouldn't like it, but really, it only
made sense. "I'll bring that down to you straightaway,
Uncle."

But Uncle Harold was already losing interest. He
didn't look up from his papers but only waved her on
once more.

Jane left, entirely relieved. Now that Uncle Harold didn't

have to worry that she was going to bankrupt him with her shopping, he would likely forget all about her again.

Jane found that she much preferred it that way. Especially since Uncle Harold was sure to disapprove of any interest she might have shown in that scandalous cad, Mr. Damont.

Not that she was interested any longer.

Absolutely not.


Dalton led Ethan on a circuitous route to a semicircular room high in the attic of the club. He opened the door and waved Ethan through.

"My secret office," he said.

"Secret from whom?" Ethan asked. "I've only been a Liar for half a day and I already know about it."

"Precisely," Etheridge said ironically. "Please, take a seat."

Ethan was dying to sit. In fact, he rather thought he'd like to lie down and moan after his session with Kurt. Instead, however, he found himself refusing the chair. "No, thank you. I'd rather stand."

Etheridge sat and folded his arms over his chest. "Why don't you trust me, Damont?"

Ethan met his gaze levelly. "Why don't you trust me?"

Etheridge almost smiled. If Ethan hadn't seen the big lord turn to putty for his lovely wife, he wouldn't have interpreted the easing of Dalton's jaw for the pleasant expression it was doubtless meant to be.

"You know, my lord, I happen to think I'm the perfect addition to your gang. Your lot could use some livening up."

To his vast surprise, his lordship nodded. "It has been a long road back. We lost a number of good men this year. I think that new blood will help them look toward the future."

"What happened?" Ethan wasn't sure he wanted to know about Liars dying. He liked his life expectancy right where it was—which wasn't all that long, come to think of it.

Etheridge folded his hands on the desk. "We had a non-Liar working in the club as manager, bartender, and so on. Jackham wasn't a bad fellow, by all accounts, but somehow the enemy got to him. He gave up the names and locations of most of the men before he realized what they were going to use them for. When men started dying, he quit informing and tried to come back to us. I think he truly regretted it, but it was too late by then. He came to a bad end in the Thames, we hear."

Ethan frowned. "Jackham? I thought the traitor was a bloke named Denny?"

Etheridge grimaced. "Denny? No, he was never one of us. Just a gossiping valet that the men handed back and forth until we discovered that he was telling tales to the Voice of Society."

"And will this Denny fellow end up in the Thames as well?" What a bloodthirsty lot the Liars were!

Etheridge tilted his head. "Why do you care?"

*Because I want to know in which direction to run for my life.* "I don't. I'm simply curious, that is all."

Etheridge leaned forward suddenly, his eerie silvery gaze becoming intense. "Damont, there is something more that I haven't told you."

*Why am I not surprised?* "And that is?"

"There is more than one kind of spy, Damont. There is the sort that infiltrates a place like Maywell's, possibly as a guest or servant, who simply watches and reports on every detail that goes on around them."

"That sounds like what I'll be doing."

Etheridge shook his head slowly, his gaze never leaving Ethan's. "I wish you to work another way. I want you to be a double spy."

Ethan frowned. "Double for whom?"

A slight smile eased the corner of his lordship's

mouth. "I want you to get Maywell to recruit you as a French spy, so that you can find out about his organization and feed him misinformation from our side."

This was appalling. "Why would he do that?" Ethan asked in horror.

Etheridge gazed at him for a long moment, then shrugged. "For the same reason we would, I suppose. You've a useful combination of talents."

Ethan took a deep breath. "I think I liked the sound of the first sort better. I'm very good at watching." If he was merely watching, he could keep an eye on Lady Jane and the other ladies, just as a safeguard.

Etheridge sat back. "Fine. Watch at first, if you like. But I don't think it will be long before Maywell tries to draw you in." He pinned Ethan with his gaze. "If he offers a chance, take it. If he gets that far and receives a refusal from you, he won't dare let you live."

Ethan swallowed. "How do you know that?"

Etheridge let out a breath. "Because that's what I would be forced to do. That's why we have never let anyone in until we've been absolutely sure of their loyalties."

*Until you.*

Etheridge didn't say the words out loud, but Ethan heard them all the same. Sobering thought, to go along with all the other sobering thoughts that had been conjured in this secret office in the attic.

"If you're trying to scare me, you've wasted your time." Ethan shrugged. "I've been scared since I walked in here this morning."

Etheridge nodded. "Good. Stay that way. It might keep you alive."

Overwhelmed, Ethan shook his head. "You're a fanatic, do you know that? The world is black and white to men like you. Our side is good, their side is bad—even though their side is made up of ordinary men, just like us."

Etheridge considered him with half-lidded eyes. "That ability to see the shades of gray is going to come in useful as a double spy—if it doesn't get you killed first."

Ethan snorted. "So what is the life expectancy of a double spy these days?"

Etheridge looked down at his hands, then back up to meet Ethan's gaze. "I guess we'll find out, won't we?"

Despite Etheridge's grim-reaper manner, Ethan found himself enjoying the rest of the afternoon spent in the Liar's Club. He was invited to the kitchen to partake of Kurt's *coq au vin* with Collis, Phillipa and Phillipa's son, Robbie (although how such a young woman could have a strapping lad of ten, Ethan didn't dare ask), and Fisher.

There was one thing he couldn't stop thinking of, however. How could someone who was close to these people suddenly become their enemy—ending up in their sights, as it were?

"These blokes, Jackham and Denny—"

Phillipa shuddered. "Don't mention Mr. Jackham to me, if you please. I still have trouble going up ladders after what he did to me."

"What did he do to you?"

"He dangled me off a rooftop by my cravat, thank you very much."

Ethan stared. "Cravat?"

She shrugged, a boyish gesture. "It's a long story."

Robbie grinned. "Flip was done up like a lad."

Ethan wrinkled his brow. "You call your mother 'Flip'?"

Phillipa sighed. "The story just gets longer and longer."

Ethan grinned. "It's one I'd love to hear someday."

Collis kicked him under the table. Ethan sent him an exasperated glare. "What? That wasn't flirting, that was just talking!"

Phillipa only looked amused. "You could flirt all day and likely I'd never notice. That was one social skill I never mastered."

Out of sheer habit, Ethan leered. "I would be happy to teach you—ow!" He rubbed his shin. "Yes, well, that time I was flirting. Old habits die hard."

Collis snorted. "Not as hard as you will if you don't stop."

"All right, then, if Jackham is off limits, tell me about this Denny bloke?"

Collis held up a hand. "He worked for me as valet."

Phillipa nodded. "And before that, he worked for James."

"And before that, for Sir Simon last spring!" Fisher put in.

Ethan blinked. "Three employers in one year? Good God, what did you lot do to the poor wretch? Can you imagine being shuffled around like that, unwanted and unappreciated? Was he that bad a valet?"

Collis looked uneasy. "Well, no. He was quite good actually. Everything was always done to perfection."

Phillipa had to agree. "I didn't like him, but James always looked very dashing—which isn't easy for James. He tends more toward the rumpled-farmer air."

"He was quite clever as well," added Fisher. "If I recall correctly, he came up with some of the more original nicknames in the club."

"Nicknames?" Ethan looked around the table. No one had said anything about a nickname. "Do you all have one?"

They nodded, even Robbie.

"I'm the Phoenix," Collis said.

"I'm Gemini," added Phillipa.

Ethan blinked. "You're a twin?"

She shook her head. "It's a—"

"Long story," Ethan finished for her. "Right." He turned to Robbie. "And you?"

"I'm the son of the Griffin," Robbie explained. "So I'm the Cub." He looked a bit peevish. "Da said that might change someday."

"Let us hope," Ethan agreed. He looked at Fisher. "What about you?"

Fisher gazed back at him. "Why, Fisher, of course."

Ethan blinked. "Oh. I thought that was your surname."

Fisher nodded happily. "It is. Didn't that work out nicely?"

"And Kurt is . . . ?"

"The Cook. No better knife man in all the world." Collis grinned. "I wouldn't think too long on that if I were you. You'll have nightmares."

Ethan leaned back. "True." He was beginning to have a few already. "So do I have a nickname as well?"

They all looked a bit uncomfortable. Collis shrugged and grimaced. "Well . . . it doesn't really work that way. One day someone will simply start calling you a name . . ."

Robbie nodded. "And then it will stick."

Fisher agreed. "The way Denny named that Chimera bloke, just before you all took off on that trip down the Thames."

Collis looked surprised. "Oh, is that where that came from? I'd wondered." He turned back to Ethan. "We don't usually nickname the enemy, but we needed something to call the rotter aside from 'the enemy mastermind.' That was a bit of a mouthful."

They were back to Denny, which was fine because Ethan was beginning to want a nickname and he didn't like that. He'd never been much of a joiner. "So you lot mistreated and disrespected a servant who worked hard for you?" Ethan shook his head. "No wonder he turned on you."

Collis frowned at his *coq au vin*. "I never saw it from that perspective."

"A valet depends on the master for everything." Ethan

rolled his eyes. "That's why they call them 'dependents.'" He pointed his fork at Collis. "You're lucky all he did was carry tales. I would have come up with something much more fitting."

"As in?"

"As in red pepper in your drawers, or thistle spines in your stockings, or—"

Collis held up both hands in defense, laughing. "Hold on there, evil one! You have a mind like a villain!" He looked over at Kurt, who was working more magic on the giant cooker. "Kurt, aren't you still looking for an apprentice? I think I have a candidate for you."

Kurt raised his leonine head to consider Ethan without expression. "Not much of a fighter." Then he grunted. "But fast," he said wistfully.

Suddenly feeling a bit chilled, Ethan leaned over to Robbie. "What does Kurt do around here besides train fighters and cook?" he whispered.

Robbie grinned evilly and drew his finger across his throat, accompanied by a wet slicing noise made in his mouth. "Assassin!" he whispered back, with rather more relish than Ethan thought was precisely healthy.

"Er, right." Nightmares indeed. Ethan looked back up at Kurt. "Thank you, sir, but no, thank you."

Kurt gave a shrug that reminded Ethan of mountains moving and turned back to his bubbling pots.

After excusing himself from the luncheon, Ethan decided to get back to the real world. He was expected at Lord Maywell's tonight. As he was about to leave, he realized that he'd left his walking stick in the cellar.

He trotted quickly down the stairs and spotted the stick immediately—then just as promptly forgot it again.

Clad in nothing but close-fitting trousers and a tight weskit, Rose Tremayne was performing some complicated exercise on the great mat. She moved slowly and gracefully, as if in a dance, her arms and legs seeming to take precise patterns in the air.

It was one of the loveliest things he'd ever seen. She was grace and perfection with her bare arms sweeping slowly through the air in a great arc—

Ethan picked up his stick and went slowly back up the stairs. Rose was a lovely thing indeed.

*I wonder what Lady Jane would look like in trousers?*

# Chapter Twelve

As Ethan left the club and strolled to the corner to catch a hack, he looked about him with new eyes. He was a Liar now, one of them, inside—perhaps for the first time in his life.

He smiled to himself as he passed a school. His eyes barely took in the sign over the gate. "The Lillian Raines School for the Less Fortunate." Now why did that sound familiar?

Well, that wasn't him, was it? He was feeling quite fortunate indeed. Then his shoulder throbbed where Kurt had landed that single massive blow. Painful, but all in all, well worth it. He was a Liar now.

Ethan was so wrapped in the warm glow of camaraderie that he had no idea how closely he was being watched.

Jane opened the door to the second parlor with a polite smile pasted on her face. Simms had told her that a gentleman caller awaited her there. It was probably just Billingsly—not worth disturbing her aunt for chaperonage. She'd simply pop in and tell the fellow that she was terribly busy doing . . . something.

There was no one to be seen, only a gaily colored hatbox on the table. She stepped closer to look for a delivery tag.

"For Lady Jane Pennington. In apology for a regrettable misunderstanding."

Oh, no. It couldn't be. Jane lifted the lid of the hatbox.

It was. The garish bonnet lay tenderly wrapped in tissue, in all its awful glory. "Oh, dear," Jane murmured as she lifted it out. "It's even uglier than I remembered."

"Thank heaven," drawled a deep voice behind her. "I thought it was just me."

Jane whirled to see Mr. Damont lurking behind the parlor door. "What are you doing here?"

He bowed. "It is lovely to see you again as well, my lady."

Jane blushed angrily, then pushed the bonnet back into its box and thrust it out to him. "Take your gift. I want nothing to do with it."

He peered down at the crushed straw. "You broke it!" he accused.

Jane looked down. She had indeed. Now doubly embarrassed, she glared up at Mr. Damont. "Look what you made me do!"

He scoffed at her. "I did not!"

"Oh!" A gentleman would never refute a lady! "Yes you did!"

He folded his arms. "Did not."

She plunked the box back onto the table and planted her fists on her hips. "Did too!"

He grinned. "Did not." His tone was high and childish.

She snickered, then bit her lip. "Did too!"

He stamped his foot. "Did not."

She laughed out loud, then clapped a hand over her mouth. "I hate you," she mumbled.

He tilted his head. "Do not."

She took a deep breath, then gave it up. Throwing her arms out, she shook her head with a smile. "You're right. I don't hate you."

He smiled rather sweetly. It left deep creases in his cheeks. Her breath left her at the sight. She sometimes forgot how very handsome he was. Recovering, she blinked. "So that was a misunderstanding this afternoon?"

He held up one hand in a vow. "Absolutely. I wished to solicit a female perspective on something I have at home, that is all."

The blush returned. Jane pressed both hands to her cheeks. "I thought—"

He nodded. "I know, but I promise, I have no etchings."

Chuckling, Jane shook her head. "You can always make me laugh, even when I really don't want to."

"Am I forgiven, then? You don't think I'm a cad who would proposition a respectable woman?"

She looked up at him teasingly. "Well, I wouldn't go that far . . ."

Something crossed his expression and he made a small movement, almost a flinch. Jane hesitated. He really meant it—he really cared what she thought. She shook her head quickly. "I don't think that at all," she said honestly. "I was mostly embarrassed at—" *At being caught staring at your trousers.* Well, perhaps honesty had its limits.

She clasped her hands before her. "I don't think ill of you at all. You've been very kind to me, and Serena. I think you are a very nice man."

He blinked. "That is going a bit far."

She nodded. "I agree. I take it back."

This time he was the one to laugh involuntarily. He shook his head. "Who are you, Lady Jane? Where in the world did you come from and are there more of you there?"

Jane paused. Mother had told her not to reveal too much about herself. "I have been living in Northumbria for several years. And no, I don't believe there are many girls there like me."

She hadn't meant to let that tiny stream of loneliness leak into her voice. Perhaps he hadn't noticed. She looked into his eyes and saw that he had. Moreover, he'd understood. Jane looked away.

This was more than she was prepared for. She suddenly wasn't sure how she felt about being alone in here with this man—who had already kissed her once, and now showed an unfortunate ability to sympathize with her. Of all the men in London, why a lowborn gambler?

It must end now, before this attraction—or affinity, or whatever it was—became something more. That would not be beneficial, for either of them. "Mr. Damont, I think you should go now."

He drew back. "What? I thought—"

Jane took a deep breath. "Whatever you thought, you were mistaken. I don't wish to continue this conversation. Please leave."

He gaped, then threw out his hands. "You run hot, then you run cold. You are the most confusing, mystifying, bloody-minded female I have ever met!"

Irked, she folded her arms beneath her breasts. "I'm sure you mean to be insulting, so I shall find great pleasure in taking your comments as complimentary."

He threw up his hands and swung away from her. "Why me? I've lived a good life! I don't kick dogs and small children! I've never taken a penny from someone who didn't deserve it!"

"Do be careful not to exaggerate, there," she drawled.

"I'm not exaggerating," he protested. "I only play blokes who don't deserve their own good fortune!"

"And what do you think constitutes 'not deserving'—inheritance?"

He huffed. "I have nothing against those who inherit. It's those who use what they were given to do harm or to take advantage of those who have less."

She dropped her arms. "Is that true?"

He shook his head and flopped into a chair. "Of course it's not true," he said. "Why would anything that comes out of my mouth be true?"

"I'm sorry," she said, her tone gentle. "I didn't mean to insult you."

"Well, you did." He scowled for a moment, then turned a sunny smile on her. "Lucky for you I don't hold a grudge."

She laughed and shook her head. "Then you are, indeed, a better person than I, for I hold them long and well."

"Who do you have a grudge against? Is it someone evil? Shall I cheat him for you?" he asked eagerly

She pressed her lips together but it didn't hide the smile. Ethan sat back again, basking in the fact that he could make Lady Jane Pennington smile against her will.

"You really are a good sort, Janet. I do hope we can be friends."

"I'm not sure that's possible," she said slowly. "I've never heard of a friendship between—"

This time he definitely flinched. "Between a lady and a merchant's son?"

She frowned slightly. "Between a man and a woman."

"Oh, don't worry about that," he said airily. "I've scads of women friends."

She was silent for a moment. "I'm sure you do."

She rose and clasped her hands before her. "It grows late, sir. I think I must say good-bye now."

"Here now, Janet!" *Bloody smooth, old man. What a thing to say!* Ethan rose and crossed to her. "I didn't mean—I wasn't talking about those sort of—"

A heavy step sounded in the hall outside the parlor. Although she had nothing truly to hide, Jane shot Mr. Damont a panicked look. "My uncle!"

In one lithe movement, Mr. Damont slipped back behind the door just as it opened.

"Jane?" Uncle Harold pushed the door open wide. A bit too wide. Jane winced and hoped Mr. Damont hadn't taken the impact of the doorknob anywhere too important. Uncle Harold glanced around the room. "What are you doing in here? I thought I heard voices. Is someone in here with you?"

Jane gestured to the hatbox. "Simms told me I had a caller, but when I came in, all I saw was this gift."

Uncle Harold peered at the crushed bonnet without much interest. "Didn't like it much, did you?"

"Not at all," Jane said quite truthfully.

Uncle Harold was examining the tag. "What's this misunderstanding about?"

"I cannot be sure," Jane said vaguely. "I believe I took offense to something a gentleman said."

Uncle Harold scowled. "Who?"

Blast, she was afraid he was going to ask that. "One of the gentlemen who was here last evening, I think. I don't recall all of them very well." All too true. Beside the shining sharpness of Mr. Damont in her memory, the other fellows faded into an insignificant blur.

"Humph." Uncle Harold seemed to lose interest. Jane couldn't imagine why he'd expressed any in the first place. Why, after all these months, was he finally exhibiting curiosity into her affairs?

Then again, thinking of the way Mr. Damont's very presence made her palms damp, perhaps the word "affairs" was ill-chosen.

"Carry on, then," Uncle Harold said, his tone already bored. "See you at supper, my dear."

"Yes, Uncle Harold." Jane remained where she was, standing in the middle of the parlor with a vapid smile on her face, until her uncle's heavy footsteps faded down the hall. Then she let out a breath and dashed to shut the parlor door once more.

Mr. Damont was plastered to the wall, his eyes clenched shut and his hands crossed protectively in front of him. Jane pursed her lips and looked away. "He is gone, sir."

Opening his eyes, Ethan stared at Lady Jane Pennington, paragon of aristocratic ... well, pretty much everything, and accomplished bald-faced liar. "You hoodwinked him."

"I did not," she objected serenely.

"You did so. You hoodwinked him like a professional."

She sat elegantly on the sofa, not looking at him. "I did no such thing. Everything I said was the absolute literal truth."

"I know," he said with a sigh of ecstasy. "That's what made it so beautiful." He moved to stand before her, bouncing on his heels. "Let's do it again!"

Her calm finally faltered. She stared up at him. "What?"

"Let's do it again! Let's go find someone else to lie the absolute literal truth to. I want to see it one more time."

A reluctant laugh broke from her lips. "No, thank you. One black mark against my soul in one day is enough."

"Oh, come on. I know! Let's go find a vicar! Or a bishop!"

Her jaw dropped. "You are incorrigible."

He grinned down at her conspiratorially. "So are you, Lady Proper Pennington. You enjoyed that and you know it."

She looked away, but the corner of her lips quirked. "I did not."

He leaned close, a good bit closer than was proper. "Yes you did," he said, his voice a caress. "You're very good at being bad, Lady Jane."

She gave him a push, and rose from the sofa to pace the parlor. "And you're insufferable."

He laughed and fell into step beside her. "Thank you. I do try."

She rolled her eyes as she walked on. "Years of diligent practice, yes?"

Ethan only grinned down at her. She was such an odd mix. Half proper lady, half clever minx. Add a good dollop of sarcasm and he was captivated. If she wasn't careful, he was likely to find himself proposing something wicked after all, something most improper and vastly enjoyable to them both.

He sighed. No virgins. It was a bloody good rule and he was going to stick to it.

He only wished he could remember why.

"Mr. Damont," she said quietly. "Have you ever considered being more than that?"

"More than what?"

She turned to gaze up at him. "More than a gambler and a place card?"

*Place card.* The description struck home. He turned away.

She moved to follow him. "You could do it. You're clever—and you already know so many influential people!"

He moved away, but she persisted. "You could take up the law—or the Church!"

That was too much. He turned on her. "Good God, Janet, what do you expect of me!"

"I expect more, that is all!" She did not back down before his frustration. "I expect that you would use your intellect and talent for something other than your own enrichment!"

"Why should I?" He felt compelled to defend his position, even though the battle was one he'd never truly won, even within himself, and even though he'd taken steps today to become much more. "Why must I exert myself so? What has the world done for me that I must do for it in return? For that matter, what of you? What do you use your mind and talents for but to decorate the world by being in it?"

"I am not decorative!"

"Bloody hell you're not!" Ethan frankly yelled. "You're a confounded beauty and you know it!"

She froze, her mouth already open again to protest. She looked completely gobsmacked, staring at him as if he'd just grown green fur. Ethan was seized with a wild desire to kiss those parted lips.

She shook off the surprise. "Why do you not simply stop? Do something else?"

God, she was like a bull terrier! "I say, you're right! I'll do it!" Ethan opened his arms and turned a circle. "I'll simply quit cards entirely and become a ship captain . . . or Prime Minister . . . or . . . I hear the job of King is open!"

The glint of approval that had begun to appear in her eyes dissolved as she realized he was mocking her. She folded her arms and glared, her gray eyes flashing. "Sod."

Ethan bowed formally. "At your service, my lady."

"There's nothing wrong with honest work, Mr. Damont."

He threw himself back into his chair. "You'd know all about that, I suppose," he muttered around the cheroot he was lighting. He drew the smoke in deeply. "Being Lady Jane and all."

She stayed where she was, standing rigid and disapproving with her arms folded. "Yes, being Lady Jane and all, I do know all about that."

He snorted, watching the ribbon of smoke rise. "Janet, you don't even button your own clothing."

"Mr. Damont, you know nothing about me."

He glanced at her. "Then tell me. Tell me how you carry your own bathwater and sew your own gowns and cook your own supper, Lady Jane." He didn't bother to stem the sarcasm dripping from every word.

She tilted her head. "I don't have to prove any such thing to you. I know what I have done and I know what I am. Until my Uncle Christoph passed away last year, I lived like a pauper. All this," she waved a hand to indicate her fine gown. "All this came to me quite lately, I fear."

Ethan's brows came together. "You're telling me the truth, aren't you?"

She smiled. "Absolutely."

Ethan smiled back, catching on. "But you're not telling me all of it, are you?"

She blinked at him, clearly irritated. "Why, Mr. Damont, would you accuse a lady of lying?"

"Yes," he said. "I would. But not you. You, I would accuse of telling the absolute literal truth, Janet."

"Don't call me that!"

He frowned up at her. "Call you what?"

"You may address me as Lady Jane, or 'my lady.'"

Now she truly was angry. Pink spots had appeared in her pale cheeks and her eyes flashed like lightning behind a storm cloud. Damn if she didn't look fine like that. Intriguing. He stood, stubbing out the cheroot he hadn't smoked, and approached her slowly until he stood an arm's length away.

"Janet," he called in a low voice. Her eyes narrowed dangerously. Ethan loved living dangerously. He took another step. "Janet," he murmured.

She twitched, her hands itching to slap him, he knew. Still, she only glared at him, as if trying to prove that she was above reacting to anything done by a low creature such as him. He couldn't resist the challenge.

He took another step and stopped so close before her that if she inhaled too deeply, her bodice would touch his waistcoat.

She took a deep breath, proving him right. Her eyes flickered. She took another. And another. Ethan could feel her nipples hardening against him. Without taking his gaze from hers, he smiled wickedly. "Don't wear two little holes through the silk, Janet. This is my favorite weskit."

Her hand did fly then. Ethan took the first slap willingly, because he definitely deserved it, but when she drew her hand back again, Ethan was faster. He caught her hand, curling his fingers around her wrist in a gentle but implacable cuff. "My turn," he said softly.

Her eyes widened and she drew back. He raised his other hand—

—and gently cupped her cheek in his palm. She froze but he could feel a trembling begin deep within her. His fingertips slid into her silky hair and suddenly Ethan passionately wanted to see it down around her shoulders, streaming over her bare breasts, splaying over his pillow—

He stroked his thumb down her cheek to her top lip. So pink, although he was positive she wore no lip rouge.

"You're all milk and satin and strawberries, do you know that, Janet?" His thumb caught her full bottom lip down and her lips parted.

Jane could not move. Never, never in her life—oh, dear God, she couldn't breathe, couldn't think—

His palm was hot on her cheek, his thumb leaving prints of fire on her lips. Without will of her own, her tongue flicked out to taste the salt on his skin. He was brandy and fire and male . . . and had she really done that?

His eyes went hot at her tiny permission. She couldn't take her gaze away. Oh, God, she'd done it now—

His hand slid to the back of her neck and his mouth came down on hers.

# Chapter Thirteen

———— ◈ ————

She melted in his hands. Virtuous, wholesome Lady Jane Pennington turned to hot wax at his touch. She flowed against him, surrendering to his kiss as if his mouth on hers were all she'd ever wanted in her entire life. It was bloody intoxicating, that's what it was.

Victory and arousal pumped through Ethan's veins, roared in his ears, drowned out his reason. He let go of her wrist and wrapped his arm hard about her waist, pulling her to him, needing to feel her body against his. She was lithe and liquid and willing, oh, so willing—

She kissed him back, awkwardly and fervently. Her hands came up to dive into his hair, clinging to him, pulling him closer. He groaned into her mouth, her hot, sweet, untutored mouth—thank God, she was a quick study. Her kiss deepened, her lips plumping and her tongue venturing to mesh with his—closer, he had to get closer.

The wall came up against Jane's back and she was grateful for its pressure molding her more closely to Ethan's hard, hungry body. His knee pressed between her thighs, pinning her with her own skirts to the wall. She gladly rode his hard thigh astride, the pressure of it jolting through her. Soon she would sink into him, for she was dissolving in his heat. Her bosom was pressed hard

to his chest—she ached, needed to rub away the ache—
she writhed against him.

He made an animal sound at her motion. His hand left her
neck to wrap around her breast—yes, that was what she
wanted, his touch, his rough demanding caress, his fingertips
plucking at her nipple through her bodice. No, she wanted
him closer, touching her, she wanted her breast to be as bare
as her cheek, to feel the heat of his palm, the coarse texture
of his thumb, the hot, wet suction of his mouth—

*What am I doing?*

Cold reality rushed through Jane. Ethan Damont had
his tongue in her mouth and his hand on her bodice in
her aunt Lottie's second-best parlor in the middle of the
afternoon.

Jane placed both hands on his shoulders and shoved
with all her strength. Mr. Damont went staggering backward, his eyes wide with surprise. He caught himself instantly and straightened, his chest heaving. She was
breathing hard herself, as if she'd run a race when she'd
never taken a step.

Actually, she'd taken a rather large, unwise, regrettable step . . . one she was quite sure she couldn't take
back. "I—I cannot—I do not—" Her heart wouldn't stop
racing. Her body ached. All she wanted was his touch. All
she wanted was to find a dark room and submit to his
every caress. She scarcely recognized herself.

"I fear I no longer know who I am," she said quietly.

Her admission went through Ethan like a shot, over-
powering his own anger and ardor. The note of loss and
confusion in her voice—he had done this to her. He had
wanted to break her, he realized. He'd wanted to batter
down her barriers.

He'd wanted to win.

Looking at her standing there, breathless, her priceless
composure in pieces about her feet, her hands visibly
trembling, he felt no victory, only shame.

He passed one hand over his face. "Janet, I'm—"

"Please do not address me so." Her demand was quiet this time, soft and defeated. Her tone made his chest ache.

He exhaled, then bowed slightly. "My deepest apologies, my lady," he said formally, without a trace of mockery. He straightened. "I fear I have overstayed my welcome. Please excuse me."

She nodded graciously but silently, gazing somewhere just over his right shoulder. Ethan left the parlor feeling as though he had viciously kicked Zeus.

Simms was standing in the front hall. "His lordship has been expecting you, sir." Although the butler must have known that Ethan had been alone in the parlor with Lady Jane, the man gazed at him without comment.

As, of course, any butler should. Only Jeeves felt it necessary to criticize him. Right now, Ethan rather felt he deserved a good dressing-down. Unfortunately, there was no one to condemn him.

No one but himself, that is.

Lord Maywell lounged in his chair like a prince on a throne. Ethan had to admit that the man had a certain air about him. In fact, he reminded Ethan of his own father— watchful and exacting. The only difference was, he would never have seen that light of assessing approval from the eyes of his father.

Ethan reminded himself to be wary. If Lord Maywell was, indeed, some sort of espionage mastermind, then it wouldn't do to underestimate the man. Just because someone was a lord didn't mean he was necessarily useless. Just look at Etheridge.

So Ethan assumed a careless air of his own, lounging in his own chair as if he were still the detached gambler with no ties and no loyalties. It was a comfortable and familiar skin to live in.

Now that he was out of the environment of the club, he was beginning to forget that brief sensation of belonging. One afternoon did not a family bond create, after all.

"Tell me something, Damont—where do you stand on this issue of pulling British troops out of the Americas?"

Ethan twirled his unlit cheroot in his fingers. After spending time wrapped in the endless haze of smoke that surrounded Maywell, he was beginning to lose his taste for the things. He stared at the ceiling. "America . . . America . . ." He shrugged. "Isn't that where the tobacco comes from?"

Maywell narrowed his eyes. "You have no opinion on the American war?"

Ethan waved his cheroot at his lordship. "Too bloody right I do! I say it's time to end that bloody mess and get the price of tobacco back down!"

Maywell chuckled at that. "I'll bring that up at the next meeting of the House of Lords. Maybe that'll light a fire under some of those old sticks." He drew on his cheroot, making the tip glow in the dim room.

Ethan wondered if he was supposed to laugh at that, or if Maywell even recognized his own pun. Abruptly, he found himself wearying of the cat-and-mouse wordplay between them. He wasn't going to play.

"I have to admit, my lord, that I don't give a monkey's arse about the war, or Napoleon, or the Americas. Not only do I have no opinion, but I don't really want to hear your opinion either." He leaned back, eyeing his host.

Maywell eyed him narrowly. "You don't care at all? You have no patriotic passion? No fervor for the preservation of Mother England and the status quo?"

Ethan spread his hands. "What has the status quo ever done for me?"

The fact that it was the truth did nothing to ease how hollow it sounded in Ethan's own ears. If this was no pose, if this was no act . . . then he must truly be the most worthless, parasitical lout that ever walked the earth. He was beginning to think Etheridge was right about him all along.

"Hmm. Interesting." Maywell blew out another cloud of smoke, obscuring his face except for those glinting eyes. "Let us change the subject then, shall we? Tell me, have you ever frequented one of the bordellos located near Westminster?"

Ethan knew there were some "shops" near the palace that sold more than cravats and Chinese tea. He shook his head. "I've always favored Mrs. Blythe's establishment, myself."

Maywell grunted. "That's not one of mine."

"Yours, my lord? Do you mean one of your favorites?"

Maywell pursed his lips. "I mean, I don't own that one."

Oh-ho. Ethan's ears pricked, although he was careful not to show it. "I had no idea you were in the business, my lord." The man had five daughters, for God's sake! "Have you found it profitable?"

Maywell grunted. "Financially they have yet to truly pay out, but otherwise . . ." He spread both hands, his smug expression implying some great profit other than monetary.

As in . . . what? Surely the man didn't find it spiritually rewarding? Ethan decided to bite. "What other sort of profit is there?"

"Information." Maywell pointed at Ethan with his lit cheroot. "The only real power in the world lies in controlling information. He who knows the most, wins."

Ethan could not hold back a disbelieving snort. "So this is a scholarly pursuit? Do you have naked ladybirds reading aloud to their clients?"

Maywell smirked. "You'd be surprised what some of these gentlemen pay for."

Ethan thought back to his own history of energetic sexual exploration. "I sincerely doubt I would be." He smiled. "So if the information is not being disseminated by the ladies, then it is being collected. Am I correct?"

Maywell nodded smugly. "And who do you think is spouting all this pillow talk?"

Westminster . . . the center of the British government. The two Houses of Parliament, the Guard, the Home

Office, which ran national security and the war effort—

"I say," Ethan breathed. "That's brilliant." It was, in an entirely evil way. All those overworked, frazzled officials— a clever, sympathetic woman could get a great deal out of such men.

*Careful! You're not supposed to know Maywell's a traitor!*

Ethan examined his nails. "So you are a blackmailer, then?"

That even surprised Maywell. His lordship started and went rather pink with indignation. "I am not a blackmailer!"

"So then why? What do you need all this information for?"

Maywell said nothing for a moment. Then he leaned forward and placed his folded hands in the precise center of his desk blotter. "Damont, you are a man of many talents. You have experience in certain aspects of the world that I do not. You are clever and clear-sighted, unclouded by soggy sentiment."

"Thank you," Ethan drawled. "I think."

"I could use a man like you, Damont."

Oh, no. Here it came, despite his efforts. In fact, it seemed almost as if his declaration of apathy had sealed Maywell's opinion of him—in precisely the opposite way Ethan had intended.

"I'm sure I don't know what you mean," Ethan said uneasily.

Maywell smiled, a toothy predator's grin. "I think you do. You came to me, don't you recall? Why do you think that was? Do you think it was mere happenstance that you came to my house the evening of the ball?"

Ethan shrugged. "I had my reasons."

Maywell smiled slightly. "As well I know. Luckily, all that your friends from the Liar's Club found were the records of a mission I have little faith in anyway."

*Maywell knew.* Ethan went cold. Nevertheless, he kept

his expression unconcerned. Never had he needed his poker face more. "What friends? I don't frequent the Liar's Club."

Maywell steepled his fingers before him. It reminded Ethan eerily of Dalton Montmorency, although one could not imagine two men more different in make and manner.

"Mr. Damont, I have no wish to put you on the spot. Let me tell you all about your friends." He raised one finger. "One, they operate from behind the smokescreen of a gentlemen's club. Two, they recruit from all levels of Society, for which I commend them. Three, they know about me, as I know about them."

Ethan swallowed. Maywell definitely looked like the Chimera to him. On one hand, he'd found out what the Liars wanted to know. On the other, he was probably going to die before he got to tell them. "A pretty tale," he said, striving to keep his tone mild. "I only wish I knew what you were talking about."

Maywell nodded. "You may continue to pretend if it helps you to do so. I wouldn't want you to betray your comrades—"

Something must have slipped past Ethan's guard and crossed his expression, for Maywell's eyes narrowed.

"Ah. They are not your comrades yet, then. Interesting. Could it be that I have found a man who does not exhibit the loyalty of a hound to his master? If you do not love your master . . . then he must keep you on a very tight leash." Maywell gave Ethan a kind smile. "I could cut that leash for you."

Ethan remained as still as possible. He'd underestimated Lord Maywell, he could see that now. Dalton had done so as well. Maywell's offer made every rebellious strand of Ethan's personality tighten with longing. He hated being dangled on a string, no matter for what cause he was hung.

"I have no master," was all he could force from his tight throat.

Maywell regarded him with a raised brow. "No, not since you escaped your father."

Ethan jerked slightly at that, a tiny motion that Maywell did not miss. The man's expression went kindly and he leaned forward, placing his hands flat on the desk.

"Damont, you think us worlds apart, you and I—but I tell you that we are the same beneath the labels the world has pasted upon us. I was the third son, the spare for the spare. I grew up knowing that there was no chance for me to be the man I could be. No true title, no substantial inheritance, no lands I could husband into any real power. An empty title, a tag given to any son of a duke, that left me dangling between worlds. I could not even turn my hand to business, for to do so would bring the scorn of my kind." He grunted. "My kind . . . a more worthless lot I've never encountered."

Hearing his own feelings echoed by Maywell made Ethan feel strange, as though he'd thought he was staring a hobgoblin in the eyes, only to have it turn into his own reflection in a mirror. He blinked to break the spell of Maywell's words.

"I'm sure your lordship's life has been very difficult," he said blandly. "I'm sure I cannot imagine." Although he could. *"Dangling between worlds."*

He himself had been dangling so long he couldn't remember what it felt like to have the earth beneath his feet. He hadn't belonged, truly belonged, since he could recall. He'd been plucked from the society of his own kind by the time he could talk. "I don't want him to sound like a street urchin," his father had said often enough. "He ought to sound like a lord."

He'd been caged by tutors and dancing masters and fencing masters and fed only the manners that his father selected for him. A gentleman's diet—a rarefied menu indeed.

Yet even the lowliest gentleman tutor had been superior to him in caste, and had never let him forget it. For the coin his father paid into their poor gentility, they would teach him what he needed to know—but the one thing they all made sure to educate him in was that no matter how hard he worked, no matter how long he studied and practiced and performed, he could *never* be one of them.

Maywell had continued speaking. Ethan pulled his mind back from old hollow thoughts to reorient himself on the man who held Ethan's life in his hands.

"Does that sound like sense to you, Damont? Empty-headed lords running England's greatest asset, her fertile lands, into ash and sand. Courtiers plying an even more empty-headed prince with women and favors, while men with sense watch this country get further and further indebted and depleted fighting Bonaparte!"

His first goal was to live. His second was to find out as much as he could for the Liars. Ethan spread his hands in a world-weary gesture. "What else are we to do? It has always been this way. It always will be."

Maywell narrowed his eyes and leaned forward again. "It does not have to be, Damont. Do you think that if Napoleon wins, he will keep this current power structure in place? He is a self-made man. He believes that a man's mettle is shown by what he does, not his name or title. Do you think that he'd tolerate these soft-handed, brainless layabouts as *his* Imperial aristocracy for one single moment?"

Ethan leaned back and crossed his own hands lazily over his middle. "An intriguing notion, to be sure. But does not Paris still hold lords and ladies galore? He has yet to do away with them."

Maywell waved a derisive hand. "Bah. They are ornaments, left in place to please Josephine. All the men who matter, all the ones with real power, are men that Bonaparte has brought up through his ranks, men that have proven their grit on the field and in the halls of power." Maywell sat back, mimicking Ethan's unconcerned pose.

"Men like us, Damont. Men with sense, who see the world clearly—who see how ridiculous the social order is and how it depletes us."

Becoming interested in spite of himself, Ethan tilted his head. "Yet you, my lord, are exactly who would lose by such a revolution. I find it hard to believe you would really give all this up." He waved his hands to indicate his surroundings.

Maywell let out a bray of actual laughter. "All this? All this crumbling house and this back-bending debt and this fight to marry off five girls before anyone discovers that even the dresses on their backs are borrowed?"

Ah, finally a truth that Ethan could understand. Maywell's position, encumbered by responsibilities of family and rank, was everything Ethan had always abhorred. The idea of ending up this way, weighed down, owned—the very thought nigh to made him shudder with revulsion.

"And you believe that if Napoleon wins the day, this would change?"

Maywell smiled. "It will change. I have it on very good authority that my efforts will be well rewarded. I will get everything I deserve and more." He peered closely at Ethan. "As could you."

Ethan smiled easily. "I already have everything I deserve."

Maywell pursed his lips. "Do you really?" He tapped his fingertips together. "I'd like us to conduct a little experiment. Tomorrow morning, I want you to walk up to the gates of Carlton House and request a private audience with the Prince Regent."

A surprised laugh burst from Ethan's lips at such an outrageous impossibility. "Why walk? Why not fly?"

Maywell smiled. "I thought as much. Only trust me, Damont. Indulge me on this whim. I assure you, it will be an illuminating experience."

Maywell stood. Ethan followed, since it seemed the interview was over. All he wanted to do was get out of that house. He'd not thought he would find the whole matter so disturbing . . . so destabilizing to his usual careless equilibrium.

Ethan was nearly out of the study when Maywell called him back. "By the way, Damont—Jane has been invited to dine with friends of ours tomorrow night. I would appreciate it if you would escort her there and back."

Ethan blinked. Escorting respectable young women anywhere was not usually something requested of him. In fact, if he recalled correctly—never.

Then again, if he was working for Maywell now, it might be expected that he take on some of the responsibilities of an employee—like a steward or a man of business. After all, Maywell hadn't said he was to accompany Jane to the dinner party as a guest, but more like a bodyguard.

He nodded. "Yes, my lord. It would be my pleasure."

In fact, it would be a good opportunity to apologize to Jane. Again.

# Chapter Fourteen

Lord Harold Maywell watched Ethan Damont take his leave without escorting him from the room. Reaching into his pocket, he brought out a fine cheroot. It was from his last case of them. Thank goodness he would soon be rewarded for all his hard work.

The girls were going to break him otherwise. Resentfully, Lord Maywell thought of the money wasted into nothing by his older brother's son. All of it gone and the lands seized for taxes—lands that had been in the family for more generations than that callow boy had years. Stupid young sot.

What he himself could have done with those resources and a bit of common sense . . . well, his daughters would be headed for the futures they deserved, marrying well and happily instead of putting themselves forward for the masculine leavings of Society.

By the time Napoleon came sailing over the Channel, Lord Maywell planned to have worked himself high enough up the chain of command within the network that he would be made a marquis at the very least.

A faint sound came from across the room. The small round-faced man stepped out of the shadows of the curtained window embrasure and into the circle of light thrown by the candelabra.

The small man looked at the door. "When I told you I saw him leaving the Liar's Club, I thought you were planning to kill him."

Lord Maywell leaned back in his chair, smoke wreathing his already whitened hair. "I thought about it. It did seem a waste. After all, his talents could come in just as handy for us."

"They got to him first."

Maywell took the cheroot between his fingers and gazed at it with satisfaction. "But I have something he wants."

"The girl?" The smaller man scoffed. "No disrespect to Lady Jane, my lord, but Damont's reputation precedes him. He has no problem with obtaining female companionship."

"Yet he could never lay claim to a lady—especially not with the blessing of her family and friends." Maywell inhaled another long draw on the cheroot. "True welcome in Society is the one thing Damont can never have—unless I give it to him."

"You'd do that? You'd give him your blessing and your niece and all her vast inheritance—"

"I might. Or I might simply let him think I will." Maywell rolled his cheroot in the ash receptacle that his wife insisted he keep in his study. "I think Jane likes him as well."

"Do you really concern yourself with what a mere girl wants when the very future of England is at stake?"

"No. But her willingness will be a great lure for Damont. He will want to please her."

The small man snickered. "From what I've heard, he ought to be good at that."

Maywell stiffened. "Don't be crude. That is a lady you speak about."

The small man bowed. "My apologies, of course. I forgot myself. Allow me to change the subject. What about the larger plan?"

"We aren't ready yet," Maywell protested. "There are still preparations to be made."

"We are as prepared as we are ever going to be," the small man insisted.

Maywell shook his head. "Let me obtain the loyalty of Damont first. I have the feeling we're going to need him."

"Then you took a great risk, sending him to Court. What if that secures his loyalty to the Crown instead?"

Maywell's lips twisted. "You don't understand Damont the way I do. What he discovers there will send him reeling right into our grasp."

"Are you sure?"

"Oh, yes. If there is one thing on earth I am sure of, it is that Mr. Ethan Damont is about to turn traitor against England forever."

Jane pressed a hand to her mouth, unable to believe what she was hearing. She'd heard her name as she passed the closed door of her uncle's study and had been stunned to hear that her uncle was considering encouraging Ethan Damont to court her.

Surprised delight had coursed through her. She had pressed her ear to the door to hear more—she wasn't accustomed to eavesdropping, but after all, the topic concerned her greatly—only to freeze with icy horror as she listened to the rest of the conversation. Now, she felt sickened by what she had heard.

Uncle Harold was a traitor—and worse yet, he was planning on turning Mr. Damont traitor as well!

Jane turned to run as lightly as possible from the hall, only to stop cold before reaching the stairs. She had no one to turn to —no one to tell. How could she go to her aunt with this story?

Aunt Lottie would think her malicious or mad, but she would certainly not believe her. Her cousins—they were too young and innocent to hear such things. Besides, what could they do against their own father?

Mother would know what to do.

Yes. If Jane posted a letter first thing tomorrow, she

ought to hear back from Mother very quickly. Jane ran carefully up the stairs, doing her best to let no one hear her passing. Once safely in her and Serena's room, she pulled out her writing case and began.

"Dear Mother, I have just learned the most disturbing thing . . ."

Serena dawdled over her evening biscuits and milk, unwilling to go upstairs to bed just yet. She'd been up to her room a few moments ago, only to find Jane bent avidly over her writing desk, pen scratching wildly, ink everywhere.

When Jane first came to visit, Serena had been very happy, especially when it meant that she was moved into the largest, nicest bedchamber with her cousin. It had used to be Augusta's room and Augusta had lorded it over all of them that she no longer had to share a bed.

Jane was usually good company. Serena liked to hear about her life in Northumbria, although it was difficult to get Jane to talk about her years in the Dowager House.

Serena pictured someplace brooding and romantic, with windswept moors and towering dark clouds. Jane had laughed at her when she'd said that.

"There is wind and there are clouds indeed, but I doubt you'd find it so romantic when you were trying to keep your bonnet in place."

Sometimes Serena suspected that Jane purposely suppressed all romantic urges, just to be practical. Serena wasn't fond of practicality. Practicality meant doubling up bedrooms and the youngest daughter getting the most elderly of the gowns and cheap shoes from Shepherd's Market that looked just like the expensive ones from Bond Street but fell apart after a few wearings and pinched horribly until they did.

Finally, Serena couldn't force herself to maintain interest in her stale biscuits and left the room to dawdle her way down the downstairs hall.

The door to Papa's study opened a few feet ahead of her and a familiar figure hurried out with barely a polite nod in her direction. Serena sighed. It was only Papa's man of business, that small, round-faced fellow who came and went at all hours.

The study door remained open, so Serena peeped in to see if Papa was in an expansive mood. She saw him leaning back in his chair at his desk, blowing rings of smoke over his head and smiling slightly.

Encouraged, Serena tapped timidly on the doorframe. "May I come in, Papa?"

Papa smiled warmly at her and Serena relaxed. She knew Papa favored her over the others, but she was also fairly sure that was because she was careful never to nag at him for more gowns and shoes. One had to be careful to catch Papa in just the right mood, or he could be as gruff as a bear.

She ran to him and twined her arms about his neck, laying her head on his shoulder fondly. "You are working very late, Papa."

"And you are up late yourself, Angel," he said, patting her clumsily on the shoulder.

Serena closed her eyes, breathing in the smoky, sandalwood Papa scent that surrounded him. Such moments came rarely and Serena treasured every one. Some girls had loving papas and some did not. Serena knew she should feel fortunate that every once in a while, her papa was actually hers. She only wished such moments came more often.

"Why aren't you in bed, Serena?"

She sighed into his shoulder. "Oh, Jane is writing another letter. I think she is upset about something, for she is nearly breaking the nib of the pen."

She thought she felt him stiffen. "What would Jane have to be upset about? She seemed fine when I spoke to her this afternoon."

"I don't know. I looked over her shoulder but all I could see was a line about overhearing something."

Papa's hand dropped from her shoulder and she felt him shrug her off.

"Get off to bed now, Serena," he said shortly.

Sighing, Serena straightened. She would have liked another few seconds—but never mind. If she was good and sweet and careful not to nag, then sooner or later she would be welcomed back on that broad shoulder again.

The next morning, Ethan dawdled on Pall Mall. The Royal Guard was in high evidence near and around the Prince's residence. Carlton House didn't have literal gates, of course, but there may as well have been a moat with no drawbridge before him, so vast was the gulf between mere Ethan Damont and George IV.

Finally, he tossed his cheroot into the gutter and took a breath. It was a ridiculous errand, one he was sure Maywell had sent him on for one reason only.

"Time to teach the merchant's son his place," he muttered to himself. A conservatively dressed, bespectacled fellow scurried by at that moment and cast Ethan a curious glance. With a twist to his lips, Ethan watched him approach the Guard and be whisked indoors. "Now why didn't I wear my royal underling suit? Oh, that's right," he muttered to himself. "It's being cleaned."

He sauntered forward. The Royal Guard were a tall lot, all muscle and rigid spine. The two men standing on either side of the entry were no exceptions. Ethan blew out a low breath. What did they feed these blokes, elephant's milk?

He stood his tallest, which helped some, and pasted an arrogant smile on his lips, which helped more. "Hullo, lads. I've come to ask for a private audience with the Prince Regent."

They didn't laugh, he gave them that much.

"Your name and business, sir?"

Ethan swept off his hat and bowed facetiously. "Ethan Damont. I am no one of any influence or importance whatsoever. I've no business at all. I'm simply here on a whim."

The guard on the right glanced back over his shoulder at the gatekeeper, who bent to busily check something. After a rustle of pages, the gatekeeper raised his head. "He's on the list. Let him through."

Ethan blinked. "I'm what?"

The Royal Guard stepped apart, creating a space in the wall of muscled imperturbability. A bemused Ethan wandered through, his mind racing. What list?

Once within the doors, he stood quite still, too stunned even to look about him for a moment. Then he came back to himself enough to blink at the grandeur around him. He stood in an entry hall that could have held his own fine house and had room for part of the garden as well. Gilded molding created panels on the walls that each held an individual mural depicting—apparently—the visitor's entrance into heaven.

Well, that had yet to be seen, hadn't it?

A bewigged, beribboned, and begilded servant stepped up to him. "If you'll follow me, sir."

Ethan nearly whistled. The man's white satin livery with gold-thread trim was blinding. Various obnoxious comments concerning its resemblance to cake icing rose to Ethan's lips, but he said nothing as he was led down a grand hallway that was wider than his house. Eventually the servant stopped before an ornately carved door and stepped through. Ethan could see only the man's shiny rear end as he bowed deeply. "Mr. Ethan Damont!"

Someone murmured something in the room and Ethan found himself gestured inside. He imagined he was going to find himself before some officer of the Crown who would demand an explanation.

Instead, he entered the room to find himself face-to-face with the face on the coin—the face of the Prince Regent of all the British Isles, George IV, who was smiling genially at him, Ethan Damont!

"Hello, Ethan," His Royal Highness said in an oddly familiar voice. "Rescued anyone else from a dungeon lately?"

Ethan gaped, breathless with shock. Finally, his numb lips formed one word.

*"Codger?"*

Jane carried her letter downstairs this morning instead of allowing the chambermaid to do it. She meant to see it posted straightaway.

Just as she reached the bottom of the stairs she saw Robert, dressed to go out, collecting the rest of the outgoing post from its customary spot atop the table in the entry hall. "Robert, are you going to post those?"

"Yes, my lady. Is there something you'd like me to post for you?"

Jane started to hand him the heavy letter she'd composed to Mother. It had taken several sheets of paper to tell all the details she'd held back before concerning Mr. Damont. She'd included everything this time, from their first meeting under the elm to yesterday's bewildering encounter in the second parlor. She'd laid herself naked in her plea for help, but Mother would understand. Mother *must* understand. Jane had no one else to turn to.

Robert reached out to take the letter. After a moment, Jane released it uneasily. Then she scoffed at herself. She was seeing conspiracy everywhere. What could happen between here and the Post Office? Robert certainly wasn't going to read her letter. He was no wicked henchman. Robert was a pleasant, rather nondescript fellow who carried parcels and tea trays and letters to the post.

Nevertheless, Jane watched him leave the house, then moved to the window in the front parlor to watch him march purposefully down the street toward the Post Office. Only when he was finally out of sight around the corner did Jane relax her vigil. The letter was well on its way. Help would soon arrive.

"Codger, eh?" The Prince Regent's eyes flashed at Ethan with amusement. "Most people call me 'Your Highness' or even 'Your Royal Highness.' On occasion, a few people whom I hold in great affection are permitted to address me as 'George.' " He waved Ethan toward a velvet chair and sat himself down before a vast tray of breakfast. "You, my dear Damont, are the only person on earth who has ever called me 'Codger.' "

Ethan stumbled toward his chair, unable to take his eyes off the prince. The last time he'd seen the man he knew only as Collis Tremayne's stout old uncle—whom Ethan had immediately dubbed "the Codger" with his usual irreverence—had been after he'd dug the battered and bruised old fellow out of his iron manacles and released him from the cellar of a munitions factory owned by a traitor.

"Good God," Ethan gasped. "That munitions fellow, the one who beat you up and chained you—"

The prince nodded. "Louis Wadsworth," he said around a mouthful of food. Ethan supposed if one was the leader of the British Empire, one didn't have to bother with table manners. The Prince pointed his fork skyward. "In the tower now."

"Too bloody right," Ethan breathed. "Did he know—"

The prince shook his head. "No more than you did. It was a priceless moment when he figured it out—rather like just now." The Prince smirked at Ethan. "I thought you'd figure it out sooner or later, although to be honest, I rather thought it would be sooner."

Ethan barely noticed the dig. His mind was swirling with the knowledge that he was sitting in the presence of the Prince Regent, watching him eat sausage and toast, and surviving having called him a codger. It all left him rather breathless.

"I think I need to sit down," he said weakly. "Oh, that's right, I am." He took a breath. "Perhaps I need to lie down."

The Prince chuckled. "So, Damont, what brings you here today? If you didn't know that it was me you rescued a few weeks ago, what possessed you to waltz up to my guard like that?"

Something clicked in Ethan's mind. Maywell had known. Somehow, through some channel, Maywell had known what Ethan had not.

As had the Liars. Ethan's gut went cold. Etheridge and Collis and even Rose had known what precious cargo they had carried from that dungeonlike cellar. Known all the while and never told Ethan, though his life was every bit as endangered as theirs.

Not a word, not even yesterday after he'd sweated blood and bullets to pass their bedamned tests—

They still didn't trust him enough to welcome him in truth. He could almost have laughed if it hadn't hurt so badly. So much for brotherly camaraderie. So much for belonging. It turned out Ethan was just a tool after all.

"It was a whim," he told the Prince dully, betrayal writhing like hot lead in his belly. "It was only a whim."

# Chapter Fifteen

When Jane stepped into the carriage with the help of Robert, she took one look at Ethan waiting there for her and turned right around. "I am suddenly feeling a bit ill, Robert—"

Ethan leaned forward to touch her gloved hand where it rested on the doorframe. "Lady Jane, please . . . I would very much like to escort you to your supper this evening."

Jane hung there for a moment, undecided between stepping down and stepping in. Finally, what decided her was the thought that here was perhaps her last opportunity to detach Mr. Damont from her uncle's web of deceit before Mother removed her from the house.

She sat down and eyed him warily, for fresh in her mind was that fascinating, disturbing moment in the second parlor. They would be every bit as alone together now in the carriage, for the footman clung to the back and the driver remained on the fore.

"Light the lantern, if you please, Robert," she ordered. Robert leaned in to fiddle with the small carriage lantern that hung down from the ceiling to light the interior.

"Sorry, my lady, but it's empty of oil. It will take a few moments to fill it."

Jane blew out a breath. "Then never mind. Thank you, Robert." She arranged herself carefully on the seat, head high, gloved hands clasped demurely before her. When Robert had closed the carriage door and they felt the carriage shift as he boarded the boot, Jane could not resist a suspicious glare at Mr. Damont.

"Did you arrange this?" Her gesture indicated everything from his presence as her escort to the empty reservoir of the carriage lantern.

He laughed darkly. "Why, Lady Jane, I must protest! I hate to disappoint you, but I am neither as nefarious nor as clever as you seem to think. Although I shall be sure to remember the bit with the lantern in the future, should I ever wish to accost a lady in a dark carriage—"

Jane moved to knock on the ceiling of the carriage to get the driver's attention. She found her fist cupped in Mr. Damont's palm, his fingers gently caging hers.

"I'm sorry," he said quietly. "I find I'm in a black mood tonight." He released her hand and leaned back. She lost sight of him in the shadows of the carriage. "So, my lady, where are you off to this evening?"

Jane sighed. "I am representing the family at Sir Arnold's musicale this evening. Aunt Lottie and the girls decided not to venture out tonight and it was left to me, since we had already accepted the invitation."

Actually, the girls had been forbidden to attend by their father for some unfathomable reason and had spent the evening drowning each other in tears of protest.

Except the reason suddenly wasn't unfathomable, was it? Mr. Damont's presence as escort explained a great deal. Uncle Harold was throwing them together, hoping to use her to further draw Mr. Damont into his traitorous snare.

"What is your explanation for being here, Mr. Damont?"

He shifted slightly but she still could not see his face. "I believe I have become something in the way of a family retainer to his lordship," he said. "I am not to accompany you inside as a guest so I believe my role is to be something of a guard through the city streets."

"Ah." It sounded plausible enough, but for the fact that no guardian would ever submit his ward to being unchaperoned in a carriage with an attractive young bodyguard. Mr. Damont did not seem quite clear on that point, however, and Jane decided not to enlighten him.

She made a face. "I'm beginning to believe that one's level of impropriety depends solely on if anyone is watching," she murmured to herself.

"You're becoming as cynical as I am," Mr. Damont said.

"Impossible," Jane shot back. Then she sighed. "Still, I do wish we had not such a plethora of rules governing us. I trust you, but this arrangement—"

"You trust me?"

She gazed at him for a long moment, a small smile playing on her lips. "I find you entirely trustworthy, Mr. Ethan Damont. Does that truly surprise you?"

It did surprise him. It shook him to his very soul. "But—but why? You know who I am . . . you know very nearly everything about me!"

She crossed her arms. "What would your point be?"

"No one trusts me! Not after the first quarter of an hour, anyway!" He ran a hand through his hair. "Nor should they—and nor should you!"

Jane gazed at him, true perplexity on her face. "Ethan, what are you talking about?"

"I'm talking about my being a cad, that's what I'm talking about!"

"You? A cad?" She laughed in disbelief. "Where did you get such a notion?"

Only from everyone he'd ever encountered in his life— apparently, with the exception of Lady Jane Pennington.

Disturbed, he turned to look out at the passing night. He did not deserve her trust—did not even want it! After the way he'd practically assaulted her yesterday, how could she claim to have such faith in him?

The silence stretched between them as the carriage moved slowly on, making Jane feel every shift and jostling of her thighs. She forced her awakening body to desist and turned her attention outside.

There was a great deal of traffic out tonight. She could have walked to Sir Arnold's in half the time of course, but ladies did not walk the city at night, not even in the rarefied area of Mayfair.

She felt restless with the physical tension between them. Did he feel it too? He seemed not to, for he sat motionless and silent in the shadows opposite her. She, on the other hand, could not seem to keep still. She found herself leaning forward to peer through the small square window every few seconds and her fan was going to be in shreds long before they reached their destination.

"You look very nice tonight, Janet." His voice came low and velvety across the darkness to her like a touch.

Yet how could he see—

Jane looked down at herself to realize that her constant leaning forward had pressed her breasts high into the neckline of her gown until they nearly spilled out. The square of light from the passing of other carriage lanterns threw her bosom into high relief framed by the black outline of the window.

She quickly pressed herself back against the seat, out of the light, but it was too late. Those few words, in that softly suggestive voice, had set her pulse to pounding. She could feel his eyes on her. She knew he was admiring her breasts, probably thinking about how he'd held one in his hand—

She closed her eyes against that memory, but she could not shut it down the way she had over the past day. Now, here, with him, the heat came flooding back, washing over her, melting her deep down inside until her thighs relaxed involuntarily in response to the pressure within.

"Ethan . . ."

Hearing his name murmured in Jane's husky voice sent bolts of arousal ricocheting through Ethan. She'd never called him that before.

"Say it again," he urged, his voice low and hard with heat.

"Ethan," she said obediently, coating his name with a sensual obedience that promised much, if he dared to take it.

If he dared . . .

If he dared to make her hate him. After all, she was a lady, gently born and sheltered. It shouldn't be too hard to offend her so deeply that she'd never claim that ridiculous level of trust again. He was a cad, by God, and he was quite prepared to prove it.

"Lean forward, Jane," he ordered in that same heated murmur. "Lean forward and let me see you."

She did, slowly, so that the light crept over her bodice and dipped gently between her breasts, turning that perfect skin to milk in the lamplight.

Ethan leaned forward as well, and watched distantly as his own hand reached to trail one finger along the lace edge of her bodice. He halted just before making contact with her skin, then drew back. She swayed forward as if to follow his touch.

"Milk and satin and strawberries, Janet," he murmured.

He could hear her deep longing breaths. He had power over her at this moment. In her innocence and trust, she had handed him the keys to make her wish she'd never laid eyes on Ethan Damont.

"Touch your skin, Janet," he coaxed. "Let your fingers be like the light that travels over it."

Slowly, hesitantly, she raised her hand to her neck. Ethan wished he could see her face, but she was half in shadow. He was forced to imagine the way her closed lashes lay on her pale cheeks, or how the pink tip of her tongue might come out to moisten her parted, panting lips.

His arousal surged at that but he made no move to touch her. "That's right, stroke that place just there, below your ear. I want to kiss you there. I want to move behind you and lift your hair to press my lips just there."

He watched her fingers trail slowly over her own skin, imagining his own there, or his mouth. "Let your hand trail down now." His own breath was coming fast now. "Touch the soft valley between for me, Janet."

Jane followed his every direction slowly but willingly, entranced by his low voice and by the fact that she knew he watched every motion. It was a wicked, tantalizing game that fell just within the bounds of decency. Not truly wicked, really, at least not yet. And she was so warm inside, so liquid smooth and dreamy, as if she were asleep in her bed and this was all some blameless midnight imagining . . .

"The lace is covering too much, darling. I cannot see. Tug the lace down, just a bit . . ."

Jane inhaled deeply as she obeyed, knowing that her breasts would swell to the limits of the bodice. She wanted to tantalize him, wanted him to see, wanted him to watch.

She heard his breath catch and felt power surge through her. She was the one he wanted, the one he watched, the one making him take broken breaths.

"More," he begged, and she obeyed. She pulled the lacy edge of the bodice down to her nipples, going weak at the feeling of the cool evening air on her sheltered skin.

"Yesss," he hissed urgently. "Show me, Janet. I want to see."

Almost without thought, she tugged ever so slightly more and allowed her hardened nipples to spring free of the bodice.

"You're so beautiful, Janet. So fine and lovely, like a goddess in a garden. I love to look at you."

Jane dropped her head back, letting him look his fill. She could hardly bear the need that pulsed within her but she could not break the erotic spell he cast. She wanted him to tell her what to do, how to tantalize him. If he told her, if she was only obeying his mesmerizing voice, if he stayed there in the darkness—then it was only a dream, only a wicked, luscious dream of what might be.

"I can't touch you, Janet. I want to, but I can't. You must touch yourself for me, darling. You must put your hands on yourself once more, just for me."

Jane felt her own chilled fingers move to rest over her own heaving breasts. The sensation made her shiver.

"Does that feel good?" His voice was so urgent, so full of dark command, yet so gentle she could not resist him. She could only make a tiny obedient sound of agreement, a small animal cry that seemed distant and alien to her own ears.

"Touch your nipples, my love. Take them between your thumb and forefinger, yes, just like that. Can you feel how rigid they've become? That means that you like this. Do you like this, Janet? Do you want more?"

She could only breathe an aching sound.

"I'll take that as a yes, Janet. I'll take that as a sign that you want to roll your nipples between your fingers gently for me. Are they hardening still more? Can you feel the way the sensation goes directly through you, to that warm, soft place between your thighs?"

She could feel that very thing, and she was grateful to him for putting words to the sensation for she'd forgotten how to speak, how to think, how to do anything but obey that wicked deep voice that seemed directly connected to her will.

"Free your breasts completely, Janet. Pull your pretty little cap sleeves down to your elbows and set your breasts free. I want to see them sway with the motion of the carriage."

She did it gladly, for it was difficult enough to breathe without the confines of her gown. The sleeves captured her upper arms tightly to her torso, lending a further help-less element to her dream state. She was bound, captive, she was not responsible . . .

"Hold them high, darling. Cup them in your hands and

hold them, feel how heavy and warm they are. I love your breasts, Janet. Hold them for me."

She did so, offering them up for him. Would he never touch her? Would she never feel his hot hands on her chilled skin—would he never ease this throbbing ache within her? She squirmed on the seat, unable to bear the mounting pressure of her own excitement.

"Do you want more? Let me help you."

*Yes, oh, please yes . . .*

She waited to feel his hands on her. Instead she felt her skirts rustling and then the cool evening air was on her thighs above her garters. She drowsily opened her eyes to find the hem of her gown piled high in her lap and Mr. Damont back on his side of the carriage, veiled in darkness as before.

"Let your breasts down now, my lovely one. Let them move with the motion of the carriage while the cool air makes your skin crinkle up, just for me."

Jane let her hands fall to rest in her lap. Her elbows were still trapped by her drawn sleeves and she could feel the velvet of the seat against her bare back, brushing softly with every jolt of the carriage.

"Let your knees drop open just a little for me, Janet. Melt for me, darling . . ."

Her thighs opened and she was thankful, for it eased the throbbing just a little.

"Run your fingers along the tops of your stockings, pet. Show me how high they ride above your knees . . ."

Jane let her fingers trace the small scalloped edge of the stocking tops from the top down around the outside of her thighs.

"Now the other way, darling."

Her fingers trailed obediently between her thighs. When her wrists made glancing contact with her center she flinched at the jolt of pleasure that went through her.

"Slide your fingers higher, darling. I wish I could stroke your silken thighs, but I cannot. I can only watch while your hands do what I cannot. Where would you like my touch, sweeting? Would you like to move higher?"

Jane spread her hands flat over the insides of her thighs, wishing they were his large hot hands instead. He had a delicate touch for such a big man. If he were stroking her thighs, he would move slowly higher, moving his fingertips in small circular motions, just like that.

"Higher, darling . . . higher. Do you ache for me? Show me where—show me where you want me to touch you . . ."

Gasping with need, Jane pressed her crossed hands against the very center of herself. A delightful surge of pleasure coursed through her at even her own touch.

"Your pantalets are lovely, Janet. I like the old-fashioned ones that hang separately from the waist. I like the way they part just so . . ."

She could hear how breathless he was, how strained his gently commanding voice had become. He ached as much as she did. The thought fired her arousal higher.

"Part them for me, Janet," he whispered, his voice gone quite hoarse. "Part the cotton with your fingers—"

The carriage jolted to a stop in the traffic. The bump joggled Jane's fingertips past the parting of the pantalets, dipping her touch deeper—

She gasped in surprise and almost withdrew her hands, almost awoke from the spell . . . until Ethan's voice pulled her back.

"Shh. Don't fret, darling. I want to touch you there. I want to feel your flesh turn damp on my fingers." His tone was no more than a hoarse whisper now, a dark, desperate voice putting words to her most base fantasies. "I wish I could slip into you, past your velvet mound, past your soft gates, to that secret place . . . do you know that place, Janet? Can you find it for me?"

She did know, for she'd found it before, in the dark, guilty privacy of night. Yet this was different, better, *more*. Ethan was with her, watching her, sending her

body far beyond her own previous fumblings with pleasure. The knowledge that he watched her, aching for her
until he could barely speak, owning her with his erotic
commands—this captive performance for him was something she could never have conceived of alone.

"Touch yourself there, darling. There, where it has begun to swell and harden, just like your sweet strawberry
nipples—stroke yourself for me. Let me see you come
apart for me . . ."

She did it, everything he asked of her and more. She
abandoned herself to the pleasure of her own hand, barely
aware of the way her head rolled on the cushion back,
scarcely conscious of the small, hungry cries coming
from her own panting lips.

"Faster, Janet. Fly for me."

She could feel herself nearing the edge, so close, so
desperately, achingly close—

"Now, Janet!" His voice was a searing, feverish growl.

As if she'd only been waiting for his command, she
felt herself flung from that precipice, flying quivering off
into a starry sky, falling, crying, sobbing . . . to drift
slowly to rest, her heart pounding, her mouth dry, her
thighs still twitching as the last tiny shocks ran through
her body.

She took a gasping breath, then another, as if only just
now remembering how to breathe . . . remembering her
name, remembering herself . . .

Remembering that she rode in a carriage traveling the
streets of London with Mr. Ethan Damont sitting across
from her, watching her every move.

# Chapter Sixteen

Ethan, sitting in a state of torturous arousal across from her, could see the moment that Jane came back to being Jane. She inhaled sharply, released a panicked, humiliated whimper, and began to desperately wrestle her gown back over her exposed body.

Ethan watched shamelessly as her crushed skirts were pushed down over her limbs. He did not even pretend to avert his eyes as she struggled to pull her bodice up over her bare breasts. No, he deserved every moment of such agony. He wasn't going to spare himself a moment of it.

Besides, he was quite sure he'd never see Jane again after tonight, much less be privileged to gaze upon her full, pale breasts or soft, milky-white thighs . . .

Had a man ever died from unfulfilled arousal? He deserved to die, he thought distantly as the pounding in his swollen groin refused to abate. Jane hated him quite thoroughly now, he had no doubt. He'd accomplished his mission. She would now be sure to keep her blue blood far from his bad blood, no matter if he begged her for forgiveness on his knees—not that he would ever have the heart to try to reach out to her again.

The carriage pulled to a stop. Blearily, Ethan realized they had reached their destination. Had it truly been only a half hour since they'd left Maywell House? Three quarters of an hour at the most, he realized. He felt as though he'd lived a lifetime in this carriage with Jane—the lifetime he'd never be able to have with her, perhaps. Was that hell? An eternity of not having what you most wanted in life?

Light from the house warmed the interior of the carriage. Across from him, Jane had repaired herself better than Ethan would have believed, considering her riotous abandon only a few short minutes ago. Aside from a few loose strands of hair and somewhat crumpled skirts, she looked much the same as when she'd entered the carriage that long lifetime ago.

Robert had scarcely touched the door before Jane bounded from the carriage and into the waiting doorway of Sir Arthur's house. After handing her over to the butler waiting there, Robert came back to the still-open carriage. "Will you be going in, sir?"

"No." Ethan didn't elaborate. Jane would be inside for hours . . . hours that he needed to himself at this moment.

Robert only blinked, then went to the front of the horses to lead them back around to where the others waited for the guests inside. Robert and the driver would join the Boswells' servants for a bite and a pint of beer, if the hostess was a kindly one.

Left sitting in the dark, Ethan finally allowed himself a single, dragging, pained inhalation. Jane had defeated him as well, if she only knew it.

He'd always known there was no chance for him to have what Collis had, or what Etheridge had. He wasn't that sort of man—the sort that women came back to, at least for more than momentary satisfaction. None had ever loved him. Why would they?

He was no more than his father had always said— weak, selfish, immoral. He'd done his best to live down to that every day of his life, until he found that it was nothing but the absolute truth.

Then along came someone . . . someone like Lady

Jane Pennington . . . who made him dream of having more, of being more—

Which was no good for either of them. Sooner or later, he would fail her. He was quite sure that, sooner or later, she was going to want more than he had to give. She would come up empty, as had anyone who had ever depended on him.

So he'd tried to protect her from that tonight. He'd meant to break her, to shock her, to push past her limits and offend her so deeply that she would run from him forever.

Yet Ethan found himself a broken man as well. God, she'd been so trusting, so lovely, so openly, wildly responsive . . .

Nothing in his wicked and varied past could have possibly prepared him for the privilege and transcendent honor of guiding Lady Jane Pennington on her first voyage of sexual discovery. Nothing he ever experienced in the future could possibly compare.

He was a ruined man.

Ruined for any woman but the single one who could never possibly feel for him again.

"What have I done?"

Lady Boswell rushed out to greet Jane as she mounted the front steps and entered the front hall. The musicale was already in progress, to judge from the screeching soprano currently sharing her talents.

"I'm sorry to be so late," Jane blurted. "The traffic—"

"Jane, dear! Are you unwell?" Lady Boswell blinked at her worriedly. "You look so feverish!"

Jane turned to catch a glimpse of herself in the entry hall mirror. Good heavens, no wonder her hostess was so alarmed. Jane scarcely recognized the pale reflection with the bright feverish spots burning in both cheeks. "The carriage jostled so." She pressed her hands to her face. "I—"

*I don't want to be here, I don't want to be in London, I*

*don't want to be alone anymore. I want to go home. I want
to see my mother and I will never, ever see her again.* The
tears began to well up inside and Jane was afraid that if
she began to weep, she would never stop. She would turn
London into Venice with her tears.

That thought brought a bark of wild laughter to her
lips. Lady Boswell looked at her as if she truly were mad.
At this moment in time, Jane could not swear that she
was not.

"I think I—I must return home," she managed to say.

Lady Boswell nodded emphatically. "Yes, dear. I think
you should. I'll have your uncle's man bring the carriage
around again . . ." The woman nearly ran from Jane.

Jane almost laughed again. *Her uncle's man.* Owned
by her uncle, bought and paid for with Jane herself, willing chattel that she was!

*Her uncle's man.* Such a vast understatement of the
facts all but made Jane sit right down on the marble front
steps and screech with furious, agonized laughter. She bit
it back, digging her teeth into her bottom lip until it was
sure to bleed. She didn't care, she only wanted not to become more of a spectacle than she already was. Several
people had come into the front hall and were watching
her weave her way back outside. Tomorrow, the town
would be abuzz with the incident of Lady Jane Pennington and her carriage sickness.

She nearly began giggling again. If they only knew!

Only the thought of remaining on display for one more
dangerous moment could compel her to get back into that
carriage with Ethan Damont. At least with him, she need
not hide her confusion or her pain. At least with him, she
could freely vent her wrath—

*And why is that?*

Oh, dear God. It could not be that she trusted him
*still*? How could that be, after the way he'd humiliated
her—after what he had done to her?

Worse, after what he'd commanded her to do to herself?

And she had done it. Horror swept her as she recalled her own simplicity. She'd mindlessly, willingly obeyed every word from his lips, every erotic command, every delicious, wicked, pleasurable—

As the carriage crunched its way back around the front of the house to roll before her, Jane came to the startling realization—nay, the stunning, shocking *certainty*—that if he asked, she would do it all again.

Ethan could not believe it when the carriage door opened and Lady Jane clambered right back in only moments after getting out.

"What are you—I thought the carriage was being moved—"

"It is," Jane said flatly. "It is being moved back to Maywell House."

Ethan nearly panicked. He hadn't counted on having to face her again so soon. His groin was still on fire for her, his thoughts had barely worked their way through the first loss of her. He was depending on those hours to get his thoughts in order, to decide what to say, to shield himself against her pain—

Why didn't she seem to be in pain? She ought to be writhing with humiliation, speechless with agonized shame . . .

He knew he certainly was.

Jane, however, sat ramrod straight on her seat across from him. Her chin was high, her eyes dry, her glittering gaze fixed on his.

*Trouble.* That was the only bit of sense that made it through Ethan's confusion. When a woman looked at a man like that?

That meant trouble.

"Mr. Damont—"

A surprised laugh burst from him. "Please," he said helplessly. "Call me Ethan."

She frowned. "Mr. Damont," she said firmly. "There is something we must discuss."

Although he was quite sure of her meaning, he pretended nonchalance. "I can't imagine what that would be." Damn, he was tired of pretending.

"We must discuss your association with my uncle, Lord Maywell."

"Well, I have to admit, I didn't expect that." Shaking his head, he eyed her with surprise. "I thought you were going to berate me for . . ." He made a vague gesture around the inside of the carriage.

Lady Jane brushed that topic briskly aside. "That is not important, sir."

Not important? The sheer hopeless bloody *importance* of it had been enough to nearly bring him to tears a few moments ago. Ethan tapped two fingers over his lips. "I cannot seem to predict anything anymore," he mused aloud.

"No. What is much more pressing is the fact that my uncle is trying to suborn you, Mr. Damont. He is a traitor to the Crown." She sat back, all virtuous dignity and dogged righteousness. She was rescuing *him*. It was damned sweet, that's what it was.

He nearly opened up to her right then and there. He almost told her everything from the moment Rose Lacey knocked on his door to this afternoon at Carlton House. He *longed* to tell her, actually.

*What if this were a test?* The black insidious thought, once arrived, would not leave. What if this virtuous fervor, the last hour's erotic bravery, the parlor, the milliner's shop, even the goddamned tree—

No. No, it couldn't be all some complicated net of her uncle's weaving. It wasn't possible!

Except that it was. After all, here she was, alone with him in this carriage, coming back for more again and again, no matter that his behavior would send any proper virginal young lady screaming from him.

These suspicions made him feel a bit sick. Was Jane

part of Maywell's plan? Was she even a willing convert, sacrificing herself for the cause, submitting to his advances out of some twisted duty—

It was too much. There were too many strange factors, too many warped players. He could not keep them straight anymore. Etheridge and his Liars? Collis and his lies? Rose? Maywell? *George?*

And Lady Jane Pennington standing at the front of it all, a freckled, strawberry-blond whirlwind of sensuality and temptation, tailor-made to pierce right through a cynical gambler's hard-won defenses . . .

She was simply too good to be true. Therefore, she must not be.

So Ethan leaned back, crossed his arms over his chest, and played along. If this was a test, then by God, he would pass it.

"You're too late, my lady. I have already decided to join your uncle wholeheartedly."

"No!" She leaned forward, all her cool determination gone. "You cannot mean that, Ethan! You don't understand! He's on the side of the French, of *Napoleon!*"

Ethan nodded easily. "Yes, my lady. I know. I think it a most worthy endeavor."

*"No."* She leaned into him, putting her hand urgently on his knee. "I will not permit you to do this! You are too good, too honorable—"

He interrupted her with a harsh laugh. "You can say that, after what happened tonight?"

"Ethan, listen to me. Uncle Harold cannot—must not—succeed! You—you could help me stop him!"

Help her stop Maywell? What an absurd suggestion for a Society debutante to make. Now he was sure she was a plant. "I don't see what you are so upset about, Lady Jane. I'm sure your uncle has provided you with an appropriate future in Josephine's court." Now he was simply taking cynical pleasure in baiting her—but a bloke needed to take his pleasure where he could.

She sat back, her face the very picture of disappointed confusion. "I know you don't really want to do this," she said, her voice husky with frustration. "I *know* this. I must make you see . . ."

Abruptly, Ethan wearied of the entire farce. "Jane, you cannot stop this—"

In one swift movement, Jane reached for him, catching his lips with hers. Ethan gasped slightly, his lips parting as he began to pull back. She grabbed both his ears and deepened the kiss, her tongue plunging with sweet awkwardness into his mouth. His hands gripped her head, fingers plunged into her hair—when had he reached for her?—and he kissed her back with all the need that threatened to drown his soul. Her arms wrapped about his neck as if she would never let him go. *Thank God.*

He pulled her down to lie across his lap. Holding her—oh, dear God, how had he ever lived without it! Caressing her—life was warm and welcoming again. She was cool silk beneath his hot hands, submitting sweetly to his touch. Then she ripped his cravat from him and flung it across the carriage. Things went a bit mad after that.

She squirmed on him until she faced him directly, without ever taking her mouth from his. She rode his lap as he pushed her skirts high, baring her thighs to his touch. He ran his hands up her soft skin to slip behind her, holding and caressing her bottom as she ground herself clumsily onto his groin. Her hands roved over him, fumbling with the buttons of his weskit, tearing his shirt from his trousers, tugging ineptly at his trouser buttons—

Then he was poised at the center of her, like a barbarian at her welcoming gates. She went soft and giving, hovering over him as her moistness warmed him and her curls feathered across the top of his aching erection.

The thought crossed his fogged mind that he was a bounder, taking an inexperienced virgin in a carriage this way. Although it could be argued that she was taking him. He let her drop a tiny bit, until her hot opening kissed the tip of his cock and she writhed in excited protest in his grasp. His mind went quite blank with lust and need at that point. There was nothing in his thoughts but the first thrust, the way she would wrap tightly about him, the pounding race to completion—

*And then what?*

*What will become of her?*

*What of you? What will you become?*

He tried to shake off the voice. He would be no worse than he was now, than he had always been. He wasn't noble, for Christ's sake. He wasn't honorable, or good, or even very nice.

Which didn't explain why he thrust her from him to land in a tumble of lacy petticoats on the seat across from him. With one fist he pounded the ceiling of the coach. "More speed, man!" he shouted. His voice was thick and harsh with unfulfilled desire. Across the short, eternal distance, Jane batted her skirts down from over her face to glare at him.

"Why did you stop?" Her voice was a mere breathless gasp.

"Repair yourself," he growled.

She tried to wriggle into an indignant pose while tugging her bodice back to decency. It didn't work at all. She ended up slipping to the floor, twisted in her gown, frustration wrinkling her brow. He bent to pick her up and set her on her feet. His heart pounded at the heady scent of her readied body and the gleam of humiliated tears in her eyes. God help him, she was so damn sweet.

Too good for him by half.

He set her to rights with experienced hands, even pinning her mantle back over her shoulders, and plunked her into the opposite seat, as far from him as the carriage would allow. Not that it would matter. The distance between them was so great that he could never cross it, not truly. Making love to her would only ensure that she would be cast from her own future.

"I am too . . . disadvantageous for you," he said, forcing his voice to easy conversation level. His casual tone surprised her, he could see. The carriage was nearly at their destination. He must make it good and permanent this time. "I am too everything for you, Lady Jane Pennington," he continued, infusing his voice with a jaded drawl. "Too experienced, too world-weary, far, far too decadent in my tastes. You are delightful in your way, there is no doubt. Anything fresh and young is enjoyable, for a short while. But now your continued importuning is only embarrassing us both. My loyalty is quite unswerving, I assure you." That might even be true, if he could ever pinpoint just where that loyalty lay.

She was staring at him, her eyes wide in the uneven gleam from the swaying lanterns hung outside the carriage. It twisted within him that he had hurt her, that he *must* continue to hurt her and drive her away.

They arrived at their destination at that moment. Ethan was grateful, for the clatter and upset involving disembarking would surely drown out the way his body still hummed with wanting her. She looked away from him at last, her gaze going out the window to see that the carriage once more stood before her uncle's home.

Her front door was open, casting a golden pathway down the marble steps for her. A manservant came to open the carriage door for her with a bow. There was little she could do to argue with him now, he'd ensured that. Her head bowed with apparent resignation, Jane pulled the hood of her mantle up to cover her hair and wrapped it tightly around her to hide her disarray. Then she stood to give one hand to the man waiting for her.

Ethan let go a soundless sigh of relief. She was going, taking away her tempting self and taking with her all the painful dreams of an impossible future that she inspired.

Then one small hand reached back to take his in an iron grip and he looked up into her hooded face. Her eyes gleamed over a small predatory smile. "Don't underestimate me, Ethan Damont," she whispered fiercely.

Then she was gone in a flutter of dark blue wool. The golden doorway closed on him, the carriage began to move—and Ethan sat there, cradling the feel of her warm, determined handclasp tightly in his fist.

# Chapter Seventeen

The man sat before the fire again. This time he leaned forward with his elbows on his knees, gazing into the coals as if seeking an answer there.

The gambler was becoming unpredictable. Could the fellow maintain his focus long enough to finish the task at hand, or would it be better to sacrifice that particular chessman and begin again?

It would be difficult to find another operative with the gambler's particular mix of skills and social level. Difficult, but not impossible.

Yet a great deal of time and effort had gone into the present game. All of that would go to waste if the gambler had to be dealt with before the strategy came to fruition.

The man closed his eyes for a moment to rest them from the dull glare of the coals. He'd been so sure the gambler would succeed—and the fellow might yet do so.

Many things teetered in the balance—a great load for one morally fragile man to bear. The danger could be eliminated in a single move.

It seemed a final test was in order. A test that would tell, once and for all, the steadfastness of the gambler.

And if he failed . . .

Well, that was the nature of the business. The fates of

nations overruled the destinies of mere mortal men. The game was worth more than the sum of its pieces.

Fortunately, the gambler would never see it coming.

Ethan hadn't made it out of the circular drive before the carriage was stopped. The door opened and Lord Maywell himself stuck his bushy white head inside, ruddy and out of breath.

"Damont, there is a problem."

When the housemaid came to tell her that her uncle wished to see her in his study, a flutter went through Jane's stomach. She'd thought she had managed to cover her disheveled state when she had come in.

After pleading sudden illness, she had escaped to her room and had already changed from her evening gown to an older, soft muslin. She felt as though she were a completely different person than the girl who had left the house those few hours ago. Such heat. She never knew she bore such fire within her. It confused and delighted her at once. Her thoughts were still too jumbled and chaotic to sort through. She had hoped she could avoid seeing any of the family for a while, especially her uncle.

The ruthless gleam that sometimes came into her uncle's eyes shimmered before her as she descended the stair. The unease did not dissipate at the sight of her aunt and cousins lining the hall to her uncle's office.

Her aunt did not meet her eyes as she walked slowly by her. Serena was the only one who could not look away. Jane's youngest cousin glared at her with hot betrayal in her tear-reddened eyes.

They are angry with me, she realized. How could they know—

Had Mr. Damont told all? Her stomach churned. Even after everything, she would not have thought it of him.

For some reason, Serena's fury upset Jane more than the thought of her uncle's reaction. She'd never had sisters, never had girls close to her own age to grow up with, and now she never would.

Then the study door was before her. A whisper of silk sounded behind her. She looked over her shoulder. Her aunt and cousins were gone.

The study was not well lit. Only a single candle on the mantel lit Lord Maywell's face as he stared into the glowing coals. "Not well done of you, Jane girl," he said, his voice a growl. "Not well done at all."

"Uncle, I—"

"Silence!" He turned to her, his features a half-mask of light and shadow. "You've said quite enough."

Then Jane saw with horror that Uncle Harold held in his hand the long, detailed letter she had posted to Mother this morning.

Oh, God help me. Jane bit her lips. She would plead nerves, she decided. She'd been overwrought by—by homesickness. Or she'd had a nightmare and been carried away by her fears—

All entirely silly reasons. She only hoped her uncle still thought her merely a silly girl. Then she saw it—that icy edge of heartlessness that only she seemed to notice—and her belly turned to stone.

She was going to die.

"Silly girl," her uncle said easily. "Silly, overwrought, thoughtless girl. To weave such a fiction about your own dear family. Why, you must be as mad as your mother, mustn't you?"

His words confused Jane for a moment. She'd thought she was about to be gutted like a fish. She'd thought he would want to destroy anyone who discovered his treasonous activities.

Then his meaning sank in and Jane realized what he meant to do.

"No," she breathed, her voice choked by bone-deep fear.

"Oh, yes." Lord Maywell took a seat behind his desk. With a flourish, he took a pen from the inkstand and dipped it into one of the wells. "A stroke of the pen by your oldest male relative will have you safely tucked away in Bedlam by morning—at least when accompanied by a sizable bribe."

Bedlam—the madhouse. Jane could not breathe. Mother had never received the last letter. As far as Mother was concerned, Jane would simply have disappeared. Mother would never look for her in Bedlam.

Uncle Harold shook his head sadly. "A bribe that I shall have to pay for from your very own accounts, of course. 'Tis only to be expected that I should pay for your care from your inheritance. Money and madness—those are your legacies, my dear." He signed the paper, each scratch of the pen abrading Jane's nerves further.

Then he leaned back and wove his blunt fingers together over his girth. "We took you and treated you as one of our own daughters," he said piously, although the dark flicker she saw in his eyes might have been guilt. "I only hope I've acted quickly enough to prevent your infected mind from contaminating my own dear girls."

Jane slid one foot sideways. She wasn't too far from the door and she was fairly sure she could make it out of the room before her uncle could manage his bulk around the desk. If she could beg shelter from a boardinghouse long enough to send word to—

"If you run," Uncle Harold said sadly. "If you run and scream and carry on, it will only strengthen my case that you have become deranged."

He was right. She didn't care. She turned and dashed to the door. Her hand was on the knob when heavy footsteps behind her ended with her being snatched back from freedom with both arms wrenched behind her.

Two of her uncle's burly footmen held her pinned between them. She hadn't seen them, so closely had she concentrated on her uncle's eerie performance. She fought them, as hopeless as it was. All she needed was for one hand to slip, for one second of a lessened grip—

They stood stolid and silent, letting her fight herself to exhaustion like a badly tamed horse. Finally, she sank to her knees, sickened by her own weakness, terrified beyond her own control.

She was not going to die. She was only going to wish she was dead.

Lord Maywell stood from behind his desk, where he'd watched her struggles with regretful eyes. She wanted to scream at his hypocrisy. The packet of commitment papers was neatly sealed with a large waxen *M*. "All settled now, my dear?" His tone was everything kindly. His false affection made her want to vomit.

She wondered wearily if doing so would in any way deter her guards. Looking up at the crude, grim features of the footmen, she rather doubted it.

Lord Maywell opened the door and woefully waved them through it. "I've a man outside who will take her to Moorfields," he told the men. He handed them the commitment papers. "Give him this and tell him to consider himself permanently engaged."

Jane could scarcely keep her feet beneath her as the two men hurried her out of the house and into the darkening dusk where the same unmarked, unlit, closed carriage awaited. She considered letting them drag her, but as it was she felt as though her arms were nearly wrenched from their sockets.

She needed to stay fit and watchful. From what her uncle had said, only one man would accompany her to the asylum. Her chances were better against one, better yet if they left her unbound. Her only goal now was to appear as weak and unthreatening as possible.

The footmen tossed her carelessly into the waiting carriage, sending her tumbling onto her seat like a sack of potatoes. No sooner had Jane fought off her own tumbled skirts and fallen hair than she was sent sideways again by the horses' sudden departure.

Hands grasped her in the darkness, pulling her against a hard male form. Jane cried out and struggled anew, despite her vow to appear helpless.

"Shh, Janet. Be still."

Joy leapt through her at the sound of Ethan's voice. "I am saved! Oh, Ethan, you clever darling!" She turned in his arms to plant ill-aimed kisses on his face, laughing damply with relief through tears of fear.

He hesitated, then he pushed her gently back to her seat. "I can't imagine what makes you say that," he said slowly.

In the confining darkness of the carriage, Jane felt a thrill of renewed fear. No, it couldn't be—not Ethan too? Her heart aching, Jane pressed herself back against the velvet cushions, her eyes straining to see him in the dimness.

"You are not saving me?"

He shifted. "Not at the moment . . . no."

"But his lordship means to put me in the asylum!"

He cleared his throat. "It is not my place to interfere in a family matter. I'm sure your uncle—well, I'm sure he knows what he's doing."

"But I'm not mad!" she cried.

In an instant, his palm covered her mouth, unerring in the darkness. "You'll not convince anyone by screeching like a fishwife."

Jane closed her eyes against the fear that surged within her. Ethan would never do this if he knew. All she needed to do was tell him the truth—but he would not listen to a madwoman. He was quite correct. No one would.

So she drew a deep breath through her nose, and then another.

"That's good," Ethan said soothingly. "It will all go better if you stay calm."

The cool sympathy in his voice cut through her. Ethan never talked to her that way. He provoked her, he teased her, he even frankly insulted her—but he never spoke to her like a simpleton.

The cruel injustice was too much for her for a moment. A single hot tear fled from beneath her lids and trailed down her cheek to his hand. He snatched his hand away as if she'd scalded him.

Jane opened her eyes, blinking back the other tears that threatened. She could not spare the time to cry. If things did not go well, she could look forward to many long days of incarceration in which to indulge in tears. If things did go well, she'd have no reason to cry.

Please, God, let things go well!

Across from Jane, Ethan pressed his own back into the cushions, pushing himself as far from Jane and her tears as he could. He could not give in to his compassion for her. There was more at stake here than one rather odd young woman.

Unthinking, he rubbed his hand where that single tear had burned him. Jane was a sensible sort—usually. The thought of her crying made him feel terrible for what he was about to do.

"I don't want to go." Her whisper floated across the space—the infinite and insurmountable chasm—between them.

Ethan shut down the ache caused by the quiet fear in her voice. "No one imagines you do. Yet I do believe it is for the best."

Jane's heart sank as she finally saw the resolve behind his light tone. Ethan wasn't just doing as her uncle told him—he was acting from his own conviction. There was no persuading a man when he'd taken that stand.

"God save me from a man who believes he is 'doing the right thing,'" she said, weary desperate laughter seeping into her voice. "You win, Ethan. I'll go to Bedlam without a fight."

"I'll hold you to your word," he replied cautiously. She seemed resigned, however, for she merely leaned her forehead against the window frame and gazed blindly into the night.

At least she was not weeping. Silence settled into the carriage, making the sounds of the clopping hooves and squeaking chassis all the louder. Ethan fingered the papers in his pocket. Now didn't seem to be the time to tell her that the entire matter had been his idea.

Bethlehem Hospital was a hospital, after all. A nice, safe place for Jane to wait out of danger while Ethan finished his mission. It was a good plan, and much preferable to Lord Maywell's half-formed ideas of murder.

Lord Maywell was doomed, he had no doubt of that. All Ethan needed was a bit more time to worm his way further into the man's trust. When all was done and the dust cleared, there would be plenty of time to retrieve Jane.

Jane's outrageous accusations—all right, they were only too true, but bloody ill-timed!—could have botched the entire matter. Ethan's own intervention with the Bedlam idea was the reason why Jane wasn't dead or dying at this moment. Maywell would not stop at murder, Ethan would wager his house on that.

No. He firmed his intentions with the conviction that Bedlam was a hospital. A safe place, out of Maywell's hands and out of danger.

Jane would keep just fine there.

Bethlehem Hospital for the Mentally Disturbed was the thing of myth in the city of London. There had been a "Bedlam" of one sort or another for hundreds of years, from the days when insanity was considered part and portion of holiness.

Different locations, progressively larger and more modern buildings, yet all still operated upon the methods of the cautionary tale of old. "Be thou sound and be thou chaste, or thou shalt end thy days in Bedlam."

Jane knew what manner of place Bedlam was, even if Ethan did not. She knew that, as in days of old, the insane were considered living words of warning and, as such, were put on public display.

And perhaps, for a few, the mad provided some semblance of warning. Perhaps a few sensitive souls left Bedlam and saw their lives in a new light—lives that could be changed and improved for the betterment of all.

Jane knew all about madhouses. Her own mother had nearly died in one, after all.

Dark memories and choking fear wrapped tightly about her throat, making it cruelly difficult to breathe.

When the carriage drew near to the hospital, Ethan turned to Jane for one last attempt to draw her out of her misery.

When the carriage pulled up to the front gates of the asylum, Ethan immediately began to have second thoughts. The place was grim in the darkness with its entrance lighted only by a few sputtering lamps.

"Oh, look," Jane said faintly, incipient hysteria in her voice. "I'm home."

Ethan rubbed his hand across the back of his neck to still an uneasy chill. Well, likely any place would look unimpressive in the dark like this. They probably didn't get too many new patients in the middle of the night.

The gatekeeper didn't seem very surprised to see them, however. "State yer business," he said, without much seeming to care what that business was.

Ethan leaned out the window. "Lady Jane Pennington is being brought for treatment."

The gatekeeper blinked. "Treatment, is it? That's a new one." He shook his head. "Well, then, you'd best go on in."

The gate creaked open with ominous groans and the carriage rattled on through. As they approached the entrance, Ethan eyed the building worriedly. The more he saw, the less he liked it.

A uniformed couple came to stand on the front steps to greet them as the carriage rolled to a stop. Ethan stepped out first, then handed Jane down gently. The driver moved the carriage forward out of the way.

"Is that the patient?" The woman attendant stepped up.

By way of explanation, Ethan handed the nurse the packet of papers that Lord Maywell had given him. The doorway stood open, letting a reassuring wash of golden light over them all as they stood on the drive. He breathed a little easier. This didn't seem so bad.

The two attendants nodded over the papers, then took Jane by both arms to lead her away.

It was too soon. Ethan held up a hand. "Wait—hold on!"

The two attendants did not stop hustling Jane swiftly away. Jane was only able to cast one panicked glance at him over her shoulder before they'd whisked her away through the great double doors.

Behind him, the carriage had parked and the driver jumped down. For a moment, silence fell. The horses held their feet still on the gravel, and the carriage gave up on its many creaks and protests.

In that silence, Ethan finally heard it. A sound like the faraway sea. With horror, he began to realize what it was.

From behind the thick imposing walls of Bedlam came the faint ongoing symphony of insanity. Male roars, female screams, the endless rattle and bang of iron to iron.

Ethan had been to the Royal Menagerie once as a boy. He remembered it well, for he'd been much disturbed by the hopelessness of its inhabitants. While his family had milled through the walks, seemingly unperturbed by the sights and smells, a sound had started up. Perhaps it had begun in the cage of the lion—or perhaps one of the monkeys began to screech—but in the end, it seemed every animal trapped there had added its cries to the cacophony. It had swelled around Ethan until he could feel it vibrate his very bones and teeth.

Until now, it had been the most terrible sound he'd ever heard.

He had to see . . .

He took the grand entry staircase two steps at a time. There was an anteroom first, where two leering sculptures of madness guarded the great double doors. Ethan passed them by with no more than a glance. With both hands, he hit the latches of the great oak doors at a run, flinging them open in his rush.

The noise hit him like a hot wave. His crashing entrance only spurred the madness higher, until the screeches and howls echoed off the great arched ceiling two stories above.

His eyes wide, his breath coming up short, Ethan gazed upon hell on earth. Cages lined the gallery where he stood, cages of women in limp gray gowns and straggling hair. Some stood at the front bars, reaching toward him with dirty hands as they cried out unintelligible pleas. Others lay inert, perhaps sleeping, although they gazed eyes open at nothing at all.

Down the gallery, past an iron gate, Ethan saw brawnier hands reaching out. That was where the loudest roars came from—the caged men.

The smell hit Ethan then and he recoiled, his hand covering his mouth and nose as he backed away from the combined filth of two hundred unwashed bodies. With shaking hands, quite unable to draw another stinking breath, Ethan pulled the heavy double doors closed with a slam.

He leaned against them for a moment, sucking in a breath of relatively clean air.

The mob voice came directly through the heavy oak, vibrating through his hands, scraping his every nerve raw.

He could never leave Jane here.

"Jane!" He ran back into the anteroom, looking wildly around for some clue to where the two attendants had taken her. *"Jane!"*

A burly guard in the Bethlehem Hospital colors came into the anteroom through a small unobtrusive door. Ethan bolted for it, but the guard blocked him.

"Sorry, sir. The visitin' hours be tomorrow durin' daylight."

Ethan ignored him, mindlessly shoving at the heavy fellow, trying desperately to get through. *"Jane!"*

Angered, the big man pushed him back. "Tomorrow! Ye can get in tomorrow!"

"I have to get her out of here!"

"It said in them papers that you're just deliverin'. It said that no matter your objections, the lady is to be kept until his lordship says otherwise."

The guard crossed his arms over his chest. "You'll not be gettin' anyone out if ye don't have the papers," he said menacingly. "Now get on. Ye can see her tomorrow."

Frustrated, Ethan backed up a few steps. "I'll be back for you, Jane!" he called with all his strength. "I'll be back!"

Behind him, he heard the din of the menagerie rise to new levels in response. The noise and the fetid air and the guilt made him sick, until he had to stumble back out into the cool, clean night.

What had he done?

# Chapter Eighteen

With a push more violent than necessary, the male attendant shoved Jane into one of the cages that lined the upper gallery. She tripped over the trailing hem of the gown she'd been given that was vastly too large for her. The cheap gray flannel tore at the waist with a weak ripping sound.

She could not quite fully stand, for the second-gallery cages were somewhat shorter than the first, although they seemed wider. Still, she kept her feet, and clapped one hand over the tear, pressing the fabric close to her body. She'd been through such indignities in the last hour that her small modesty might seem ridiculous, yet still she covered her bare skin from the gaze of the guard.

He shrugged and shut her cage door with a clang. There was apparently only one key for all the cages, for only a single fat iron key hung from his belt.

He held it with thick fingers and locked the crude iron padlock with practiced ease. The sound of the click made Jane flinch, but she said nothing. By now she knew that no pleadings or promises would sway either the male attendant or the nurse assigned to see to Jane.

Only when his heavy footsteps had faded along with the light of his lantern did Jane allow her knees to weaken. She ached from her struggles against both her uncle's footmen and the Bedlam attendants. She wrapped both arms about her knees and pressed her forehead down upon them, willing the noise to stop, willing herself deaf to the mad riot around her.

With the departure of the guard, at last the inmates settled to a random mumble of insanity and Jane could think.

When she'd seen the doors close on Ethan's protest she'd known she had no chance. She'd not been allowed to reach him, for the attendant's thick arm had come around her waist, pulling her from her feet.

The next several moments were a blur, but she'd come out of them with a few new bruises and a renewed feeling of helplessness.

The nurse had ordered her carried to a room occupied by a fireplace and a number of crude iron tubs. There Jane was stripped and forcefully bathed despite the fact that she was already cleaner than the scummy water she was thrown into. She'd fought the nurse until the woman had threatened to leave the bathing to the guard.

Quailing from such a fate, Jane cursed herself for her own girlish weakness. She wished she were stronger, or faster, or more persuasive. Yet many large men were incarcerated in Bedlam—who was to say they did not wish the same?

Finally Jane decided she was simply going to have to be resilient and sturdy instead. She was no Augusta, who had never been so much as chilled in her life. She had survived Northumbria winters with little food and no coal. She'd managed to keep her mother in some dignity and comfort despite their poverty.

She could survive Bedlam.

For a while.

As Maywell's carriage rumbled back into Mayfair, Ethan pressed both hands to his head, trying to shut out the memory of that choir of madness. He had to think!

He had to rescue Jane from that place. The thought that she had already spent hours there made him ill.

He could go to the Liars—

In his mind he saw Etheridge's cool expression as he talked about sacrificing someone he could not trust. What if the spymaster decided that Jane could not be trusted? What if he ordered Ethan to leave her where she was? Which of course, Ethan would disobey—thus setting himself against the Liars. He cared little for the danger to himself, but what would happen to Jane? Her uncle was a traitor. She would likely already be guilty in Etheridge's cold-as-marble estimation.

He could go to Collis. Collis owed him—

*"I'm a Liar, Ethan. My loyalties lie here."*

Right, then. He was on his own. But how could he get her out of there? Nausea roiled through Ethan at the thought of Jane caged like a beast. Getting her out of there was all that mattered. To hell with the Liars and their ridiculous intentions for him.

To hell with Maywell's plans and national security.

He had to undo what he'd done to her.

*Think!* Anyone could get into Bedlam. There had been a sign at the entrance demanding an admission fee. Pay a penny a head to see the animals in the zoo.

The problem was not how to get in.

The puzzle was—how to leave in the middle of the day with a woman at his side?

Unless . . . unless he went in with one . . .

He rapped on the ceiling. The small trapdoor opened and the driver looked down at him. "Yes, sir?"

"I've had a long night," Ethan said casually. "I'm in need of a bit of relaxation. Take me to Mrs. Blythe's House of Pleasure."

Jane sat on the floor of her cell, in the corner farthest from its door. It helped a little to think of it as a cell, and not as a cage. Less degrading somehow. A prison cell implied a crime committed. A crime committed implied a person of some dangerous capacity. A criminal might be strong and fearsome, not helpless and cowering.

She was a prisoner, a dangerous one who must be kept contained in a cell for fear of her criminal nature. She took a deep breath and tried to feel dangerous.

It was a silly game, but it helped. A bit.

She needed something to keep her calm for she must think. How could she get out of here?

*Ethan will come.*

He hadn't wanted to leave her here last night, she was sure of that. She had heard him calling her name. She took a breath. Ethan *might* come. Then again, he might not.

She'd already examined every inch of the ca—the cell. The door was hinged on the other side, in the direction in which it swung. The padlock was large and crude. Jane had heard of locks being picked by hairpins, but she had none. Her entire net worth consisted of a cheap flannel dress, soft felt slippers, a much dented tin chamber pot that didn't bear touching, and a worn blanket that she'd confined to the other corner of the cell when she'd spotted the wildlife present in it. Better to sleep on the bare bench.

Nothing to use for a key. Nothing to use for a weapon. She didn't want to hurt anyone—with the possible exception of the crude male attendant—but she would use a weapon if she had to. If she'd had one.

A bit of string tied her simple braid at the end. Jane untied it and examined it closely. It was useless, being only ten inches long. She sighed, wrapped it twice about her wrist, then experimented with pulling her long hair over her face to hide from observation.

A useful disguise perhaps, but she did not like it. She might be in Bedlam, but she would retain herself for as long as she could—she simply was not the sort of woman who let her hair hang in her eyes.

She rebraided it neatly and used the string to tie it up again.

After what seemed a thousand hours, an elderly woman came past the cages, pushing a cart. The cart contained loaves of dark bread and tin cups of watery soup.

Jane made no attempt to be dainty about the coarse fare. She'd eaten worse and much less of it. It was important to maintain her health and strength against the filth all around her. She drained the cup before handing it back to the woman and took her hunk of dry bread back to her corner.

The meal seemed to revive the woman to Jane's right, although the limp form to her left had her worried. The first woman stirred to glare at Jane through rheumy eyes.

"Gimme yer bread!" A grimy hand reached through the bars.

Jane started and cringed, then remembered—*dangerous*. She slapped the woman's hand hard until it withdrew. When the sanctity of her cell was restored, Jane gave the creature an even stare. "If I've hurt you, I apologize. If I have more than I need, I will be happy to share. But if you put your hand in here uninvited again, I cannot promise that you'll get it back."

The woman blinked, then gave a rusty chuckle. "Yer a canny lass. You'll do all right, for a while. Not like 'er." She indicated the too-still inhabitant of the far cell, then shrugged. "At least the stupid cow stopped 'er singin'. Near to drove me mad."

The woman went back to her bread, chuckling at her own joke. Jane eyed the other cage with pity. The feeding nurse had taken the cup of soup away, but the hunk of bread still lay on the floor, not six inches away from the woman's limp hand. Jane saw the woman on the far side reaching for it with one scrawny arm. She would have protested, but the other inhabitant hadn't a chance of reaching it. Jane could, but not even her own survival would induce her to steal. That thought settled firmly within her, comfortable from long use.

She would not fall from her own set of standards, no

matter what. She'd survived without falling before, she could do it again. At least this time she had no one to look after but herself.

When the relative amusement of eating the bread had been drawn out as long as it could, and not even a crumb was left, Jane began to have trouble ignoring the clamor about her. The voices rose and fell, and had been never-ending even in the dark of night. The incessant banging on the bars began to chip away at Jane's reserve of cool rationality. She leaned both elbows on her knees and pressed her hands over her ears.

She shut her eyes and prepared to wait out the rest of the day.

That morning, Ethan appeared at his appointed time at Lord Maywell's freshly bathed and apparently at his ease.

Maywell eyed him carefully as Simms let him into the study. Ethan bowed genially. "Good morning, your lordship."

Maywell nodded, then waved Ethan to a seat. Ethan sat with a well-satisfied sigh. He knew his lordship's driver would have reported on the midnight visit to Mrs. Blythe's. In fact, he was counting on it.

"I hear you had an enjoyable evening after—"

Ethan would have laughed if he hadn't been so consumed with cold, calculating fury. Lord Maywell couldn't even bring himself to speak of what he had done, the hypocritical bounder.

"Yes, I did. Your niece was safely ensconced in the hospital and I felt the need for a bit of company. Should I not have used your carriage?"

"No—no, that was quite all right. You sent it back in good time."

Ethan could see that Maywell was wondering if he'd underestimated Ethan. Ethan wasn't feeling particularly charitable. Let the old schemer wonder.

Maywell cleared his throat, placing his folded hands

before him on the desk. "Damont, I believe in rewarding loyalty. You've showed that, true enough. I know it wasn't easy for you to take my niece Jane to Bethlehem Hospital. I know you're partial to her."

Ethan nodded slowly, thinking of Lady Jane Pennington climbing into his lap last night. His cravat seemed to tighten. *Partial*—that was a bit of an understatement.

Lord Maywell leaned back in his chair, watching Ethan through narrowed eyes. "I've an offer for you, son." He smiled slightly. "You don't mind me calling you that, do you, my boy?"

Son. Ethan hadn't heard the word in a very long time. Part of him, long buried along with any hope of hearing that word so fondly spoken again, responded. Maywell would know that about him. He shook his head silently. *Twisty old bastard.*

"I've a passel of daughters, but the fates never saw fit to give me a son," Lord Maywell mused aloud. "It's a real lack for a man to have no son."

Ethan cleared his throat. "I wouldn't know, my lord."

"I'll be blunt, Damont. I want a man inside the Liar's Club. I know they sent you to me, hoping I would recruit you. They thought you would make a superior double spy."

Ethan swallowed. This man was very frightening sometimes. "I've told you, my lord. I don't frequent—"

"The Liar's Club. Yes, I know you have. Simply listen to what I have to propose."

He leaned forward, white whiskers bristling earnestly. "I'd like for you to go back to the Liars, carrying certain information that I have prepared. It will be true—at least, for the most part. True enough to convince them that you have been successful. In return, they will give you misinformation to feed me, I'm sure. It is what I would do. Bring it to me anyway, for sometimes it can be as useful to know what the opposition is trying not to hide as it is to know what they are trying *to* hide."

Ethan frowned. "How very . . . intricate. If I were to do this—which I could not, for I don't frequent the Liar's Club—but if I were, what makes you so sure that I would choose to heed your orders and not theirs? How could one leader ever be sure of a double spy?"

Maywell didn't answer immediately. Instead, he leaned back in his chair and drew on his cheroot and focused a narrow gaze on him. Ethan tried to match it with a level one of his own, but he feared the man saw inside him all too well.

For what it was worth, Ethan knew Maywell understood what it was like to be the unwanted son, to feel the scorn of the family, to long for their acceptance and to finally realize that there was no reprieve but to try to establish a dynasty of his own.

"I think it's time you took a wife," Maywell said lightly, as if he were not reading Ethan's very thoughts. "I think you've shown your worth to me. I care nothing for this matter of rank and title. I follow good old Napoleon's creed, that a man is who he proves himself to be. A man of constancy and honor—now that man is as good as a lord in my book." He took a deep pull on his cheroot. The smoke swirled between them, hiding his lordship's eyes from Ethan's view. The haze seemed to take shape in his imagination until Ethan could almost see his future in that writhing air.

Maywell continued, his voice as low and soft as a mesmerizer's. "As good as a lord—good enough to wed a lady . . . Would you like that, Damont? Would you like to wed Jane, to stand proudly by her side, welcomed by her relations, defended by my standing against whatever Society may want to say about it?"

Longing swept Ethan, stealing his breath like a blow to the gut. To wed Jane—to be her husband, to be part of her family, to be given her hand with her family's blessing, to live out his days beside her and his nights in her arms . . .

All he had to do was join Lord Maywell in his secret

crusade—a cause that Ethan himself did not entirely lack sympathy for.

To be truthful, what did he owe the Liars? Or for that matter, the Crown, or even England herself? He'd spent his adulthood fighting for his own survival, for every scrap of respect and acceptance, yet he'd never truly belonged anywhere.

Lord Etheridge had seen this in him, he realized now. This was the spymaster's fear, this was the source of his reluctance to invite Ethan fully into the Liars. That lack of trust hit Ethan a further blow, contrasting rather unfavorably against Maywell's offer.

Grimly, Ethan wondered if Etheridge would ever know that it was his own suspicions that had driven Ethan away.

With a start, Ethan realized that he was seriously contemplating it. He would step over the line he had straddled for too long, he would cross to the other side, he would betray his country freely—if it meant he could possess Jane.

His gut twisted. Jane, for his very own. He could get her out of Bedlam this afternoon, he could ride right up to the doors with all the proper papers and Jane would be free—and his.

Maywell, the evil bastard, had known just what key to turn.

His cold control nearly shattered, Ethan bowed his head and stood. "My lord, if I could—if I could take a little time to think on this . . ."

Ethan had not been home for two days, yet still Jeeves had the door wide and stood at the ready. In no mood for their usual banter, Ethan merely nodded at him as he strode by him.

"Pardon me, sir, but you have a guest."

Ethan stopped short. He never had guests. "Who is it?"

"It is a Mr. Tremayne, sir. He is waiting for you in your study, sir."

Collis. Ethan worked his jaw for a moment, then turned. He marched into the study and tossed his hat down on the desk. "Tremayne," was all he said by way of greeting.

Collis was leaning on the mantel, toying with the coals with a poker. He looked up and blinked at Ethan. "Damont, old man! Where have you been?"

"Maywell's," Ethan said shortly. "Where else?"

Collis folded his arms before him. "How about Carlton House, for starters?"

Ethan halted in the act of looking for his decanter. It was upstairs, of course. He turned to Collis. "I figured it out. Thanks so much for letting me in on it."

Collis nodded. "George told me."

George. *"A few people whom I hold in great affection are permitted to address me as 'George.'"*

Ethan didn't smile. "How is the old codge?"

Collis was watching him carefully. "He is well. He's concerned about you, however. He seemed to think you were upset by the discovery."

Ethan threw himself into the chair behind his desk. "Upset? Why would I be? You had your reasons for lying to me. National security and all that."

"Yes, national security and all that." Collis looked relieved, until he began to peer more closely at Ethan. "There is something bothering you, isn't there? Is it Maywell? Is it the case?"

Ethan leaned his head back on his chair and closed his eyes. Collis had been his friend since they were both in short pants and skinned knees. He wanted to confide—to confess—and most of all, to confer. What should he do about Jane?

But Collis was a Liar, through and through.

And Ethan was not.

"The case is going well. Maywell seems to trust me quite a bit already."

"Really?" Collis sat forward eagerly. "Has he offered you a position in his organization yet?"

*Yes, he has.* "No, not yet."

Collis looked disappointed for him. "Well, don't worry. I know you can do it."

With a few more encouraging words that Ethan responded to vaguely, Collis left with a relieved smile on his face. "I'm glad you understood about the George bit," Collis told him as he left. "I'm glad you know now. George likes you. He trusts you to keep the whole affair close."

Ethan nodded and smiled, nodded and smiled, until Collis was gone and he was finally alone.

He'd lied to the best friend he had. Ethan wasn't even sure why he lied. Hell, he wasn't even sure what side he was on. He was lying to everyone, left and right, just as he always had.

So why did they keep trusting him? Didn't they understand what sort of man he was? Didn't they realize he would only disappoint and betray?

The way he had disappointed and betrayed Jane.

Into his arms, into Bedlam, and, if he gave in to temptation, into marriage.

*And Jane would hate him for it.*

Yes, she would. Loyal little Brit that she was, she would despise him.

He could win her over, part of him argued. He could use her desire for him against her. He could make her want him, over and over, until he burrowed his way back into her heart as well.

*Like a worm.*

She would be his. That was what truly mattered, didn't it? Possessing her, wedding her, freely and openly laying claim to the only woman he had ever loved?

*And destroying her in the process.*

He could not do it.

Even as he'd smiled, even as he'd leaned forward to present his hand to Lord Maywell, even as he'd smoothly stated his intention to think on his lordship's most generous offer, Ethan had been giving his magnificent Jane away.

Love was a cruel mistress, it seemed—an even more demanding one than Luck. He found it surprising that he was not more shocked at the consuming love he felt for Jane. He'd mocked love and he'd fled it, so why was he love's willing servant now?

The answer was simple, so simple he was mildly surprised he'd never realized it before.

Because love was Jane. She was everything that made life good—like lazy mornings and soft words and a kitten's purr. Whether she spent those mornings in his arms or not, the world needed Jane more than it needed him.

So very simple indeed.

If being the man she wanted him to be meant losing her—if being true to her meant stabbing himself through the heart—then so be it.

Heartbreaking loss and peace filled him in equal measure. He would remain true to Jane and to England—and to hell with Maywell and the Liars.

He would remain alone.

# Chapter Nineteen

A murmur of voices, very different from the clamor of madness, drew Jane from her corner at midday. She knelt at the front of her cell and gazed down to the lower gallery.

Visiting hours had begun. Bright color swirled past in a river of well-dressed humanity flowing down the walkway. Bedlam was all gray, from the uniforms of the attendants to the sooty, grimy walls themselves. To see the bright skirts and redingotes of ladies, and shimmering colorful waistcoats of gentlemen in the sunlight streaming through the high windows made her slit her eyes against the brilliance.

She did not close them entirely. This would be the time when Ethan would come. Already some of the observers were making their way up to the second gallery. Jane tried to search the crowd for him, but without the help of her usual height, she could not see over the people who came to stand before her own cell.

"This one is not so foul as the others," one lady called to her fellows.

"Indeed she is not," replied another woman. They came close to peer at Jane through the bars. They held their skirts high from the dirty floor, freely showing off their lace-clad ankles.

Jane revised her original opinion. These were not ladies, these were painted demireps, parading on the arms of their admirers. She answered their rudeness by glowering right back at them.

"Look at her stare at us," said the first woman. She squinted at Jane. "Wills!" She tapped her escort sharply on the shoulder, never taking her hard gaze from Jane. "Wills Barstow, make her stop staring!"

Wills, a pudding-faced fellow of about twenty-five with evidently more money than taste or brains, rapped his walking stick on the bars. "You there! Don't stare at the ladies!"

Jane slid her even gaze to meet his. "I don't see any ladies, do you?"

The two women gasped, obviously appalled at the accusation. Jane barely refrained from rolling her eyes. "If you object to being accused of lack of gentility," she advised them cordially, "then perhaps you should refrain from wearing so much paint." She folded her arms, tsking softly. "And showing so much of your limbs in public? Now what would your mothers think of that?"

"Here, here!" Wills was really angry now. His face reddened and he stuck his walking stick through the bars, swinging it at her.

There would never be a better opportunity. Jane grabbed at it as it swished by, barely missing her in the confines of the cage. The second swing struck her knuckles hard, making them bleed, but she did not lose her focus on the stick. If she could only grab it—

One of the uniformed attendants stormed up. "Oy, sir! Don't be swattin' at the inmates! Some do-gooder'll see them bruises and fuss at us for mistreating the wenches!"

Wills reluctantly pulled his stick back from Jane's reach. She glared at the attendant who had ruined her chances of getting a weapon. He surprised her with a swift kick through the bars. His heavy boot struck her just below the knee, causing her to cry out and fall to the ground.

"See there?" The attendant nodded with satisfaction. "That won't show."

The painted women snickered. Wills spat at Jane's collapsed form, spraying the side of her lowered face. With a jerk, she raised her head and glared at him. He took a step back from her fury.

"Your name is Wills Barstow," Jane said in a low voice. Dangerous. "You shop on Bond Street and pick your women up in Shepherds Market. You live in Mayfair in a fine house and every afternoon you wake up and wonder if this is all there will ever be to your life."

Wills gaped in horror, his face becoming absolutely ashen as he hurled himself back three steps.

"By God, she's a—a witch!" He swallowed, hard, then turned on his heels and ran, leaving his companions to follow him as they would.

Jane smiled slightly and sat back in her corner.

The woman to her right, who had watched every moment with fascination, gazed at her in alarm. "Oy, 'ow did you know all that?"

Jane tilted her head at the woman, smiling sweetly. "Didn't you hear what he said? I'm a witch."

The woman scuttled back as far from Jane as she could get. Jane felt a slight qualm for frightening the poor wretch, but it was really best for all concerned if Jane was left entirely alone.

She wished she did have magical powers, instead of just the power of acute observation.

Wills's name, she'd heard from the ladybird. The second and third things she'd surmised from his clothing and the maker of the women's shoes. Mayfair was a pure guess, but the last was something she'd recognized in his empty, dissatisfied gaze—something she'd experienced herself once upon a time.

It was odd, but she hadn't felt that way since she'd met Ethan Damont.

Speaking of Ethan . . .

She let her head drop onto her folded arms, shutting out the asylum as best she could. "Where are you, you rotter?"

Light footsteps stopped outside Jane's cell. "Look at this beggarly creature, darling," said a cool feminine voice. "Isn't she odd? Not at all like the others."

Jane remained as she was, with her forehead lowered onto crossed arms over knees pulled high. For most of the day, she'd managed to avoid being singled out by the spectators. She'd discovered that if she bored them, they went away. Surely visiting hours must be ending soon. She bit her lip and tried to seem as dull as possible.

A heavier tread joined the first. "Oh, I don't know, my sweet," a masculine voice drawled—a voice Jane knew as well as her own. "They all seem much the same to me."

Ethan. At last! Jane jerked her head up to see him gazing at her calmly from outside the cage. His arm was wrapped about the waist of a beautiful woman—another painted ladybird like the earlier ones, but this one was truly lovely. From the cheeks and hair that peeped out from beneath her deep bonnet, her coloring was much the same as Jane's, but there the resemblance ended. Jane knew when she was outclassed.

She could only blink stupidly at them for a moment. Then she shook off her surprise and forced down the silly twinge of hurt at seeing Ethan with someone else. "Eth—"

He cut her off smoothly. "Do you think that bothersome guard can see us from here, my love?"

Jane opened her mouth, but the other woman answered. Jane flinched, then berated herself silently. Ethan had never addressed her so. There was no reason for him to start now.

"Yes, I believe he can. In fact, the bounder has been watching me ever since we passed him."

Ethan looked away from Jane and gazed passionately into "My Love's" eyes. "I don't care," he murmured huskily. "I cannot wait another moment to take you into my arms!"

"Oh, darling!"

"Oh, Bess!"

Before Jane's disbelieving gaze, Ethan and the other woman—Bess?—dissolved into a grasping, torrid embrace.

If this was a rescue, it was a damn poor attempt! What was he trying to do, make her vomit her way out of Bedlam?

Jane's cage rattled. She looked back to see that Ethan had pressed his ladybird up against the bars while passionately kissing her neck.

Apparently, this was nothing so new in Bedlam, for the other inmates were beginning to cheer the couple on. "She's an 'ot one, sir!" "Best put out that fire afore she burns the place down!"

Jane was about to demand an explanation when she saw Ethan working his way down Bess's neck to kneel at her feet. For the first time, Jane noticed that the gown Bess was wearing so well was a good ten years out of date. The waist was cinched and the skirts were outrageously full. If Jane had been wearing it, she'd have been laughed off the street.

Unfortunately, Bess looked lovely in it.

Ethan went to one knee and gazed worshipfully up at Bess. "My darling, I must!"

Bess tossed her head impatiently. "Go on, then, my stallion!"

Jane looked from one to the other, completely perplexed. Was Ethan going to propose? He was trying to kill her, wasn't he?

It wasn't a marriage proposal. It was much worse. Ethan flipped Bess's hem high and dove underneath.

Jane clapped one hand over her mouth in shock and plastered herself to the back wall of her cell. The woman's skirts flowed over the entire front of the cage. There was nothing to see but Bess with her back pressed to Jane's bars and her head rolling from side to side with ecstasy. Ecstasy that had been denied to Jane, yet!

One day she was going to make her way free of this place, and when she did, she was going to hunt Ethan Damont down and kill him!

Then something else caught her attention at the front of her cage. A fold of Bess's full gown had lapped over the catch and lock—and there was something going on under that fold!

Reason finally beat down her shock and—admittedly—jealousy. Of course, Ethan would never come here simply to flaunt another woman in front of her! He had a plan!

Relief spun through Jane, making her dizzy with it. Her clever Ethan! And here she'd been vowing revenge! How silly! She would wait to kill him until *after* she thanked him.

She heard a faint metallic click and a jingle. Then the door to the cage inched forward slightly, digging into the folds of Bess's gown. A manly hand came up from under the hem and beckoned her forward with one finger.

Normally, Jane would not have been inclined to insinuate herself beneath the skirts of a prostitute, but today was not a normal day. She eagerly wiggled through the narrow opening in the gate and slipped under the wall of scarlet brocade. Above her, Bess continued to carry on, her cries of ecstasy growing louder.

Jane found herself in a stuffy, dimly red-lit space crowded with skirt hoop and the blessedly pantalets-clad limbs of another woman. And Ethan. He pulled her to him to greet her with a hard desperate kiss. As she pulled back, a small damp laugh broke from her. "Hello to you too, Mr. Damont!" she whispered.

"Take off your gown!"

Jane blinked. "Not until we're married," she shot back.

Ethan started. "What?" Then he shook his head. "Janet, I'm not—"

"Ah, sir?"

The deep tones of the burly guard's voice close by froze them both. Jane was sure they were caught until she realized that Bess's cries would have covered up their own hissed whispers.

Ethan gazed wild-eyed at Jane. "Y-yes?" he called out. "What is it?"

His tone was that of a bored aristocrat being disturbed by an unwanted servant. Hysterical laughter began to rise within Jane. She pressed one fist to her lips and gazed helplessly at Ethan while her shoulders shook.

"Visitin' hours is near gone, sir."

Ethan shot Jane a warning look, but she could tell he was having trouble restraining his own sense of the ridiculous. "I see—ah, yes. Thank you, my good man."

From above them, they heard Bess purr. "Yes, thank you most kindly. We won't keep you but a moment longer." The entire dress heaved with the force of Bess's sigh. Jane's giggles soured as she thought of what a sigh like that would do to the woman's substantial décolletage. Such effect was apparently not lost on the guard either.

The man cleared his throat with obvious difficulty. Jane hoped he managed to wipe his chin as well. "All right then—I'll just go on then and . . ."

"What a wonderful idea," Bess cooed. "You go on then."

Jane had never heard so much sexual promise conveyed in so few words. "I'm going to have to practice that," she murmured, as she heard the guard's footsteps move hesitantly away.

Ethan's hand came over her mouth. Instead of protesting, Jane surprised herself by wanting to melt into the hard warmth of that hand. She was tired of being brave. She wanted to be held and told everything was going to be fine.

Ethan came close to whisper into her ear. "Everything's going to be fine," he said softly. Then he slipped back out from their silken cage and was gone. If it hadn't been so stuffy in there, Jane would have felt cold with his absence. How did one man give off so much heat?

Above her, Ethan began to coo nonsense to Bess again. "Let me hold you for just one moment more, my sweet, just one precious moment more . . ." Then the toes of his boots appeared beneath the flounced hem next to Jane's hand. Jane glared at those boot tips with narrowed eyes. "That's close enough," she muttered. Close enough to pull Bess into his arms, apparently.

"Oh, my darling! Oh, my sweet!" Various wet sucking sounds ensued.

Ethan and Bess sounded as though they were having entirely too much enjoyment. Jane crouched low and sourly considered elbowing the man she loved in the kneecap. If she didn't do it too hard, he wouldn't be permanently crippled, would he?

"I must have you, my darling, my love!"

The gown bucked and swayed around her. Jane bit her lip. She knew it was false—or at least hoped it was!—but she didn't think she could bear much more.

Then Bess dropped to her knees next to Jane. "Hullo, dearie!"

Jane started wildly. "But—!" She looked up. The gown was still being clenched by a passionate Ethan. She heard his amorous murmurs continue. She looked back at Bess, who was clad in nothing but a chemise and pantalets.

"Quickly now," Bess urged, tugging at Jane's gray flannel gown. "Get that thing off and give it to me."

Jane could only stare stupidly at her. "But I've nothing underneath!"

Bess smirked. "Trust the voice of experience, dearie. You won't die of it. Besides, I'm giving you mine."

Finally, the entire, mad lovely plan bloomed in Jane's mind. "Oh, my."

Wasting no more time, she pulled the oversized gown over her head and thrust it at Bess, keeping her blushing face averted.

She felt Bess push something small and thin into her hand. She looked down. Hairpins.

"Pin that braid up," Bess urged as she scrubbed at her face paint with a handkerchief. Beneath it, Jane was surprised to see an ordinary freckled snub-nosed face emerge. Bess grinned at her. "Go on! Get up there. He can't carry on like that forever!" Then she smirked cheerfully at Jane. "Although he's been known to try." Then Bess pulled her own hair down and felt beneath the hem for the cage door. "Be seeing you, dearie."

Jane stopped trying to hide her nudity long enough to put a hand on Bess's arm. "Will you be all right?"

Bess blinked as if she hadn't expected Jane to care. "Oh, sure. I'll take myself a rest cure for a few days, and then—" She held up an iron key just like the guard's. In fact, Jane rather thought it *was* the guard's! "I nicked it off his belt just now!" Bess winked. "Don't worry, dearie. It'll be worth it!"

Then she flipped up the hem and was gone. Jane heard the lock clink back into place.

"Janet!" Ethan's urgent whisper came down through the neckline of the gown. "Get your lovely arse into this dress!"

Fortunately, Jane was intimately acquainted with the construction of such dresses, since she had refitted and resewn her mother's old gowns for both of them over the years. Her mother had taken every single stitch of clothing with her when she and Jane had made the trip to the Dowager House, for that wealth of wardrobe had supplied the two of them with fabric and trims throughout the following ten years. Jane's mother had drifted through the rotting rooms of the Dowager House clad in the same costly gowns as she had always worn, as if she walked in halls of gold.

As Jane eased her way up the statuesque gown, she bit back another semi-hysterical giggle. She'd done her share of silent cursing at recalcitrant hoops and corsets over the years. She felt as though she ought to apologize to every single one as she popped up through the gown that was going to save her life.

She eased her head up to peer at Ethan, who was glaring at her through the open neckline.

"Hurry it up, will you?" he hissed at her. "That guard could come back to the upper gallery at any moment!"

"Close your eyes," Jane told him.

Ethan shut his eyes obediently—at first. Then, as he felt her begin to rise and fill the empty dress in his arms, he found himself compelled to open them the tiniest slit. After all, he'd never claimed to be a gentleman!

She was completely nude. He could see directly down the dress to nearly every part of her elegant, rose-tinted body. She was having a bit of trouble fitting her arms into the sleeves from that angle and Ethan got an eyeful of round pert breasts that swayed very temptingly with her every movement. She glanced suspiciously up at him a few times, but Ethan had spent years on his poker face. He knew she could not see past his lashes to his slitted eyes and he knew that no sign of his rousing lust was displayed upon his face.

He should have thought of this method years ago. All he'd ever needed to do to get a woman naked was to rescue her from Bedlam.

Finally Jane managed the sleeves and rose to her feet completely. Her head popped out and Ethan released the dress enough to do the tiny buttons up the back.

Oddly, his hand shook far more this time than when he'd undone them for Bess.

Jane was looking down at herself in dismay. Ethan tried not to be irked that she ignored the fact that she was wrapped in his arms.

"I've not half the bosom to fill this bodice," she hissed.

Ethan finished the buttons at last and clapped the fallen bonnet on her head.

"No one will notice," he said absently, as he tried to tie

the ribbons beneath her chin to hide her face. Damn his trembling hands! What the hell was wrong with him?

Jane cocked her head at him. "Bess," she said in a normal voice. "Will the guard notice I've lost a stone in bosom?"

Bess popped up behind Jane, peeking between the bars. "Too right he will. I doubt the bloke ever even looked at my face."

"What do you think then?" Jane was still talking to Bess, her voice calm as if she were discussing the weather in her own parlor. "Have we something I can fluff myself up with?"

Bess considered her with narrowed eyes. Ethan gave up on the ribbons. He suddenly felt a bit left out, even though Jane still stood within the circle of his arms.

"I know," Bess said. She crouched on the floor for a moment, fumbling beneath her hem. Then she stood with twin bundles of fine knitted silk in her hands. "My stockings," she said as she handed them through the bars to Jane. Then Bess quirked a brow at Ethan. "They cost fifteen pence apiece. You can add them to my account."

Ethan nodded. "I will, Bess." He looked down at Jane's freshly altered bodice. "Heavens, those are fluffed. Do you lot do that sort of thing often?"

Both Jane and Bess snickered. "If they only knew, eh, duchess?" Bess said to Jane.

Ethan looked up to see the guard approaching again. "Time to go."

Jane reached a hand through the bars to clasp Bess's. "Be safe," she urged her.

Bess blinked. Ethan could imagine her surprise. Usually women like Jane would cross the road before they'd allow their skirts to brush Bess's. "I will that," Bess said huskily. "Best you be off, duchess."

Jane tucked a last strand of hair beneath the bonnet and tied the ribbons with swift precision that mocked Ethan's attempt. She took a deep breath and smiled at Ethan nervously. "Do I look all right?"

She looked beautiful, bizarre gown, shadowed eyes, and all. She looked like everything he'd ever wanted and knew he'd never have.

Ethan smiled softly down at her. "You look—"

"Oy! I seen it all, you know!" They all turned to stare at the woman in the next cage. She had her arms crossed over her flat chest and a smug look in her eye. "What's to keep me from telling that guard what you done?"

Ethan's breath left him. Damn and blast. The old cow was going to give it all away.

Bess bridled. "Mayhap the fact you're as mad as a gin tinker?"

Jane held up a hand to quiet Bess. The guard was close enough now to hear them. She leaned closer to the other woman's cage. Ethan could barely hear her—something about "bread" and "every day."

The woman nodded and sneered at Bess, who rolled her eyes in response. "Yes, the old sot can 'ave my bread," she agreed. Then she ducked down to the back corner of the cage, assuming the leave-me-be position that Jane had held most of the day. The approaching guard didn't so much as spare her a glance.

"I've got to put you out now, sir," he said diffidently.

Ethan wasn't fooled. Damn right he ought to be diffident. Earlier, Ethan had slipped the fellow half a crown to be left with his inamorata.

If he slipped him any more, the man might become suspicious that something more than public licentiousness was going on. So Ethan merely nodded dismissively and offered Jane his arm.

Her hand was trembling when it came around his bicep. He noticed that she kept her face down and her chest high. The guard seemed duly appreciative and they passed him by without incident.

At any moment, Ethan expected discovery and outcry. Down the stairs, along the lower gallery to the heavy double doors to the anteroom. No cry came. The two statues loomed over them like the final guards preventing their escape. Ethan pressed one hand over Jane's as they stepped through the front door of Bedlam to the top of the grimy marble steps outside.

He was surprised to see that the watery afternoon sun was still quite high. What had seemed like suspenseful hours had only been minutes.

And now Jane was free—or at least she would be once they drove out through those menacing gates.

Uri was waiting in the drive with the carriage, one hand ready at the door. Ethan felt Jane pull at his arm. He could feel the urgency in her, the compulsion to run for the carriage in a final race for escape.

"Easy, love," he said softly. "You're a bored demirep, remember. You've got all evening to cross that drive."

He felt her inhale carefully and her death grip eased. She descended the stairs with an air of ennui worthy of the stage.

Uri bowed and helped her into the carriage. Ethan nodded at the footman as he climbed in after her. Jeeves trusted Uri and, for whatever reason, Ethan trusted Jeeves.

"Take us home," he ordered.

Uri nodded and soon the carriage began to roll. Ethan looked down to discover that at some point in the last few moments, Jane had taken his hand in hers, fingers entwined. Though she stared out the window, her expression apathetic, her fingers clutched his with all the power of her fear.

Ethan marveled. She'd seemed so cool during the escape from the cage and the donning of the dress, he'd almost forgotten how frightened she must be.

And rightly so. Bedlam was no place for a lady. Nor for Bess, for that matter.

They drove sedately beneath the arched iron gateway and the gatekeeper closed the gates behind them, shutting out the sane world from that of madness for yet another day.

Jane started slightly at the deep clang of the closing gates but otherwise remained still as they drove toward the river and the bridge.

Ethan leaned over but could not see her face for the depth of the bonnet. "Janet? Are you all right?"

Slowly, she unlinked her fingers from his and raised her hands to the bow beneath her chin. She calmly undid the ribbon and pulled the bonnet from her head, setting it carefully aside on the seat beside her.

Then she flung herself into Ethan's arms.

# Chapter Twenty

— ◆ —

"I knew you'd come," Jane cried. "I knew it!" Then she leaned back and glared tearfully at Ethan. "How could you leave me there?"

He pulled her close. "Shh, I'm sorry. I'm so sorry, Janet. I didn't know. I thought it was a good place, a safe place. I only wanted to get you away before your uncle did something terrible—"

She shuddered. "I think I would almost rather have been killed," she said, her voice low and horrified.

He pushed her bonnet back to cup her cheeks in his hands. "You don't mean that. You should never, ever mean that."

Her face crumpled. "You don't understand, you don't know . . ." Her wails disintegrated into nonsense as she dissolved into sobs.

"What? What don't I understand? I know it was an awful, frightening place, but you knew I was coming back for you, didn't you?"

She shook her head furiously, wiping at her face with the back of her hand until he pulled out his handkerchief. For several long moments, she sobbed helplessly into it as he held her, stroking her hair and saying he knew not what to comfort her.

Finally, she drew a deep broken breath, and then another.

She stiffened a bit in his arms so he released her. Wiping her eyes and nose with his handkerchief, she straightened to gaze at him with reddened eyes.

He smiled gently. "Your nose is running, Janet."

She laughed damply and dabbed at it. "I fear this is ruined," she said about his handkerchief.

"Better it than you," Ethan told her.

She shook her head. "You must think me the most ridiculous infant."

"Why?" He stroked a damp strand of hair back from her cheek. "Because you held on with gritted teeth and iron will until *after* you were out of danger? There are soldiers on the battlefield who cannot claim that."

She sighed. "It was not so bloody and awful as that . . . only grim and loud and cold. I think I was safer in the cage than out, to be truthful."

"Then what is it? Tell me, Janet. Help me understand."

She took a deep breath. "It is something of a family secret. Lord Maywell did not want anyone to know, for it could have hurt my cousins' chances for marriage . . ."

"Yes?"

She looked him in the eye. "My mother went mad. After my father died and his brother Christop became marquis. She lost everything that she'd built her life around.

"We were sent to the Dowager House—a grand name for the hovel that awaited us. Since the practice of keeping the previous duke's wife out of sight on some distant estate had fallen by the wayside a hundred years ago, it quickly became apparent that no one had put one penny into the property since then. It was a damp and rotting ruin."

Jane shrugged. "Mama simply never accepted it. She would pretend—or believe—that nothing had changed, that my father was only briefly away, that we still lived in the grand house on the estate, that we still had servants to take care of every little thing, that we were not near starving and freezing every winter—"

She shook her head as if to erase all that. "I did my

best to take care of her and to pick up after her. I traded everything in the Dowager House that I could, trying to keep us in food and coal." She laughed shortly. "What I couldn't trade or sell, I burned in the hearth for heat. It was difficult at first, but then my uncle stopped sending even the smallest stipend—" Jane clenched her fists. "Then it became much worse. And Mama couldn't help. Her will was too weak, and her mind."

Ethan listened in horror. "Jane, how old were you?"

She folded the battered handkerchief neatly. "My father died when I was fourteen."

"Good God." Ethan was devastated. He had thought his childhood stark and unloving, but he'd never gone hungry in his life. He could see her, thin little strawberry-blond child, picking up after her mad mother, keeping the poor woman from harm, carrying silver and china and whatnot to trade for food . . .

"Oh, Janet." He pulled her into his arms again, tucking her head beneath his chin. "Oh, poor little Janet."

He could feel her shake her head. She pulled away. "No, I survived. I know how to master hardship." She looked away, biting her lip. "It is madness which frightens me. To fade away like that . . . that I could not bear."

God, what had he done to her? He had thrown her into her own personal hell. If he lived forever, he swore he would never let anyone hurt her again.

Especially not him.

"Yet your mother recovered," Ethan reminded her. "I saw that letter. You weren't writing to a madwoman. She recovered her mind, and you recovered your fortune, did you not?"

Jane looked down at her hands. "I am considered to be quite the heiress now," she said obliquely.

She raised the handkerchief to her eyes again, then smiled damply up at him. "I'm sorry. It is only that I am so very weary . . ."

Gently, careful to be completely brotherly, Ethan

pulled her closer to lay her head upon his shoulder. "Then rest on me. I'll see you safe."

She allowed it, remaining there until he felt her go limp with exhaustion. Only then did he put his arm around her to support her against the jostling of the carriage. As night fell on them, he remained unmoving all the long way back from Moorfields to Mayfair, unwilling to wake her from her peaceful slumber.

When the carriage arrived on his street, he rapped on the trapdoor. "Drive past to the alley in the rear," he told the man. Someone might be watching the house, but Ethan thought they just might be safe enough going in through the back in the dark.

Jane was still quite limp. Ethan didn't rouse her, but lifted her into his arms. When he disembarked in the alley, he was unsurprised to see Jeeves there, holding a lantern with one hand and the garden gate open with the other, without a trace of surprise on his face.

"Uri can take the young lady, sir," Jeeves said, as if he often took delivery of unconscious women in the evening.

Ethan let out a small gust of laughter. "What *did* you do in your former employ, Jeeves—work for a circus?"

Jeeves nodded serenely. "One could say that, sir."

Uri, a giant blond fellow, Cossack by the look of him, stepped forward to take Jane. Ethan strode right past him. "I shall manage."

"I'll have a room made up in a moment, sir," Jeeves said.

"Don't bother," Ethan muttered. "She'll be in mine."

Jeeves's brows shot up at that. "Yes, sir. Shall I make up the sofa in your study for you, sir?"

Ethan didn't answer, for he was already on the stairs. In his chamber, he found a fire in his hearth and his covers already turned down. He turned from the bed and placed Jane gently in the chair.

Jeeves appeared in the doorway with a tray holding a steaming teapot and a plate of biscuits. "Will the young lady be requiring a physician, sir?"

"No." Ethan straightened and gazed down at her. Her hair spilled tangled and lank over the ugly, outdated gown. She had lost a slipper somewhere in the rescue and her bare foot was filthy and scratched.

"She's only weary." Ethan turned. "But I think she would like a b—"

Uri appeared behind Jeeves toting two huge steaming buckets.

"Bath," Ethan finished weakly.

Mrs. Cook bustled in. "Uri, fetch the tub and put it next to the hearth. Mr. Jeeves, would you find something for the miss to change into? I'm set to burn that awful gown, I am." She turned to Ethan, her round face crinkling into a smile. "Good evening, sir. Now, go on. Get out."

Ethan blinked. She waved her apron at him as if she were shooing chickens. "Go on with you now. You didn't think you were going to help her bathe, did you?"

Ethan stumbled back from her domestic vehemence. "No! No, of course not—"

The next thing he knew, he was out in the hall with Jeeves and Uri and the door to his own chamber was firmly shut in his face.

He turned to glare at Jeeves. "So that is Mrs. Cook?"

Jeeves nodded serenely. "Yes, sir. Isn't she a marvel?"

Ethan was in no mood to agree, but even his protectiveness could not argue with the sense of letting a woman tend Jane. Mrs. Cook would cosset her, he could tell. Jane deserved a bit of cosseting right now.

So he bit back his irrational protest and went down to his study for a brandy—but of course, that was locked away from him as well.

He stood in the center of his study without tea, without brandy, and without Jane. "Oh, this is my house all right," he said out loud. "I can tell from the lack of respect."

Finally, Mrs. Cook came to tell him that she had put Jane to bed. "She's a bit worn out, but I got some tea down her and she's sleeping off all her troubles." Then she folded her arms beneath her mighty bosom and glared at him. "What are you going to do about her things?"

Ethan blinked. "What things?"

Mrs. Cook nodded. "That's right. What is she supposed to wear? She can't live in your dressing gown."

Jane was wearing his dressing gown? It would be too big for her, but the green velvet would look very well on her indeed—

Mrs. Cook interrupted his wayward musings with a pointed throat clearing.

"Can you find her some things tomorrow, please? Anything you think will do, just have it charged—" No. He'd forgotten. There would be no charging of feminine things to Diamond House. He shook his head. "I'm sorry, but she'll just have to make do . . . unless you have something to lend to her?"

Mrs. Cook looked at him as if he were not only miserly but mad. Ethan could hardly tell her the truth. She was a respectable woman, a quality servant. She would never put up with such nonsense, nor would Jeeves.

No, he would have to keep it secret for as long as possible that, as of this afternoon, he hadn't a penny to his name.

Jane slept like a woman, not a child. Ethan looked down at her in the light of the single candle he held. There was really no other way to phrase it. She did not curl up small, nor did she fling her limbs out with abandon. She lay in a pose of strength and grace, on her back with one hand at her neck, fingers curled loosely at her collarbone, and the other hand resting across her stomach, atop the green velvet covers. Her face was smooth and still, not at all like her usual vibrant flickering expressions. She looked beautiful and somber, like a Renaissance angel.

The kitten jumped up on the bed with that peculiar bursting suspended-on-a-string way it had. Ethan scooped it up before it could disturb Jane and cupped it to his side. A loud purr erupted from within his hand.

He ought to leave her be. He ought to go down to his made-up sofa in the study and get some rest.

Instead, he pulled the fireside chair closer to the bed and sat down with the kitten in his lap to watch Jane sleep.

The breakfast table groaned with savory treats. Apparently, Mrs. Cook felt that Jane was too thin.

Ethan sat across from her and they both did their best to compliment the cook by making some small dent in the plenty.

Ethan seemed to be trying to hide some of it in his pocket.

Jane was hard-pressed to define the precise cause for the awkward silence between them this morning . . . other than the fact that she'd spent the night in his house, in his bed, and now sat at his breakfast table clad in his dressing gown.

She'd never been in this strange half-intimate, half-wary position before. So she ate silently, hoping that Ethan knew what to do about it.

As the heavy hush stretched on, it became clear that Mr. Ethan Damont hadn't a clue.

Out of the corner of her eye, Jane spotted Ethan's hand again slipping surreptitiously to the pocket of his dressing gown.

"If you don't like kidneys, why do you suffer them at your table?" she asked, unable to bear her own curiosity any longer.

He assumed an innocent expression. "I do like kidneys." He popped a forkful into his mouth and chewed with every sign of enjoyment. "There."

Jane gazed at him suspiciously for a moment, then returned her attention to her own plate.

When his hand slipped once more to his pocket, Jane sighed and put down her fork. "I cannot help it. I've tried my best to ignore it, but I must know." She pushed back her chair before the butler could reach her and strode around the table. Ethan leaned back warily as she approached.

She put out her hand. "Give it to me."

Ethan blinked sweetly up at her. "Why, Lady Jane, I've no idea what you mean!" Jeeves made a tiny choking noise behind her. She ignored him and focused her entire attention on Ethan. Her hand remained extended, unmoving, until finally he let his shoulders slump in resignation.

"Oh, very well." He reached into his pocket. "Here."

He plunked something warm and fuzzy and squirming into her waiting palm. Jane gasped in shock. "Ethan Damont, you should be ashamed!" She shook her head at him furiously. "Giving kidneys to such a baby!" She tucked the kitten protectively under her chin. "That's far too rich a fare! Jeeves, room temperature cream, if you please," she ordered briskly.

"Yes, my lady." Jeeves reappeared almost instantly with a saucer and a small pitcher. Jane made a place next to her plate.

"Oy!" Ethan protested. "That's *my* moggie!"

Jane reluctantly untucked the kitten from her neck. "Well . . ." she said slowly. "Very well, if you promise not to feed her any more ridiculous fare until she is old enough to digest them."

"He," muttered Ethan as he repossessed his kitten. "The proper address is 'he.' His name is Zeus."

"Zeus? *Zeus?*" Jane sank to her chair, one hand over her mouth. Her shoulders shook. Bloody hell, she was laughing at him again. While he waited for her to subside, Ethan stroked one finger over Zeus's head while the kitten made short work of the cream.

Finally, he could bear no more. "Are you quite finished?"

Jane waved a languid hand his way. "Al-almost!" she gasped.

Zeus plunked his tiny bottom on the fine table linen and clumsily began to wash the splashed cream from his face with one tongue-dampened paw.

Jane slid back in her chair, her arms crossed over her aching midriff. "The mighty hunter has returned from the kill. Zeus." She snickered again. "Tell me, is he the one with delusions of grandeur, or is it you?"

Ethan shot her a disgruntled glare. "What's wrong with the name Zeus?"

"Not a thing," she retorted gleefully, "if you're a thirty-stone lion on the veldt."

Ethan folded his arms. "Well, I see no reason to call him 'Precious' or 'Fluffy,' or some other embarrassing title which will someday require him to trounce numerous other toms in order to prove his manhood."

Jane blinked. "Why, Mr. Damont—I do believe I just caught you considering the future!"

Ethan drew back. "I did no such thing!"

"Yes you did. You obtained a cat and named him for who he would be, not who he is. You planned ahead!" She fluttered her lashes and sighed dramatically. "I'm so proud."

Her antics pulled a reluctant laugh from him. "You're obnoxious, my lady."

She simpered at him. "And I feel the same for you, kind sir!"

It was a brief return to the way they had been. Disturbed, Ethan stood and scooped Zeus up by his round, full little tummy and deposited him in the customary pocket. "I hate to interrupt your entertainment," he told Jane. "But I fear I have work to do."

She sobered immediately. "You're not returning to Maywell House?"

He shrugged. "It would raise suspicion if I did not. I'm sure his lordship is awaiting my report."

"How will you explain my escape from the sanitarium?"

"You have not escaped yet, remember? Bess will let herself out when she sees fit." Ethan shrugged. "Even then, I was told to deliver you to the institution. I did so.

Whatever happened after—well, that could hardly be considered my fault, could it?"

"They'll know someone helped me."

"No, they'll *suspect* someone helped you. The guard never looked at my face with all those distractions. I'm sure that I'll come under suspicion, for his lordship has noticed my partiality to you. The best way to allay those suspicions is to continue to behave as I have been—a willing convert to his lordship's cause."

She reached out and caught his hand as he walked past her. The spontaneous gesture stopped him in his tracks. With urgent fingers, she pulled him a step closer. "Take care, Mr. Ethan Damont," she said softly. "I should be very unhappy to lose a friend so recently found."

They had touched more intimately in the past, but that moment, with her ungloved fingers very nearly twining with his—the profound vulnerability of her slender hand in his—made him catch his breath.

Jane felt him cling to her hand for the merest second. Then he smiled slightly, a mere twist of his lips. "And I feel the same for you, kind madam." His low, soft voice was a startling caress.

Then he was gone.

# Chapter Twenty-One

———— ◆ ————

Jeeves was waiting in the hall with his hat and walking stick when Ethan descended the stairs.

"How long will the young lady be staying, sir?"

Ethan halted. "To be honest, Jeeves, I don't know. I haven't been thinking very far ahead lately."

Jeeves nodded. "Yes, sir. Then might I suggest that you make preparations to keep her for some time?"

Ethan blinked at him. "Jeeves, are you suggesting that I *should* keep her?"

"She is a very fine young lady, sir. I'm sure one doesn't come across such a treasure often. One wouldn't want such a lady to get away."

Ethan laughed slightly, shaking his head. "Not matchmaking now, are you, Jeeves?"

"Sir?"

Yet, Jeeves was quite correct on one point. "Ah, Jeeves, it would be wise . . ." He rubbed the back of his neck, not quite sure how to phrase himself. "I think it would be best if the young lady didn't leave the house at all. Could you see to that?"

Jeeves nodded, his eyes as untroubled as a still pond. "I'll tell Uri and Mrs. Cook as well, sir."

Ethan frowned. "Er, yes. All right." Wasn't it a bit appalling how his staff wasn't blinking twice at the notion of keeping a woman prisoner in the house? After all, he didn't pay *that* well.

"Pay" made him think of bills, which made him think of not being able to pay them again.

Oh, well. No matter. In the words of the valiant Bess, "It were worth it."

The breakfast room felt cold when Ethan was gone. Jane pulled her borrowed dressing gown more tightly over her neck. Ethan's scent rose up from the rich velvet—mingled tobacco and sandalwood and Ethan.

When had she become so familiar with the scent of him? When had the touch of his fingers become something rather necessary to her existence?

She wanted him not gone, not on his way to Lord Maywell's house. She would not call that man "uncle" any longer. His betrayal of her cut even more deeply than his turncoat activities—perhaps because loyalty to England was a large and abstract concept but loyalty to family was something one could see and hear and feel when it was gone.

Like the loyalty she'd developed toward her aunt and those five dear, silly girls. Worry for them rose within her, and for Bess, still in the asylum.

Yet, for all her bonds to her relations, most of her worry rose for Ethan, going back into that viper's hold.

The butler came back into the room and took his customary place behind the master's empty chair. She smiled tremulously at him.

"I fear you are stuck with me, Jeeves."

She was surprised at the faint pained expression that passed over his face. "What is it? What did I say?"

He seemed appalled that she had noted anything unusual. "Forgive me, my lady," he said quickly. "It is only that name."

She blinked. "What name? Jeeves? Is that not your name?"

"No, my lady. The master calls me 'Jeeves' out of his own preference for the name."

"He actually renamed you? More to the point, he renamed you Jeeves?"

"Jeeves will do." The butler sighed faintly. "The master does enjoy his little jests."

"I know." Jane snorted. "He calls me 'Lady Pain.' "

"Oh, no, my lady. The master did not dub you thus. You are well-known by that name."

Hurt stabbed her. "I am? But why?"

Jeeves gazed at her evenly. "I daresay it is because of your letters of refusal to your suitors."

Jane frankly gaped. "Letters? *Suitors?*"

"You seem quite taken aback, my lady. Did you not pen some rather pointed letters of refusal to the young gentlemen who sought your hand?"

"My hand?" Jane became aware that she was causing an echo. "Forgive me, Jeeves. It is not that I doubt you—but I have no idea what it is you speak of!"

Jeeves lifted a brow. "I see. Well, then, my lady, it seems someone has been acting on your behalf in this."

"Someone like his lordship," Jane muttered. She found herself furious anew. "I cannot believe—"

Except that she could and did believe. Lord Maywell was capable of virtual murder of a relation. She would not have lasted long in Bedlam, at least not as the person she was. Was not that a more ruthless act than driving away a few young gentlemen in order to keep his hands upon her supposed inheritance?

True—but *Lady Pain*?

A flush of humiliation rose. She pressed both palms to cool her cheeks. "What people must think of me!"

"Oh, I shouldn't worry about that, my lady," Jeeves said calmly. "They'll forget all about it once they learn that you spent the night with the notorious Ethan Damont."

Jane jerked her head up at that. "Jeeves, please! No word must get out—"

Jeeves nodded evenly. "That's better, my lady. What's done is done. His lordship will get his just deserts, I've no doubt."

Jane laughed ruefully. "I suppose that was a bit silly, worrying about my name."

"Yes, my lady. Come, you are chilled. Mrs. Cook has mentioned that she would be glad of a bit of company in the kitchen if you're so inclined."

Mrs. Cook was a cheerful sort, round and bubbly like the pots cooking on her stove. The kitchen was fragrant and warm from the day's baking that sat cooling on a rack.

Jane felt swept away to long ago, when she'd pester the cook in the kitchen and get a hot bun in return for leaving the cook to her work.

Mrs. Cook sat Jane down with a cup of tea and a bun and a sympathetic smile. Jane's eyes burned at the kindness. "Thank you, Mrs. Cook—" She gazed up at the woman in worry. "Is that really your name, or has Mr. Damont renamed you as well?"

"Oh, not to worry, my lady. I've been Sarah Cook for so many years now I've forgot whatever I was before. Husbands, they come and they go."

Jane sipped her tea and gazed at Sarah Cook with wide eyes. "How many husbands have you had, if you don't mind my asking?"

"Oh, no, dearie, I don't mind." Sarah thought for a moment. "Well, let me think . . ."

Jane laughed into her cup. "I beg your pardon," she sputtered.

Unperturbed, Mrs. Cook folded her hands over her midriff. "'Tis a funny thing, to lose track like that. If I'm counting only the ones I took before the cleric . . ."

The story of Mrs. Cook's scandalous and varied romances took up most of the morning, and by the time she'd finished relating the demise of her last "but not least, oh my, no!" spouse, Jane was feeling much more herself.

"I don't suppose you know where I can find some clothing?" As fond as she was becoming of Ethan's dressing gown, she'd prefer not to still be wearing it when he returned. There was something a bit too intimate about lounging about wrapped in his scent all day.

Mrs. Cook's expression went a bit sly. "I did send a message to a friend last night that I had need of a few things . . ."

Ethan strode through the front door of the Liar's Club with a nod to Stubbs, the doorman, and made his way directly up the stairs to the rear of the upper hallway.

Appearing from nowhere in particular, Collis caught up with him as he was searching for the trigger of the secret door.

"Hold on, there, Damont!" Collis came up level to him and lowered his voice. "It's customary to look both ways first, old man."

Ethan obediently looked behind him. There were no public patrons anywhere about this early. That done, he shoved at the secret spot with the heel of his hand.

"Not there." Collis stroked one hand down the crease between two panels. It was nothing but a thin, dark line, but the door clicked obediently. "Now push."

Ethan did, and the door sank in and slid to the side. "Counterweights?"

"Hmm. Installed a hundred years ago. They're a real horror to repair, let me tell you. One can hardly get at them."

"Not interested, Tremayne." They passed through to the Liar side. "Where's the Gentleman?"

"Himself is up in the attic with Herself. No Liars allowed."

Ethan grimaced. "I thought she was expecting?"

Collis laughed. "Just you wait until you're married."

Ethan shook his head. Never. But Collis clapped him on the back and said, "Wait for him in the office. I'll ring the bell to let him know something's come in." He peered at Ethan. "Something has come in, yes?"

Ethan nodded shortly. "I wouldn't be wasting his time."

Collis grinned. "Excellent. He'll be very pleased." He turned away.

Ethan shrugged off the sting of the friendly blow to his shoulder. He didn't care if Etheridge was over the moon. He only wanted this over so that Jane could be safely out of it.

Ethan was in the not-so-secret office for less than a minute before Dalton entered.

"What do you have for me?" Boyish eagerness flashed in those eerie silver eyes and his color was high. Ethan blinked. His lordship looked very nearly human.

"I have the addresses of several pleasure houses near Westminster that are being run for the purpose of squeezing pillow talk out of government officials," Ethan said, handing him the list. "Do keep that quiet until I'm—" *Out of it.* Except that Etheridge didn't want him out of it. "Until I'm more securely in position."

"Maywell has offered you a place?"

"Oh, yes. My job is to be a Liar. He knows all about you lot. He wants me to spy on you for him."

Etheridge's eyes widened. There was some satisfaction in seeing his mightiness gobsmacked with surprise. Ethan felt it only distantly, but found it pleasurable anyway.

"Bloody hell," Etheridge whispered finally. Then his eyes sharpened. "What did he offer you?"

It was an obvious question. His lordship wasn't dim after all. Ethan shrugged. "He offered me his niece's hand in marriage."

Etheridge frowned. "Why in hell would he do that?"

Ethan only gazed at him evenly. "Because I could never attach a lady of that caliber on my own."

Etheridge pursed his lips. "Is she very beautiful? And an heiress, I suppose."

Ethan nodded. "She's the daughter of the ninth Marquis of Wyndham."

"Wyndham?" Something flashed in Etheridge's eyes. "That's . . . interesting."

"I told him I would consider his proposal."

"You did, did you?" Etheridge watched him closely. "That would be quite a conquest."

*Especially for a man like you.* Etheridge didn't say it but Ethan heard it echo clearly in the small room.

Ethan didn't take offense. He no longer cared for Etheridge's opinion. He shook his head. "I'm not interested in marriage," he said flatly.

Surprisingly, Etheridge grinned, a swift friendly flash. "I've heard that before. In fact, I'm quite sure I've said it."

Then he went back to the cool lordly manner of before, to Ethan's relief. "An offer like that could sway many men. So . . . which side are you on now?"

Ethan met his gaze. "England's." Jane's England. Not Maywell's, not the Liars'. The one where a certain bright candle could burn safe and long.

Etheridge nodded shortly. "Is there anything more?"

"No." Ethan donned his finest poker face. "What more would there be?"

The spymaster tilted his head. "I see."

Ethan looked away. Those damned silver eyes . . .

"I'm due at Maywell's now. You wish me to accept his proposal, I take it?"

Etheridge smiled slightly. "I wish you to *appear* to accept it. I'm not sure actually wedding the niece would be wise."

Ethan stood. "I told you." He spread his hands. "I'm not the marrying kind."


As he walked up the steps to Maywell House, Ethan prepared himself. It would be nearly as difficult to lie to the perceptive Lord Maywell as it had been to Lord Etheridge.

"I am bloody tired," Ethan muttered to himself as he stood at the door, "of lords."

He took a deep breath, then lifted the knocker.

Simms answered and regarded Ethan coolly. "His lordship is not receiving at the moment," he informed Ethan. "This evening will be more convenient for him."

Ethan nodded pleasantly. "Then please tell his lordship that I will see him then." He turned on his heel and trotted down the steps once more. "Bloody damned tired," he muttered, "of lords."

Back at Diamond House, Ethan found himself eagerly mounting the steps. He had all the day to be with Jane—

Except that would not be wise. He had already proven several times that he was incapable of being alone with her without someone having their clothing tampered with.

No longer. He had vowed he would not harm her, and ruining her would most definitely count as harm.

Jeeves had the door open, of course, so Ethan breezed by him with a swift greeting. "Is the young lady in her room?"

"Yes, sir. She and the young master wore themselves out with a bit of string earlier. The young lady decided they could both use a nap."

Ethan smiled and climbed the stairs eagerly. He wanted to see Jane—just to see her. He wanted to know how she'd spent her morning and if Zeus had made her laugh. He opened his door, eager to see if she had suffered any ill effects from her ordeal and if she—

Jane sat on his bed with an unconscious Zeus in the dip of her skirts, stretching a sheep-gut penis sheath between her fingers. She looked up at him, her brow furrowed. "I've been at it for an hour," she said, frustration in her tone. "But I cannot fathom what this is for!"

Ethan had been introduced to sheepskin sheaths at the tender age of fourteen by his most memorable tutor, a young man named Luther. Luther had been hired for his pedigree—he was the youngest son of the youngest daughter of the old Earl of Gatwick. To all appearances, Luther was a model young gentleman, courtly of manner and articulate when Ethan's parents were about. It was not until Luther proposed to take Ethan on their first excursion to view the masterworks hanging in the Royal Academy that the young pupil saw his new teacher's true nature. They only bothered to view the nudes.

Luther was as dissolute a wastrel as Ethan had ever met, then or since. Fond of the darkest of pleasures and strongest of spirits, Luther gave Ethan a day and night he'd never forget.

They'd started at one of the more ordinary pleasure houses. Luther had chosen a buxom redhead for himself and a pert blond miss for Ethan. Her name was Tilly and her nature was enthusiastic. Ethan had left her presence feeling quite pleasantly corrupted.

In retrospect, Tilly had been a virtuous nun in comparison to their further adventures. Jessamine was next, with her love of being spanked with the flat of a hairbrush. Then there was Lisette of the black lace stockings and odd-smelling cheroots—she was an expert in the fine art of erotic bondage, she told him, and proceeded to demonstrate for him with another woman.

On it went, that twenty-four-hour fall into sin and depravity. From one house of pleasure to another, with a brief stop at one house of pain, where Ethan learned that even he had his limits.

Still, it was overall a very satisfying experience. In the course of one rotation of the earth, young Ethan Damont experienced more than most men did in a lifetime. Not all of it did he deem repeatable, but some of it he did practice enthusiastically, again and again as his fortunes allowed.

But not accompanied by Luther. All it took was one event of Ethan coming home smelling of smoke and sex and sin for his father to fire Luther immediately. Ethan still remembered his tutor's parting words.

"There are men who live and there are men who simply think about it. Promise me you won't think too much." Luther had picked up his satchel and moved toward the front door, only to turn again. "And wear the damn sheaths, lad. They'll keep you from catching bastards and the pox!"

Ethan had taken that advice to heart. With the aid of very little thinking, a great deal of living, and a rather impressive hoard of sheepskin sheaths, young Ethan Damont had set out to conquer the world—or at least the female portion of the population.

And yet, somehow he had forgotten about the sheaths in the side table drawer when he'd established Jane in his chamber.

"Ah . . . that is a . . ."

She looked up at him, blinking expectantly. "A what?" She looked back down at the flimsy thing in her hands. "It reminds me of sausage casing," she said, shaking her head. "But it is closed at one end and it is very short."

*Short?* "It is not!"

She nodded with great assurance. "Yes it is. Sausage casing is just *yards* long. Haven't you ever made sausage?"

"Ah . . . no," Ethan said faintly. "I cannot say that I have."

Jane laid the pale thing across her fingers, then—oh, God, he was going to die—rubbed it sensually against her cheek. "It is so soft. And flexible." She wiggled it at him. "Is it to keep things in? Things that you don't want to get wet?"

"I need to sit down," Ethan blurted. He bolted for the chair and sat, lifting one ankle over his knee to hide his bulge.

"Are you unwell?" Concern lit her eyes. She scooped the kitten to the pillow and began to clamber off the bed toward him.

It wasn't until then that Ethan noticed what she was wearing—a very fine sprigged day gown that he would swear he had seen somewhere quite recently.

"Where did you find that dress?"

She looked down at herself. "Mrs. Cook brought it to me. It's lovely, isn't it?"

"And where did Mrs. Cook find it?"

Jane sat back on her heels and tilted her head. "I don't know, Ethan. Why don't you ask Mrs. Cook if you're so interested?"

Ethan exhaled, smiling slightly. "I'm sorry, my lady. I'm only concerned that someone might question why I need a fine gown in a very slender size for my cook."

Jane shook her head quickly. "Sarah would never endanger us, Ethan." Then she planted her fists on her hips. "And I thought you were past calling me 'my lady'?"

Ethan looked down at his hands. "I simply think it is wise that while you're here—well, that we keep our distance from each other."

"Why?"

"Well, because—" Ethan sputtered. "Because you could be compromised, that's why!"

Jane's jaw dropped and she gaped at him. Then she blinked. "Um, Ethan . . . I do hate to break the bad news, darling . . . but you've seen more of me than I have. I have spent the night in your house, in your bed. I think I passed 'compromised' several days ago."

Ethan shook his head, vehemently. "No. As long as you remain a maiden, a man would be mad not to overlook those small objections."

She gazed at him, her smile disappearing. "Because I am an heiress, you mean."

"Of course."

She looked away. "Hmm." Seeming rather deflated, she climbed down off the bed and walked to the door. "Uri has made up the guest room for me. I believe I shall rest in there."

She was unhappy about something, but Ethan knew he was right to insist on retaining the formalities. Living with her was going to be hard enough without exchanging tender pet names.

There was one thing—

"My lady?"

She stopped at the doorway and turned eagerly. "Yes?"

Ethan held out his hand. "I believe you have something of mine," he said.

"Really?" She blinked at him innocently. "What would that be?"

Oh, she was evil. Ethan pursed his lips so that he would not laugh. "My sausage casing."

"But I have no sausage casing. Sausage casing is just—"

"Yards long, yes, I know." He wiggled his fingers. "Give me my soft, flexible, thing-to-keep-things-in-so-they-don't-get-wet."

"I'm sure I don't know what you mean." She turned to go out the door. "I wonder if Uri knows what it is . . ." she murmured as if to herself.

"Jane!" Ethan stopped himself and began again. "My lady, may I please have my . . . my . . ." He couldn't do it. He could not stand here in his bedroom in the middle of the day and say "penis sheath" to Lady Jane Pennington. "Oh, what the hell—keep the damned thing!"

She dimpled at him. "I know what it is, Ethan." She leaned forward, her eyes twinkling. "I figured it out," she whispered loudly. "About the time you had to sit down!"

With that, she was gone, dancing lightly down the hall, her laughter trailing after her like music.

# *Chapter Twenty-Two*

❖

The day wore on, with Ethan keeping to himself for fear of giving in to his constant impulse to kiss Jane. He had never done just that, he realized. He had never simply kissed her breathless, with his arms around her but his hands kept to himself.

He wanted to, just once, just to prove that he could—except that he was very much afraid he couldn't.

So he dawdled in his study while Jane charmed his butler, cook, and footman. Even Zeus deserted him, pattering after Jane's bright smile like another willing slave, but with fur.

It occurred to him that he had never seen Jane so lighthearted. It almost seemed as though she felt set free from more than just Bedlam.

Finally, after hearing trilling laughter for just a bit too long from belowstairs, Ethan could not help but make for the kitchen. For the first time since he'd hired Jeeves, no one had brought him his tea, or his news sheets, or emptied his ashes. Of course, he had scarcely been smoking—couldn't bear to, after suffering Maywell's choking cloud—but his servants didn't know that, for none of them had checked!

They were playing a child's game. Uri was blindfolded with what looked to be Ethan's handkerchief, turning circles with his arms outstretched. Mrs. Cook and Jeeves sat in comfort at the kitchen worktable, while Jane danced around Uri, pulling corn husks from where they stuck out from his livery while avoiding Uri's reaching hands.

Ethan scowled. Uri was a handsome bloke, if a lady liked her man oversized and washed out. Of course, Lady Jane Pennington would never trifle with a footman.

Except that she was smiling and laughing and touching Uri . . .

Ethan cleared his throat. Jane went still and Uri yanked off the blindfold. Jeeves and Mrs. Cook looked at him as if he had erupted from the floor like a master-shaped volcano. Rising, they began calling him "sir" and acting like servants again.

Which was precisely what he'd wanted, of course.

With an exasperated noise, he waved his hands. "Oh, just carry on!" He turned and left the kitchen, feeling ridiculous now.

Returning to his study, he decided to practice a few of the moves Feebles had taught him, just to keep his hands busy. There were hours to go yet before he was to report to Maywell, and Ethan was beginning to get nervous. He'd had the impression that his lordship was eager for an answer. Why then had he put Ethan off for an entire day?

Unless somehow Bess had been discovered.

Worry teased at him, making his fingers clumsy. He turned his focus on picking pockets, draping his own surcoat over the back of a chair and trying to pull out his own things without setting the fine wool in motion.

Finally, his focus sharpened and he was able to faultlessly pull several items in succession. He stepped back, much calmer and rather proud. Too bad Jane could not have seen—

Clapping came from behind him. He whirled to see Jane perched on the edge of his desk, applauding him.

"How did you get in here without my knowing?"

She smiled. "I can move very quietly when I wish." She

hopped down and stepped forward. "That was amazing!"

He couldn't help puffing slightly under her praise. God, he was pathetic.

She peered at his coat-and-chair victim. "Can you teach me?"

"Well, it takes a light touch . . ."

With only a few demonstrations, she managed a very nice pull, gleefully swinging his watch before his eyes when he could have sworn that she missed entirely.

She kept practicing as he watched with amusement. It occurred to him that some folk might not see the humor in teaching a highborn lady to pick pockets, but Ethan thought it might be useful. He was a firm believer that there were no useless skills.

Evidently, Lady Jane Pennington felt the same, for she persisted until she could pull a watch and a clip full of pound notes at the same time.

Exultation filled her. "Look! Look, I did it!" Jane exclaimed gleefully. Ethan smiled and clapped, laughing along with her.

Then she stopped, looking down at the stolen loot in her hands. Picking pockets . . . picking locks. "I know what I want to learn," she said, looking up at him. "Teach me to pick a lock. I never want to be put in a cage again."

Ethan nodded. "Of course."

She let out a breath, smiling. Within minutes, they were on their knees before the study door with the picks he had used on the Bedlam cage, doing it over and over until she got the knack of it.

"Of course," Ethan had said, as if she'd asked him to carry a parcel or open a door for her. Most men would demur, would deflect, would disapprove of a lady knowing such a low and unworthy thing.

But Ethan said "Of course." He understood, without needing the tiniest explanation. She could tell him anything.

*So tell him.*

He was about to show her another technique when Jane put her hand over his. "Ethan . . . I need to make a confession."

Ethan wasn't fond of confessions. Confessions inevitably changed things. "I don't want to know," he insisted.

"You need to know," Jane said. "You could be in danger because of me. You need to be armed with all the facts of the case."

Case? Ethan began to feel an uneasy motion in the pit of his stomach. What kind of woman used a word like "case" in that manner?

Jane had seated them both on the sofa there in the study. Close, but not touching. She sat very straight and gazed at him very directly.

Damn. He really hated it when she did that.

"Ethan, do you remember what I told you about my mother?"

He nodded. It had only been last night.

She took a breath. "My mother never recovered her wits. She died nearly a year ago, as deluded as ever."

Ethan felt terrible for her. "I'm sorry," he said gently, putting his hand over hers. "You—"

Letters to Mother. Long, detailed, informative letters to Mother.

"Oh, no!" He jumped up and moved away from her.

She followed him. "Ethan, 'Mother' is a code name—"

Ethan put his hands over his ears. Damn, he'd known she wasn't what she seemed! He'd known, yet he'd ignored his suspicions, even when the truth spat in his face.

Jane came to him and gently pulled his hands down. "Ethan, please listen."

He gave in weakly. He might as well hear it all. They were both going to be dead either way. Maybe she was right. Maybe it was better to be a well-informed corpse.

Jane gazed at him earnestly. " 'Mother' is the code

name of my spymaster. Do you know what a spymaster is, Ethan?"

He grimaced. "I believe I've heard the term."

"I was planted in Lord Maywell's house to report on his everyday activities. I didn't know why at first, but we now know that he is working against the Crown."

"That we do."

She took both his hands in hers. "Ethan, I know you don't truly want to be part of that." She gripped his fingers, her manner urgent. "You can get out, right now, and I can help you."

He began laughing at that, until he collapsed back on the cushions of the sofa. "She's a spy. Oh, God, of course she is." He rolled his head to look at her. "You have no idea how funny that is."

She was sitting very straight, staring at him with a furrowed brow. "There is nothing funny about it. Mother says I'm an excellent operative."

"Operative, she says." Ethan chuckled helplessly. *"Mother!"*

It was funny, until he began to think back over all the lies, all the moments—like in the carriage. Dear God, she wasn't one of *those* female spies was she, like the ones working in Maywell's brothels?

Sobering, Ethan recounted every moment. "What were you doing in the tree?"

"Trying to get closer to some suspicious activity in a room that was supposed to be locked," she said.

That was the night of the ball, and it had been Rose in that locked room.

"What were you doing on the terrace? And near my house?"

She looked down at her hands. "Investigating you."

"And when you kissed me in the carriage?"

"Suborning you," she said very quietly. Then she looked up. "But I really wanted to."

He stared at her. "Are you even really Lady Jane Pennington?"

"Oh, yes." She nodded earnestly. "I am Lord Maywell's niece in truth."

He eyed her distastefully. "You spied on your own family?"

She did not avoid his gaze. "It bothered me, especially after I became fond of Aunt Lottie and the girls. But I did not make Lord Maywell's choices for him. I could only do my best to protect England from him."

Ethan snorted. "With your own two little hands, eh?"

She shook her head. "You're mocking me because you don't understand. I have a mission. Nothing can precede that mission."

He flinched. "A mission. No, you're quite correct. I cannot understand a mission that willingly sacrifices people that you—" He looked away. "That you care for.

"What about being an heiress?"

She shook her head. "I never actually lied about that. It was simply assumed, because I am a noblewoman with expensive gowns—"

His lips quirked cynically. "Provided by Mother."

"Yes." She gazed at him. "You're angry."

He laughed harshly. "What powers of observation you possess! I see now why you were chosen to be a spy."

"Why?"

He gaped at her. "Why? Because—because you're a walking, talking, begowned lie! And . . . you're a lady, and a virgin, and beautiful—"

She narrowed her eyes at him. "So my sole usefulness is to adorn the foot of some lord's table?" She stood, pacing angrily before him. "You're judging me by the same standards that you've been rebelling against all your life." She tossed her head, raising her chin in defiance of his scorn. "I'm not ashamed of one single thing I've done in my life. Can you say the same?"

He rose as well, facing off with her angrily. "Can I say that you have no shame? Oh, decidedly."

She crossed her arms before her. "If I have fallen off some pedestal that you chose to put me on, then I'm sorry. I never asked to be idolized that way."

He opened his mouth to retort with some cutting jibe—and found he had nothing to say. She was quite correct. She had never put herself forward as a model of propriety. Her opinions had more to do with her own value of humanity than any alignment with Society's strictures.

She smiled slightly at his hesitation. "You and I are more alike than you realize, Mr. Damont. You have created your own rules to live by, as I do."

"I do as I please."

"Yes, you do. It pleases you to gamble and cheat anyone you think deserves it. You womanize and scandalize and generally leave a trail of moral havoc wherever you tread." Her smiled warmed. "Yet I also know that it pleases you to save young girls from embarrassment at the dinner table and carry kittens in your pocket and flirt with your cook to make her smile. You cannot even sacrifice a prostitute like Bess to Bedlam, but must make a plan for her own escape." A frown crossed her brow. "That reminds me. What did Bess mean when she said 'It were worth it'?"

Ethan looked away, then back. "You're changing the subject."

She folded her arms. "That I am. And you are trying to change it back. Why?"

He blew out a breath and shrugged casually. "Bess was paid for her time."

"Hmm. Paid well, I imagine." Her eyes narrowed. "Your butler mentioned to me that you've recently come into some considerable wealth. I know for a fact that you cheated Lord Maywell out of a quarter's income. Yet today you could not pay the bill from the fishmonger."

Damn. One day in his house and she was into everything. Ethan tried for another careless shrug. "My fortunes do tend to vary. It is the nature of my occupation."

"Oh, really? So you had a loss at cards? You?"

Damn. It had sounded reasonable until she said it like that. "So I paid Bess off. She can retire, you're free, and I—" *I don't hate myself for putting you in that awful place.*

"How much?"

Cornered, Ethan threw out his hands. "All of it! Every farthing right down to the change in my weskit pocket! What does that prove?"

She looked away, blinking quickly, then looked back at him. "That you are not as bad as you think," she said softly. "And neither am I."

Bloody hell. Her eyes glowed when she looked at him like that. As if he were the tallest, strongest man she had ever seen. He didn't know whether to kiss her or run from her.

She solved his dilemma by stepping closer and placing a tender hand on his cheek. She may as well have clapped him in irons, for he could not move away.

"You could join my spymaster, Ethan. You could be so much more than you let yourself be, if you would only see with your own eyes, not your father's."

That went deep, like a spear to his gut. He gave no sign of it. "I am what I am."

She shook her head sadly. "Life is not a game you have to cheat at to win."

He pulled away from her touch. It took all his strength. "It is when the cards are stacked against you."

She raised a hand to his cheek. He flinched and she lowered it, just as he'd meant her to.

"Ethan, my lost friend . . . don't you see? There are no cards. There is only the coin within you that is of any value. How you choose to spend that, or waste it, is the only challenge that exists."

"Then how do I win?"

"There is no win or lose. There is only the question—what do you want to gain with that coin? What sort of man do you want to be?" She turned then and left the room, leaving the sweet burn of her touch on his skin and a riot of confusion in his chest.

Something tore deep in his chest as he watched her go. "You're wrong there, Janet," he whispered to the wisp of her scent that still clung to the air. "There is definitely a high chance of loss."

The hall clock chimed in the silence. It was time to go back to Maywell's.

As Ethan approached Maywell House for the second time that day, he was definitely feeling like some sort of puppet on a string. It was a sensation he loathed from deep in his past.

This time, however, there was an entire handful of puppet masters twanging his ties.

After he was admitted into the house by a very distracted Simms, the first member of the family he encountered was Serena. She was perched halfway up the stairs, dressed in her night rail and wrapper, sitting on the step with her knees drawn high like the child she still sometimes was.

Her eyes were red and her face was so long that Ethan went to the railing and folded his arms on it casually. "What is the matter, pet?" he asked gently.

Serena shot him an angry glare. "It's all your fault."

"What is, little one?"

She rubbed at her eyes with the back of one hand. The gesture reminded him of Jane.

"You took Jane away," Serena accused.

Ah. Ethan nodded carefully. "Yes, I did. Your father felt she needed treatment." He felt low for feeding Serena such a load of codswallop, but he could hardly tell her the truth, that her father was a—

"I think Papa is doing something wrong," Serena whispered, her round face a mask of pain. "I think maybe Jane was right."

*Damn you, Maywell, for doing this to your family!* Jane was right about that as well. This mess was his lordship's doing, of his own free will.

"Are you bad too?" Serena's heartbroken question cut through Ethan like a knife blade.

"I—I try not to be." It was the best he could give her.

"Can you find Jane? I think she's lost."

Ethan went still. "Lost how? I took her to the hospital myself."

Serena shrugged. "I don't know," she said miserably. "I just heard Papa shouting, 'How could they lose her?', and then the little man came out and asked us all questions." She sniffled. "He wasn't nice at all."

The tears were falling again. Ethan could hardly bear her crumpled little face. "Serena, don't worry. I—I don't know what happened at the hospital, but Jane is very smart. She can take good care of herself."

Serena blinked, as if she had not thought of that. "Jane is clever," she said slowly. "So you think she got herself out and ran away?"

"Ah—" That was a bit too close to the truth for Ethan's comfort. "If she did, do you think she would want you to tell?"

Serena sat up a bit straighter. "No." She sent Ethan a watery smile. "I don't think you're bad," she said shyly. "I think you're very kind."

He ought not to have tried to comfort her. Damn, the tears did it to him every time. "Go on to bed, pet," Ethan said. If she was asleep, she couldn't talk too much.

She nodded and ran up the stairs, her braids flying.

Ethan made his way to Maywell's study unannounced. When he entered, he saw his lordship at his desk with his head in his hands.

"My lord?"

Maywell looked up. "Ah, Damont," he said in weary greeting. "Our problem has bred a litter of brand-new problems."

"Do you mean your niece, my lord?"

Maywell nodded. "I thought she was far too curious from the start, but her coming here was so good for my own daughters. I thought there was no possible way she could have been reached by the opposition. She's been locked away in the north for ten years, for pity's sake!"

Maywell toyed with some papers on his desk. Ethan recognized Jane's concise and complete letter to "Mother."

"I ought to have been reading all her mail," Maywell muttered. "But the first dozen or so were all so bloody boring . . ."

Clever Jane. "What is the problem now, my lord?"

Maywell pursed his lips. "Let me see . . . first, Jane is not in Bedlam any longer. Oh, yes, I know, you delivered her just as I asked. I confirmed that personally. Somehow or other, she escaped. The bloody hospital tried to pawn some poxy ladybird off on me! As if I don't know my own niece!"

His lordship took a breath, visibly calming himself. "And now that I have made inquiries, I find that Jane's mother is deceased and has been for many months." He picked up the letter. "I underestimated her because she was just a girl. That mistake may cost us everything, Damont."

With relief, Ethan realized that Maywell did not suspect him in the least. And why would he? If Ethan had wanted Jane, all he would have had to do was ask.

"My lord, I came this morning to give you my answer. I accept your offer."

Maywell gave a grunt of dry amusement. "I'm sorry, son. It seems that your reward has been returned to her previous owner."

Ethan blinked. "So you believe that she was rescued by

this person she was writing to?" It was an excellent idea. One that Ethan should implement immediately himself. Give Jane back to—

"Mother." Maywell peered up at him. "I would very much like to know who that is, Damont."

"So would I, my lord. So would I."

# Chapter Twenty-Three

Jane sat curled up before the fire in Ethan's room. She had her own room now, of course, but Ethan's room was comfortable and lived in. His books were on the shelves, his razor was on the stand, his cream silk sheets smelled like him . . .

Not that she had been sniffing. She had simply happened to notice it when she'd woken this morning.

Mrs. Cook came bustling in with a tea tray. "There you are, my lady. Why are you sittin' in the dark?"

Jane looked at the motherly woman, missing her mother—both the gently mad one and the one from before. "I think I've made a terrible mistake, Sarah."

Mrs. Cook smiled with sympathy. "There's only two times in a woman's life when she says that, my lady. When she's married the wrong man or when she's let the right one go."

Jane rubbed her face with her hands. "What about when she's driven the right one away?"

Sarah patted her on the shoulder. "That counts too, love." Jane leaned into that sympathy for a moment. Then Mrs. Cook straightened briskly. "So—what are we goin' to do to drive him back?"

Jane wrapped her arms around herself. "I don't know. He insists on treating me like a lady."

"Oh, my. That is bad." Mrs. Cook hissed thoughtfully between her teeth. "Have you tried touching his face? That works a treat."

Jane nodded.

"Hmm. Have you tried kissing him?"

"Yes."

Mrs. Cook pursed her lips. "Well, then. I'd say it's high time to bring out the cannon, my lady."

Ethan left Maywell's without much useful information for the Liars but feeling reassured that his lordship had no idea that Jane was ensconced in Diamond House.

He had time, it seemed. Time to get Jane to tell him who her contact was. She'd avoided that before, he'd noticed. If he could get her back into the safety of her own fold, then he would not have to worry about Maywell or the Liars taking her away.

He wondered if he ought to tell Etheridge that there was a rival spy network in London? What would Dalton make of that? He might already know.

Yet, somehow Ethan didn't think so. Jane acted as though there were no one else in the world who could stop Maywell but her. Etheridge had virtually said the same about Ethan. If the two spymasters were on speaking terms, then surely they would be sharing information?

Bloody black-and-white thinking—it was forever biting those blokes in the arse.

When the hack reached Diamond House, Ethan hopped briskly out, only to see his doorway dark and unwelcoming. No Jeeves?

His gut went to ice. Then he reminded himself of that afternoon's singular lack of tea and news sheet. Likely it was only Jane, distracting his servants with a game of hide-and-seek.

Except that when he entered, the house was dark and far too silent. Servants were always making noise—steps on the back stairs, footfalls in the halls, Mrs. Cook's cheerful humming, Uri's tuneless version . . .

Swiftly, warily, Ethan checked every room on the ground floor. No one. Belowstairs was just as empty.

He'd been wrong, oh, God, he'd been so stupid and wrong. Maywell had come, or the "little man"—whoever that was—had come and cut his servants' throats and taken his Jane away.

Ethan grabbed a great carving implement from the knife block in the kitchen. He climbed the stairs with soft, silent steps. The upper hall was quiet and dark—

But for the slight glow shining from beneath his bed-chamber door.

Jane? Full of fear, he burst through his own door with an outraged roar.

Only to find the scene set for romance, with a fire glowing on the hearth, flower petals on the counterpane, and one very lovely Lady Jane Pennington asleep in his bed.

Oh, thank God! He ran to the bed and swept her into his arms. "Oh, Janet, I thought—"

She blinked sleepily at him and draped one soft arm about his neck. "Ethan? I'm sorry, I fell asleep."

Thinking of his amateurish roaring entrance, Ethan shook his head, laughing. "Janet, you sleep like the dead."

She smiled sweetly and twined the other bare arm about his neck. "How do you know?"

Her skin was warm against his neck . . . and his hands? He looked down.

Abruptly all the blood left his brain to head to other more useful parts.

Jane was completely naked in his arms.

Ethan forgot to breathe for one long sensuous moment. He spread his hands open on her bare back, pressing her close while he took in her warm, womanly scent. She responded like a sleepy cat, curling into the shape of him, melting into him. God, she felt good—

*No. I vowed never to harm her.*

He pulled back from her, but her soft sleepy embrace suddenly turned to iron. In his urgency, Ethan lost his balance and fell back onto the carpet. Since Jane didn't let go, this had the added complication of pulling her nude body free of the covers in order to plaster it all over his on the floor.

"Jane, no," he gasped. "This is—we cannot—"

She writhed on top of him, fulfilling half a dozen fantasies on the spot.

"No." It took all his will and most of his strength to unwrap himself, yet somehow he managed it. Leaving her tumbled on the carpet, he scrambled to his feet and backed away.

She squeaked and grabbed the counterpane to pull over her body, but not before his memory was branded forever with the sight of her bare, slender beauty lit by the fire's glow. He shut his eyes tight. *I will not harm her. I will not harm her.*

"Well, I'm bloody well going to harm *you*," he heard her say with vast exasperation.

He covered his face with his hands. He could not let her disarm him now. She was going back to her spymaster in the same condition in which she'd left: alive, untouched—well, mostly—and unharmed.

"What have you done with my staff?" he asked Jane.

He heard her snort derisively. "Well, I haven't sliced their throats and dumped them in the Thames, if that's what you're wondering." Her voice was close now. She was standing next to him, probably still wearing nothing but green velvet counterpane.

He kept his eyes clenched shut. "I might, since you're implying they left willingly."

"They took a holiday, that's all. They'll be back tomorrow."

"They had best not return. They're sacked."

She laughed at him. "They are not."

No, they weren't. One didn't sack a cook of Sarah's

quality without proof of poisoning first. Even then, Ethan would probably give her three or four opportunities to reform.

He could smell her scent. She was very close. "My lady, please go back to your room."

"Why?"

"Because you're too good for me," he said desperately. "I'll only bring you down, you must know that."

She was very quiet for a moment. He almost thought she had already left when he heard her whisper.

"I'm beginning to think that you're too good for me."

The stark loneliness in her voice was too much for him. He lowered his hands, but she was gone.

It was very late when Jane crept back into Ethan's room. From the looks of things, Ethan had been wrestling with temptation.

That or a bear.

The room was nearly dark but for the glow from the coals. There was enough light to see the shattered glass, the empty brandy decanter, and Ethan's naked form sprawled on the mussed coverlet.

He lay face up, with one arm stretched up over his head and the other lying lax across his flat stomach. It looked as though his last conscious act had been to pull a corner of the silk bedcover across his midsection before he'd fallen into a brandy-laced sleep.

There was no doubt he was naked beneath, however, for the coverlet revealed a slit of naked hip that glowed golden against the cream silk. Jane wrapped both hands around the bedpost and leaned her head against the cool wood, filling her eyes with unguarded, peaceful Ethan.

Where was his charming façade now? Where was his defense of wicked humor? His face was handsomer without the knowing twist of lips and the jaded gleam in his eyes. He looked younger and more hopeful somehow, as if he had yet to see his dreams defeated.

Jane's heart ached to see the defenseless arch of his exposed neck and the way his lax fingers curled hopefully around nothing but air. Ethan asleep was tragic and superb—an unblooded warrior still dreaming, still eager to fight the honorable battles of life.

She stepped closer, letting one hand slide from the bedpost to trail along the cream silk. Her fingers came across the fold of coverlet that hid the rest of him from her view. She toyed with it, desperately curious but unwilling to unveil him without his consent. It would not be fair, would it, to view him naked and defenseless while she was still covered?

Almost without thought, her other hand went to the knot of her own belted wrapper. The cord seemed to undo itself under her fingers. The silk slid from her shoulders to the floor with a mere whisper of sound. She wore nothing beneath.

Fair was fair. She gave the coverlet a tiny tug. It slid partway to reveal more rippled stomach muscle and the top of a powerful thigh. She gave it another pull to show her the trail of dark hair that arrowed down his body to parts most intriguing, but there the cover stopped, held down by the hand that rested across it.

Jane studied that hand for a long moment. Would he wake if she touched him to move that hand? Furthermore, would that be truly fair, when he was not touching her in equal amount?

Feeling very much that she was stepping across a line that could never be uncrossed, Jane placed one bare knee upon the featherbed, then the other. She sat back on her heels and considered the fact that she was in bed with Ethan—naked Ethan at that.

She was compromised by anyone's reckoning now, wasn't she?

So why did this feel anything but dishonorable, anything but right and true and perfect?

The answer was simple. Because this was Ethan, and she loved him.

She loved Ethan Damont, shady gambler and rogue of the highest order, champion flirt and man without means that he did not cheat for. She smiled. He was everything she'd been brought up to avoid and disdain—yet there was no man she knew whom she esteemed more.

"You think you are so very worthless, my love," she whispered. "And yet you blaze like your name—the Diamond."

A wave of powerful emotion swept her and she reached for his hand. Not to move it aside, not to satisfy her curiosity, but to gently entwine her fingers with his and to let the heat of his palm warm hers. The heat seeped into her and ran through her veins, filling her with peace and assurance.

Yet, how could she get past Ethan's stubborn insistence that she be preserved for—for whom? For some pasty-faced young lord, or worse, some pasty-faced old lord? For some idiot who constantly gambled and *didn't* win?

How could she get past his defenses? How could she make him hers? If she made him give in by seducing him, then she would only make him more sure of his own bad nature.

She had to allow him to be good and honorable on this front, or she would shatter the new man he was trying to be.

She could let him be, let him say no. She could accept his choice and then when everything was over—let him go?

That was simply not an option she was willing to consider.

*What about taking him against his own stubborn will?*

If Ethan were bound, then he'd have no choice. If he had no choice, he could not blame himself for ruining her.

If she took away his chance to protest—was that not what he truly wanted?

She considered the sash from her wrapper. It was quite long. The tassels at the end of the cord went nearly to the floor. Long enough to bind one hand, go behind the head-board, and come down to bind the other.

Before she could think better of her scandalous plan, she pulled it from the wrapper where it lay on the floor. The cord was twisted silk and would bind most comfort-ably, she was sure. She made a sliding loop like the one she once used to hobble the old mare while she cleaned the stable. Like the mare, Ethan was probably best caught by surprise, so Jane left the loop loose around his wrist while she passed the cord behind the head of the bed, then pulled it carefully back through.

His other hand was not resting so high on the bed. Jane did not want to risk moving it herself. Looking around, she spotted a stand of peacock feathers decorating the mantel. She plucked one from the display and used it to tickle Ethan just below his elbow. His response was just what she'd hoped for—he restlessly shifted his arm higher, bringing his wrist into range of her cord. She slipped the other loop over that hand and eased the knot down to bind his wrist.

Moving quickly, she trotted around the bed to do the same to his other wrist. There. He was bound, forced to hear her out.

What she had not expected was her own response to seeing him thus, naked and vulnerable before her. A thrill of excitement went through her. Ethan kept still for her exploration and pleasure? It was a secret dream she'd not even realized she had.

Still holding the jewel-toned peacock feather in her hand, Jane clambered aboard Ethan's bed—then, on a whim, clambered aboard Ethan himself.

He shifted sleepily beneath her, his hips rising to grind

gently on her center. A shock of pleasure went through her. Scandalous images flashed across her mind.

She could ride astride him like in the carriage—dear Lord, what a thought!

She wanted him to shift again. She used the feather as a braver surrogate to trace a path down that trail of fine hairs across his belly leading beneath the covers. She was rewarded by another writhing shift of him beneath her.

Emboldened, she let the feather caress his powerful chest and trace the muscles twining up his raised arms. He sleepily tried to move his arm away until it met the resistance of the cord.

Ethan woke abruptly, alarm singing through his body.

He tried to move, only to find himself bound and pinned by a slight weight. Blinking rapidly, he tried to focus on the shape above him. Someone—

"Shh," said a soft voice. "Be still."

"Jane?" Incredulous, he let himself fall back on the pillows. While it was a relief to find that he wasn't being murdered in his bed, he felt an entirely new sense of foreboding. "Jane, what goes on here?"

To his astonishment, she waved a peacock feather at him. He shook his head. This was one of the stranger positions he'd woken to in his life. Then he focused his attention on Jane herself and the breath left his body. She sat astride him, her straight ladylike posture adding a bizarre flavor to the fact that her hair hung loose over her naked body. He could clearly see from the valley between her breasts down to where her nest nuzzled against his own covered groin. He found himself distracted by the charming way her navel crowned the slight swell of her soft female belly—

Then he came back to himself. "What the bloody hell is going on here?"

His roar echoed through the house. Excellent. Jeeves would come running. Thank God for interfering servants. He'd found a use for them at last.

Except that no one came. Not Jeeves, not Cook, not even that dour bloke, Uri.

Then he remembered. She'd sent them away.

She gave him a little slap with the feather. "They are not coming."

Ethan snapped at the irritating thing. "Stop that."

She smiled slightly. A dangerous gleam appeared in her eye. "I won't. And you cannot make me."

Ethan swallowed. "Jane, this is by far the worst idea you have ever had."

She raised the feather to tap it meditatively against her chin. "I don't think so. I think I'm brilliant. I have you right where I want you."

He shook his head. "Jane, you don't want me."

She stroked the feather down his stomach, tickling the fine hairs that grew there. "Yes I do."

"It won't be worth it, Janet. Yes, we could give each other a night of pleasure, I won't deny that. But nothing would come of it but your own ruin. I'm not a gentleman, remember? If I ruin a woman, she stays ruined."

She tilted her head curiously. "Have you ever ruined a woman?"

"Of course I have!" He hadn't actually, but this was no time to appear honorable. "I've broken more reputations than I can remember!"

"Oh, really?" She looked impressed. "Virgins strewn by the side of the road, is it?" She smiled meaningfully. "Good. Then you'll be very practiced at it." The feather began to get a bit close to home. Ethan panicked.

"Jane, I don't love you," he blurted. "You bore me! In fact, I can barely look at you!"

"Oh?" She considered that for a moment. He had hopes that she'd be hurt and back away from this horrendous plan. Then she smiled and he knew the game was up.

"If you can't look at me, then I suppose there's no need for me to stay covered." She pushed her long hair back over her shoulders, leaving her bared in all her elegant, graceful glory.

She was the goddess Diana, the huntress, and he was her prey. Ethan knew he was the most fortunate man on earth at this moment. She whisked the covers away.

And she was the most doomed woman in the world.

# Chapter Twenty-Four

"Jane, stop this!" Ethan pulled against his bindings, but the clever minx had made the cord so that it tightened if he struggled. He fought them anyway, until the bed frame creaked in protest and the veins in his arms stood out. Jane merely rode him out, sitting peacefully astride him until he tired. Finally, he lay back, gasping but not defeated. He had to save her from herself!

Then he saw what she had in her hand. The sheepskin sheath caught the firelight behind its filmy translucence. Yet there was no need to worry. She'd never get the trick of rolling it onto him without practice.

She was regarding it contemplatively. "If this were a stocking that I was putting on . . ."

Ah. Well, that might very well count as practice. He watched with mounting horror as she rolled it rather expertly into a stiff disc. She displayed it proudly. "There, what do you think?"

"I think you should stop this n—" His voice left him with a gasp as she wrapped her fingers round his cock and gently squeezed.

"I've been admiring this tonight," she said thoughtfully. "I liked it quite a bit before, but now I find it much more interesting."

Ethan gritted his teeth, straining backward in an effort

to control his growing erection. "No, Jane. I won't—"

She stroked her hand up and down. "Do you like that? Does it feel good?" Her voice was soft and mesmerizing. He recognized the tone instantly as the one he'd used on her in the carriage.

Oh, God, he was going to pay for that now. And he *still* wasn't able to touch her!

Jane wrapped her hand firmly around Ethan's staff, enjoying the silk-over-steel feel of it. His body quivered as his member jumped in her grasp. "What does that feel like?" She didn't really expect an answer and she didn't get one.

If the sheath was a stocking and his staff was a leg . . .

The flexible cover rolled neatly down over Ethan's staff. Jane realized a bit too late that she ought to have waited. Now she could not directly feel his skin, nor could he directly feel her touch.

Unfortunately, her hands were shaking badly now. The feel of him in her grasp, the way his straining body looked in the fire's glow . . . she was becoming more aroused by the moment herself.

"If you can't feel through that, I suppose I'm going to have to touch you in other places . . ."

Leaving his encased staff lying stiffly against his stomach, she moved up his body to his chest. "My breasts are tingling," she whispered to him. He clenched his eyes shut and turned away, but his breathing quickened. "Do you remember how you made me touch myself for you?"

A low, primitive groan came from deep in his chest. Jane leaned over him, using all the words and intonations he had used on her. "All I wanted was your touch that night . . . all I wanted was for you to feel how hard my nipples had become." She let her breasts trail across his bare chest. The sensation of his chest hair against her rigid nipples made her whimper even as he gasped wordlessly.

He'd stopped pulling at his bonds, she noticed. She pressed her breasts harder to his chest, straddling him again to make better contact.

His staff leaped beneath her, nearly slipping into her dampened center. The sensation made her freeze above him as the tiny shocks went coursing through her.

"You aren't fighting anymore, darling. Do you want me now?"

His jaw worked, but he didn't answer. Yet his hips rotated upward, pressing him closer to her. Experimentally, she reached between them and grasped him in her hand. She wanted to touch herself again, the way she had before, but he wasn't watching now.

If he would not open his eyes, then she would touch herself with him, so he could feel it instead.

Using his pulsing rigid staff instead of her own fingers, she began to press and rotate the thickened head against her pleasure spot. Her own slickness soon coated his staff and her own shaking fingers, until her grip began to slide rather wildly as she drove herself higher.

Lost in pleasure, she took a moment to realize Ethan was hoarsely calling her name. "Janet, oh God, Janet—ride me! Please, please, take me in—"

Half mad with arousal, halfway to her own satisfaction, Jane thoughtlessly obeyed. With one motion, she positioned him at her slit and began to drive her body down on his long, thick staff without a care for her own virginity.

"No!" Ethan's urgent cry just barely reached her in time. She halted, breathless, nearly crying with need.

"No?" she gasped.

"Oh, yes," he growled. "But slowly, darling. Go carefully."

Jane obeyed, slipping the thick round head just slightly into herself. Even that short length began to stretch her with a burning ache.

"Slowly," he breathed into her hair, for she was bent low over him. "Don't hurry. You'll feel it when you're ready for more of me."

Now that she had him partially within her, she realized

how daunting his size truly was. She wasn't frightened, nor would she have stopped if Napoleon himself had burst through the door, but she did wish she dared to untie him so she could feel his strong arms about her.

No. Stubborn, so-sure-he-was-right man would stop. He would get up and leave her like this, swollen and aching, just to save her for some imaginary highborn husband she would never want to have.

She pressed him another inch within her. Gasping, she buried her face into his neck. He turned his head to kiss her hair. "Rise up and down," he whispered. "It will ease me in."

She did as she was told, bracing her hands on his broad, muscled chest. Every stroke stretched her further, even as every withdrawal slickened and soothed her.

Then he could enter her no further. "Ah, Ethan," she whispered. "I think I'm full."

His breathless laugh rumbled up through her body as well. "No, sweeting. This is the part where I break your maidenhead."

She swallowed. It wasn't alarming, precisely, but he did seem to go on and on. "What do I do?"

"First, hold very still."

She braced herself above him.

"Now, kiss me."

Oddly, she had not kissed him yet. She lowered her lips to his in a soft caress—

He surged upward in a sudden thrust of his hips.

Jane felt him burst through, driving deep within her. She cried out, just a small cry that he took into his own mouth.

He kissed her softly. "Shh, shh. Now relax for a moment. The pain will ease—"

She shook her head. She felt soft and liquid, wrapped around his thickness. "There is no pain. I want to—" She rose and fell on him, again and again.

It burned, it blazed, it sent wracking shudders through

her until she could hardly continue. She heard Ethan crying out her name, his voice hoarse with passion.

She felt that precipice approach, the one he'd led her to before. There was some pain now, just a hint of ache behind the pleasure, but she knew she must reach the edge soon . . .

Ethan cried out and surged beneath her, inside her. He swelled and throbbed, adding the last bit of pressure she had needed—

She cried out as she flung them both over the edge, unable to stop her rise and fall, unable to do anything but call her lover's name, her love's name—

*"Ethan!"*

Jane awoke to the feel of something warm and damp between her thighs. She roused and opened her eyes to find Ethan sitting next to her, tending to her with a cloth.

She smiled sleepily at him. "Hello, darling."

He did not smile back. "Hello, my lady."

She tried to sit up, to reach for him—

Only to find that she was the one now bound with silken cord.

She eyed her beloved with wary eyes. "Ethan, what is this?" Something was wrong.

He glanced up, then went back to his task. "I would think you'd recognize the technique."

His touch was infinitely tender as the cloth cleaned and soothed her.

"I'm sorry, Ethan—"

He went still. "No you aren't."

She hesitated, aware that this was a time for the truth. "No, I must confess that I am not. Not for loving you, or making love to you. I am happy. I am only sorry that you cannot be happy as well."

"The only thing I am happy about is that you had the sense to use the sheath," he said. "At least there will be no bastards."

She blinked. "Oh, is that what it is for?" If she'd known, she certainly wouldn't have used it.

He stared at her. "What did you think it was for?"

She shrugged with difficulty, since her hands were bound above her. "I thought it was for pleasure."

"No." He looked away. "It actually feels a bit better without it."

Jane's jaw dropped. "It gets *better*?"

He let out a single gust of helpless laughter and dropped his head into his hands. "My lady, what am I going to do with you?"

Jane frowned. What was his meaning? "I want you to make love to me," she said. "I want to stay in your arms until I die of it."

He nodded, gazing at her with dark, hooded eyes. "That, my lady, I can provide."

He lowered his mouth to her.

Jane started at the first touch of his lips there. Shock rippled through her. She pulled at her bonds. What was this—this outrageous—

His tongue slipped through to her pleasure spot and all coherent thought left her mind.

Soft, slippery tongue, circling over and around, then back, then again. He created suction, making her entire body convulse. Her thighs opened, spreading her helplessly before him, open and wet and exposed for him—and then he made her forget she ever had any concept of shame.

She writhed and bucked and mouthed helpless sounds as he tortured her beautifully with his tongue, lips, and teeth. The sensations consumed her, devoured her, made her forget everything but the wild untamed ecstasy of his kiss on her.

"Oh, dear God! Please, Ethan! Oh, please, I need you so!"

He went very still, his head still bowed over her. She could see his bare chest heaving and the sheen of perspiration that told her he wanted her just as much. He was nearly trembling with it. The sight of his muscled, rippling arms tensing as he hesitated—how she loved his chest, his arms, his shoulders. Soon he would move up her body, release her from her bonds, and hold her tightly in those corded arms while he drove himself into her—

"The sheath—" His words were a gasp of need.

Jane tossed her head on the pillow. "Forget the sheath! I want you. I want your child and your name!"

He froze in the act of reaching for the night table drawer.

*"No."*

At first that breathless pained word made no sense to her. Then, as he moved away from her slowly, as if every movement caused him physical pain, she drew in a disbelieving breath.

"No?"

"No." He rose from the bed and stood with one arm braced on the bedpost as he visibly fought for breath and control. His naked back gleamed. His snugly fitted black breeches outlined his body, a body made to love hers. Jane simply couldn't understand.

"But . . . I . . . I need you so, Ethan," she gasped, too breathless and deprived to speak. "P-please, come back."

He whirled to glare down on her then. Jane drew back in shock. The dark blaze in his eyes was something she'd never seen before. He looked wild, furious, and deathly, blackly amused.

"She begs." He wiped one arm across his brow. "I begged, too, I think. Little good it did me."

A bleak chill began to creep through Jane. She turned her head, unable to meet that gaze. Her vision blurred behind a hot wash of tears. She pulled against her bonds. "Free me," she demanded, her voice thick. "Free me at once."

"Free yourself, Lady Jane," he said flatly. "You're only trapped in a bit of twist. A child could figure it out."

Jane realized that he was quite correct. A mere swivel-
ing of her wrist untwisted the loop of cord enough for
her to slip each hand free. She hadn't truly been bound
at all.

She slid from the other side of the great bed, towing
one of the cream silk sheets to cover herself. She fumbled
with her underthings and drew her gown over her head,
but could not manage the buttons. Her hands were shaking from arousal and fear that she had done something
that Ethan would never be able to forgive.

Somehow, she had struck him to the core—a deadly
blow, by the look in his hot, dark eyes.

When she was as decent and armored by her clothing
as she could be, she took a breath and turned back to him.

He was standing with his back to her, still half-naked,
at the window staring out into the night. One hand was
braced on the embrasure, the other held a nearly empty
glass of brandy. As she watched, he tossed the last swal-
low back angrily, then tossed the glass carelessly to the
cushion beneath the window. It bounced from the stiff
horsehair and fell to the floor with a shrill crack. The
noise made Jane's raw nerves jump.

"Oh, look," Ethan said without a shred of concern in
his voice. "I broke it."

Jane couldn't breathe. She felt as if an iron band were
wrapped about her ribs, constraining them like barrel
staves. She swallowed. "Ethan—" she began.

He turned his head, putting his expressionless profile
against the night. "Why would you think we could
marry?"

"I thought—I hoped—I thought if I overcame your objections, that . . ." She trailed off.

"That what? That I would miraculously transform into
the gentleman that I am not and drop to one knee?"

Jane stepped forward. "No! No, it was nothing like
that! Ethan, please don't think—"

He turned then. Never had she seen such blank fury in his eyes. "Then what was it, Jane? What did you hope to accomplish here tonight?"

"I hoped . . . I hoped you would . . ." She shrugged helplessly. "I hoped you would allow me in."

He laughed darkly, shaking his head. "There is no 'in,' Jane. Even if there was, there would be nothing of value to you there. You persist in fooling yourself."

"Don't say that, Ethan! I love you! I know that you care for me, that you love—"

"Dear God, Jane—*leave me be*!" His tormented howl echoed in the silent house. Jane recoiled.

His breath came harshly as he visibly forced himself to calm. He ran a frustrated hand through his hair, then raised his head to gaze at her levelly. "Lady Jane, I don't know how to be more clear."

Jane backed away a step. "Ethan, don't—"

He straightened completely, his expression calm and his gaze even. "I don't love you, Jane. I never will. Not now. Not ever."

Jane felt her soul curling and dying around the edges. His gaze, his manner—he was absolutely convincing. Could it be that he truly didn't love her?

The pain took her breath away. She wanted to turn and run from the room, from the house, from his blank, vaguely pitying gaze. Yet she could not stop fighting.

"You're lying, Ethan." She fought to sound as sure as she desperately needed to be.

He shook his head slowly, his gaze never leaving hers. "I have never lied to you. I never led you to believe that I would play a part in the saga of Lady Jane."

Jane gave a damp, angry laugh. "No, you've never lied to me. You have only lied to yourself!"

"Meaning?"

She looked away, drew a broken breath, then met his eyes once more. "You tell yourself that you don't want more. You tell yourself that the life you have carved out for yourself is all you want—or perhaps that it is all you deserve, or are allowed—"

He reacted, finally, drawing back in denial. "You have no idea what you're talking about."

Jane wiped a hand across her face, flinging her tears away angrily. "I know you, Ethan Damont. I know that within you is trapped a man who wants so much more from this world that he is fair to dying from it!"

He paled then, the darkness in his eyes nearly frightening. She saw one emotion chase another through that darkness. Hope and aching need fled before killing self-loathing and denial.

Her heart broke into tiny china chips when she saw denial take the fore.

"You simply refuse to see it, don't you, Lady Jane? You cannot force this. You cannot wave your elegant, aristocratic hand and command this into being. All the stubborn will in the world will not overcome the fact that *I don't love you.*"

The cruelty of it struck her like a lash, but she would not fail him now, now when he needed her the most. The man within could not—would not even try to—prevail unless she convinced him that nothing could drive her away. The only way to do that was to match his every bitter blow with love.

She met his gaze with level and relentless compassion. "Perhaps you don't love me." She lifted her chin and squared off against the enemy. "But I am not going anywhere. I am staying right here. So you're just going to have to go on pretending that it's me you do not love."

His eyes flared. "Very well. I will." He approached her, his step slow and implacable. Hot hard hands gripped her shoulders and he drew her to him. It was like leaning into a furnace of pain and contradiction. His body wanted her again, she could feel it. His soul cried out for her, she could see it behind the demon in his eyes. But his face—his beautiful dark angel face—was ravaged by anger and disbelief. He had a formidable will, her Ethan. Her love was more so.

Now Jane would finally grasp that he was not the man she thought him. He was not good. He was not honorable. He was *not* worthy.

When he crushed her to him and drove his mouth down on hers, she did not fight him or struggle against the discomfort he was causing her. She only very slowly, very gently ran her hands up his straining arms and across his shoulders, until she cupped his jaw softly in her palms. When he would let her, she kissed him back. When he would not, she suffered his bruising kiss unresisting. The fire began to build within her even so, astonishing her with its heat. It could not be that she enjoyed such treatment!

Yet there was no denying the effect his touch had on her, even such angry caresses. Perhaps it was because she could feel the need behind his bruising grip on her bottom, she could feel the ache within him as he rubbed his groin crudely against her.

"Do what you will," Jane said, gasping as his hands wrapped over her aching breasts. She covered his hot hands softly with her own. "I will always be here."

He flinched, the first crack in the wall he'd built so well about himself. Softly she put her hands on his cheeks and turned his gaze back to meet hers. The crazed shell of his certainty was shifting, breaking, like a frozen river in spring. Soon he would flow freely into her arms. She could not give up now.

She gazed into his eyes with all the force she could muster against her own hurt and trembling desire. "I will always be here," she repeated slowly. *"Always."*

He almost gave in. She could see the awe and faith flare behind his eyes, like a new spark.

Thudding footsteps sounded in the hall. They both turned in astonishment as, a fraction of a second later, the door crashed in under the force of several burly men.

Ethan thrust Jane behind him, crouching in a fighting stance though he had no chance against so many.

# Chapter Twenty-Five

———————————— ◈ ————————————

Ethan stood bound and bloodied, held by two of Lord Maywell's least injured flunkies. Jane was held in the grasp of another who bore battle scars of his own. They'd been forcibly dressed as well.

Serena, it seemed, had reassured her mother, who in turn had reassured her fretting husband.

Maywell paced before them. "You dared to touch a lady—ruin a lady, at that. You've always reached too high, Damont. This time you lost your footing and fell."

Ethan gazed narrowly at Maywell. "So all your fine talk of equality was nonsense. I should be surprised—but I'm not. You like your privileges just fine, don't you?"

Maywell glared. "Ideology is one thing. Presumption is something else altogether." He gestured to his men to bring Ethan along. "You want so badly to live like a gentleman, Damont. I'm going to give you the chance to die like one. A duel at sunrise in Hyde Park. How is that for an aristocratic end?"

"No!" Jane struggled wildly in the hands of her captors. Ethan wanted to tell her not to bother but she wasn't looking at him. She was staring at her uncle, incredulity written all over her face. "Why? You care naught for me. Why should you give a damn if I take a lover?"

Maywell hooked his walking stick over his elbow and

tugged his cravat straight, a baffling glint of panic in his eyes. "A lady would have suffered in Bedlam until the day she died, rather than be unchaste," he said sadly. He cast Jane a look of pity. "The inheritance is a sham, isn't it? There was no more in that account than my daughters could go through in one day's shopping. Do you think anyone will take you now, an impoverished, ruined lady? Good God, girl! Don't be so naïve. Do you think this cit gives a damn about you?"

Jane didn't so much as glance Ethan's way. "He loves me. Don't bother trying to convince me otherwise. If he couldn't, you've not a chance in hell."

Maywell tsked. "Such language. Oh, well. I suppose it isn't your fault. I'm told that the mad have no control over their tongues. You've been slipping away from us for a while now, haven't you, dear? This penchant for unchaste behavior. Then, running away from your home and loved ones?"

Jane flinched. "You threw us together, remember?"

Maywell shook his head. "A true lady would not have given up her virtue in less than a week! You really are a brazen little thing, aren't you?" He gestured his men to bind her hands behind her back. "So it's back to Bedlam for you, Jane. I've put them on notice that they're not to permit another escape. They've informed me that they have the means to chain their more recalcitrant inmates. Of course, you have Damont here to thank for Bedlam—that was his idea."

Jane blinked. The flush of anger on her face paled so abruptly that it hurt Ethan to see it. She looked at him, finally, staring at him as if he were a stranger—as if he'd been moved from her side to face her across that endless gulf once again.

He closed his eyes. "Maywell, you're a vicious bastard."

Maywell sighed. "Just like you, Damont. Two of a kind, remember?"

Ethan tilted his head, giving Maywell a baleful look. "You might want to remember that, my lord."

Maywell stiffened, then gestured sharply. The henchmen pushed them out of the bedchamber and out of the empty house.

Hyde Park was perfectly quiet but for the condensing fog dripping from the trees. The carriage wheels crunched over the gravel and the horses' tack jingled loudly in the silence. There was no one about, forcing Jane to give up on her half-formed plan of shouting for help.

She remained quietly in her corner of the carriage, doing her best not to attract attention to the fact that she was twisting her wrists carefully behind her. Her uncle's flunkies, perhaps intimidated by her rank, had not bound her as tightly as they might have.

The rope that had burned her skin had finally turned it numb. Jane put the numbness to good use, pulling until she felt the coarse rope dampen with her own blood. She kept quiet and simply went on twisting.

The carriage pulled to a halt sharply, sending her off balance and nearly into Ethan's lap across from her. She jerked back from touching him and pushed herself farther away with her feet.

"Jane, I—" His murmur was cut off when Maywell's men pulled him from the carriage to fall on the ground at their feet. Jane felt the thud of his body as if she had taken the fall herself, but she could allow nothing to interfere with her concentration now. Her wrists slipped this way and that within her bindings. Soon . . .

On the ground, Ethan gazed up at Maywell. "I can hardly manage a duel like this. No one is going to believe that I died in a fair fight with my hands bound."

Maywell nodded. "No one is going to believe you died in a fair fight no matter what. You're a shopkeeper's son—"

"Clothmaker, actually," muttered Ethan.

"People will be more aghast that you actually had the nerve to participate in a duel of honor than they will be that you died of it. That's only what one would expect."

"Due to the inborn superiority of the upper classes, you mean." Ethan spat out dirt and grass and laughed openly. "Inbred, perhaps. You lot do insist on marrying your cousins."

The first crack appeared in Maywell's sorrowful armor. He raised his foot swiftly. The kick did away with Ethan's ability to breathe for a moment. He wheezed harshly. "Lovely boots," he gasped. "Who is your shoemaker?"

"Why do you care?" Maywell snarled. "You'll never buy another pair."

He cut a hand sharply at his men. "Get him up. I want this parasite dead before the sun rises."

As he was pulled to his feet, Ethan cast one last look back into the carriage. Jane sat hunched in her corner, staring over his head at nothing at all.

No last look of longing, no words of farewell. He'd really done it this time. Even though he was fairly sure he was about to die, the one thing he wished was that she hadn't learned that he had put her in Bedlam.

Everyone had a limit of forbearance. Even the forgiving Lady Jane Pennington. Of course, most girls would hold commitment into an insane asylum against a bloke. It was only to be expected.

Yet somehow he hadn't. Somehow, he'd apparently expected that there was nothing that could turn his Janet against him. Somewhere deep inside him, at some point, he'd begun to believe that her love was real—that she would love him until the day they both died of it.

Since it appeared that day was today, he was a bit disappointed that she couldn't have stretched her adoration out a few more hours at the very least.

*You're a lowborn rotter and you don't deserve a bloody second of her love, so just shut up and get yourself and her out of this so you can try to win her back again.*

A lovely plan. Unfortunately, he hadn't a chance in hell of doing it. He was bound, unarmed, and surrounded by Maywell's men in the middle of a deserted park.

Then his bonds were cut with the swipe of cold steel. Startling hope bloomed within him. "One down," he whispered to himself.

He was marched to the center of the clearing. Apparently Maywell wasn't willing to wait for dawn. Torches and lanterns lit the circle of thugs.

"Make it look right," Maywell called as he climbed back into the carriage. "Pace it out."

So Ethan was stood back to back with another man, then paced out from the center. "One, two, three—"

"Fifteen, thirty-four, seven," Ethan chanted with them. That earned him a smack to the head that sent his ears ringing, so he desisted. Still, he laughed in their faces when they had to start over.

"Ten!" the man next to Ethan said defiantly. "It was right that time, you bloomin'—"

"The pistol!" Maywell called.

To Ethan's complete disbelief, a finely worked dueling pistol was put into his hand. *Two down.*

"Don't get yer 'opes up," the man beside him sneered. "It's got nothin' but black powder in it. It wouldn't look real if you didn't have powder burns on your hand."

*Ah. Back to one, then.*

It occurred to Ethan that he was actually going to die. Here. Now. He found that his former disinterest in his future had evaporated.

He wanted to live. He wanted it most powerfully.

Above all, he didn't want to die with his last words to Jane hanging over them both. What if she spent the rest of her life thinking he had meant what he'd said?

Ignoring his captors, Ethan threw back his head. "Jane!" he shouted.

She did not answer, but he did hear a pained cry come from the carriage. The vehicle was rocking madly. There must have been one hell of a fight going on in there. Ethan pulled at his captors' grip, helpless to go to her.

"Jane!" he shouted at the carriage. "I lied! I lied, Jane, just like you said!"

The carriage bounced a last time and stopped with a final cry, cut off horribly short.

Ethan's heart wanted to stop. *"Jane! Jane, I love you!"*

Sickened, he waited for a reply of some kind, but nothing came.

Maywell opened the carriage door and lowered his bulk to stand on the gravel. Ethan craned his neck, but could see nothing in the dark carriage behind the man. "Well?" Maywell cried to his minions. "What are you delaying for?"

Ethan's "opponent" stepped up and raised his pistol obediently. Ethan raised his in response, hoping against some chance that there had been a mix-up with the pistols. All he wanted was to go to Jane in that horribly silent carriage . . .

The flunky aimed and Ethan saw his finger tighten on the trigger.

A shot rang out.

The man opposite Ethan went spinning off to one side, his shot going wild. Another one of Maywell's men dropped from the wild bullet.

His opponent had been shot. Ethan didn't try to analyze any further than that. He turned and discharged his black powder charge into the face of the man at his right.

With a roar, the man staggered back, clawing at his face. Ethan used the spent pistol to cosh the bloke over the head. Out of ideas, he threw the pistol wildly at the man to his left. Incredibly, it hit him square in the forehead, taking him down like a sawn tree.

Unarmed again, Ethan rolled out of the way of the firefight. When he reached the cover of the trees and darkness, he circled around the clearing to where he thought his mysterious rescuers might be.

There was only one man, standing in the shadows, juggling what looked to be at least four pistols, his silver hair gleaming in the light of the remaining torches.

*"Jeeves?"*

The butler turned. "Good evening, sir—"

Ethan saw one of Maywell's men rise and aim. "Jeeves, get down!" He threw himself at the butler.

Something hard hit him, spinning him away from Jeeves. The butler jumped up and fired, then ran to where Ethan lay on the ground.

"Ouch," Ethan said faintly, clutching his arm. "That smarts."

"Yes, sir. I imagine so, sir." Jeeves helped him to his feet.

"Well, what do you know," Ethan gasped. "Winged in a duel in Hyde Park. All my gentlemanly aspirations have finally come true. My father would be so proud."

The clearing was pandemonium. Men were shooting in every direction, waving pistols and torches and shouting. Apparently only that one man had had the sense to figure out where the bullets were coming from and he was on the ground, not saying much.

"Come, sir. This way." Jeeves made to guide Ethan from the park.

"Jeeves, no. He still—" Ethan staggered. "He still has Lady Jane!"

Jeeves pulled him on. "I don't believe he will harm her, sir."

"No, Jeeves! I can't let him put her back in Bedlam, I—"

Other hands had him now, larger, stronger ones he couldn't resist. They rushed him into a waiting carriage that sped off down High Street, leaving the park and Jane far behind.

Ethan stumbled into the Liar's Club on Jeeves's arm. There was no one in the public area, for it was nearly dawn. Even the rotters were in bed at this hour.

Not so the men in the back room. Several jumped up to help Ethan to a chair without so much as demanding explanation.

In a moment, more men rushed in, some clad in dressing gowns and caps. Kurt loomed over Ethan for a long moment before turning away. Relieved, Ethan spared enough energy to wonder where a bloke like that had his nightshirts made. What yardage!

Then the scarred giant was back, this time with a tin pan full of steaming water and gleaming, dangerous bladed instruments. They looked eerily like devices of torture. Ethan began to push himself to his feet. "Sorry, sir. I must be go—"

The room dimmed and slid sideways. Dizzy, Ethan allowed hands to push him back down. Jeeves tugged off his blue coat, now shot through with a bullet hole and soaked with blood that would never come out.

Pity. The room turned another circle. He'd really fancied that coat . . .

Agony ripped through him, starting at his shoulder and echoing through every fiber of his body. He jerked back from the thick, blunt fingers that probed at his wound. The giant pressed him flat again with very little apparent effort and single-mindedly went back to his quest, ignoring Ethan's incoherent cursing.

Someone tipped brandy into Ethan's mouth, but he spat it out. He couldn't allow his mind to dim, not when Jane—

"Jane!" Was that labored croak his own voice? He grabbed at Jeeves with his free hand. "We have to go back for Jane!"

Just then the giant twisted something inside Ethan,

rather like a time key of pain, and blackness pulled Ethan
in. Even as the room faded, he heard Jeeves's sedate
voice. "Do not worry, sir—we will find her."

"Jeeves?" he muttered as he faded out. "What are you
doing at the club?"


Ethan came to as Jeeves and the giant were wrapping his
shoulder. They finished and stepped back.

"Move tha arm," the giant grunted. After a moment,
Ethan decided the man had asked him to try moving his
arm. He couldn't easily, for his shoulder was wrapped
tightly, but he rolled it forward slightly. It throbbed fiercely,
but Ethan could tell it wasn't as serious as it had seemed
when he was losing so much blood. He looked up at the
man. "Thank you, doctor."

The man grunted and showed several broken teeth.
"Doctor." He grunted again, then turned and walked away
without another word. Jeeves nodded serenely. "I believe
he likes you, sir."

Ethan wisely did not comment on that dubious statement. "Jeeves, did I tell you to bring me here?"

The butler looked thoughtful. "No, sir. I don't believe
you did."

Jeeves had been referred by Lillian something-or-
other . . .

Lillian Raines. Just like the school across from the club.
And of course, his name wasn't really Jeeves, it was—

"Pearson."

The butler raised a brow. "Yes, sir."

"You're a Liar, aren't you?"

Pearson nodded. "In an honorary capacity, yes, I suppose I am."

Ethan closed his eyes. "Sarah Cook?"

"She and I both work for Sir and Lady Raines, who run
the Liar Academy."

"Uri?"

"Uri works for the Gentleman, sir."

Ethan's jaw worked. "Tell me, Pearson . . . are my underdrawers my own, or are they borrowed from the Prime Minister?"

"Only you would know that, sir."

"Where is Etheridge?"

"His lordship is conferring with some of the men in the next room, sir."

Ethan rose shakily. Taking a deep breath, ordering his knees to tighten up, he strode into the next room to confront Lord Etheridge.

"How can you just sit here talking when one of your own people is in danger?"

Etheridge turned to him. "Who is in danger?"

"Lady Jane!" God, had no one been listening?

Etheridge tilted his head. "I don't know Lady Jane."

Ethan scoffed. "You don't know anything about Lord Maywell's niece, the only other spy that the government has been able to place there besides me—"

*"What?"*

Ethan wavered slightly. Etheridge pushed him toward a chair. "Explain."

"No!" Ethan stood. "No more explaining, no more testing, no more performing! For God's sake, *just trust me*! We have to get Lady Jane out of Lord Maywell's clutches immediately! If you want your Chimera, Lady Jane is the one who can give him to you!"

Etheridge looked around the room. "You heard the man. Arms and knives."

He turned back to Ethan. "Where would he take her?"

"Bedlam," Ethan answered instantly, then hesitated. "But that would be too easy, wouldn't it? The way he told us, repeating it several times—"

"It feels like a decoy?"

Ethan nodded sharply. "Yes."

Etheridge gazed at him levelly. "Then Maywell House it is."

# Chapter Twenty-Six

❖

When pistols continued to fire, Jane slipped quietly out of the other side of the carriage. Crouching next to the fore wheel, she could see her uncle's boots silhouetted against the torches. Past that, she could see several men milling around two bodies on the ground.

Neither was wearing a blue coat. Nor was Ethan among the standing. He'd escaped! For a brief instant, Jane indulged in her relief, clenching her eyes shut and pressing her cheek to the cool, gritty rim of the carriage wheel. She'd feigned collapse to fool her uncle, but her head yet ached from his blow.

Then she began to work her way into the darkness, keeping the carriage between her and the men. She crept sideways, unwilling to take her eyes off the clearing for an instant. It was too bad she was wearing such a pale gown. Now would be a very good time to be dressed in a nice sensible brown dress. She could only hope to get out of sight before anyone thought to turn around.

Her heart was pounding with fear and tension and she thought she just might vomit from the strain of seeing Ethan held at gunpoint, but all in all she was doing quite well. Finally she was able to put a small grove of ornamental trees between her and the torches in the clearing. When they blinked out of eyesight, she ran for her life.

She stumbled and fell, rose and ran on. She was less worried about noise than she was about getting as far away from Lord Maywell as possible. There was no time to worry about trying to find Ethan in the darkness. She had no idea which way he'd run in the confusion.

Although the park was cultivated and not very wild at all, the trees were mere dark trunks against deeper night. She was repeatedly slapped across the face by low-hanging branches, but she only ducked and ran on, sweeping her hands before her in the darkness.

Then she heard splashing and the sleepy clucks of waterfowl ahead of her. She tried to remember her excursions to the park. Had she made it to the Serpentine already? She slowed, listening.

The ducks and swans seemed to settle, which only made her wonder what had disturbed them. Her own headlong passage? Ethan? Her heart leapt, then she halted warily. What if it was something more sinister?

For a long moment, the only sounds were the final flutters of sleepy birds and her own labored breathing. Jane turned in a careful circle, all her senses straining. There was no sound of pursuit, no outraged roar from her uncle, no light from hunting torches . . . there seemed to be no one else in all the world.

Jane let out a slow, even breath. For lack of anywhere to sit, she dropped to her knees right where she stood. She let herself simply breathe for a moment, then she pressed cool palms to her hot cheeks.

She had to think. How was she to get herself out of this? Where was she to go? Her uncle would assume she would try to find Ethan, she was sure of that. For her part, she had no objection to doing just that. The only problem was, she had no idea where to look. Ethan was too clever to return to his house now. He would know Maywell would be watching it.

*Scratch.* Jane jerked back as a small flame flared

within feet of her. Blinking against the sudden glare, she scrambled backward, away from the small man who held a burning stick high to light his face.

Jane scrabbled backward over the damp grass until her back came up against a tree. The little man came no closer.

"Oy, there, milady," he said gently. "No need for that. I'm on the right side, I am."

"Everyone thinks they're on the right side," she pointed out.

The fellow chuckled rustily. Then the small light went out, accompanied by a heartfelt curse from the little man. Taking advantage of his distraction, Jane began to rise, working her way around the tree trunk as she slowly crept to her feet.

Then the small light flared again, catching her in midcreep. She dropped her hands in frustration. "How do you keep doing that?"

The tattered little man smiled shyly. "The bloke what made 'em calls 'em 'frickshun' matches." He shrugged. "I don't know what that means, but they sure light up a treat!"

Then he looked around them warily. "I don't like making so much light out in the open. Will ye come with me? I've got a place for you to hide."

Jane hesitated. The little man was strange indeed, with his tatters and his sweet, broken-toothed smile and his seemingly magical matches—but somehow she was finding it difficult to be frightened. She reminded herself that he could have already alerted Maywell if he'd wished, yet he hadn't. Now he was offering safety.

She bit her lip, but to be truthful, she didn't really have anywhere else to go. Slowly, she nodded. He gave her a quick encouraging nod back, then reached for her hand. "I've got to lead you, my lady. Sorry, my hands are dirtyish."

Jane nearly laughed at his gingerly concern, when her own hands were filthy from her own crawling escape. She smiled carefully instead and tucked her hand into his.

He blew out the match, which had been burning much too close to his grubby fingers. "That's a relief, that is," he said conversationally in the darkness. "My 'ands are my trade, so to speak. Wouldn't want to dull my fingers with burns."

Jane followed him carefully. She didn't know how he did it, but he managed to lead her without causing her to encounter so much as a fallen stick with her sore banged toes. They moved toward the water, as evidenced by the sponginess of the soil and the small wet sounds of the man-made lake lapping gently at its bank.

The man lifted the hand he held, showing her the obstacle before them. They ducked under something about waist-high. He released her hand and encouraged her to crawl beneath it.

Then he scratched another friction match to life to reveal where they knelt in the mud. "You can wait here while I fetch yer chariot." He blinked hopefully at her. He really was quite dear.

Jane looked about her in approval. "We're under the footbridge! How clever."

She could have sworn the little man blushed as he pulled a stub of candle from his pocket and held it out to her. "It ain't likely to be seen, if you're afraid of the dark."

She almost reached for it, then shook her head. "No, we had best not take that chance. I shall be fine. I'll stay here and rest until you come back."

He nodded in approval, then blew out his match once more. "I'll be comin' right back for ye, I promise, my lady."

She heard him crawl out from under the footbridge, but then he was gone as soundlessly as he'd come.

Jane wrapped her arms over her drawn knees and

dropped her forehead down. She was exhausted, her wrists throbbed, and she was fairly sure she'd just crawled through swan droppings.

But she was safe, at least for now. She only hoped Ethan was doing as well as she was.

By the time Kurt was out of his nightshirt and the assembled Liars were armed and gathered, Stubbs the doorman stood waiting in the alley behind the club with the reins of several horses held in his blunt fingers.

Ethan blinked at the assembled mounts. "We have horses?"

Dalton nodded as he mounted a black gelding. "After those carriages nearly lost the day for us last time, I looked into buying our own hostelry." His grin sliced the darkness. "It lies a few streets over, looking like any other. We actually make a bit of money from renting the lesser horses out."

Ethan gave his mount a sour glance. "Even the horses have secret identities. You lot are mad, through and through."

Dalton tilted his head. " 'You lot'? Don't you mean 'we Liars'?"

Ethan only turned his mount away to join the others trotting from the alley's mouth. As the group took to a canter through the dark streets, Ethan bent low over his horse's neck and kept to the fore. He didn't want Lord Etheridge's camaraderie. All he wanted was large numbers of men and arms to throw at anything that stood between him and Jane.

*"We Liars."*

How seductive that phrase was. It was almost enough to make Ethan believe, for just a moment, that he was not alone.

*Can you not feel them at your back? You could be one of them if you wished it. This is what it feels like to belong to something larger than yourself.*

The siren call of that bond pulled at him. Ethan shut it down cruelly. They did not truly want him, and if they knew how close he'd come to joining Maywell, they would likely kill him.

Yet, for the first time in his life, he did understand what drove men like them. Having a higher goal made everything so clear for the first time in his life. He knew precisely what his purpose was. Jane must be kept safe. And because Jane loved England, Ethan would do whatever necessary to keep England safe.

There were no shades of gray any longer.

Jane looked dubiously at her chariot. Her tattered savior had pulled up a moment ago in a squeaking pony cart. In the back of the cart sat a large shabby trunk, the sort that one might take on a long voyage . . . if one were inclined to pack one's things in a filthy container that had apparently taken part in the fine art of chicken farming. Small downy feathers still clung to the whitish droppings that dotted the interior.

"Swan droppings, chicken droppings," she murmured to herself as she climbed in. "I suppose I should be grateful you didn't hire it from an elephant keeper."

Feebles shook his head quickly. "Oh, no. I didn't hire the cart. I don't believe in money, y'see."

Jane shot the little man a last astonished look before the lid came down, sending her into a darkness even more complete than that of Hyde Park at night. Curled on her side, Jane suddenly wished that the trunk *had* held an elephant, for then it would be much larger.

She'd never cared much for close spaces before her adventure in the madhouse, but now the tight quarters brought back dark, howling memories of Bedlam and the constant fear that she had not admitted to. She was caged again, helpless, vulnerable—

*Breathe.* The trunk was solid, but had formed a few gaps between the planks through its hard use and evidently long lifetime. Air seeped in slowly, but Jane found she could breathe well enough, despite the smelly quality.

"I want a bath," she whispered, just to comfort herself with the sound of her own voice. "I want a bath and a cup of chocolate and a bed with Ethan in it."

She closed her eyes and tried to imagine those things, and not the way the trunk reminded her of a cage, or a coffin—

"A bath with lavender soap and big fluffy toweling, all warm from hanging about the fire . . ."

The cart began to move and Jane's discomfort found an entirely new level. She was jostled painfully, portions of her coming into bruising contact with the trunk with every step of the pony.

"I . . . want," she said between clenched teeth, "an axe!"

When the Liars neared the portion of Mayfair where Maywell House was located, Dalton slowed his mount and held up one hand for the others to fall to a brisk but near silent walk.

Ethan itched to race to Jane's rescue, but he had to admit that a secretive approach was more sensible. Maywell had to suspect that Ethan would gather the Liars. The last thing they needed to do would be to race in, pistols high, and force Maywell into acting against Jane.

As it was, Ethan desperately feared that the man already had. She'd been so silent in the carriage, as if she weren't even there any longer . . .

Ice squeezed his heart, threatening to halt the beat of it. His Byzantine-minded, shocking, achingly beloved Jane was well. She had to be, for if she wasn't, then there was no reason for any of this—not the Liars, not the war, not his own existence.

So he kept with the Liars as they quietly passed down the last sleeping street before Barkley Square, then dismounted and even more silently split into three different directions to surround Maywell House.

By the time Ethan and Dalton made their way to the square, Stubbs had already extinguished the nearest lamps by the simple expedient of shinnying up the poles and blowing beneath the leaded-glass shades.

Kurt led one division of lethal-looking blokes to the rear alley behind the gardens and mews. Collis took up guard in front of the house, with two men on each side of the front door and more in the shadows of the park beyond. There was no more than the briefest rustle of leaves and tiniest glint of distant lamplight on blades.

"I don't like this," Dalton muttered. "Too much chance of exposure. I want the Chimera, but I don't necessarily want the world to know I have him."

Ethan gazed at him evenly. "The Chimera is in there. If you want him, take him. I only want Jane."

Dalton narrowed his eyes. " 'Jane,' is it?" Then he nodded sharply. "Very well then."

Dalton raised his hand to order attack—

A shimmer of light caught Ethan's eye. He caught Dalton's hand back down. "Wait—look."

On the second floor, facing the square, a single window remained lighted. Ethan pulled the floor plan from his memory. *Jane's room.* As they watched, a female figure passed before the light, the same motion that had caught Ethan's eye the first time.

*Jane?* All Ethan could see was a shape, until the light caught on hair the color of firelight on silk—

"Hold your men," he commanded Dalton as he stepped around him. "I'm going in first."

Dalton grabbed him back. "I don't think so. Maywell has a great many burly servants. I think they might object."

Ethan pointed up. "She's alone, I'm sure of it."

Dalton eyed the figure in the window again, his jaw working. "It's risky."

Feeling suddenly full of fire and light, now that he knew Jane was very nearly in his arms again, Ethan grinned fiercely and threw his hands wide. "Risk? That's mother's milk to me. I'm a gambler, remember?"

Dalton snorted. "Go then. Secure her and then signal us. If we can, we'll get her out before we take the house."

"And her cousins?"

Dalton nodded. "All the ladies, if we can. Go."

Ethan went, slipping between shadows in his finest run-for-his-life-and-winnings manner, until he made it to the front wall of the great house.

In a popular style, there were heavier stone blocks delineating the corners of the house. Ethan considered using these as a sort of ladder, but then quickly discarded the notion. Jane's window was too central. There was no way to tell if he'd be able to move across once he was up there.

Ivy vines grew close and thick over portions of the front, one of the few signs of neglect that Maywell had allowed to encroach on the exterior. Even so, Ethan banished that idea at once. Agile, tree-climbing Jane might manage that route down, but her more sedate cousins would break their ladylike necks.

The only option that Ethan could see was to climb the portico itself and follow the ledge to beneath the window. The danger there was that the roof of the portico was in plain sight from the other bedchamber windows. If anyone happened to look out at the wrong moment . . .

It was the only feasible way. Quickly, Ethan clambered up the columns fronting the portico and pulled himself over the ornate molding decorating the lintel. He had one bad moment when what he thought was a carved-stone acanthus leaf crumbled under his grip, nothing but moldy plaster. For a moment that felt quite a bit longer than that, Ethan hung in space, dangling from one hand while he scrabbled for a better grip.

Most of the carvings were of cheap plaster—more of Maywell's deceit. Ethan was much more careful where he put his hands after that.

He made the roof of the portico with no more incidents and looked down. There was no sign of the Liars, yet Ethan knew that nearly a dozen pairs of eyes watched his every move. He gave a little wave to indicate that he was fine, then moved quickly to the ledge. It, thankfully, was stone, although it was slimy with soot and pigeon droppings.

When he reached the window, he saw that it was not locked. He tried to peer in, but the window was fogged with condensation from the cool damp night. He could see little but a white-clothed form sitting before the fire with head bowed. With one hand bracing against the aperture, he pushed the window slowly open.

The girl before the fire didn't look up. Her quiet sobs explained why she hadn't heard his entrance. Ethan began to smile with relief. "Darling—"

The girl turned with a gasp to blink at him through tear-blurred eyes. "M-Mr. Damont?"

Ethan's heart shrank with sudden cold. "Serena?"

# Chapter Twenty-Seven

Feebles drove his precious cargo carefully through the just-rising streets of London. There was naught but milk carts and window washers at work now. The street lamps still burned, where they'd not run out of oil overnight, and the first glow of dawn was still just a promise in the dirty eastern sky.

He'd done a right job of keeping the pony steady and the cart from bouncing much, but he knew the lady would be black and blue all the same. That was a shame, for she was a very kind lady. He liked the way she looked right at him, as if he weren't nearly invisible after all. Miss Rose did that too.

Finally, St. James's Street came and went. All the best gentlemen's clubs were there, like White's and such.

Which was why the Liar's Club wasn't. The Liars lived on the edge of this small area of fancy entertainments. They weren't for the solid blokes who lived at their clubs to avoid their managing wives. The Liar's Club was for them what thought they was mad and bad.

Morning traffic was picking up. Feebles steered the pony around a number of carts unloading meats and greens for the kitchens of the clubs. This was a good time to get to the Liar's Club. No one would look twice at a delivery right now.

The dignified façade of White's faded into the dimness behind them. White's looked like a right fancy place all right.

Feebles took a deep breath, already anticipating the scent of Kurt's morning baking. He'd get the lady out and fetch her a bun with his own hands when he got her to the club.

White's could keep their marble steps and fancy front door. The Liars had the best cook in all of England.

The carved door of the club finally came into view and Feebles pulled the cart to a careful stop. He clambered over the back of his seat to kneel next to the trunk. "We're 'ere," he told it.

"Let me out," came a thin voice from within. "It's getting harder to breathe."

Feebles bobbed his head, removing his cap from habit, though she could not see him. "Hold out one minute, milady," he urged. "I'll get some extra hands to carry you in."

When he passed through the kitchen into the back room of the club, Feebles found the place deserted.

Worried now, Feebles spared a moment to ring the bell to the attic. There was no response, and himself *always* responded to the bell.

Bouncing on his toes with anxiety, Feebles wondered what he ought to do with the lady. Not that he had much choice. He'd have to open the trunk in full view of the street to let her out. Better soon than later, for even now the milk carts and such were making their rounds.

He scurried back through the kitchen and the front room to the street door. "I'll have you out in a miller's ounce," Feebles muttered as he opened the door and stepped outside. "My—"

There was no cart, no swaybacked pony, and no trunk waiting on the street outside.

Feebles paled. "Lady?"

· · ·

When the cart had finally stopped, Jane had let her aching muscles relax. There wasn't one part of her that wasn't cramping or bruised.

Worse, the air was getting thick. Apparently the cracks weren't enough ventilation for this long an occupation of the box. "In just a moment," she whispered to herself, "they'll carry you in and open you up and lift you out and you can stretch—"

Without warning, the cart jerked forward violently. Unprepared and unbraced, Jane was flung headfirst into the side of the trunk. The sickening knock faded after a moment, but the wild jostling went on. Desperately bracing herself with her hands and feet, Jane tried to minimize the impacts but she was brutally tossed despite her efforts.

Her rescuer had told her to remain quiet, and so she had, but Jane could bear it no longer. "Let me out!" she cried at the top of her lungs. "Stop! Stop and let me out!"

Her cries were met with an instant increase of speed. The cart was swaying wildly now, the trunk actually bouncing across the bed of it. Every bounce was a new punishment on old bruises. Jane felt as though she were going to vomit. Only iron will and the thought of the added nastiness in her cramped prison kept her jaw locked.

Her breath labored harder now than before as her panic began to steal her self-control. Gasping, she used her upper hand to bang against the trunk lid. "Out!" was all she managed. "Out!"

The endless ride went on. Jane wept tears of helpless pain and panic as her air thickened and her body throbbed.

The little man had betrayed her after all. She wasn't going to see Ethan. She wasn't ever going to escape this trunk. She was very much afraid she was going to die.

*Ethan.* The blackness threatened to take away every thought but that one. She wanted to live, she wanted to be with Ethan and have dark-eyed children and spoil them rotten and . . .

Unconsciousness rendered what mercy it could as the darkness took her mind.

Augusta dangled from Ethan's hands, her feet kicking fretfully in the air. "I changed my mind," she hissed at him. "I want to go back up!"

Ethan gazed coldly down at Jane's cousin. "You go down slowly, or you go down quickly. It's all the same to me."

"Augusta!" Serena's hiss came from below where she waited in the shadows with the rest of her sisters. "Augusta, just shut it and climb down, or I'll tell Mama that it was you who borrowed her best bonnet and ruined it!"

The fact that such a trivial threat worked would have amazed Ethan at any other time, but now all he wanted was to get Jane's beloved cousins to safety so that he could go beat her location out of her traitorous uncle before the man was hanged for treason.

The fact that he and Serena had convinced the other girls that Ethan still worked for Lord Maywell caused him not the slightest moment of guilt. It was just as Jane had said. Maywell had made his choices. All he could do was to try to protect the girls from physical harm. Their reputations had been lost the day Maywell had made up his mind.

Augusta finally wrapped her feet around the column and slid down it into the waiting arms of Kurt. One look into the face of the giant shut her up quite nicely. Once on the ground, she ran timidly into the embrace of her sisters. Stubbs rushed the girls away down the street, wrappers and shawls fluttering. They looked a bit like geese hurrying before the goose boy.

Ethan quickly made his way back along the ledge— the journey now grown rather boring with practice—and took up his position in the room, with his pistol raised and his ear to the door.

Below him, he knew the Liars would be entering silently through any window or door that would yield to their craft.

Kurt's men would be heading for the attic servants' quarters in order to immobilize the most dangerous of the burly footmen. Collis would be securing belowstairs, disabling any guards or early-rising servants from rushing to his lordship's defense.

Where Dalton would go, Ethan cared not at all. Ethan himself only had one goal.

Maywell's study, where his every instinct told him Maywell would be waiting for him.

With utter disregard for the thuds and howls that echoed through the house, Ethan beat a path down the stairs to the main floor. He surprised one frantic footman who was running clad half in livery and half in nightclothes. He swung his pistol up in a panic at the sight of Ethan.

Ethan didn't bother to stop and discuss the matter. He raised his own pistol swiftly to clip the other man in the lower leg and ran on.

Dalton appeared at his side, his goal apparently the same. "Nice shot," the spymaster said as they rounded the corner. "I thought you didn't know how to handle a pistol."

"I said I hated them," Ethan shot back. "I never said I didn't know how to use one." He ran ahead, but not before he heard Dalton make a sound of amused surprise.

The other Liars had made their way quickly through the house. Collis and Kurt joined Ethan and Dalton just as they neared Maywell's study. They all halted just outside the door and listened.

Dalton stepped aside and motioned Ethan forward. Another time, Ethan might have made an acid comment about providing human cover for the others, but tonight he merely stepped up and gave the sturdy door a mighty kick. With the full force of the Liar's Club behind him, he charged into the room to face down Lord Maywell.

The sight that greeted them stopped all the men in their tracks. Lady Maywell sat in a chair before the fire, all grace and serene bearing, with a pistol firmly held in her hands aiming right at Ethan's brain.

Stretched before her on the rug, his own brain bleeding sluggishly into the carpet, lay Lord Maywell, traitor, schemer, and soon-to-be corpse, by the look of him.

Lady Maywell didn't seem very upset about her husband. She only gazed calmly at the mass of armed intruders with her grip on the pistol quite still and unshaken.

Ignoring the pallid form on the floor, Ethan stepped forward. If ever he needed his infamous charm, it was now. Maywell had little life left in him and Ethan had the sinking feeling that there was no one else who knew where Jane was.

"My lady," he said soothingly as he approached. "My lady, may I have the pistol, please?"

Lady Maywell turned her gaze down to her hands as if she hadn't really been aware of what she held. She tilted her head slowly, then opened her hands to let the pistol fall to the floor.

Ethan didn't think he was the only one to tense in preparation for the firearm's accidental discharge, but the pistol only thudded harmlessly onto the carpet.

"I believe that was already fired," Lady Maywell said distantly.

"Er, yes," Ethan murmured. "My lady, may I?" He indicated the man on the floor.

For the first time, Lady Maywell gave her attention to her husband. "He's dying." Abruptly her foot flew out to deliver a sharp kick to Maywell's lax arm. "Stupid, selfish *man*." She looked up at Ethan as if he were the only other person in the room. "You know what he was up to. His blasted games! Cards and conspiracy, that was all he cared about! He was on his way to ruining us all, robbing my daughters of their future!"

Ethan exchanged a glance with Dalton. After all their investigation, had the Chimera been taken out of the game by his own wife?

Ethan moved to kneel at Maywell's side. The man's face was ashen, his skin purpling grotesquely around the bullet hole in his temple. Yet, still he breathed.

Nothing could rouse him, however. Kurt examined him, lifting his eyelids to inspect his pupils, which were large and mismatched. The giant looked up at the spymaster and shook his head definitively.

The air seemed to leave Ethan's lungs. He turned urgently to Lady Maywell, who had watched this activity dispassionately. "Where is the small man?"

She blinked vaguely at him. "Who?"

Barely resisting the urge to shake the woman, despite his sympathy for her, Ethan gritted his teeth. "His man of business, his partner in treason, the small man with the round face?"

Lady Maywell blinked. "Oh, yes. I recall him now. Isn't that odd? I know he came here often, but he always seemed so forgettable—"

Ethan was in agony. "My lady?"

She stopped to consider, then shook her head. "I don't think I've seen him tonight. Harold came home quite late."

"Lady Maywell, *where is Jane?*"

She blinked, startled. "Don't you know? Harold said he was going to fetch her back, that you'd taken her from Bedlam without his permission—not that I blame you, for I regretted that as soon as Harold sent her off with you— but you should have had more care for her reputation—"

Ethan turned away, sickening despair clenching at his gut. Jane gone, God only knew where, and the only one who knew lay silent and dying at his feet.

Hopeless fear seized Ethan. He was too late, he had lost her, by God, he'd killed her as surely as if he'd raised the pistol himself!

He turned to Dalton, his eyes wild with dread. "Etheridge?" Please, let the spymaster have some sort of plan. Ethan would sell himself, his soul, his everything to the Liars if only Dalton could find Jane.

Dalton Montmorency, Lord Etheridge and spymaster, took Ethan by both shoulders and gave him a shake. "Not yet," he said, gazing into Ethan's desperate eyes with quicksilver intensity. "It isn't over yet."

Ethan took a breath, strengthened by the understanding in Dalton's eyes. Dalton loved his lady, possibly every bit as much as Ethan loved Jane.

He sent a searching look toward Collis, who nodded once, sharply. "There's still time."

Collis understood. Collis had Rose. Bolstered by the knowledge that these two men—all these men—would not stop, would never stop, until Jane was found, Ethan caged his rampant terror at Jane's fate and put it aside, deep within him. He could still feel it gnashing at his heart, but he forced his mind to calm until he could gaze back at the Liars with nearly the same control he saw in their eyes.

Time to go to work, he saw around him. Time for the job now, time for the fear later, if ever.

He nodded once. "Right. What now?"

"Let me through, ye big buggers!" Feebles's breathless protests reached them first, before the smaller man pushed the larger Liars aside to reach Ethan and Dalton.

He halted before them, gasping. "Lady Jane—I found her in the park—"

Hot jets of joy shot through Ethan. "Where is she?"

Feebles shook his head. "I had her in a cart—got her to the club but then I lost her. The bastards took her right out from under my bloomin' nose—the cart went east, the milk driver on the street saw that much—"

Dalton stepped up. "When?"

"Not an hour past, milord."

Dalton nodded briskly at the men. "Get the horses. We'll cover the city east of the club. Someone had to have seen something."

Feebles nodded eagerly. "The pony, milord—'e 'ad a black spot on his arse, looked the very image of the Prince Regent, like an 'ead on a coin."

Dalton blinked, then shrugged. "All right, lads, there you have it. A pony with the Prince on his arse. What are you waiting for? Mount up!"

Collis held out a hand to indicate Lady Maywell. "What about her ladyship?"

Dalton rubbed his chin, considering. "Would you call that murder or patriotism?"

Ethan burned to ride after Jane. "The law isn't our problem, is it?"

Dalton slid him an indecipherable look. "Not strictly, no."

Ethan opened his hands. "My lady, did you shoot your husband?"

Lady Maywell gazed back at him calmly. "No. I found him thus."

Ethan turned back to Dalton. "There you have it. His lordship was shot by an intruder. Since his traitorous activities will end with his death, I see no reason for the Liars to have further involvement in her ladyship's affairs. Let her call the magistrate and let us get our sorry selves out of here!"

Dalton regarded him sourly. "Is there anything else?"

"Oh, yes." Ethan turned to Collis. "Get her ladyship's daughters back in the house, will you?"

For the first time, Lady Maywell showed some animation. She turned on Collis, mother tiger to the fore. "My girls? What do you mean? Where have you taken my girls?"

Ethan left Collis behind to explain, running from the house with Dalton fast on his heels.

It wasn't over yet. Jane was locked in a trunk somewhere in the city, east of the Liar's Club, being pulled
along by a royally blemished pony.

Once, Ethan would have found all this darkly amusing.
Right now, he felt only driving urgency. There would be
no laughter left in him if he didn't find Jane.

# Chapter Twenty-Eight

Jane woke to find a strange, small man briskly slapping at her cheeks. She flinched away, then blinked suspiciously at the man leaning over her.

She was fairly sure it was not the same strange, small man who had put her into the trunk. She sat up clumsily, almost losing her balance. It was raining, an icy fall of water that dripped onto her face and hair from the tattered roof over her.

She was moving, she realized. She was half-lying on a seat, riding in a two-person surrey that currently lurched down a dark road. The only light came from the two cheap lanterns attached to the sides of the surrey. A dingy brown horse pulled them sluggishly, his soaked coat and slatted ribs showing harshly in the swinging light.

The small man sat back and smiled grimly at her. "It is about time you awoke, Jane. I thought perhaps you had died in that trunk." He didn't sound terribly upset about that possibility.

Jane pressed herself back against the corner of the seat, clinging to the jostling surrey frame with one hand. "I—I know you, don't I?"

The man didn't bother to look at her again. "Do you?"

"You—" She peered at him. "You work for my uncle!"

Something flashed across the small man's face, turning

his profile frighteningly grim for a moment. Then the distant amiability returned. "Rather, one might say, he worked for me," the man said cheerfully.

"You?" Oh, dear. If her uncle had considered her a danger and had threatened her life, then what might her uncle's superior do with her? Her stomach chilled as Jane realized that *this* was the mysterious Chimera.

There was no possibility that he was going to let her live.

"I'm sure I don't know anything about Uncle Harold's business." It was a feeble attempt, but worth a try, nonetheless.

Unfortunately, the small man only snorted. "Please, do not trouble yourself to deny that you spent your entire visit with your family investigating your uncle for someone in the British government. Robert has been giving me every bit of mail that left the household for the past several months. It was I who had Robert bring that last letter to your uncle's attention." He slid a look toward her. "What, no demure protest? No insistence that you were only writing to your dear old mum?"

"Very well," Jane said slowly. "I won't deny it."

He shook his head. "*Mother.* Do you know, for a time you actually had me believing you were nothing but another silly debutante?" He pursed his lips. "Mother . . . now, who could Mother be, do you think?"

Jane remained silent. If he didn't know who she worked for then perhaps she yet had a chance. If she were him, and she had someone who worked for the other side in her possession—well, someone other than Ethan, that is. *Ethan, Ethan, darling, where are you?*—she would keep them alive and well until she had squeezed every drop of information out of them that she could before she killed them.

For a moment, she was distracted by the thought that she might actually be capable of killing. How dismaying.

The surrey rocked and jolted, catching her off guard.

She fell against the small man. He shoved her back hard, nearly casting her right out onto the road. Jane caught herself by the iron handhold on the side used to pull oneself into the surrey, barely keeping herself from a spill. Her braid dangled dangerously close to the open chimney of the carriage lantern. With effort, for her body ached horribly, she pulled herself upright once more.

A moment later, she was wondering if perhaps she ought to have let herself fall. Her bruised body protested as the surrey jolted onward down this endless, deserted road . . . Where were they going?

In the thin light from the carriage lanterns, Jane could make out nothing but large, featureless, dark buildings set a short way back from the road. They had large plain doors, like those of a barn. There was no light anywhere, as if no one lived here.

A warehouse district, perhaps, like down by the docks. Buildings that amounted to little more than sturdy walls and roofs to keep the goods dry until they could be loaded onto the ships . . .

Oh, dear. Ships.

Fear gripped her soundly for the first time. "Where are you taking me? Why slow yourself down with a—" *Hostage.* She halted, biting her lip. Best not to give the fellow any ideas. "With an unwilling companion?"

The small man made a chucking sound at the horse, which ignored him but for a defiant swish of its filthy tail. Jane envied the creature its insouciance. After all, the small man wasn't likely to kill his only mode of transportation. She only wished she could be so confident of her own fate.

"I have a ship to catch—or rather, *we* have a ship to catch. A cabin of our very own all the way to San Sebastián. There's someone near there who I'm sure would love to meet you."

Jane's heart sank. San Sebastián lay on the coast of Spain, nearly on the border with France. *He is taking me*

*directly to Napoleon himself.* The idea of being squeezed
for information began to take on a new shade of horror.

"I've made considerable mischief in my time here, but
I have not achieved certain goals I was given. I think
you'll go some way toward making up for any shortcom-
ings when we arrive in Paris." He chuckled dryly, a sound
like sand on her nerves. "Do you know, this particular
ship is carrying weapons to the British troops?"

He smiled at her. "Do you not enjoy the irony?" When
she did not respond, he shrugged. "It required a hefty
bribe to get aboard," the small man said, shifting the reins
to one hand in order to pat his pocket. "I was forced to
clean out his lordship's safe box to buy this passage. War-
time does drive prices up terribly, doesn't it?"

Jane didn't like the sound of that. Uncle Harold was as
tightfisted as only a self-indulgent man could be, willing to
waste a fortune on gaming, unwilling to part with a farthing to buy decent shoes for his daughters. To clean out
Lord Maywell's safe box, said Lord Maywell would have
to be quite definitely dead.

"Oh, poor Aunt Lottie," Jane murmured.

The small man laughed nastily. "She's better off and
I'll wager she knows it."

That reminded Jane. All the members of the family
must have seen the small man at some point. Horror rippled through her. "You haven't hurt them, have you? Aunt
Lottie and the girls?" Suddenly Jane felt more than capable of murder. She found that bleakly reassuring.

But the small man only snorted. "Why would I?
Bloody lot of work, when they'll never be able to recall
more than the fact that I wasn't tall, or handsome, or particularly well dressed."

Unfortunately, Jane knew her cousins would say precisely that. If a fellow wasn't viable prey in the husband-
hunt, he might as well not fully exist to them.

"The British aristocracy are fools," the man went on.
He hunched his shoulders and put a peevish look on his

face. Instantly, he was transformed into a young fellow not yet twenty, with the sullen attitude to match. "Whot you lookin' at?"

It was very eerie. He looked nothing like the ordinary middle-aged solicitor Jane had first seen in the halls of Maywell House. Then he straightened, peered down his nose at her, and spoke in cultured tones. "Is there something amiss, my lady?"

Jane blinked. Put him in the proper clothing and he could pass in the finest ballroom as a member of Society.

The man relaxed, letting the lordly demeanor slide from him like an unwanted cape. He sent her a bland look, once again the chilling, unemotional kidnapper.

No wonder he wasn't worried about being recognized by the ladies of Maywell House. It was just as well for them, for that obliviousness had saved their lives.

It was not, however, such a good thing for Jane, for how could Ethan find her if he didn't know who had taken her?

She sat back, considering her options carefully. There was no one about to hear her call for help, there was no way to leave a clue about what ship she was on, or even that she'd been carried off English shores at all! She would simply disappear, leaving Ethan to wonder forever.

She was afraid yet again, she realized. It was a familiar sensation. She'd been frightened for a great deal of her life—frightened of what would become of her and her mother, frightened of discovery while in London, frightened of Bedlam, of her uncle, of dying in the trunk . . .

The anger, on the other hand, was something new. It erupted within her like a long-dormant volcano, looking for any fissure to vent through.

Slowly, Jane turned to stare at the man sitting beside her on the seat of the surrey. Yes, she found the idea of killing rather easy to contemplate at the moment. She turned back to stare at the dark buildings around her without awareness, for her entire attention was focused on her outside hand.

She felt her way along the side of the surrey to the rusted fixture that held the lantern. The heat rising from the sooty glass shield scorched her bare hand and the loop of wire handle above it seared her fingers and palm as she gripped it.

She made no noise, only maintaining her vacant stare, as if she had given up, as if she had let all the fear of her lifetime wear her down to helplessness.

The rusted catch of the fixture resisted her. Her fingers were burning as she twisted the wire against the stubborn catch. She slid a glance toward her captor, then pressed her free hand to her belly and groaned.

He shifted his attention to her. "What is it?" he snapped.

Jane shook her head wildly, then clapped her hand over her mouth and twisted convulsively to lean over the side of the surrey. She was distantly proud of her own realistic vomiting noises.

"Oh, for pity's sake," her captor said scornfully behind her. "If you're the seasick sort, I might just have to kill you right now."

Jane ignored him and continued retching spasmodically as she fumbled with the carriage lantern clasp with seared fingers. At last, it came free.

With all the strength left in her battered body, Jane swung the oil-filled lantern in a two-handed arc directly at the small man's face.

He was too quick for her. He ducked away swiftly, leaving the lantern to smash harmlessly against the back of the seat. It bounced, slipping from Jane's grip to fly forward. In a burst of fury, the small man had Jane by the throat. "I think I *will* kill—"

The horse screamed in alarm. Both Jane and her captor froze, turning their heads to see the horse's tail aflame from the leaking lantern that had struck it. The hapless nag reared and hopped in its traces, sending Jane and the small man jolting wildly on the seat. Then, with another fearful scream, the horse bolted.

Her captor released Jane to grab for the reins that now flapped wildly behind the horse. A part of Jane urged her to grab the side of the surrey and hold on—but the fury that swept her made her turn on her captor with all the pent-up rage of being beaten, kidnapped, crated, and jostled until she simply couldn't bear one more moment. She flew at him with teeth bared, clawing at his face and neck, nearly throwing both of them from the wildly racing surrey.

He beat her back mercilessly, until her ears rang and she tasted blood in her mouth, but she could not stop. She struck him with fists and open hands, without design or even thought. Only her rage fueled her, rage at being made afraid one too many times.

The out-of-control surrey careened wildly, rising up on one wheel, then slamming back down. Jane was thrown back against the seat back. Her captor took the opportunity to deal her a brutal blow, stunning her nearly unconscious. She slid away from him, barely aware that he now scrabbled frantically for the loosed reins.

The chance came too late, for the surrey began to overturn. With a cry, the man sprang free. Jane could not react quickly enough. The world spun over and over, until her head came in contact with the cobbles and all went black.

# Chapter Twenty-Nine

Collis and Ethan found the pony in a grimy hostelry a mile east of the Liar's Club. In his panic, Ethan had resorted to dismounting and grabbing every man he saw by the lapels. "Have you seen a pony with Prince George on his arse?"

He definitely qualified for Bedlam now.

At last, astonishingly, one fellow had blinked, sputtered, then said, "Yes, sir!"

The pony and cart had been traded to the hosteler for a horse and surrey, with the addition of an outrageous pile of coin. The hosteler was unrepentant. "'E said 'e 'ad to get his sister out o' the chill. Said 'e was takin' her somewhere warm by ship. She looked ill enough to me. 'Ow was I supposed to know she were kidnapped?"

Ethan tried not to think about what condition Jane might be in to be so obviously ill. She was alive and he was finally on the right trail. Still, he sent Collis an anguished look.

Collis nodded. "I'll send word to Dalton at the club. He'll have Dr. Westfall waiting for her." He looked around. "Ethan, we should gather the others."

"The others are on their own," Ethan said grimly. "Let them catch up as they can. Didn't you hear the hosteler? Even with a lame horse, it would only take an hour to reach the docks from here! They're nearly there now!"

He put his foot into the stirrup and mounted his horse. "You can wait if you like." With that, he reined the horse around and kicked it into a gallop, heading in the direction taken by the mysterious man with the "ill sister."

Jane ached from the top of her head to the soles of her feet. For a moment, that was all she was aware of. Then other sensations rose to the fore. She was cold. She was wet.

She shifted her body away from the wet only to realize something else. She was pinned beneath something heavy. Alarm coursed through her, bringing her entirely to consciousness.

She was facedown on the muddy ground, her cheek half-submerged in a puddle. Something—the surrey?—lay across the backs of her legs. It didn't hurt, but she could not move. She pushed her upper body up out of the mud as best she could and looked around her.

The overturned surrey covered her like a canopy. The rain had stopped but the dark and deserted road beyond was still soaked. The other carriage lantern must still be burning, for Jane could see light from beneath the edges of the surrey.

A sound behind her made her twist to peer from under the other side. The small man was mounting the bedraggled horse bareback, having stripped it of its traces. Other than a singed tail, the horse looked to be in better condition than Jane was.

Jane almost cried out to him for help but stopped herself. He obviously thought her dead or too injured to journey with him. Let him think so. She was fine where she was, only damp and uncomfortable and sore, aside from the pounding in her battered skull. Only let him get out of earshot and then she would bring London itself down with her howls.

She carefully lay back down, keeping an eye on the horse's hooves as it was turned away from her. She watched it leave the circle of weak light from the lantern and listened until she could no longer hear the stumbling clop-clop of the poor thing's hooves on the cobbles.

She forced herself to wait just a bit longer, counting backward from one hundred. Her gown was soaked through to her skin in front and she was beginning to shudder violently from the chill. Inhaling deeply, she began to cry for help with all her might.

She shouted, she bellowed, she screamed so loudly she had to cover her own ears against it—yet there was no response.

The frantic horse had carried them past the warehouse and customs district into the marshland surrounding this area of the docklands. It was a wasteland, where her cries only mocked those of the seabirds inhabiting the marsh.

Finally, her throat sore and her ears ringing, Jane let her forehead fall onto her arms. The cold ate through her, multiplying all her aches and shading her fear with grim necessity. The surrey pressed fiercely into her flesh and her position—her ever bedamned *helplessness*—made the panic begin to rise once more.

She braced her hands on the cobbles and tried again to pull her legs out from beneath the surrey. Then she twisted frantically, trying to shove at any part of it she could reach, hoping to dislodge it. She jostled it mightily, only to feel it settle more firmly down onto her.

"No!" She tried again, harder, rocking it to and fro above her. Nothing happened. Breathless, she stopped and tried to control her panic. She would be found soon. After all, she lay to the side of a finished road. Roads carried traffic, so all she had to do was try to stay warm until someone passed—

A sharp familiar smell drifted beneath the surrey. Jane sniffed, trying to place it. As she watched, something began to drip down the side of the surrey to land on the marshy ground before her eyes.

Rain?

She touched a finger to it, then lifted it to her nose.

Lamp oil? Oh, no.

In her struggles, she must have spilled the lantern's reservoir. That could be dangerous if the oil set fire to the surrey's wooden frame.

Jane held very still. At first, she saw nothing, heard nothing. She relaxed slightly. If it was only spilled oil, she had nothing to worry about.

Then she smelled the first wisp of smoke.

Ethan trotted his horse eastward down the dark corridor of warehouses known as Commercial Road. If this was, indeed, the route Jane's captor had taken, it would have provided complete secrecy at this time of early dawn. Later the place would be bustling again with the transfer of goods to and from the docks, but now it was as silent as a grave.

The road forked and Ethan paused. To his right, the warehouses continued, clear to the East India Docks. That way would provide excellent cover for a kidnapper.

To his left, the road traveled over unused marshland. It was a fast route to the docks, bypassing the warehouses, with open spaces all around and no shipping-industry traffic to block it. Most passengers likely went this way.

As he hesitated, he heard hoofbeats coming up from behind him. He didn't bother to turn. He knew who it would be.

Collis reined in his horse next to Ethan. "Shall we split up then?" he asked without preamble.

Ethan nodded, relieved. There were some advantages to this partnership, it seemed. He rarely had to explain anything to Collis.

"I'll go to the left." He had no real reason for his choice, only that the windswept dimness seemed to call to him.

"I'll ride with you," Collis said. He signaled for some of the others to take the right-hand route and rode beside Ethan at an easy canter.

For some time there was nothing to see but gray mist. Ethan was forced to slow them to a stumbling trot, for the horses could not see ahead at all.

"I'm thinking we ought to have stopped for torches," Collis muttered.

Ethan peered ahead. "Someone has a fire going up ahead. Probably some mudlarks warming their hands. We can take a burning brand from that if you like." He wasn't willing to stop, but this snail's pace was eating at his nerves. He wanted to fly after Jane. They had to catch up to them before they reached the ships or they would never find them in the sea of masts waiting at the docks.

He urged his horse faster, toward the small orange fire in the distance. Someone must be burning wet wood.

The smoke from the wet wood and the scorched horse-hair-stuffed cushions sliced into Jane's throat like a knife. She coughed and gagged, but never stopped her frantic activity.

Reaching as far as she could, for she'd already used up everything near her, she scooped up another handful of sloppy black mud and smeared it energetically into her hair.

Above her, the fire crackled and smoked. On the bright side, the surrey was quite wet. On the dark side, the wet wood burned anyway when covered in lamp oil and smoked mightily while doing so.

She had already coated what parts of her gown she could reach. She was fairly sure that her exposed ankles and calves were sufficiently dampened from the mud around her.

The smoke filled the canopy of the overturned surrey, floating like a threatening black fist above Jane. She twisted herself to lie as close to the edge as possible, gasping for the cleaner air that the flames above her pulled beneath like an inefficient draft.

Suddenly, it wasn't dark beneath the surrey any longer.

Twisting, Jane gazed up in horror as the floor began to burn through. As she watched, the fire found the drier interior and flared with hot new life.

Ducking her head, covering her hair with her hands against the falling shower of sparks, Jane screamed until her burning lungs gave out.

Ethan held up a hand to halt the others. "Did you hear that?"

Collis pulled his horse back and turned his head. "What—"

But Ethan was gone, kicking his reluctant horse into a full gallop. The fire ahead was brighter now, larger. As Ethan neared it, he saw with horror that it was a surrey matching the description of the one taken by Jane's captor—what was left of it, anyway.

The thing was overturned and engulfed in flames. Ethan flung himself from the saddle, ripping his coat off as he ran.

"Jane! Jane!" Oh, God. She could not be inside, could she? Had he heard a scream coming from it or had it only been a seabird's cry?

A single small cry came from beneath the crackling roar of the fire.

"Jane!" He dove at the surrey, slapping at it with his coat, trying to find some way to her. Hands pulled him back. "No! Let me go! She's underneath!"

Collis and several Liars dragged him back from the flames. Ethan struggled desperately. "No! No, she's—"

"Ethan, it's too late," Collis cried hoarsely. "It's too late!"

Ethan fought against their restraining hands, punching and kicking wildly. They dragged him to the ground, pinning him there with the weight of several bodies.

Collis shouted for the others to find water and the Liars scattered to fill their hats with any standing water they could find.

The surrey burned on, lighting the scene with hellish orange light.

Suddenly the pile of bodies surged upward. "No!" Ethan fought his way free, taking down any man who reached for him with Herculean strength. He laid Collis out with a merciless blow to the jaw and ran to the flaming surrey.

Careless now of the heat, he took hold of the side of the surrey. The metal trim was so hot it seared right into the flesh of his palms. He didn't release his hold, but only ducked his face away from the flames that danced over the undercarriage.

With a single mighty heave, he lifted the surrey up and pushed it over.

It fell crashing and splintering upright onto its flaming wheels, leaving only a blackened still form behind it on the ground.

Cold water splashed Ethan as he fell to his knees next to Jane's body. Without much caring, he realized that his sleeves were on fire. The Liars around him beat the flames down, using wet hats and coats to put them out.

Then, when he was no longer aflame, they backed silently away, leaving him next to the burning surrey with Jane.

"Janet?" His voice broke in his throat. Horrified, he reached one hand to her blackened hair, expecting it to crumble to ash beneath his touch.

Instead, his fingers met wet slime. Mud? Just then, she sputtered hoarsely.

Ethan gave a laughing, startled gasp. He reached for her, pulling her limp, soaked, muddy form into his lap. "Janet?" He pushed her filthy hair back from her face with equally filthy hands. "Janet, breathe, my darling. Breathe."

He felt her chest heave mightily and held her while she coughed out the smoky air filling her lungs. As she gasped and choked in his arms, Ethan let his forehead drop to her wet neck as he clutched her tightly to him, rocking her in the light of the flames, surrounded by a circle of cheering men.

Jane lived. At this moment, it was enough. It was more than enough.

Jane drew one blessedly cool breath after another, safe in the circle of Ethan's arms. The skin of her arms was scorched and she was fairly sure she'd lost some hair, and her head pounded like a smith's hammer on an anvil, but she was alive and she was with Ethan.

Finally, her breath came slower and easier, though her lungs still burned. She opened her eyes to see Ethan's dirty face hovering over her own.

"You're a sight," she said huskily.

He laughed damply, clutching her more tightly. With wonder, Jane realized that his face was streaked with tears.

"You're a much worse sight," he said, his voice choked with emotion.

Jane realized that his shoulder was wrapped in bandages beneath his open shirt. She reached one hand to touch, then pulled back when she realized how dirty her fingers were. "Are you injured?" Her voice was only a croak.

He blinked down at the bandages as if he'd forgotten all about them. "Oh." Then he shook his head. "I'll be fine."

Someone laughed nearby. Jane turned her head to see a handsome dark-haired man grinning at them and rubbing his jaw. "I thought you couldn't fight," he said to Ethan. "You took out six of us with a bullet wound in your shoulder!"

"I never said I couldn't fight," Ethan replied absently, stroking the mud from Jane's cheek with his thumb. "I said I didn't want to."

The man laughed again. "Until now."

Jane blinked at the man, confused. Then she abruptly remembered something. "Oh!" She fumbled in her pocket, her scorched fingers clumsy. She pulled out a strip of sodden card paper and handed it triumphantly to Ethan. "Here!"

He let go of her long enough to take it from her. Her heart ached to see his burned and blistered fingers. He held the nasty wet thing tentatively. "What is this? It's ruined, I'm afraid."

Jane smiled and laid her head on his shoulder once more. "Good, for that is your Chimera's passage ticket off English soil." She heaved a blessedly deep breath and closed her eyes. "I picked his pocket, just as you taught me."

The man stood in the fog's concealment, watching the group gathered around the burning cart. He'd made it to the ship in time, only to be put off when he'd been unable to prove he'd bought passage.

Check and mate. There would be no obtaining the passage ticket now. Of course, there were other ways of returning home.

Ire swirled within the man as the Liars succeeded in rescuing Lady Jane. He'd sacrificed the gambler Maywell, one of his best pieces, in this game and he'd still been neatly checked.

He felt his pulse pound with unaccustomed fury. Odd. He usually managed to keep his emotions cool, but the bloody damned Liars—

The man took a deep breath. He was the Chimera, the myth, the man of many faces who appeared and disappeared at will. And not checkmated, not yet.

As his anger diminished until not a ripple of emotion marred the glassy pool of his concentration, the man smiled slightly. If he was not meant to leave this damp, stinking island yet, then so be it.

There was always work to be done here. At the moment,

he rather relished the idea of taking on the Liars again. And if they thought him struggling to find his way out of the country . . .

His smile widened, but did not reach his flat pale blue eyes.

Time to set up the game once more.

# Chapter Thirty

———— ◈ ————

Jane leaned her head against the back of her chair and allowed her eyes to close for a long, lovely moment. She was clean and wore a borrowed dressing gown, seated before the fire in a bedchamber in a most curious place, a gentlemen's club, of all things.

She strongly suspected that this was the same club Mother had told her about, but she was playing innocent for now. Later, however, Mr. Ethan Damont had some explaining to do.

Her hands were bandaged and all her scrapes and cuts and bruises—there was a dismaying amount of them—had been inspected and dressed by the gruff, kindly Dr. Westfall. She raised her head and opened her eyes to smile at the man, who was even now putting his supplies back into his doctor's bag.

"How are Mr. Damont's hands, Doctor?" She'd ridden back to the club in Ethan's arms, before him on his horse, but when they had arrived, he'd handed her over to the other Liars without a word. She hadn't seen him since.

Dr. Westfall grunted without turning. "His hands are burned, of course. The damned fool, sticking his hands in the fire. Most people learn better before they turn two."

Jane began to protest that he'd been injured saving her, but the good doctor only raised his hand to stop her. "No, my lady, I don't want to know. I don't ask, and this lot doesn't tell, and we're both the happier for it."

She smiled, understanding all too well. "Will he recover full use of his hands? They were so blistered . . ." The memory made her trail off as she pictured the raw, seared flesh of Ethan's magnificent, talented hands.

The doctor did up the clasps of his bag, finally turning to her. "My lady, Mr. Damont will recover eventually. And when he does, I fully intend to win back the small fortune he took from me earlier this year." The man's eyes twinkled despite his gruff tone. "Now, does that please you?"

Jane smiled. "Yes, Doctor."

He strode to the door. "You've the constitution of an ox, my lady, but even you must rest now." He wagged a finger at her. "You'll not stop the headaches until you do."

Jane pressed a fluttering hand to her throat and batted her lashes. "An ox? Why, you are too kind, sir!"

The doctor let out a single booming bark of laughter as he opened the door. Mr. Tremayne was waiting outside and Jane saw him give the doctor a startled glance.

The doctor brushed past him with another grunt, although Mr. Tremayne greeted him politely. Then Mr. Tremayne tapped politely on the doorframe. "May I enter, my lady?"

Jane leaned forward eagerly. "Yes, if you tell me how Ethan is, Mr. Tremayne."

Collis glanced away. "Oh, he's all right. He's probably resting now, as you ought to be."

Jane gathered herself up. "I don't want to rest. I want to see Ethan." She started toward the door. "Will you take me to him?"

Collis stopped her with a gesture. "Damont . . . well, you see . . . he has this cat . . ."

Jane frowned at him. "Speak, Mr. Tremayne."

Collis sighed. "Ethan isn't here. He went home."

Jane's heart sank. "He went home? He left me here, without so much as a word?"

Collis shrugged. "I'm sure he would have said good-bye, but with the doctor here . . ."

Jane narrowed her eyes. "Mr. Tremayne, you seemed fluent in English before."

He blinked at her, then flushed. "My God, you are a ferocious creature, aren't you? I think you two might very well deserve each other after all."

Jane nodded. "Thank you. I think so as well. Now tell me why he left, and pray do not wax inarticulate."

Collis folded his arms and grinned at her. "He said, and I quote, 'I've caused quite enough wreckage in her life.'"

Jane sighed. "I knew it. I knew he was still trying to chuck me."

Collis tilted his head to smile at her. "Well, are you simply going to stand there and let him?"

Jane's head ached. In fact, her entire being ached, within and without. She felt weak. Drained. How could she keep fighting Ethan's persistent retreat from her? How could she bear to lift up her sword again?

She pressed a hand to her forehead. "I think—I think I'm going to have to think about it tomorrow."

Collis seemed disappointed, but he nodded. "Very well, then. I'll leave you to rest." He turned to go but stopped at the door. "By the way, Dalton sent a message to your cousin to let him know you were safe and sound."

Jane froze. "My—my cousin?" How had they known?

Collis looked at her oddly. "Yes. The current Marquis of Wyndham is your cousin, isn't he?"

Jane let out a horrified breath. "Mr. Tremayne, I need my clothes, quickly!"

Ethan let himself into his empty house, fumbling the key with his bandaged hands. The burns hurt, but the physical pain was only a dull echo of the ache in his chest. He felt as if his ribs would cave in from the pressure of it.

The house seemed more empty than it ever had before.

Ethan gazed about him dispassionately at his most prized possession. Bricks and mortar, that was all he saw now. Yet it was more than Jane had.

He went to his study and went straight to his desk. There, in an inner drawer, he found what he sought. He pulled the inkstand closer and clumsily uncapped the ink using both bandaged hands. Then he pulled a sheet of foolscap from another drawer and wrote silently for a long moment, his customary scrawl even larger and less legible than usual.

He folded it, but didn't bother to light a candle to seal it. There was no Jeeves, so there was no fire in his hearth, no lit candles awaiting him. There was only a cold, empty house that he didn't want anymore.

Jane had come bloody close to dying because of him. More than once, actually. She'd told him the story of her journey in the trunk while they'd ridden back early this morning and he'd been horrified at how close she had come to suffocating.

He'd made one stupid mistake after another. They were all so obvious now. He rose from the desk and threw his scorched, bullet-ridden, bloody coat to the floor of the study as he made his way to the brandy.

His first had been to remain in London for one minute after Lord Etheridge had made his "proposal." He ought to have been on the first ship to the West Indies.

His second, third, fourth—oh, God, his infinite mistake!—had been to give in to his attraction to Lady Jane Pennington. He'd been weak, desperate, breaking every one of his own rules three times over. Damn, the brandy was upstairs. "No virgins. No virgins. No virgins," he muttered to himself.

"Too bad you didn't remember that earlier."

Ethan whirled, raising his ridiculously muffled fists in defense.

A man not much older than himself sat in Ethan's chair, before Ethan's cold hearth in Ethan's study. His sharply cut features had a watchful quality as he gazed stonily at Ethan. Zeus slept on the man's lap, lounging on his back with all four white paws in the air. The traitor.

"Who the bloody hell are you?"

The man remained seated, disregarding Ethan's fury entirely. "I'm here to talk to you about a certain virgin."

"Jane?" Too late, Ethan realized he ought to have kept his bloody mouth shut.

The man nodded. "Apparently. She spent several nights here with you, I hear." He tilted his head. "Unchaperoned," he added sourly.

*"Who the bloody hell are you?"*

Ethan's front door burst open and light, running footsteps sounded in the hall, footsteps Ethan knew all too well. He turned. "Janet?"

She halted, disheveled and breathless, in the doorway. She was so beautiful his chest hurt anew. "Oh, dear," she said faintly when she saw the two of them.

"Hello, Jane," the man said, his tone warming only slightly.

Ethan couldn't believe it, but Jane actually paled. "Hello, Stanton," she said diffidently.

Ethan blinked. Diffident? *Jane?*

He turned back to the intruder. "Who the bloody hell are you?"

"Stanton" raised a brow. "Persistent fellow, isn't he?" he said to Jane.

Jane moved forward. Ethan could have sworn she was trying to put herself between him and this balls-forward Stanton bloke.

"Ethan . . ." Jane turned to him with a careful smile. He hated that careful smile.

"Ethan, meet Mother." She took a breath. "And my cousin, the eleventh Marquis of Wyndham."

Ethan let out a breath. "Oh." He turned to Lord Wyndham. "Why didn't you just say so?"

Jane turned back to Wyndham. "Stanton, I can explain—"

A new voice echoed in the hall. "Wyndham!" Dalton appeared in the study doorway. If Ethan was not very much mistaken, his lordship was somewhat out of breath.

Lord Wyndham gazed curiously at Dalton. "Etheridge?"

Dalton entered and nodded at Ethan, greeting Jane as well. "My lady." Then he faced off against Wyndham. "If you want to destroy this man, you'll have to go through me," Dalton declared. "He's one of mine."

Lord Wyndham showed a trace of astonishment. "He's a Liar?"

Ethan felt rather astonished himself. "I'm still a Liar? I thought you only wanted me to infiltrate Maywell House!" He was stunned. They still wanted him?

At that moment, Collis appeared in the doorway, not quite so breathless. "I figured Dalton had everything in hand," he said easily. He blinked at all of them. "What, you didn't need me, did you?"

"If I might get a word in edgewise?" Jane's voice had regained something of its usual acerbic tone. She turned to her cousin. "Stanton, I'm simply worried that you've the wrong idea about Mr. Damont." She took a breath. "He never laid a hand on me," she stated definitely.

Ethan had to pause and admire such a nicely delivered bald-faced lie.

Wyndham turned to Ethan. "What have you to say to that?"

Ethan feared he wasn't going to lie nearly as professionally as Jane. And yet—he'd never actually used his bare hands, had he? He turned to Wyndham, the picture of a misunderstood gentleman. "I vow to you all—I never laid a hand on her."

Jane smiled proudly at him. He only nodded back as serenely as Jeeves—er, Pearson.

"Not only that," Jane went on. "The only reason Lord Maywell didn't kill me days ago was because of Ethan's—er, Mr. Damont's—influence on him." She sent Ethan a slightly irritated glance. "Mr. Damont is an excellent operative. I never suspected a thing."

Wyndham narrowed his eyes at Dalton. "About that . . . why wasn't I informed that Maywell was being investigated?"

Dalton matched Wyndham's gaze. "Why wasn't I informed that you and Lord Maywell were related through your cousin?"

Collis cleared his throat and raised one hand like a dutiful student. "Pardon me, but I want to know how Lord Wyndham knows about the Liars."

Jane let her gaze drift back to Ethan, standing so upright and alone among the others. All she wanted to know was if Ethan still loved her, as he had shouted to her in Hyde Park.

She took a step toward him, but before she could say anything, Ethan reached for a folded paper on his desk. He handed it to her without a word.

Jane took it and silently unfolded it. One sheet was the legal deed to Diamond House.

The other was a statement in a rather hideous scrawl that stated the transferal of ownership of Diamond House to the sole possession of Lady Jane Pennington, signed by Ethan Damont.

She looked up at Ethan, hope blooming in her heart. He would never give up his house—not unless he meant for them to share it!

"I want you to have it," he said stiffly. "I—I don't want it any longer and you've lost so much—"

Vast and infinite disappointment swept Jane. He wasn't asking her to share his home. He was giving it to her as a parting gift.

"Where are you going to live?" Her voice didn't break,

she was surprised to notice. Oh, that must have been her heart that shattered, she thought dully.

"I thought I'd take an extended journey to the West Indies," Ethan told her distantly.

Jane narrowed her eyes. "Isn't that where men flee to escape their debts?"

He blinked at her in surprise. She saw the first glimmer of comprehension cross his face. He indicated the deed. "Is that not enough repayment?"

Jane crossed her arms and tapped the folded deed against her chin. She became aware that the others were watching them. She cared not a whit. "No," she said firmly. "It is not."

Ethan drew back. "What else do you want from me?"

"Zeus," Jane responded instantly. "I want Zeus."

Ethan's jaw dropped. "But—" Then his face hardened. "Of course. I can hardly take him with me, after all."

Jane was disappointed. She was going to have to raise the ante, it seemed. "I want the house, Zeus, and . . ." She glanced at Lord Etheridge and Collis, then she smiled. "And ten years of indentured servitude." She pointed at Dalton. "To him."

Ethan scowled. "What?"

Collis snorted. "She wants you to be a Liar, you idiot."

"The commitment is usually for life," Dalton drawled. "But I'll take that ten years and raise you another cat." He rolled his eyes skyward. "God knows we have enough of them running about Etheridge House."

Ethan held up his hands. "Wait just a moment—"

"I'm not finished yet," Jane snapped. "You owe me. You admitted as much yourself. Is that not so?"

Ethan cleared his throat and looked away. "Yes. I owe you. I'll serve ten years in the Liars."

Jane nodded briskly. Her cousin was watching her closely, but for all that she owed him, she would not give up Ethan. "I want you to smile more often." She ticked each item off on her fingers. "I want a decent proposal of marriage. And sometimes..." She leaned closer to Ethan, although she truly did not care who heard her. "Sometimes," she whispered loudly, "I want to be on top."

Ethan put both hands over his face and laughed helplessly for a long moment. "Janet, you're killing me." His voice was muffled but she could already tell he was smiling. Then he dropped his hands and inhaled deeply. "No more running."

His eyes were shining so brightly that Jane felt her own chest grow tight. Love, for the first time unfettered and unrestrained, shone from his eyes like a beacon through the fog.

He dropped to one knee and took her bandaged hands in his bandaged hands. "I have no name, no fortune, nor even much value as a man. All I've ever had that was of any worth is this house and my cat. If you'll have me, Lady Jane Pennington, then all I have is yours."

Jane shook her head. "I'm sorry, that isn't enough. You're supposed to tell me how much you love me."

He smiled sadly up at her. "Would you believe me? I've been known to lie on that topic before."

She arched a brow. "Try."

He bowed his head for a moment. "I don't think I could keep breathing for a single day if you weren't," he said, his voice husky with emotion. "I don't think I could bear to pass one moment of my life knowing that I hurt you, or that you were hurt because of me. I don't think I could watch another sun rise if I didn't watch it with you."

He looked up at her at last. "Is that love enough?"

Jane nodded, her eyes filling. "It'll do."

He smiled at that. "Then, my lady, we have a deal."

They solemnly spat on their palms and shook on it. Then he stood and pulled her into his arms.

Jane fell headlong into his kiss—until someone cleared his throat behind her.

"Oh, hell," Ethan murmured against her mouth. "I forgot about them."

Jane chuckled and hid her face in Ethan's neck.

Lord Wyndham sighed. "A Liar in the family. Oh, well, I suppose it could be worse. He could be a—"

Collis held up one finger. "Better not say a tradesman's son. Or a dandy. Or a card cheat."

"Oh, hell," Wyndham murmured faintly. "Maybe she ought to marry him soon, before he gets any worse."

Jane giggled. "Or before I do," she whispered to Ethan.

# Epilogue

———— ◇ ————

Jane peered curiously about her as Lady Etheridge led her through the secret portion of the Liar's Club. "Are you sure it is all right for me to be here?"

Clara smiled. "Considering that you are marrying the Gambler and are already an operative for a member of the Royal Four—"

Jane's eyes widened. "Shh! Ethan doesn't know about them," she whispered.

Clara eyed her with amusement. "Don't you think you ought to tell him before the wedding next week?"

Jane thought about it. "Hmm. No," she said firmly. "He has enough adjustments, with the prince trying to knight him and everything." She sighed. "Have you heard all the details of his rescue of the Prince Regent? It's such a thrilling tale—"

Clara held up a hand. "Yes, dear, I have. Several times." She led Jane down a hallway. "We'll just pop up to the attic for some drawing supplies and then you can describe the Chimera to me. I've become quite good at using other people's descriptions . . ."

But Jane wasn't listening. She'd stopped before the notice board, her eyes locked on a drawing already placed there. "That's him," she breathed.

Clara hurried back to her. "What?"

Jane reached out to touch a drawing of a sullen young man, not more than twenty, with a round face and peevish expression. "That's him. That's the Chimera."

Clara went very still. *"Dalton!"*

Lord Etheridge and Ethan Damont came barreling down the hall. "What is it? Are you unwell?"

Clara took down the drawing, her hands shaking as she pulled the pins from the paper. She handed it to Dalton.

"The Chimera," Clara said slowly, "is Denny."

Take a sneak peek at

*Surrender to a*
*Wicked*
*Spy*

*Book Two of the Royal Four series*

Coming October 2005

# *Prologue*

———————— ❖ ————————

Lady Olivia Cheltenham fell into the Thames and was rescued by a Viking god. Rather, she was pushed in—by none other than her very own mother—and the Viking god saved her. Rather, he tried to. Sorry to say, she ended up saving him.

When Olivia felt her mother shove her over the railing of the bridge, she had what seemed like a very long time to consider the reason on the way down. Mother had never shown signs of being homicidal before, so she didn't think that was it. Nor had Olivia done anything more offensive than ask repeatedly why she was being required to stand on a bridge and look at the Thames for hours on a chill, windy day. Therefore, the only explanation could be that there had been an eligible bachelor within sight.

As the icy water closed over Olivia's head, wrenching her bonnet off and taking her breath away, Olivia was forced to admit that perhaps she should be more charitable. Mother had been under such a strain lately, but surely she wasn't mad enough to kill Olivia in the hunt for a husband?

The river was not deep here, and Olivia felt her toes touch the soft bottom briefly before her natural buoyancy began to pull her upwards again. Her head broke the surface, and she took a much needed breath. This not being the first time she had ever fallen into water in her life, she had begun to strip off her spencer immediately and now she was able to pull her arms free and toss the short jacket aside to float slowly away. Fortunately, her gown would not weigh her down, for she was wearing a very light muslin without much in the way of petticoats. Mother had insisted she wear it this morning despite the weather—a fact made suddenly sinister in the light of recent events. Olivia put her mother's plotting out of her mind in favor of a more important matter—survival. She kicked her slippers away and examined her situation.

Above her, she heard her mother's horrified screams and the shouts of what seemed like a large crowd gathering, but Olivia did not waste time peering up at them. The water was so cold that it was already sending spikes of pain into her hands and feet. She ought to get out before she went numb. Turning easily with a sweep of her arms, she spotted a set of the slimy stone stairs that led from the bank down to the water every so often along the river's edge.

She was about to strike out for the spot when something large hit the water next to her, sending choking brown filth up her nose and into her open mouth. She sputtered in disgust and swiped at her face, clearing her vision in time to see a pair of great arms reaching for her.

With a kick, she avoided them easily and swam a short distance away. The arms belonged to a large, filthy stranger.

Of course, in his defense, he probably hadn't been filthy before he entered the water.

In fact, he'd probably looked very nice indeed a few moments ago. Olivia tread water easily as she considered him. If the chiseled cheekbones and firm chin visible beneath his dirty gold, streaming hair were any indication, he normally looked very fine indeed. His head remained very stably above water. Apparently he was large enough that he was able to stand firmly on the bottom. He looked like a very wet, very dirty Viking.

No, not descriptive enough. He looked like a large, wet, dirty Viking *god*.

Enter the eligible bachelor.

He swiped the hair from his eyes and blinked sky-blue eyes at her in confusion. "Are—are you all right?"

Mother's game was working. He was dutifully going to rescue her. How embarrassing. Olivia grimly decided not to play. "Oh, yes," she assured him. "No need to bother about me."

Obviously not understanding, he reached for her. Olivia evaded his grasp, swimming effortlessly aside. Unfortunately, this put him between her and the stairs, and she was already starting to shiver.

He reached again. She evaded again. He stared at her in frustration. "Will you come here so I can help you?"

"No, thank you," she replied primly. "If you'll simply move aside, I shall make my own way out."

He blinked, frowning. The river lapped at his chest much the way it did to the great immovable pillars of the bridge. "What?"

Olivia gave up. She had no time to make idle chatter with him. He was big enough to simply walk out, but she was growing colder by the moment. Striking out, she took a side tack that swept her a bit downstream of him. Of course, the great fellow reached for her again, but he seemed unwilling to take a single step, so she rounded him quickly and made for the stairs.

Halfway there, she glanced back. He still stood there, as immovable as a stone. "Aren't you coming?" she called. "The water is very cold."

He turned his head and upper body to look at her. "I—I can't."

Olivia was beginning to lose patience. Her teeth were chattering mightily now, and she couldn't feel most of her body. "I'll make sure she apologizes," she snapped. "I know it was a terrible thing to do, but I do think you're being a bit mulish now."

He blinked at her. "I have no idea what you're talking about, miss, but the reason I can't move is that my boots have sunk into the mud."

"Oh." Olivia looked longingly at the stone stairs once more, then turned back.

"No," he protested when he saw her returning. "Go on! You must get out of the water!"

Olivia ignored him, stroking swiftly to his side. "Can you not pull your feet from them?"

He blushed and looked away sheepishly. "They're very new, and they fit quite tightly. It usually requires my valet's help to pull them off."

Olivia didn't bother to hide her opinion of that sort of vanity. He glanced at her expression and shrugged. "Everyone is wearing them that way these days."

Some Viking god he was. Just her luck that the first man in London who attracted her was a vain and impractical dandy. As if he needed any help looking stunning!

Locking her jaw against the chattering that now verged on violent, Olivia reached for him. "You need to take the weight off the mud," she told him. "Let yourself lean back and try to float your weight on the water."

He frowned at her. "I think I'd prefer to stay firmly on my feet."

"I'm sure you would," she said patiently, though it cost her dearly. Still, she could hardly rail at the fellow when it was Mother who had caused the entire mess. "Trust that I know what I'm talking about," she urged him. "Livestock gets stuck in the mud at home all the time."

"Livestock?" He looked a bit miffed at that, but began to lean back obediently. She caught his wide shoulders with her numb hands, kicking fiercely as his weight began to come on her. For a moment she thought he was going to sink like a stone, but then he began to float on the sluggish current.

"Now wiggle your feet side to side," she instructed him. "You must break the suction of the mud."

He scowled at nothing in particular.

"Are you wiggling?" she persisted.

"I'm wiggling," he assured her gruffly.

Olivia was beginning to have trouble moving her limbs. She felt so heavy . . .

"I got one free," he said exultantly, stretching out his arms for balance.

Olivia kicked too slowly and sank beneath his movement. It took all her strength to push back to the surface. She wasn't chattering anymore. Her brain felt sluggish, but somewhere she managed to dredge up the knowledge that that was a bad sign.

He lurched in her grip. "I'm free!" He pulled her close with one great arm, carefully treading water so his feet would not touch down again. "Miss?"

Olivia closed her eyes. Her lids were far too heavy to hold open any longer. She hung there in his grasp, too cold and numb to save herself now that she'd saved him.

*"Miss!"*

Being one of the most eligible bachelors in London Society, Dane Calwell, Viscount Greenleigh, was actually rather accustomed to saving damsels. In fact, they seemed to drop from the sky to land at his feet in various states of distress.

The Season was nearly over, and Society's mamas were becoming desperate indeed. Unbeknownst to them, Dane had every intention of marrying this year. After all, he was in his late thirties and his wild days were long done. A man with his responsibilities needed an appropriately demure, composed, well-bred hostess and mother for his heir. Therefore, he looked on all of this attempted entrapment with amused tolerance. Still, Dane had hope that he'd find a young woman with a bit more substance before the season ended.

So when a young lady fell into the Thames right before his eyes, Dane hadn't hesitated before leaping from his horse to dive into the water next to the struggling miss.

Except that this particular miss hadn't needed rescuing, at least not until she'd nearly frozen while rescuing *him*.

She lay in his arms now as he carried her up the grassy bank of the Thames. He didn't think it was precisely proper for him to be holding her so close, but the unconscious girl's mother—who only now had thought to run back down the bridge to the bank—was currently indulging in a rather overblown fit of panic and there didn't seem to be any servants or footmen with them.

Dane wrapped his sodden coat more closely about the pale chilled form of his rescuer. Her frozen state concerned him greatly. He was feeling deadly cold himself, and he was far larger than the young woman he held.

He glanced up at the gathering crowd—where had all these people been while the two of them had been floundering in the Thames?—and picked out a mild-looking young man at random.

"You there," he called. "Fetch a hackney coach here at once." The fellow nodded quickly and ran for the street. Dane glanced at the woman he was beginning to think of as "the mother from hell" and tried to smile at her reassuringly. This only sent her into a fresh bout of sobbing and carrying on as she clung to his side. She seemed to feel that she was to blame for some reason.

There was no sense coming from that quarter, so Dane tuned the woman out.

A shabby hack pulled up on the grass. It was a pretty poor specimen and small to boot, but Dane was in no mood to care. He ordered the mild young man to load the mother into the vehicle and carried the girl on himself. Seating himself in the cramped interior, he settled her into his lap, keeping a protective hold on her.

Perhaps he ought to be ashamed of noticing that she

was a healthy armful and that she fit rather nicely against him. Still, it was refreshing to be this close to such a sturdy female. She felt rather . . . unbreakable. He always felt somewhat uneasy when he came too close to some of the more petite women in Society. His common sense told him that he was not going to crush them during a waltz, but his imagination supplied many an awful vision anyway.

So when his coat briefly fell away from the young woman's bodice during the jostling carriage ride, Dane fell prey to his manly instincts rather than his gentlemanly ones and didn't precisely avert his eyes from what the thin, sodden muslin wasn't covering very well.

Well, well. Very nice. Very nice indeed. He could safely change his description from "sturdy" to "buxom."

Dane saw her open eyes and smiled at her, glad to see that she was alert once more. She likely hadn't seen him peeking, and if she had, he certainly wasn't going to affirm her suspicions by appearing guilty. Besides, the brief glance at her full bosom capped with rosy points that pressed tightly to the translucent muslin had been the highlight of his rather trying day.

Her gaze left his, however, and slid to where her mother sat opposite them, now sobbing somewhat less vociferously.

"Mother," the girl said firmly through blue, chilled lips. "T–tell this nice gentleman that you're s–sorry."

The weeping woman uttered something unintelligible which seemed to satisfy the girl in Dane's lap, for she then turned to look back up at him with an air of expectation. Dane hesitated, having the feeling that he was the only one who didn't know what they were talking about. "Ah . . . apology accepted?" he said finally.

The girl seemed to relax. "You're t–taking all of this very well, I must say," she told him as her shivers continued. "That bodes well f–for your character. You must be a man of g–great parts."

Perhaps it was the fact that he'd recently been peeking
at her own rather "great parts", or perhaps it was the fact
that his own "parts" were becoming more and more stimulated by the motion of a curvaceous bottom being jostled against them, but the commonplace saying struck
Dane in quite a different way than it was intended to. He
laughed involuntarily, then covered it with a cough. Smiling with bemusement at the very unusual creature nestled
on his lap, he nodded. "Thank you. I might say the same
about you."

The girl eyed him speculatively for a moment, then
turned to her mother again. "Mama, you should allow this
gentleman to introduce himself to you."

"Mama" nodded vigorously, then visibly repressed her
sobs and dabbed at her eyes with a tiny scrap of lace that
truly didn't look up to the task of drying all those tears.

"That's not necessary, my dear," the woman said, with
a final sniffle. "The Earl of Greenleigh and I have already
been introduced."

Dane sat there for a long moment with a smile frozen
on his face while he racked his memory to place the rumpled, red-eyed woman across from him. Finally, light
dawned. Cheltenham. She was the wife of a destitute earl,
but the family was of excellent lineage and spotless reputation. "Of course we have, Lady Cheltenham," he said
smoothly, as if he'd recognized her all along.

Then he looked down at the self-possessed and voluptuous young woman in his arms. So this was Cheltenham's daughter . . .